CALL ME A LIAR

Colette McBeth is the critically acclaimed author of four psychological thrillers. She was a BBC TV News television correspondent for ten years, during which time she covered many major crime stories and worked out of Westminster as a political reporter.

Colette lives on the south coast with her husband and three children.

Praise for **Call Me a Liar**:

'A thrilling look at the dark side of the bright young things . . . shifts like quicksand under your feet' Erin Kelly, author of *He Said / She Said*

'A slick and pacey thriller that will keep you reading through the night' Renée Knight, author of *Disclaimer*

'I loved this book . . . It combines a furiously twisty plot with utterly believable characters. A winner' Elly Griffiths, author of *The Crossing Places*

'Blown away by the writing in *Call Me a Liar* . . . Good line after great line, and a brilliant, totally contemporary setting with bright young things way out of their depth' Jane Casey, author of *After the Fire*

Praise for **An Act of Silence**:

'I loved it. Clever, atmospheric and truly scary. Colette is the real deal' Marian Keyes, author of *The Woman Who Stole My Life*

'Sensational. Intricately plotted and emotionally tense' Clare Mackintosh, author of *I Let You Go*

'The complex nature of family relationships are portrayed with clarity and heart in Colette McBeth's *An Act of Silence*. A taut thriller' Ali Land, author of *Good Me, Bad Me*

'Dazzling. Political intrigue, echoes of Savile, with a troubled mother and son relationship at its heart' Tammy Cohen, author of *When She Was Bad*

'An intelligent psychological thriller with a new twist on the genre. A thrilling read' C. L. Taylor, author of *The Missing*

'Vivid char . . . . . . freeze the blood. I lov . . .

'One of those beautiful books where you think you've worked it all out, only to discover that you've been duped by an expert . . . I devoured it, but also didn't want it to end' S. J. I. Holliday, author of *The Damsel Fly*

'I inhaled it – literally reading it in one sitting. A beautifully written, gripping and thought-provoking book' Emma Kavanagh, author of *Falling*

Praise for **The Life I Left Behind**:

'*The Life I Left Behind* is a rare thing; a well-paced, meticulously researched thriller which is not just gripping but compassionate, too' Paula Hawkins, author of *The Girl on the Train*

'Absolutely amazing. Grip lit of the highest order. Brilliant' Marian Keyes

'A creepy and clever thriller' *Fabulous*

'Dark and clever murder tale with a twist' *Heat*

'McBeth pulls it off with aplomb' *Glamour*

'This intriguing and twisty thriller kept me reading into the night' *Woman & Home*

'McBeth's is a much better realisation of the same theme [as *The Lovely Bones*] and, psychologically, by far the more interesting accomplishment' *Independent*

'If a more affecting psychological thriller is published this year, it will be a very good book indeed' *Irish Times*

'Completely brilliant' Jill Mansell, bestselling author of *Meet Me at Beachcomber Bay*

'Fantastic' Lucy Diamond, bestselling author of *The Beach Café*

Praise for **Precious Thing**:

'Colette McBeth delivers twists and shocks with superb timing. An impressive debut' *The Times*

'An excellent storyteller . . . *Precious Thing* is more than deserving of a place on the modern thriller bookshelf' *Sunday Express*

'An interesting and original page-turner' *Literary Review*

'A cleverly crafted tale . . . If you're a fan of *Gone Girl*, you'll love this' *Sunday Mirror*

CALL ME A LIAR

Colette McBeth

WILDFIRE

First published in paperback in 2019 by
WILDFIRE
an imprint of HEADLINE PUBLISHING GROUP

1

Cataloguing in Publication Data is available from the British Library

ISBN 978 1 4722 2676 1

Typeset in Bembo by Avon DataSet Ltd, Bidford-on-Avon, Warwickshire

Printed and bound in Great Britain by Clays Ltd, Elcograf S.p.A.

HEADLINE PUBLISHING GROUP
An Hachette UK Company
Carmelite House
50 Victoria Embankment
London EC4Y 0DZ

www.headline.co.uk
www.hachette.co.uk

To Finlay, Milo and Sylvie.
The best things come in threes.

Guilty

/gɪlti/
adjective

* *culpable of or responsible for a specified wrongdoing.*

* *justly chargeable with a particular fault or error.*

* *conscious of, affected by, or revealing a feeling of guilt.*

April 2018

Judge Rupert Harwood's sentencing, Central Criminal Court, London

It is clear from the outset you have lied and deceived and shown precious little remorse for what you have done. Rather than accept your crime, you have tried to shift the blame on to others in the most callous way imaginable. It is typical of the contempt you have shown for your victims and for the court.

Be in no doubt, you will pay a high price for your actions.

PART ONE

PART ONE

One

Joe

Lewes Police Station
October 2017

Let me say this: cracking Libby's skull was not part of the plan. I can't even remember hitting her; it was more of a violent push in the deep heat of an argument and before I could do anything to change the outcome, she was flying backwards, her head making a strange metallic sound as it connected with the stone floor. *Ting!* That's the only way I can describe it, like one of those instrumental triangles we used to play in school. It was a shame about the floor too – if it had been a shag pile carpet rather than porcelain, Libby might not be unconscious in hospital. But I'm certain safety was not uppermost in their minds when they were designing that house. It was all sharp angles and hard surfaces and glinting, gleaming glass that allowed your own reflection to stalk you.

I don't mention any of these misgivings to the police, though. My solicitor has advised me it's not a good line of defence. They're hardly going to charge a floor covering with a violent crime, he says.

It's me they have in their sights, at any rate. Every question is angled towards my guilt. What I did. What I failed to do. My shortcomings – of which there are many – have been itemised and catalogued, and while individually they appear harmless enough, their combined effect in the harsh light of the interview room creates an unsettling picture. I don't doubt this is the ploy, the web the officers are spinning around me. But it is an effective one nevertheless. Having listened to their accusations and character assassinations for the best part of eight hours, I'm beginning to scare myself.

The main issue appears to be my scant adherence to the rules. Yes, it's true, there are rules of engagement when you find yourself in such situations. Say your wife or child goes missing, say you stumble across a body, or in my case, you happen to knock out a loved one, there are set procedures and scripts to follow. Firstly, you raise the alarm. You call 999. You attempt to help the victim. You account for every second spent before help arrives. *Officer, I passed wind at 2.02 p.m.* You display the correct mixture of horror, fear and sadness. You cry the requisite amount of tears. Basically, you're aiming for high levels of authenticity in every single action. Anything too forced or overly dramatic will arouse suspicion. Anything too casual and you are cold and callous. It's a balancing act and I'm no circus entertainer. I'm failing spectacularly.

I did nothing. Try explaining that one away. I tell them I panicked but even that's not true. I wasted precious minutes standing over Libby unable to compute what had happened. There was nothing left inside me, no nerves or sensory receptors to send messages to my brain. Even when finally I leant over her to assess the level of damage, I became instead mesmerised by my own face, gawping at me from the polished brilliance of the porcelain floor.

Well, look what you've done.

You thought you were special.

Turns out you're every bit as bad as the rest.

The officers say they want to know everything, but this is a lie. They want to know everything around the narrow field of their investigation, scavenging for morsels of extraneous information that will get us nowhere while blocking out the bigger picture. I have no intention of pandering to them. I could tell them Amy Winehouse was playing on the karaoke system at the party downstairs, not Amy herself, obviously, but Will's brutal destruction of 'I'm No Good', but that would be pointless scene-setting, nothing more. I could make a stab at describing the hurt Libby inflicted upon me. Her revelation chiselling into my bones. *I don't love you, I never did.* How she stood in front of me and delivered this nugget of truth. I could tell them how it burnt through the epidermis right down to the subcutis, how I thought the pain might send me mad with grief, but this would provide them with a motive, allow them to craft a neat narrative around revenge.

And this is not a story about revenge.

It's about ambition and greed, and love, I suppose, and what we do in the name of them.

I tell the officers I looked out of the window and saw the car and the two men getting into it and driving off. I tell them I ran into the hallway and that's when I saw the smoke and felt the blistering heat.

Have I mentioned the fire?

It has been suggested several times that I started it deliberately to cover up my crime, as if an assault wasn't enough for one evening and I decided to go the whole hog and burn the place down.

Let me say this clearly: I did not start the fire but someone else did.

Everyone invited to the party was meant to die in that fire.

And just because we survived doesn't mean we're safe.

Not even Libby, if she ever wakes up.

Two

Libby

ICU, Princess Royal Hospital, West Sussex

The swish of nylon. Footsteps padding the floor. The staccato beat of a heart. Occasionally, accusations weight the air, medical staff gossip, snaps of colour to brighten a daily routine: *Terrible one, this, the boyfriend is in custody. Clever bunch too. Graduates, you know. All that education and privilege. Just goes to show.*

This is the soundtrack to Libby's existence.

She has ample time to think. What else is she going to do, lying here in the hospital bed? New memories are currently beyond her reach so she plays with the old ones, gathering them up in chronological order to form a single timeline. It is this thread she unspools and winds in again, eyes trained to spot the kink.

It doesn't take her long. It is there, of course, always was, right at the very beginning. People will say it was ambition that landed her in this sorry state, but she knows beyond all else it was trust.

She trusted him.

More fool her.

She can picture him now, ploughing his lies. His face will be a picture of concern. *Tell me she's going to be OK,* he'll say to the police before taking them through a sequence of events that end in his exoneration. They'll struggle to make the calculation, to see that he is more than the sum total of his charm and intellect.

Why would the man who loved her, a man previously of impeccable character, do such a thing? Libby doesn't even have the answer herself. Yes, she has the evidence – she *is* the evidence – but it still requires serious mental contortion for her to override the past. Then there's the love; if she could speak she would ask the doctors to have it surgically removed because this is the source of her pain. The head injury, she is sure, is just a side show. But the love throbs and pulses and reminds her that everything she thought was real was nothing more than an illusion. And unless she can find a way to kill it, she can't see a way through.

Three

Joe

This is my beginning, me, Joe Hemsley. Libby has her own, and Tess too, but mine starts in Dalston, on a warm April evening, music drilling into my brain, some new group my friend had promised were awesome turning out to be nothing of the sort. I staggered outside, shaking my head to clear the noise.

'I want to wash my ears out. I can't ever unhear that,' she said. Her voice was plummy. I half expected to turn around and find a horsey specimen in a Barbour jacket but I found Libby instead. She was standing next to me on the pavement, wavy blond hair, half up, half down, undecided. A big smile like an embrace. Another refugee from the gig. 'I just asked for my money back at the desk,' I told her.

'What did they say?' She took a step closer to me. She smelt of lemons, citrus fruits. Good enough to eat.

'They said, who do you think we are, John fucking Lewis?'

We laughed about it all the way to the chip shop, and all the way back to her flat off Holloway Road, one she shared with five other girls, and the night became a morning that rolled into a night again, the time welding us together. Sometimes, it's that seamless. I'd spent the bulk of my university years calculating how to pull, bemoaning the fact my friend Rex had found true love and regular sex (not necessarily in that order) and yet I had not. What was wrong with me, I routinely asked, only to find the answers too easily – I needed to work out, take more of an interest in fashion (an interest full stop) get a decent haircut. And I'd consider them all and resolve to do something about it, before deciding I really couldn't be arsed. And then one night, one crappy band and the girl appears out of nowhere. BOOM, love had me trapped in its bubble, and I thought, maybe I'm not so bad after all.

I made a stab at restraint, counselling myself to take it slowly because how well could I really know someone in a few days and weeks? But the love wouldn't slow down, it set its own speed, an unstoppable momentum that was beyond rationale and reason and control. She peed in front of me, a form of intimacy too far in my book, until now when I rejoiced in it as a sign of our closeness. I went to see her in *Macbeth*, witnessed her appalling interpretation of Lady Macduff, and I mean truly excrutiating, stressing all the wrong words, forgetting her lines. I should have been humiliated by association but no, I loved her all the more for it. She couldn't act therefore she couldn't lie therefore we must be the real thing. Barring a revelation that she was a fangirl of Nigel Farage, I didn't see how we could go wrong. The only mark on her card was the repeated reference to changing the world. But even I could cope with a bit of idealism.

'I think you should set your sights a bit higher, don't you?' I said.

My sarcasm landed me a jab in the ribs.

'What are you going to do when you graduate, then?' I sensed Libby was more of a planner than I was. I suppose I expected a great job to land in my lap with little effort on my part. I was on course for a First in Maths and Computing, my skills were in demand, employers circling campus with offers of graduate schemes. But I wanted a break before signing up to life in an office, a bit of travelling perhaps, Libby and I bumming around South-East Asia in matching fisherman's trousers for six months. Sadly, Libby didn't share my vision. She wanted something in the bag. Her uncle had supported her through college and she needed to repay his investment, so swanning off to Vietnam for a year to live on the Mekong was not an option. This love thing was complicated, it was already forcing me to redraw my plans.

'I'm still considering my options,' I said. 'But saving the planet is right up there with a corporate job and a new car.'

It wasn't true. The idea that it was our responsibility to save the planet rattled me. I felt pretty aggrieved that all generations before us had stored up their problems in one gigantic tower of shit and we were supposed to roll up our sleeves and sort it out: the dolphins, the plastic, the pollution. In return we got to rent. Forever. Not that I shared these reservations with Libby. There was an authenticity to her tone I couldn't deny, plus she was sitting up in my bed, blinking against the sun, breasts on show, bright blue eyes circled by smudges of last night's mascara. I don't think I had ever concentrated on someone so keenly. I even deduced one breast was slightly bigger than the other, not that it bothered me. It was simply something I noted and filed away: *boobs not symmetrical.*

'I'm pleased to hear it. We've got the brains. The education. It would be a waste if we didn't do something good with our talents.'

'You're absolutely right. But can we start tomorrow?' I crawled over the bed towards her, planted my lips on hers.

'Seriously, though, what *are* you going to do?' She pulled away from the kiss and I sensed a considered answer was required.

'Get a job.' It was the best I could offer what with the boobs on show and the bed and other thoughts cramming my mind.

She closed her eyes, giggled to herself. 'I can just picture you. You'll wear a badly fitting suit. School shoes for adults. A big firm, share options. You'll be the resident genius, the one they can't let go. And you'll drive a Range Rover.'

'They're very good cars.'

She clasped her hands behind her head. She hadn't shaved, didn't mind that I saw it. It was like spotting a dodo. In my limited experience, women viewed body hair as the enemy, a natural outrage to be controlled. Everything shaved and waxed and trimmed like topiary.

But Libby was different, raw and unfiltered. She mocked my straightness, unbuttoned my reserve, breached my defences with her wicked smile and those eyes that sparkled and teased and asked, who are you and what do you want?

'Don't you want more?' she asked. I lifted her hair, kissed her neck. I'd lost concentration, needed to bring this particular line of conversation to an end.

'Life's not John fucking Lewis, you know,' I said, and she surrendered and kissed me back.

After that it became our thing, our motif. Whenever one of us complained about something, a sub-standard jalfrezi, the day not being bright enough, a cough, a cold, the other would say, 'What do you think it is, John fucking Lewis?' *The world's not perfect, deal with it.* As time went on, we spun it out; our wedding list would be in John Lewis, our kids would sleep in John Lewis bedding, and on it went. The joke provided endless possibilities that reinforced our togetherness.

Except it wasn't that great a joke really. Or at least it doesn't seem like one now.

It seems like a warning.

Four

Libby

For Libby it started with a dinner and a conversation a few months before her finals. Her and her uncle at Mama Rosa's Italian in Cobham, an unusual venue for them – he was flasher than red-and-white checked tablecloths and candles stuck in empty bottles. When Richard took her out it was always a big deal, a table at the Ivy or lunch at the Shard. It wasn't that she was averse to low-costing eating – she was a student, after all – but subconsciously she had measured his love against the grand gestures, the view, the price of a bottle of wine, which was why Mama Rosa's Italian was giving her a serious case of the heebie-jeebies.

He wasn't himself either. Shrunken. Richard was the boom of his laugh, the precise cut of his suits. He was extravagance and generosity, big watches, parties, large, shiny cars with leather seats. The master of his universe. And yet that night, his tuning was out. Not hugely, he was still recognisable, but it was enough to interfere with the overall picture. A brush of stubble coated his face and combined with the nervous twitch in his jaw, a throbbing Adam's apple, it unsettled her. He was playing out of position.

What have I done wrong? That was her starting point when life went awry, always was. If she could have been better, kinder, tidied up her toys when asked, done the dishes without moaning, perhaps her mother would still be here. Libby hadn't been enough and so she spent her life trying to be more.

Still, the wine soothed her worries, and after the first bottle she was sufficiently relaxed to broach the subject of travelling, taking some time out after her exams. Yes, she'd mocked Joe when he'd first mentioned it, but the notion had planted itself in her brain and assaulted her with images of undiscovered beaches and clear blue seas and the pair of them collecting memories as they trailed across a continent together, running for late-night buses, sleeping on ferries, waking up to new smells and sounds and views every day. But above all else, and it was this that made her drunk with excitement, she saw spread out in front of her a chunk of time where she'd be free of responsibility, of duty, of the need to be unremittingly grateful to her uncle and Dana his wife for everything they'd done for her. With Joe she could just be, and that was the glorious simplicity of it.

Except, Richard didn't do loafing around. He did purpose and ambition and goals. She took another swig of wine, waited until he had filled his mouth with a slice of pizza before she came right out with it.

'I fancy going travelling when I finish,' she said. Her words were shaky and unsure of themselves. 'Vietnam and Thailand and Burma.' She studied his expression. He was chewing frantically and she could track the progress of the pizza down his gullet. 'You know, before I settle into a job, it would only be for a short time.'

'Why would you want to do that?'

'It would be an amazing experience, don't you think?'

'Living on a shoestring? That's not my idea of a great experience, Libby. Better to get the job and get started and then you can travel in luxury.'

She searched for a line, a persuasive sentence to win him over.

'It's not about the luxury, the luxury isn't the point.'

'Then what is the point?'

'It's about . . .' She was floundering under his interrogation. She couldn't say, *It's about having no responsibility, or have you never fancied just bumming around for six months?*, because he wasn't the sort to understand. And why was it she deserved six months off when he had to work like a dog to pay for everything?

'I'd say it's best not to waste time.' Her mistake was in the hesitation. It made her vulnerable and her uncle seized the opportunity to move in and shoot her down.

Libby hadn't been aware time was in short supply. 'Get started, get some experience, earn some money, set clear goals and then go travelling if you still fancy it.' He said travelling like it was an alien word that had no place in his mouth. Libby felt the stirrings of a headache, a premature hangover. His answer had drilled through the images of sparkling seas and jungle treks and toes in hot golden sand until there was nothing left of them except tiny little fragments of what might have been. 'Oh come on, don't look at me like that. You would hate it anyway. It isn't your style. You like the good things in life.'

Was that the truth? Was that what she really wanted? For the first time Libby saw the gulf between his version of her and the one she had been free to create with Joe.

'I don't think that's . . .'

He balled up his napkin, threw it on to his plate. 'The business is in a bit of trouble. A big deal has gone wrong. It's touch and go if we'll survive.'

Libby pushed back into her chair absorbing the blow. *Now* it made sense. His appearance, the choice of restaurant, the off-key vibe. He was scared. Why else would he tell her? He must be terrified of losing it all. God, she was selfish, banging on about travelling when the man who had provided everything for her was deep in the shit. The shame made her hot. That, and the fear, because this kind of talk shook her, the way it diminished him. He always had a solution. He moved on quickly, his eye always on the next thing, the horizon. One step ahead, he used to tell her, that's where you need to be in business. The prospect of his demise frightened her more than she could admit. Richard wasn't just the man who held everyone else up – his wife Dana, Max and Tilly, her cousins, the two-hundred-strong workforce he employed – he was the man who held her up.

'Oh,' she said. Libby studied him again with the benefit of this new knowledge. 'I'm sorry.'

'It's not your fault.'

It wasn't her fault because Libby wasn't running his business, but she was one of his many outgoings and she could picture Dana berating him over all the money he wasted on her, money that could have been spent on his own children, Max and Matilda, on her, on anything other than Libby, the niece she suffered under duress. It was a bone of contention between her aunt and uncle, often on show, rarely concealed. Dana couldn't understand why he had taken her in, given her a home and paid for everything since her mother died. But who else would have looked after her? Where else would she have gone? She had nothing. The only thing she inherited from her mother were two diamond stud earrings, earrings she had never removed since her first piercing when she was ten years old. And Libby had only the faintest memories of her father, long hair, bare chested, camping together in a hot tent, the sweet, heady scent of his tobacco mixing with the smell of sausages on the barbecue. Her grandmother said he was bohemian. Her uncle called him a useless hippy. Whatever he had been, he wasn't any more. A motorbike accident had seen to that. And her mother was never quite the same afterwards; she looked faint, distant, like her signal was fuzzy. When she drowned, it was her uncle that looked after her, forked out for the private school fees, the university fees, the accommodation and upkeep, everything right down to the margherita pizza in front of her and the wine on which she had been getting merrily drunk.

'Is it that bad?' She wanted him to say no, reassure her like he always did. Smooth over her worries.

'Touch and go.'

Wrong answer. She gulped her wine, experienced the dread rising like smoke inside her. He was her gravity, the force that held her down. He couldn't lose everything.

'I can pay for this,' she said, before remembering it was all his money anyway.

'Good God, I can still afford to treat you to a pizza, but for Christ's sake, don't order dessert.' His face cracked with laughter and seeing him rebooted brightened her mood a touch. 'Sod it, let's have another bottle.' He picked up the empty one and waved it in the direction of the waiter.

Before she knew it the room was dancing in front of her, her uncle bobbing in and out of focus. It was frustrating, this drunken state, because she could sense there was something else, something that was unspoken or needed to be spoken. Shame her head was too fuzzy to work it out. Maybe he needed to cut her allowance, drop it entirely, and this was the preamble. She felt a thin sheen of sweat layer her brow. Well, she was nearly finished with her computing degree anyway, and then she would get a job. The travelling idea was now filed away as an unnecessary indulgence.

'Is there anything I can do to help?' she blurted out. It was a stupid question. She could hardly single-handedly save his business. But she wanted him to know she cared, that she didn't take his financial support for granted. 'I understand if you need to stop the payments. I can get a job, and a loan.'

'Nonsense. I wouldn't hear of it.' He poured the last of the wine into his glass and examined the sediment gathering at the bottom, before swigging it. 'But let's talk about what you're going to do when you finish university. You're a smart girl. You'll go far.'

Libby came away from that evening with a plan. A hazy one, given the amount of wine she had consumed, but it became clearer the next morning. And once she understood what her uncle expected, she embraced the plan wholeheartedly because in a small way, a very small way, it helped redress the deficit in their relationship. It gave her a use, a purpose. It also changed everything, including her relationship with Joe. But that realisation would come much later. Much later.

If only she hadn't fallen for him so hard. But even when she tried to rein back, the attraction defied her control, strange given that on paper he shouldn't have been the one for her. Not even close. She had a type; they tended to be blond although she was flexible on hair colour, blue eyes to match her own. She liked them clean-cut, sartorially savvy in a modern elegant kind of way (basically no super-low-rise jeans that revealed boxers, and no hoodies, and definitely no rugby shirts). Joe had no concept of fashion, rotated a series of washed out T-shirts including one he had received for running the Ealing 10k in 2014. He had deep brown eyes that reminded her of fat, juicy hazelnuts and his hair was dark and long and sometimes greasy, not out of design, she suspected – no one would choose that haircut – but simply because he had not been to the barbers since Christmas. And yet the thing was, Joe fitted. He fitted in every conceivable way. It made sex spectacular, made the modern elegant men who turned out to be neither modern nor elegant pale into insignificance. She had no idea it could be this good or this easy, or that she, Libby Sumner, could let go and relax and be herself. Joe didn't try to pierce her veneer in that awkward way her other boyfriends had. He didn't need to. He steamed past it, saw who she was, and by rights that should have made her vulnerable and exposed but all it did was make her feel calm. A glorious, sweeping, blissful kind of calm that flooded her veins like a drug. And even in the brief interludes when they weren't having sex, Joe still fitted; they were both studying computers, she could let her nerdiness roam free, they both liked Thai food but hated Chinese. Even the way her head slotted neatly under his chin when he pulled her into a hug was right.

After the meeting with her uncle she made several attempts at retreat. And when they didn't work she tried to make Joe retreat, feeding him reasons to go off her: The first-thing-in-the-morning kiss without brushing her teeth, the peeing in front of him and the underarm hair on show. None of them worked. Quite the opposite. It made him keener. It was almost as if he wanted the raw, unfiltered version of Libby, the one she had learnt to gloss and polish over. And that's how Joe hit her with an irresistible double whammy; she fell in love with him, but she also learnt to love herself again too.

So yes, there was the voice, the relentless inner voice, that said she shouldn't be doing this, that it was wrong and unfair, but she silenced it.

For a while at least.

Five

Joe

There was an intensity to those first few months, a sense that time was running out, that we had to grab the perfection and enjoy every glorious moment of it while it lasted. The end of term was approaching, real life looming, nights out with friends seemed like a waste, an intrusion. Libby's move to my flat came in three quick phases, first with the arrival of her toothbrush, then a change of clothes, before finally she rocked up one Sunday with a suitcase. My flat was above a chip shop in Woolwich, a location Rex and I had always seen as an advantage, unlike Libby, who professed to hate the smell of fried food. But it trumped her dwellings because it was empty, Rex having moved in with his girlfriend a few months earlier, and so we spent our time locked away from the world for revision and sex, venturing out only when vitamin D levels reached critical levels and food supplies were low. It was upon her return from one such mission that she came home armed with a poster.

'Take a look at this,' she said, thrusting it into my hands.

Are you tough enough to crack?

It was a job advert dressed up as some kind of game. The irony of the wording is not lost on me given what subsequently happened to Libby.

But this was still months before it ended badly. And I had no reason to suspect it might lead us to anything other than gainful employment. Big firms were stalking the campus. Tech startups were luring the maths and computing students with promises of equity and smoothies on tap. They were all after the same thing: fresh blood, big brains, fierce intellect, and they were prepared to pay.

'Sounds cheesy, like CBBC does job ads.' She looked crushed and I regretted my dismissive tone, made a show of giving it closer inspection.

'I thought it'd be right up your street. Crack the code, hack a system, get a job. Only this is legit.'

She was referring to my on campus business activities. Not so long ago I'd had a nice little sideline in hacking, nothing major, just helping friends and acquaintances out with their requests for a small fee. 'I'm one hundred per cent above board now.'

'Admit it, part of you misses the buzz. This way you can have your cake and eat it.'

We devoted our Friday night to the task. Or in my case, one hour thirty-eight minutes of mine. That was how long it took me to break into the system. This kind of thing was second nature to me. Libby was slower. A lot slower. After two and a half hours I brought her a glass of wine: 'Are you trying to sabotage my chances?' I backed off, went out and bought us a curry, more wine, careful not to disturb her on my return.

'I admit defeat,' she said.

I swiped the laptop from her. 'No you don't.'

It took me half an hour to get her through.

'You are a cheat, Joe Hemsley.'

'I never claimed to be anything else.'

Three weeks later, in the thick of our finals, we both received the same email: *YOU HAVE BEEN SELECTED FOR INTERVIEW...*

I don't profess to be any kind of hotel expert but I can confirm this one was especially pleasing to the eye. A huge, airy entrance, with a giant industrial staircase weaving up to the first floor. Pops of bright colour in the furnishings. The fact that I even noticed these things should tell you it was impressive.

There were five of us invited from UCL. Will, Tess, Asha, myself and Libby. I vaguely recognised Will but beyond that I had no idea we'd spent the past three years on the same campus. Libby appeared much more familiar with them. 'We don't all go around with our heads in books,' she said when I expressed surprise. Over coffee and croissants and a fruit selection designed to banish student scurvy in the bar area (think, mosaic tiles, industrial lamps, gold fittings), the operations director of Freetech, Kyle Nowak or head dreamer as he called himself, piled his plate high with melon and pineapple, ordered a chai latte and talked to us about new frontiers and horizons.

'I didn't realise we were training to be Jedis,' I whispered to Libby.

'You were targeted, do you realise that? We could have gone to any college in the country but we went to UCL because we know it produces the calibre of people we need. Why waste time with second best, that's what I say. And you guys are the cream. Go on, admit it, you're the best in your class.' Will nodded, his ego inflating with every word Kyle spoke. 'I've done my home-work. The code competition, that was just a bit of fun, entry level stuff, but I know you're all at the top of your respective classes, getting the top scores. That's why you're here.'

Kyle stabbed a piece of pineapple. He was in annoy-ingly good shape. A tan setting off his full set of American teeth. He worked out, as evidenced by his muscles rippling underneath his grey T-shirt emblazoned with *NO LIMITS* and next to him I couldn't help regretting the months spent indoors eating takeaways. Part of me hated him, the other part wanted to be him.

He directed us into a conference room – something of a downer after the bohemian vibe of the bar – and issued us with name badges. He perched himself on the edge of the desk like a newsreader.

'So what is Freetech?' He opened his arms wide as if he was the embodiment of the question. 'Who are we?' He jumped down from his ledge and paced the room. 'You want to know that, right? You want to know why we're different, what you can do for us, what we can do for you. First off, let me ask you a question. What do you want out of life?'

It wasn't a particularly warm day, and the air con in the conference room was fierce, but the sweat bubbled on my skin nevertheless. That question again, bullying me into submission. I hoped Libby would go first so I could pillage some of her answer and present her thoughts as my own.

'Joe, let's hear from you first.'

'Me?'

'You are Joe, aren't you? Not an impostor.' Will, who was sitting next to me, snorted with laughter, prompting an intense dislike in me. Libby's eyes burnt, *Don't fuck it up.*

'I'd like Liverpool to win the league.' *I can play for laughs too*, I thought, but I caught Libby's expression and it wasn't pretty. 'I want to be challenged and I . . .' the words got stuck on my lips and I had to unpick them, 'I want to make a difference.'

We went round the group, all giving variations on the same theme, each one embellishing their speech with more passion than the last.

'Well,' said Kyle, finally. 'You're in the right place, give yourselves a pat on the back. Go on then, you deserve it.' He smiled and waited until Will thumped himself on the shoulder.

'Take it in the literal sense by all means, Will, ' Kyle smiled and I laughed the loudest. Will's cheeks flamed and he swatted himself again to make it look like he had been targeting an imaginary fly but he had no one fooled.

'Freetech is a young company and you'll be our trailblazers, our brilliant young brains shaking up the tech industry. We're also part of a bigger global enterprise, a family of companies, so I guess you could say we have the best of both worlds. Think of us as the upstart younger brother, the disrupter, out to make our mark on the world.'

Begrudgingly, I warmed to Kyle. Fuck, I wanted to be him, join his movement, whatever it was on offer. I wanted the tan and the teeth. I wanted muscles underneath a *NO LIMITS* T-shirt. His oratory was on a different plane to the usual corporate spiel, fizzing with energy and purpose. Freetech, we learnt, had global ambitions, 'We want to use technology to make change happen.' He gave examples of clients around the world who they'd helped succeed in their missions, hinted at government contracts to secure fair elections. A large part of what we'd be doing was ethical hacking, breaking into clients' systems in order to test them for weakness. A more ideal job I could not have found. I felt the weight of responsibility – yes, that word again – lifting from my shoulders. Here was a job I could do, and earn saving-the-planet Brownie points too. I wanted to know how many jobs were on offer and who I had to kill to get one. Will would be first on my hit list. The longer I spent with him the less I liked him.

If I were writing a review of the day, like people do on Amazon for razors and toasters, the only negative I'd flag was the final exercise. We'd done the psychometric tests, the coding. We were all done in, cooped up too long in a room. But before Kyle dismissed us he wanted one last piece of information, a nauseating circle of trust-type exercise.

We had to reveal our greatest fear.

Why? Well, we needed to admit our weaknesses in order to be strong, apparently.

If there was a kink in this logic, I didn't spot it. Asha said snakes, and when Libby said being alone, I squeezed her hand under the table. Will's was starving, though from the look of him there was little chance of that in the near future. And mine? Dark enclosed spaces.

The letters arrived in early July. One addressed to Libby – she'd given them my address – the other to me. His and hers. It was a sultry morning, the fryers in the chip shop below mercifully out of action until evening. Every window in my tiny flat was thrown open to encourage air flow but to no effect. We'd talked of a swim, a picnic, wine in the park. In one corner of the kitchen, a bee flung itself against the pane of glass, once, twice, three times, oblivious to the escape routes all around.

'Do we open them at the same time?' Libby asked.

'What if one of us gets it and the other doesn't? Will we hate each other?'

'I have a feeling that's not going to be a problem,' she said. I admired her confidence.

Libby was right. We both got the job. We were to start five weeks from now, which really couldn't have been more perfect. A month-long holiday to loaf about, guilt-free, secure in the knowledge we'd soon be earning a sizeable chunk of money, although it wasn't *just* about the money, we'd be using our talents for the greater good. The very next day we each got an email from UCL informing us we'd got first-class degrees. If I'm honest I'd expected nothing less, but the confirmation was sweet. And that summer I remember how we couldn't stop looking at each other, because we saw a reflection of our own good luck. Not that Libby would have called it luck. There was hard work and planning. It wasn't random, she said. We deserved it. And we tried not to be smug, what with our love and good fortune and the general sense we were winning at life, but on reflection I admit we weren't entirely successful.

I suppose you could say it started with vanity. We believed we were special when the truth was we were simply vulnerable.

Six

Libby

'I got the job,' she told Richard when the letters arrived.

'I thought you might.' She could hear the smile in her uncle's voice.

'I'll make you proud.'

'You better,' he said.

No pressure.

He called her the next day in an expansive mood. 'There's a present in your account,' he said. 'Didn't I tell you there was no need to slum it? Book somewhere decent, you deserve it.'

Four thousand pounds to spend on a holiday. 'I can't accept that, not when you're—'

'Nonsense. Things are beginning to look up, Libby. And I want you to enjoy yourself before the hard work ahead.'

'If you're sure.' She knew better than to argue. He liked gift-giving, it was part of who he was, and besides, she'd given up the idea of travelling on his advice and Joe had too. The gift was her uncle's way of compensating.

A week later, she surprised Joe with a trip to Santorini. His reservations, *I should pay my own way, I don't even know your uncle*, were dampened by the inflight drinks and by the time they reached their apartment, as the sun was dripping down a bright orange sky, setting the white cliffs alight, they were silenced altogether. They spent long, lazy days, waking late, taking break-fast on the balcony, fresh bread with the most delicious mulberry jam made by the owner Eleni, who insisted they visit her brother Sami's taverna to taste the best barbecued fish on the island.

'We could stay here,' she said, lying on a lounger, her face tilted to the sky. 'It's almost criminal that we have to go back and start work.'

'I think you'll find I can be easily persuaded.' He traced his finger down her stomach, circled her belly button. 'What's the worst that would happen if we turned the job down?'

Libby didn't have to consider the worst-case scenario, it was there, swinging over her like an axe, just as it had been for years. She would be a disappointment. *So what?* she imagined Joe saying. *You don't have to prove yourself.* But he didn't understand – why would he, when his worth wasn't tied up in what his parents thought of him? But to Libby it was everything.

'I'm starving,' she said, sitting up, changing the subject. 'Let's go to Sami's place for dinner.' Eleni found them the best table overlooking the sea and they ate dorada and drank the ouzo Sami plied them with and didn't leave until one in the morning, staggering back to their apartment under a fat shining globe of a moon, the sound of the cicadas ringing in the shadows, giddy on life.

'When we get to London,' Libby said, and Joe put his fingers to her lips.

'We're never leaving this place, remember.' She batted his fingers away.

'But when we get back, let's find a flat together. Our flat. Somewhere like Hackney or Clapton.'

'Romantic. Do they have sunsets in Clapton, and fresh barbecued fish and free ouzo and homemade mulberry jam?'

'All of the above.'

'You wouldn't lie to me, Libby, would you? Just to get me where you want me?'

'Never.'

★

Day one of the job and Libby was tense. Tense on the way to the bus stop, tense as she ill-advisedly necked her third coffee of the morning.

'It's just a job, relax,' Joe said. She would not relax, and she wished Joe could manufacture a few nerves, if only to make her feel less inadequate. But that wasn't going to happen. Joe shared none of her reservations, and had the kind of innate confidence in his abilities that was impossible to mask.

Libby and Joe were first to arrive and waited in the lobby for Kyle to meet them. One by one, the others who were at the interview appeared and exchanged chat about their summers, their degrees (all firsts), and made complimentary noises about the office and its location in an achingly hip corner of Shoreditch, a few streets from Silicon Roundabout. 'Ah, the fabulous five,' Kyle said when he bounded through the lobby. He was still wearing a short-sleeved shirt in a loud jungle pattern and issued them with security passes, explaining that there were five floors in the block, each belonging to a sister company. 'Your passes won't work on any other floors and vice versa. We wouldn't want anyone poking around in our business.'

Their office was deserted and had the smell of new furniture and paint. 'Where is everyone?' Asha asked.

'It's just you and me, guys,' Kyle said. 'We're practically a startup, but we'll be punching hard, let me tell you.' He ran them through a few housekeeping rules, mainly to do with confidentiality. On no account were they to discuss their clients outside the office, 'Or even with each other, do you understand?' They nodded their assent and he moved on to the bowls of gluten-free energy balls. 'Help yourself!' He ignored Joe when he said they reminded him of turds. 'There's also free yoga on Fridays. Just up your street, Will,' Kyle said.

Throughout the morning, he called each of them into his office, a glass cube in the middle of the room, to tell them about their individual clients and the kind of testing they would be expected to do. When Libby emerged from her chat, she felt half the size, squashed by the pressure bearing down upon her. It was real now. And she had wanted a challenge, she loved nothing more than a challenge in normal circumstances, she just hadn't expected to feel such a fake. Unlike the others, she hadn't dabbled in small-time hacking as a pastime at college, she was way too much of a good girl to break the law. But the rest had all been at it, it was why they had been such attractive candidates in the first place. Kyle wasn't the only one who had done his research. She knew all about Will's activities. He had joked the FBI were after him or his online persona, and had fallen uncharacteristically quiet over lunch when Asha asked what exactly he had been up to. Asha herself had hacked her ex-boyfriend's accounts, his life basically, changing all the passwords in revenge for him posting a naked photo of her online – *I hadn't even had a wax for fuck's sake, that was the thing that sent me over the edge.* And Tess? Well, hats off to Tess, who hadn't done it for anything so tawdry as personal gain. She'd broken in to Westminster Council's system, obtained access to emails between one of their executives and Elliot Homes, the country's largest house builders who wanted to knock down three blocks of social housing to build luxury apartments in their place. When she found evidence of Elliot paying a substantial sum to another council project in return for the 'favour' she leaked the emails. Her only problem was she got caught. Quite how Tess managed to escape without a criminal record was beyond Libby. No doubt she had smiled at them. Or twiddled her hair or stretched her long, lean limbs out until they released her. Had Libby mentioned Tess was pretty? Very, very pretty.

It was clear, even in that first week, that Kyle liked Tess. No surprise there. But honestly, he could have been a little less obvious with his favouritism, hanging over her desk, praising her work – 'Thank God you're on our side,' he'd joke and she'd smile coyly and blush. When he wasn't fawning over Tess, he was fond of reminding them this was a probationary period. 'We're handling seriously sensitive information here and we have a responsibility to make sure whatever we find is secure. You don't discuss your work outside of this office,' he repeated at least twice a day. 'And we work as a team, one bad apple and we're all tarnished.'

This kind of talk made Libby sweat. Not because she wasn't trustworthy; she was the most reliable person she knew. It was simply that she was out of her depth. Drowning, more like. She lacked the guile and guts of her colleagues who could break virtual locks and slip through barriers as if they didn't exist. They could dial a number, spew lies to the unsuspecting employee on the other end of the line – *I'm the CEOs PA, I need that access now* – or cry down the phone – *My partner's abroad and I'm locked out of our account.* They played tracks of babies crying in the background to ramp up the emotion and elicit a sympathetic response from the call centre employees – *Oh, OK, just this once, I shouldn't but you sound desperate* – who would do their bidding unaware they had just been conned.

'You have to silence your conscience,' Kyle said one day over lunch on the terrace. He was addressing the group but really, she knew his words were aimed at her. 'Remember, that's why these systems are weak in the first place. More often than not it's a human weakness that allows hackers to thrive, you know; the guy on the other end of the line takes pity on the caller and before you know it, a family has lost their life savings or a company is going down the tube because they're the victim of a cyber attack. Our job is to exploit every loophole in these systems and report back to our clients. That's why they're paying us. Don't feel sorry for Maggie in HR who you've just persuaded to hand over the payroll details, think of the bigger picture. Our clients can't afford Maggie's indiscretion. Her eagerness to help has just potentially cost them millions, lost people their jobs. Focus on that.'

Libby tried. When it was her turn to pick up the phone and lie through her teeth – the social engineering side of the hack – she attempted to take herself out of the moment, think big, not small. Remind herself the client wanted her to do this, that she was trying to make them more secure in the long run, not less. It required a certain dampening of her emotions, her instinctive do-goodery, and sometimes it worked. Sometimes she'd fly through the lies, speeding along in their slipstream, and find herself exhilarated, pushing her own boundaries. And then other times her gaze would travel around the open-plan office and she'd witness her colleagues, their total concentration and immersion in the task, and there was something cold and robotic about the scene that made her shiver.

It also reminded her that she didn't really deserve to be here. She was here because someone had helped her.

She was an impostor.

Still, she had to maintain a front. Everyone else was committed to the task, knew exactly what they were doing. It was like being in an exam and having that sinking feeling she was the only one who didn't know the answer. She couldn't even tell Joe how she felt, didn't want to pour water on his fire because he was in his element, had declared the job to be a dream. And he loved the free beer Fridays, on the roof terrace where they'd find a table together, the staff from the other floors all around but never mingling. But it irked her, the fact she didn't have Joe to herself any more but was forced to share him with Asha and Will and Tess. Joe's only issue was with Will, whose vanity was off the scale. 'Someone show that man a mirror for fuck's sake,' Asha said one day. 'He actually thinks he has a chance with Tess. Can you imagine?'

Libby could not imagine Tess and Will together. Not Tess in

her floaty dresses that always seemed to reveal a flash of skin. It shouldn't have irritated her, not really – what was it to her how other people dressed? But it did. And the long hair, decorated with at least one flower accessory, the hair she was forever twisting and untwisting around her index finger. That was another source of mild aggravation. And the general way she wafted around. Waft wasn't a word Libby would normally use but it described Tess perfectly.

'What have you got against her?' Joe asked one Friday night as they were making their way home in a cab. They'd all moved on from the terrace to a club where Asha persuaded the DJ to play back-to-back Spandau Ballet for half an hour because they were the only ones there. Joe had danced to 'Gold' with Tess. Will too. Even Asha. Everyone danced with Tess. Everyone wanted to be close to her so some of her magic and gloss would rub off. Everyone apart from Libby, who guarded the bags and coats from no one at all and watched the spectacle as a knot formed in her stomach. Libby hadn't even known Joe could dance, he had never danced with her, and there he was cutting some moves (bad ones admittedly), leaning in to whisper to Tess and then throwing his head back when she said something funny.

'Don't tell me you're jealous,' he said in the cab home to Clapton – they'd found a flat when they got back from Santorini, the deposit paid by her uncle.

'Of what?'

'Of me having fun with another woman.'

'Were you?'

'It doesn't mean I love you less.'

It was their first rub, the first spark of friction thus far, and she put it down to the long week at work, the booze and fatigue. And she put it down to Tess too and made a mental note to keep an eye on her.

★

It was two days later when she saw her. Libby told Joe she was leaving for work early. She fancied a walk, decided to get off the Tube a few stops too soon and enjoy the morning. There was something wholesome about it, virtuous even, like drinking lemon water or glugging apple cider vinegar. She stopped at a stall for a coffee and that's when she saw a leg that looked long enough to be Tess's sticking out from a park bench. Red sandals on her feet. Tess had red sandals. It *was* Tess. Maybe she was enjoying the morning too, Libby thought with a ripple of irritation. This was her idea. She didn't fancy sharing small talk with her colleague en route to the office. She was about to skip away when she clocked the man by her side. Who was that? Tess hadn't mentioned a boyfriend and there didn't look to be any familial resemblance. The man was short, stubby with a shaved head. Wearing bright white trainers and a blue T-shirt. Muscles, too big for comfort. And a tattoo. Older than Tess. But she definitely knew him. She knew him well enough to argue. Tess was shaking her head and the man's face was scrunched up as he berated her. Libby had never seen Tess like this before. She was always calm – too calm in her opinion – nothing ruffled her feathers or prompted her voice to rise above a whisper. And here she was, arguing in the park first thing in the morning with a man Libby would have crossed the road to avoid.

'Shit,' Libby jumped. Tess had spotted her, raised her hand in a reluctant wave. It was too obvious to deny, and walking away would have been rude. Slowly, she made her way over.

'Gorgeous morning,' she said for want of a more original line of conversation.

'It is,' the guy said. 'We thought we'd make the most of it.'

Libby noted the *we*.

They both stood up, him resting his hand on the small of Tess's back. Up close he was marginally less intimidating. 'I'm Tess's boyfriend.' He reached out his hand to shake hers.

'Libby. We work together.'

Tess's face burnt, and Libby knew there wasn't that much heat in the early sun. She turned to the man. 'We can talk later, Libby and I really should get going or we'll be late for work.'

'All right, darling, enjoy.' He leant over towards her just as she moved her cheek so his kiss landed on her ear. Libby and Tess walked out of the park together.

'Would you mind,' Tess said, 'if I put these in?' She pulled her phone and earbuds from her bag. 'I'm listening to a podcast and it's really addictive.'

'Not at all,' Libby told her. But she did. Having witnessed the strange display she wanted the chance to grill Tess and now it was lost.

As she walked by her side towards the office, it occurred to Libby the man hadn't even told her his name.

Seven

Tess

Tomaz. The man in the park. It started with him. A meeting
months before when Tess was at her lowest. She was
scared, and he must have smelt the fear leaking out of her skin,
drenching her clothes. Tess had never been frightened like that
before, and then Tomaz came along and offered her a way out.
At least that's how he sold it. Only now it didn't seem like a way
out of anything. It seemed like a huge mistake.

This was exactly what Tess had been telling Tomaz, shouting
at him that she didn't want to do it any more, when Libby burst
out of nowhere and spotted them in the wild. Of all the people
it had to be Libby with her watchful, prowling eyes, appraising
her clothes and her hair, feeding her that look, the one that was
slightly off kilter, the one that made her sweat and think, *Does
she know?*

Tess tried to shake her off on the way to work, slowing her
pace and speeding it up in the vain hope her walking companion
might get the message and leave her alone. No such luck. Libby
was game, trotting alongside her, no doubt with an arsenal of
questions she was dying to ask. Tess shoved her earbuds in
before she got the chance and listened to anything – the anything
being Heart FM and power ballads. But still, better than an
interrogation from Libby.

Who was he?
Your boyfriend. Kept that quiet.
Didn't seem like your type.

On reflection Libby would never be so crass as to utter the last statement. She was way too polite, too nice, the type to couch her digs in a much softer fabric: *Funny, I would have pictured you with someone else.*

But the burn was the same no matter the words: *You really are scraping the barrel, aren't you?*

What stung was that whatever else Libby had got wrong, in this respect she was correct. Tomaz was not Tess's type. If you had shown the old Tess, the real Tess, a window into her current life, she would have laughed in your face. Tess had never kowtowed to anyone. She shouted loud, fought hard for causes, from her primary school petition to improve school dinners (108 signatures, thank you very much), to her letter to David Cameron (aged fifteen) urging him to 'poke his head out from his palace' and see the injustice in front of him. 'Whether rich or poor, we are all the same,' she'd written. Tess had always spoken from the heart and often shot from the hip. But for all the scrapes she had landed herself in (*Couldn't you just tone yourself down a bit, dear?* her grandmother had once asked), there was one irrefutable truth. Tess had always been Tess. One hundred per cent authentic.

Until now.

Now Tomaz was in control. That was how their relationship worked. He called the shots. He told her when they would meet and what she would do. He even suggested she adjust her wardrobe, lose the utility wear, the dungarees, the nose ring, the loud voice. *Lose yourself.* And it was happening. She could feel the fight being sucked out of her like her innards were being removed. One morning, she was sure, she'd wake up to find a floaty dress lying where she once was. If only she'd known, that first time they were introduced, what this would entail, she would have screamed in his face and told him to fuck off and lived with whatever consequences he had planned for her.

But now he wouldn't let her go. Why would he, when she

was exactly where he wanted her to be? The word *no* bounced off him like a rubber ball and Christ knows she'd thrown it at him enough times. 'A bit late for that now, Tess,' he said. 'You're in too deep.'

And for all she hated him and his fat stumpy fingers and the way he used the flat of his hand to wipe his nose, and the smell of him, the godawful tang of stale washing, she knew he was right.

She emerged from the bathroom in the office, shaking the last drops of water from her hands. Joe looked up and smiled at her. 'Not eaten it yet?' She pointed to the gluten-free energy ball sitting like a relic on his desk.

'Be my guest.'

'I'll pass, thanks all the same.'

She sat at her own desk and attempted to focus. The guilt made her insides scream. She hated herself, the treachery of what she was doing, but there was no way out. She was here to do a job.

Just not the same one as everyone else.

Eight

Libby

The encounter with Tess distracted Libby for the rest of the day – the odd pairing of boyfriend and girlfriend, the palpable tension between them, and Tess's silence on the way to the office. Downright rude, was her initial judgement, but slowly, over the course of the morning, reason wore her down and she revised her opinion. Had Tess been scared of him? Libby considered what she had seen: the possessive arm around her shoulder, the kiss Tess avoided, the flush of heat in her face. She had not been comfortable in her boyfriend's presence, and frankly Libby didn't blame her. She wasn't a big one for vibes and auras like some of her hippy student friends, but there was something negative spinning off him, an energy that sapped her own. And she hadn't failed to notice Tess turning back to check behind her as they left the park, and seeing him, as Libby did, arms crossed, eyes trailing them until they were out of sight.

By the end of the day, her imagination had gone into over-drive. Tess was not some seductress stalking the office and trading in whispers and whimpers but a woman in an abusive relationship, worn down by a partner she couldn't shake. Libby even looked for telltale bruises, scanning those long limbs that had provoked her initial jealousy (yes, she would admit it), and when she found none, she reminded herself that a clever abuser would make his mark in hidden places, the torso, the back, somewhere out of sight.

She googled coercive control, remembering it was a thing,

not just a thing but against the law: *Emotional abuse over a period of time when the perpetrator controls their victim.*

'Fancy a wine after work?' Libby asked. She was one of life's givers and she wanted to help, whether Tess realised she needed it or not.

'What?'

'A drink, do you want to go out after work?'

'Erm, I'm not sure I can.'

'Meeting your boyfriend? Don't worry, another time, then.' She waited for her reaction.

'Actually, why not. A drink would be lovely.'

This is going well, thought Libby. The bar she had chosen was filled with bearded men and bright trainers and young women, her age actually, in large glasses she suspected were worn for show rather than any optical necessity. She'd picked it figuring it would be Tess's scene but her mistake was evident as soon as she walked in. Libby felt out of place. She *was* out of place, in her skinny jeans, jeans that she feared were to these hipsters what bootcuts were to her. It was true she had not mastered the art of dressing for work while dressing cool. It contradicted all the years of private school indoctrination, *dress smart, work smart.* Even Tess looked awkward, today's dress wearing her rather than the other way around.

'It's hell in here,' Tess shouted over the noise.

'I'm glad you said that. Let's go somewhere else.'

Libby got drunk. Tess got drunk, at least Libby hoped she did. Hoped it wasn't just her glugging the wine while Tess simply pretended and watched her get sloshed. Because the next morning when Libby was nursing her hangover and searching her mind for the booty from the night before, the fresh information she had on Tess, the private, intimate stuff she'd shared, she found none. Nothing at all beyond a hatred of salted squid that only emerged because they'd ended up in a tapas bar. Conversely, Libby had emptied herself out, told her how she met Joe, shared the *not fucking John Lewis* line which really wasn't that funny if you weren't part of the joke. She'd even talked about her work, at length, the client she had, The Change Group, its CEO Marc Zimmerman. It was all against the rules of confidentiality and Libby was a fervent obeyer of rules, but she wanted to shake off her girl guide, goody-two-shoes image and Tess had invited confidence. Plus there was the wine. Lots of it.

She scrolled back to the end of the night and there she was, still dealing out personal titbits as a form of currency – the death of her mother, her uncle stepping into the breach and bringing her up – and in return she had expected to be paid in information about Tess's life. But it didn't come. Every time she manoeuvred the talk around to boyfriends and Tess's in particular, she'd say, 'Oh, there's nothing to tell. It's very boring.' Christ, she had even told her Joe was amazing in bed, her exact words, 'like no one I've had before' making her shrivel with embarrassment. And still, not a thing about Tess. It was like forking out for a Michelin star restaurant and getting a burger in return.

Tess's fresh face was the final insult that greeted her the next day as she walked into the office. It was not the face of a woman who had drunk a bottle and a half of wine.

'There's something weird about her,' she told Joe at home that evening. 'She told me nothing at all.'

'She probably couldn't get a word in edgeways.'

'Are you saying I talk a lot?'

'You know you talk a lot.'

'But you're implying I talk too much.'

'No, that's not what I'm implying.' He pulled her in towards him, his eyes laughing, inviting her to laugh at herself. But she had no intention of giving him what he wanted. Joe wasn't taking this seriously, that was clear, but if he wanted to defuse her anger he was going about it the wrong way. A simple, *yeah that's weird*, was all it would have taken. Libby wasn't in the market for reason or logic, because she knew, knew in her bones that something wasn't right with Tess.

'Why do you always stick up for her?' she said when it became clear Joe wasn't going to tell her what she wanted to hear.

'Fuck's sake, Libby, it's not a crime if she doesn't talk as much as you. I've yet to meet someone who does.'

'So it's my fault she didn't share a single bit of information about herself? You don't think that's even a tiny bit suspicious?' He had turned on the TV, found the football. 'Are you even listening to me?'

'I think you should stop over-analysing the situation,' he said, cranking up the volume with the remote, 'and I think for once you should stop talking.'

Over-analysing, that stung, Libby didn't mind admitting. It was an accusation that had been levelled at her more than once. By her aunt Dana – *Of course we want you here but boarding school would be best for you, stop over-analysing* – and by her friends who often accused her of reading too much into a missing invitation, a phone that didn't ring, a text she judged to be overly abrupt. But she had expected better from Joe, the very person who got her immediately, loved her despite her foibles, made her feel secure. *I'll show you*, she thought.

Her alarm over Tess's toxic relationship was downgraded to intrigue. 'You can only help people who want to be helped,' her uncle used to say, which was his way of neatly explaining away her mother's absence and then her death. And he was right – when was he wrong? – Tess was a grown woman who made her own choices and had to take responsibility for them, just as Libby did her own. Plus, her ongoing popularity, the obvious favouritism Kyle showed her, *nice work!* was all too much. If you took the boyfriend out of the picture Tess was too good, perfect in every way, and perfection made Libby suspicious.

You couldn't have called it stalking. How can you stalk someone when you work in the same office? It wasn't like Libby was following her home, although the thought had occurred to her for one brief moment. It was more of a heightened awareness. Bluntly put, she was conscious of Tess's every move because she knew if she watched closely enough, she'd eventually find some evidence, of what she couldn't say, just something that would vindicate her, something that she could present to Joe: *I told you she was weird, now do you believe me?*

Libby noted when Tess went to the loo, what she ate for lunch, her favourite sandwich filling – prawn and avocado – how long she took for lunch, how she wore those floaty dresses on some kind of a rotation system. There were only three, just three of them accessorised with a scarf or a jumper to make them look different, but Libby's razor-sharp eye was not fooled. And while she wasn't one to be materialistic, she did wonder why Tess didn't treat herself to a trip to Topshop to buy a few more – her earnings would certainly have covered the expense.

At one stage she questioned whether Tess's relationship with Kyle had strayed into the sexual. There was definitely a frisson between them, a pent-up energy pressing against their boundaries. Libby could only imagine what lover boy would have to say or do about it were it true. And perhaps it wasn't, but whatever was going on, Tess spent an inordinate amount of time in Kyle's office, chatting through God knows what. Libby would watch them, Kyle pushing back in his chair, hitching one leg on to the opposite knee and stroking his nascent bead, *Oh yeah, I completely agree. You are so right.* Not that she could hear them, but she was becoming skilled in lip-reading. It really was painful to watch.

*

Then again, no one was forcing her to watch them. She shouldn't have been watching. And a few days later, her punishment arrived. Had they noticed her beady eyes following them, or how her focus was elsewhere? Had her work suffered? She really couldn't say.

'Tess is going to help you,' Kyle said. 'Show you some new skills, a few shortcuts.' This, she had not expected. It came as a surprise, a hot slap in the face that brought an instant, crushing humiliation. It was one thing for Libby to be aware of her own shortcomings, but to have them noted and discussed, publicly addressed, that was . . . well, it was an outrage. She searched Kyle's face in desperation, hoping to find a knowing look, the hint of an apology, a sign of shared understanding that would make sense of what he was doing to her. But all she found was a cold authority.

'I really don't think that's necessary,' she said.

'Hey, this is a learning curve, you shouldn't be resistant to absorbing new skills.' His tone was steely and Libby wanted him to shut up because every word brought a fresh sting. For a diversion, she turned her attention to Tess and immediately wished she hadn't; that goofy grin, showing off the gap between her teeth that was oh so quirky, one side of her hair pulled back in a dandelion clip. A dandelion FFS! How old did she think she was? It was all too much. Libby wanted to rip it out, wipe the smile from her face, witness a flash of pain in those big doe eyes.

'Don't look so upset, Libby,' Kyle said. Yet more salt in the cuts. 'We're a team. We play to our strengths,' but he walked away without specifying what Libby's particular strength was.

Later, when her heartbeat had returned to something close to normal and she'd had a good cry in the loos, and given herself a stern talking-to, Libby decided she would not be treated like this and approached Kyle.

'I don't think this is a good idea,' she said. 'You're the one who has drilled us in client confidentiality. How can I possibly work with someone else, show Tess what I've been doing and not compromise security? I'm really not comfortable with it.'

She had expected him to listen intently to her reservations, reassure her or better, can the idea altogether. She did not expect him to peer beyond her, as if she was too dull to hold his attention for more than a second.

'I hear you, absolutely,' he said, although she doubted this very much. 'And I'm impressed you're taking security so seriously, but you have to trust me, there's a reason behind everything we do. Now if you don't mind, I've got a call to make.'

So Libby endured it. Three days that were torture at first, Tess leaning over her shoulder, or Libby leaning over hers as she paraded her technical brilliance. But then, despite herself, Libby had to admit she was good. Much much better than her, and it was a relief to be thrown a lifeline, shown a way around the issues she had not been able to overcome alone. With Tess's help, Libby made more progress on her client's system in two days than she had done in two weeks. By day three, when Tess had finished with her, Libby spent another two hours alone on the system, equipped with her new-found confidence, and she was in, the hack all but complete. In front of her was the proof: flickering on her screen were the CEO, Marc Zimmerman's private emails. Quickly, she glanced at them, until she happened on one that was incendiary to say the least and, her face burning with guilt, she closed the page and sent them on to Kyle as per company protocol.

'Great work, Lib,' he said. And she was so taken with the praise, she forgave him for shortening her name without her permission.

★

It was Friday and they headed upstairs to the terrace, still warm for September, London not ready to say goodbye to summer. Tess was sitting next to her. 'Thank you,' Libby said, 'for this week. I'm pretty much there.'

'You're in?'

'Thanks to you.'

'It's nothing.' Tess shrugged her shoulders. But it was; for Libby it was a whole lot more than nothing. It was down to Tess that she finally understood the pull, the adrenal buzz, the quickening pulse, the sweetness of the hack. And now she could sit drinking beer under the pink sky, shrouded in the warm glow of achievement, feeling like one of them at last. Not even Will could dampen her mood.

'Graduated from the remedial class then, Libby?' He said.

'Shut up, Will.' Asha threw a peanut in his face.

'Maybe you're not cut out for it, too nice, maybe you don't have the killer instinct.' Will wouldn't let it drop.

'Nice?' Tess said. 'I wouldn't underestimate Libby if I were you. And by the way, Kyle wanted me to help you next but I said I had my limits.'

Libby raised her bottle in Tess's direction, *cheers*. She was grateful for the intervention even if Tess had got her all wrong. She *was* nice. Everyone always said so: *Such a nice/pleasant/helpful girl*. If only anyone understood the time and effort Libby had spent living up to these anodyne descriptors, regardless of whether, in truth, she wanted to be bad, be difficult, be hard to please.

She re-emerged from her thoughts, attempted to plug herself back into the conversation, Asha ribbing some bloke she had brought back to hers the previous weekend. 'Honest to God, he kept on saying, what should I do next? So I told him, if you haven't read the manual you should leave right now. I'm not in the market for apprentices.' She roared with laughter and the others joined in, everyone except Libby who wondered how she would have behaved in such a situation. Would her niceness have dictated she say something encouraging, along the lines of, *just up a bit, you're doing fine, that's it*, when really she would have loved to have been more Asha, had the guts to say get lost.

Her focus swam back to Tess. Tess was more complex than Asha, at turns strong-willed and forthright, nervous and withdrawn. Libby watched Tess pull her bright red rucksack on to the table and rummage around inside it, clocking the gentle but noticeable shake of her hands. Was she worried about her boyfriend? Did she need to account for every minute spent away from him outside of work? Libby couldn't fathom her. And really, she decided, as Joe handed her another beer, there was no reason why she should. Not everyone was straightforward, easy to read.

'I haven't got my phone,' Tess said, patting herself down theatrically as if it might be hidden on her person. 'I must have left it in the office.' She stood up, climbed over Will to get out.

'Watch it, you're standing on my balls!'

'I think that's highly unlikely, don't you?' Asha said.

Libby watched her as she headed away from the group across the terrace, transfixed by the outline of something hard and rectangular in Tess's back pocket. Why had she lied?

Libby found herself needing an urgent pee. That was why she left immediately after Tess, two beers and her bladder was at its limit. And it so happened that the bathroom she preferred – yes, she had a loo preference – was on the same floor as their office. And so what if she moved quietly when she reached the fifth floor? Libby was always quiet and thoughtful, careful not to disturb others. And when she saw Tess in the office, she practically levitated so as not to disturb her. She didn't shout, *Your phone is in your back pocket*, because whatever Tess was doing, it was clear she wasn't searching for a lost phone, not hunched over Libby's desk, fingers tapping the keys, her face illuminated by the glow of the computer.

Nine

Tess

Tess was a surprise to herself. A few minutes before she had been sipping beer with her colleagues and laughing and joking like it was a normal Friday night. And then the lie came out before she had even given it proper consideration. 'I haven't got my phone,' and she was on her way, casting one last glance over to Libby before she left because if there was a problem it was sure to come from her. To Tess's relief, she was engrossed in one of Asha's many sex disaster stories and Tess was on her way, the lift descending, taking her to the Freetech office, her head fuzzy with beer. It was about time she delivered something concrete. She'd been working here for four weeks and until now all she'd been doing was skirting around the edges of illicit activity, watching her colleagues tap in their passwords, trying to memorise the letters. It was easier than she had anticipated because, regardless of Kyle's warnings, it was hard to distrust the people you worked alongside every day, lunched with, drank beer with, laughed with. That high level of alert was not sustainable. And Tess had worked hard to prove she was one of them, out to help, a team player. None of them would have expected her to be passing information back to a third party.

But here she was. She hadn't chosen this evening for her first steal. The evening had chosen her. It was Libby's news about the successful hack that had piqued her interest, got her juices flowing. In the previous days, while working together, Libby had been annoyingly protective of her client, careful not to show Tess anything confidential. Shame she hadn't been so careful with her password. Tess had studied her type it in at least four times a day over three days. JohnLewis62!, sweet really. Touching. It made her feel bad. But not so bad she was going to pass on the ripest opportunity she'd had so far.

She typed in the characters, waited, heart thumping as the icon spun and the display appeared before her. She was in. It was that easy. Just her in an empty office reading Libby's emails to Kyle, the summary of how far she had got, the sensitive information on her client Marc Zimmerman and his company The Change Group. She downloaded whatever she could on to a memory stick, slipped it into her pocket and headed back upstairs with a smile plastered on her face. The smile in itself was a disguise. What she wanted to do was laugh, clap her hands, burst into song. The euphoria was so alien it made her giddy. Tess had experienced the full spectrum of negative emotions of late, the self-loathing, the anxiety, the stress. But this burst of excitement flushed her system clean, reminded her of the old Tess. Carried her back to the fearless campaigning days, when life appeared in black and white and Tess was secure in the knowledge her targets deserved whatever she had planned for them. When the sense of do-goodery and righteousness shielded her like a protective armour. But this scenario she had found herself in was entirely different. She was acting on orders, under duress, someone else pulling her strings, plotting against people who were not enemies but colleagues. And she was fully prepared to be disgusted by her own treachery.

Except she wasn't.

Quite the opposite. It had been an age since she had felt this alive. And she realised then that she wasn't as good and wholesome as she'd fancied. Tess could lie and cheat and steal and still live with herself because there was a rationale behind it even if she didn't like the tactics. And it helped that there was something for her at the end of it.

'Any joy?' Libby asked when she returned to the table.

'I'm such a dick, it was in my pocket all along.'

Tomaz was happy when she handed over the memory stick. Correction; he was happier. 'Good girl,' he said. *I'm not three years old.* Tess could have happily taken each one of his fat sausage fingers and bent them back until he screamed. She didn't. Of course she didn't. That would have been counter-productive. There was a game to play, an endgame, she had to stay focused. Give Tomaz what he wanted and then she'd be free. He slipped the silver rectangle into his pocket, furtively, like she had handed him a wrap of drugs, and he smiled. Someone like Tomaz shouldn't smile. He was all teeth, teeth thrown into his mouth with little care for the arrangement. 'Now we'll see what happens.'

'I'm not so sure. I don't think—'

'It's not for you to think.'

'When will it be over?'

'When I tell you.'

She'd had enough. Five minutes in his company was five minutes too much. At least there was no Libby this time, lurking on the borders of their exchange, so she'd be saved a kiss from Tomaz. No need to pretend they were boyfriend and girlfriend. The thought made her stomach flip in disgust.

'Call me then,' she said, standing up. He beckoned her back.

'You're forgetting something.' He pulled out an envelope from his pocket, padded with notes, pushed it into her hands. It made her feel dirty. 'Don't want to see you go unrewarded.'

Ten

Libby

Libby was not going to spoil this breakfast with talk about
work. Not when breakfast at the new café round the corner
promised to be the kind of magazine-style Sunday morning that
suggested everything was good with her life. The Edison bulbs,
exposed copper pipes, reclaimed wood, signs she had upgraded
from student to working woman; goodbye greasy spoons and
takeaway chips. Plus, Sam's Spot, with its organic coffee and the
vegan breakfasts (she wasn't a vegan, but still . . .) was proof that
their decision to live in the hinterlands of Clapton was the right
one. The first sprouts of gentrification were appearing. Work
talk did not have a place at this breakfast, nor did her disappointment at Joe's reaction.

She'd told him what she'd seen on the Tube home the night it
happened. 'She was at my desk, I swear she was logged in. What
was she doing?'

She'd witnessed an eye roll, *not this again*, and countered it
with more evidence. 'Her phone was always in her back pocket.
That was just an excuse. I saw it when she left the terrace.'

'Well, firstly, if you saw her phone, why didn't you tell her?
And secondly, she doesn't have your password, so how could
she have logged in as you? And thirdly, if it's bothering you that
much, why don't you ask her yourself?'

'It's our stop,' she said, relieved to be spared a fourthly.

★

When they woke the next morning, she'd raised it once more, in the hope that a sober Joe might employ more logic than the drunk one had the night before. First, though, she brought him coffee, ran her hands through his hair, kissed him, reminded him that it was her, Libby, the woman he'd fallen for, not some mad woman with a grudge.

'Listen,' he said and she was instantly buoyed by his tone, 'maybe mention it to Kyle if you're worried. I mean if you really think she was up to no good, that is.' She kissed him again, on his chest. 'But be prepared for him to think you're mad. Or ask how you know she got into *your* system. Your desk is closest to the door; who's to say she didn't just use it and logged on as herself?' Libby was sitting on the edge of the bed now, the desire to kiss Joe having deserted her. 'Also . . .' There was an also? She didn't want there to be an also. 'If somehow Tess did have your password, he's going to want to know why.'

Why, or how? If Tess had Libby's password, it was her fault. That was the implication. Not even an implication, it was the truth. How many times had Tess hung over her as she typed it in? Stupid. Stupid. Stupid. And now she couldn't out her without incriminating herself.

Now, days later, she was still thinking about Tess and she needed to stop. Concentrate on the positives. Joe was a positive. She allowed herself an appreciative look in his direction, standing menu in hand, queuing up to order breakfast, and experienced a ripple of lust. Even Joe was improving. He'd bought himself some new clothes, had taken himself to the trendy barbers next to work where they had given him a small quiff. He was looking . . . hot. No joke. She found it hard to believe her luck. It was hardly his appearance or dress sense that had attracted her in the first place; she had fallen for him *despite* them. And now here he was, transformed into the guy that turned heads. She had herself a looker. *Sex*, she thought, *we must have it today*, and she planned the seduction in her head; an afternoon shag, after all, would be a fittingly decadent moment in a perfect Sunday. How long had it been? A few days? She counted back. It was almost a week. That was most certainly too long. The thought marred her otherwise perfect mood. He wasn't going off her, was he? *Don't be ridiculous. Don't over-analyse.* They were working now, long hours, stress; the pressure to prove themselves would surely take its toll. And it was perfectly normal for sex to become less regular the longer you were with someone. All the magazines said so. But it did mean her time with Joe alone was more precious. She spread the assorted newspapers out on the table to mark her territory. What with the café being packed and their table seating four, there was always the danger of an interloper, *Would you mind if I sat here? Yes, as a matter of fact I would mind*, but Libby would be way too polite to say so. She would shift to make space, to keep everyone happy while silently seething.

She glanced down to the newspaper's front page. *BOSS IN TAX SCANDAL . . .* It was the *Sunday Herald*. Force of habit. Or force of her uncle's habit. The paper he read every Sunday over coffee and two boiled eggs. And now here she was, following in his footsteps, even if Clapton was not her uncle's scene – *Where the hell is that?* And he was more likely to do breakfast at the Wolseley than the trendy offering that was Sam's Spot. She rummaged for the magazine sections, Style and Culture; she'd read the news later. *Who are you kidding?* She stopped, appreciated the music playing, something deep and soulful, worthy of a Shazam, she could play it later when she was seducing Joe.

TAX SCANDAL. The words in the headline bounced back to her. It couldn't be. There must be plenty of bosses in tax scandals. Still, no harm in checking. She put the magazine to one side, curiosity speeding her heart rate, and retrieved the main section from beneath the Sport and Travel.

CHANGE BOSS IN TAX SCANDAL

Marc Zimmerman, the multimillionaire campaigner and out-spoken critic of the government, is facing a blacklash after leaked emails show he owes seven million pounds in unpaid taxes.

'I got you oat milk, they didn't have soya,' Joe said, hovering over the table carrying their coffees. 'Jesus, it won't taste that bad . . . That's a strong reaction to milk. If I'd known . . .'

She held the paper up to his face, so close he blinked and stepped backwards, splashing coffee over himself.

'Easy. Probably best to read the paper when I'm sitting down and not holding two cups of steaming coffee.'

'I told you,' she said. 'I told you there was something going on, now do you believe me?'

It wasn't a question. There was no doubt. He would have to believe her now. Her client's emails had been leaked, splashed all over the newspapers with the information she had found, kept confidential and secure.

'Go on, then, tell me what this is about before you combust.' Joe didn't know this was her client. No, not even Joe. That's how strict she had been, how very careful she was to play by the rules. No one knew except Tess. It could only be Tess.

'This is my client.'

He sucked in the air through his teeth, emitting a shrill whistle. She had hoped for a more profound assessment of the situation. She wanted to pull him into her line of vision, to make him see what she was seeing. 'You were careful, weren't you? I mean, you've got all the correct security in place?'

Was he for real? 'You think this is my fault?'

'No.' His face coloured. Clearly, that was exactly what he thought. That Libby had dropped the ball. 'This isn't my doing, for fuck's sake.'

'No, you're right. It could be anyone. Anyone. That's the

point of our work, after all, testing security. Shame someone got there before us.'

Why did she have to hammer it home? Why wasn't it blindingly obvious by now?

'Someone? *Someone* did not get there before us. Don't you get it? Tess did this. It has to be her. That's what she was doing when I caught her at my computer last week.'

The teeth whistling was accompanied by a rueful shake of the head this time. 'Really? Come on, Libby. What have you got against Tess? Where's your proof?'

'I saw her.'

'OK, I see where you're coming from, but Libby, you saw her at your desk, nothing more. Maybe she left something there while you were working together last week. Maybe she wasn't logged on as you. And even if she was up to something, the problem is you have no proof. You can't just fling accusations like that around.'

'Thanks for believing me.'

'Don't be like that. I just . . . it's difficult. You have to be rational otherwise it's going to look like you've got a vendetta going on.' He reached out to touch her hand, as if a bit of contact was going to soften the blow.

She was aware of the waitress hovering a few feet away, two breakfasts in hand.

'I've lost my appetite,' she said and got up and walked out.

Eleven

Tess

'Have you seen the newspaper?' It was Tomaz's voice on the other end of the phone dragging her from her dream in which she was on a boat in the Med, surrounded by three of her best mates, their sun-crinkled faces laughing as they sailed out towards the horizon.

'Funny you should ask, but no, I haven't.' She'd been enjoying her dream, and resented Tomaz's interruption. 'Your average person is still asleep at this time on a Sunday morning.'

'It's all there,' he said, ignoring her dig. 'Marc Zimmerman in tax scandal. Now do you believe this is going to be worthwhile?'

She jolted upright, like he'd slapped her awake. 'Are you sure?'

'Nah, I'm just sitting with the paper laid out in front of me. 'Course I'm fucking sure. I just hadn't expected it to happen so quickly. But where there's money involved . . . I told you, trading in confidential information is big business. Believe me now?'

His tone was thick with glee. She pictured him crouched over the paper, a modern-day witch, delighting in the chaos unfolding before him. Delighted that he was vindicated. Was it the fun of the chase that mattered to him, or the end goal? She wanted to believe it was the latter, but . . .

'*Sunday Herald*,' he said. 'Go out and buy yourself a copy. You've done well. The boss is going to be delighted. Meet me at six thirty tomorrow, Brick Lane. I'll treat you to a curry. We need to plan what comes next.'

'I can't.' She didn't want to meet Tomaz for a curry. Even at the speed Tess ate, a meal would still require at least forty-five minutes in his company. 'I'm already meeting someone.'

'Don't let me down, Tess, not now when there's so much at stake.'

They were there, sure enough, the words in black and white in front of her. She was sitting in a café, close to her flat in Bethnal Green, the paper on the bench beside her. Every now and then she'd sneak a look down. No way could she read it in full view of the dads feeding their toddlers croissants and the people feeding their hangovers. Because they would know, wouldn't they? The very instant they saw her absorbing the story, they'd know exactly what she was up to. Her complicity, her involvement was too real, too big to conceal from anyone. She was convinced it seeped out from her like radiation.

But listen, she told herself, *you are still human.* She could still *feel*. It wasn't like the subterfuge, this sneaking around, came easily. The shock alone had made her skip breakfast, and Tess never missed breakfast, or any meal for that matter. Even now, at midday, the premium latte and the toasted sourdough she'd ordered tasted weird and bitter, almost undrinkable, inedible, which was a crying shame given it had set her back twelve pounds fifty.

But.

Was there a but?

On reflection Tess was forced to admit there was.

The development was a boost. She could feel the energy in her fingertips. Why else were her hands shaking as she took a sip of the disgusting coffee? Added to that, there was a guy next to her, and when he glanced in her direction the thought of sex had sprung into her mind. Not that she fancied jumping him there and then, nothing like that, but just the general idea of it suddenly appealed to her again after months of celibacy. Months when she'd been hollowed out and shrivelled up. She could feel her heart beating, thudding, a comforting, welcoming experience given her worry that this work, this task was supposedly killing her soul. The story in the newspaper made what she was doing real and tangible and as such, it had given her a purpose. Tess needed a purpose.

It was a stand-off between the old Tess and the new version. The old Tess would not have countenanced this line of work, not with her idealism and her clear moral lines. But then again the old Tess had also been mad for Mumford & Sons and thought Obama was the answer to world peace, so really, she wasn't to be trusted.

No, it was a sign of her maturing that she now accepted you had to compromise in life. Dip your toes in murkier water. Do bad to do good, eventually.

This was a more determined Tess. A harder, colder one, perhaps given her recent life lessons, but at least this way, she would get her shit done.

The main challenge now was going back to work on Monday, probing deeper without getting caught.

'Where's Libby?' she asked Joe the next morning when he arrived alone.

'She's come down with a bug, hopefully just a twenty-four-hour thing,' he said.

Her absence made the day unexpectedly easy. She had predicted Libby being huddled in Kyle's office talking through the impact of the leak. And Tess wanted to be in Kyle's office. Tess needed to get close to Kyle and his business dealings. It was another moral obstacle she was prepared to hurdle.

'I'm grabbing a coffee from downstairs, fancy one?' She ducked her head around his door, pushing her hand through her hair. 'Monday morning calls for double caffeine.'

'I'll come with you. I could be doing with some fresh air.'

The queue was fierce and the baristas moved languidly, too cool to act fast. Normally Tess would rail against the poor service but today it was a blessing. She calculated it would take at least fifteen minutes to achieve a takeaway chai latte (Kyle) and a double espresso (her) and this meant more time to talk.

'Good weekend?' he asked.

'Do you know, it was. One of those ones where you turn down all invitations and just chill.' She didn't mention that the invitations had stopped coming; she had turned down so many over the past six months her friends had all but given up, and taken the view that Tess had gone to ground. 'Just lazed around, had breakfast, watched a film . . . read the newspapers.' That was a gamble, mentioning the newspaper, one she knew could backfire. She turned her attention to the cakes as soon as she had uttered it; holding his gaze a moment too long could spark suspicion. 'How about you?'

'Yeah, totally chilled. I did nothing.' A likely story, she thought. *Not with those muscles, you didn't.* They were hours in the gym, not slobbing around. 'We should have hooked up, done nothing together,' he said.

The overture was a discreet one, easy enough to dismiss. But Tess registered it as progress. He liked her. She liked that he liked her. But the trick to all of this was to keep him at a safe distance. Even the new Tess had her limits.

She smiled, attempting to be coy, 'Then we'd be doing *something*.' *For fuck's sake, that came out wrong.* 'I didn't mean that . . . I just meant . . .'

He put his hand on her shoulder, 'I know what you meant.'

'Libby's not in,' she changed the subject. 'I hope it's not contagious.'

'I think we can do without her input for one day at least.' He rolled his eyes, invited her to collude.

'She told me she was making good progress last week. Sometimes you get lucky.'

'And she needed your help to make her luck.'

'Well, I'm not sure my help was welcome.'

'She give you a hard time?'

'I wouldn't say that, she's just, you know . . .' She twiddled with her hair, an annoying habit she developed when she was trying to be less like herself. The old Tess would have slapped her.

'Intense?' he prompted.

'Well, I didn't say that.'

'You don't have to, I did.'

To Tess's disappointment, Libby returned the next day, her face hard set, throwing her bag down, pivoting on her heel (vertiginous, like a candidate in *The Apprentice*) and heading straight for Kyle's glass office. It reminded Tess of watching a TV screen with the sound turned down. Maddeningly. From the body language alone she would say Libby was not happy, her finger stabbing the air, Kyle shaking his head in response. She would have spilled blood to listen to their exchange.

As it turned out there was no need. In the toilets later – Libby's pee cycle either mirrored hers exactly or there was an element of stalking going on – she waited until Tess was washing her hands. 'I know what you did,' she said.

Tess's head pulsed. *Do you? Do you really?* She opted to play it cool, lighten the atmosphere with a joke. 'I thought that's what toilets were for.'

But Libby wouldn't be derailed, and Tess took a step back, found herself pushing up against the hand dryer.

'I saw you at my desk.'

Had she? Tess hadn't been quite as slick as she'd fancied, but what of it? What could she prove? 'I was at your desk the best part of last week. We were working together, and I was looking for my phone, remember?'

Libby smirked. That look really didn't do her any favours. 'Are we talking about the same phone that was in your pocket all along?'

'Come on, don't tell me that's never happened to you? You can't see something that's been right under your nose all along?'

'I can safely say that hasn't happened to me.'

'Well, let me promise you, it won't be long before it does and when it happens, you'll kick yourself for being so blind.'

Twelve

Libby

Libby stood over the sink, splashing cold water on her face to take the heat out of her cheeks. A victory had been snatched from her grasp, a goal scored by the opposition in the dying seconds of a game. It was not in the script, this defeat, and it was agonising. How had it happened? Libby couldn't say exactly, all she knew was that with a few carefully chosen words Tess had pierced her moral certitude and lodged a kernel of doubt deep in her mind. It was as if she had detected Libby's congenital weakness, her terror of ambiguity, and targeted it with a bespoke form of cruelty; the suggestion that she knew something Libby did not, that something was heading Libby's way that would derail her plans, implode her life. *You're blind.* OK, Tess had not used those exact words but that was what she meant. It could mean everything and it could mean nothing, and there lay the torture, in the subtlety of the threat, wide open to interpretation.

A sane person would have cast it aside. Tess was simply trying, and succeeding, to wind her up. But Libby did not feel of sane mind, and frankly she did not look it either. There she was, still hiding in the loos, her flimsy shirt now wet, revealing the lace of her pink bra beneath. Her eyeliner smudged, her make-up watermarked. This was not the face of a winner. The last few days were taking their toll – her client's emails leaked to the newspapers, and the small world around her, Joe, her uncle and Kyle, failing to treat it with the suspicion it deserved.

Yesterday, she raised herself from her sick bed (a migraine brought on by stress) and visited Richard, describing at length what had happened, the confidential information on her client spilled out into the public arena, his reputation shredded as a consequence. And yet Richard hadn't appeared overly fussed; he was more concerned about the table they had been allocated, *This is not my table, my table is by the window,* than the subject of conversation when they were eventually reseated.

'I had nothing to do with it, you know that, don't you?' she said. And he laughed in her face, carried on chortling right up until the starters arrived and he popped a devilled prawn into his mouth. 'Don't be paranoid, Libby. That's the beauty of you, no one would ever believe you are in the wrong.'

This was not the reassurance she craved, and truth be told, she felt more than a little patronised, although she knew this wasn't his intention. This morning she had broached the subject again with Kyle: 'Do you think anyone here could have leaked the information?'

'Is there anything you want to tell me, Libby?' What did that mean? She searched his expression for evidence of sarcasm.

'It had nothing to do with me, but you already know that.'

'I'm keeping an eye on things, Libby. I trust everyone in this office one hundred per cent – if I didn't they wouldn't have a job – but there's no room for complacency.'

She walked away, hollow with doubt. Whose complacency was he referring to? Hers? No one had blamed her, not openly at least, but she felt somehow inept, tainted by association, and now Tess had added to the escalating sense that she didn't have a clue what was going on.

Libby suggested a film to Joe after work, fancied immersing herself in someone else's drama for a change. But she chose badly, *Molly's Game.* Not a poor film, just not the one for her mood. She wanted uplifting, instead she got a salutary tale in greed and comeuppance. It put her off her nachos. On the walk home from the Tube she prodded Joe for reassurance, hoping he would step in and supply it where her uncle and Kyle had failed. 'I feel like I've fucked up somehow. I mean, no one's come out and blamed me, but I bet that's what they're thinking.'

Joe regarded her with amusement. Joe was the office star player, just as she'd guessed, breezing through the job.

'No one has blamed you, because they don't think it's got anything to do with you.' She loved Joe's monochrome world view, but just occasionally, like right now for instance, she wished he could see the grey areas that gave normal people, the ones with hang-ups and neuroses, cause for concern.

'I wish it was that simple.'

'It is that simple. You worry too much.'

'Thanks.'

'What do you want me to say? No one blames you. Kyle says you're doing really well. Tess said you did really well last week when she was helping you.'

'You've been discussing me with Tess?' She experienced an upswell of rage. The pair of them had been talking about her progress.

'Not discussing you, it wasn't like that. You just came up in conversation.'

'And when was this?'

'We were at the café, when you were off sick the other day.'

'Cosy.'

'It was lunchtime, we both wanted a sandwich. Are we supposed to do it on a rotation to avoid each other just to keep you happy?'

The temperature between them rose, an argument on simmer. Libby didn't want an argument. She was still reeling from her encounter with Tess. But she wanted Joe on her side, backing her up. She wanted *him*. And yet she couldn't shake the sense that he was slipping out of her grasp, and every time she tried to pull him back towards her, he drifted further away. Another fight wasn't going to help but she was hurting and the hurt wouldn't let her back down. It identified points of friction and pressure and levelled accusations. 'Did you tell her that you helped me get the job?' she said. They were close, Joe and Tess, increasingly so, and Libby had no idea what was revealed or exposed in these little chats in the coffee shop.

'Of course I didn't. Do you really think I would do that?'

'I just thought you might have, you know, when you were discussing me with Tess.' They'd stopped outside a barber's, packed with late-night men, chatting, chewing the breeze. A siren blared down the street, scattering the dark with flashes of neon. Joe's expression hardened, his eyes pinned to hers.

'Is this your thing?'

'What?'

'Hurting the people who care the most?' He started walking away, the shape of him dissolving into the night, with no sense of the earthquake his words provoked.

She was still shaking by the time she reached the flat and inside they avoided each other, a feat considering its size. She made herself a coffee without asking him if he wanted one, played a video on Instagram loudly while he was watching the football. She wanted to inflict hurt, to understand what it was like to scream inside; but instead she went for petty, childish wins that made her feel worse, not better. She couldn't help herself. And this was the root of Libby's problem; her pathetic need had to be fed, her endless doubts reassured at every turn. She wanted Joe to see what she could see, that Tess was to blame, out to destroy what they had. She did not have the insight to realise she was doing that all by herself.

Thirteen

Tess

A curry in Brick Lane. Tomaz was looking suspiciously well dressed for the occasion. A polka dot shirt, a pair of chinos. Aftershave. The whole ensemble made Tess decidedly uncomfortable. Surely he wasn't persuaded by his own lies, the girlfriend/boyfriend line he had spun Libby. Tess might be done with her period of celibacy but there were some places she would never go.

'You look nice.' He shifted in his chair, sheepish, embarrassed almost. *No no no no no.* She wanted the regular arrogant Tomaz back, the one never short of things to say and orders to give. This nicer version was unnerving.

'Shall we order now?' she said. The waiter had saved her, doling out the menus just in time. 'I'm starving.' Her hunger had returned and was now working overtime to make up for yesterday's lull. Before Tomaz could ask for five minutes to decide, she shot in: 'I'll have the pakora and a naan bread, pilau rice and a lamb rogan josh.' His mouth had formed an O in surprise. 'And a side of aloo gobi,' she said to piss him off further. He was paying after all.

'Just a chicken balti and pilau rice for me.'

She ordered a Coke because wine might have sent the wrong message and immediately ploughed into recounting her day: the coffee queue with Kyle, her frequent visits to his office, how she was generally winning at the task. And then, a blow-by-blow account of her exchange with Libby in the toilets, omitting only the bit where Libby claimed to have seen Tess at her desk because that didn't do her any favours.

'Well?' she said. She had expected an intervention, some kind of facial expression that said, *shit*, or *we'll have to be more careful*. Something.

'Are you OK?' He wasn't OK, this much was evident now. Someone had taken a pin and punctured him. Her mind scooped up the evidence; the smart dress wasn't for her benefit, was it? He didn't fancy her. *Thank God* (but also, *FFS, not even Tomaz fancies me*).

'What's happened?'

There wasn't a denial, he just screwed up his face like he was already dealing with the after effects of the curry. 'It's difficult.'

Difficult? Of course it was! This whole thing had been difficult from the word go. And now they were getting somewhere, it was still difficult but at least it was going to be worthwhile.

'We need to lay low for a while,' he said.

'What are you talking about? I'm either there or I'm not. We're either doing this or we aren't. There is nothing in between.'

'You need to get out.'

Get out. He could not be serious. Not after everything she had done. But his face didn't look like he was joking.

'No,' she said. She wasn't having it. No way was he going to do this to her now. She had wanted out for months, never wanted to be in in the first place, but Tomaz had pressed home the consequences of her non-compliance and closed down the escape routes. But now, now she was invested in this. She had a purpose. 'Why? Why on earth would we quit now? It would be madness. I didn't want to do this, remember? It was your idea. And now I'm here, now I'm this close,' she pressed her thumb and index finger together, 'this close, and you're telling me you think it's a good time to call it a day. What's the matter, lost your bottle?'

He gave a wry smile, shook his head to mock her newfound passion. 'This isn't your gig, Tess. Never was. You do as you're told. There are bigger things at play here, things that have just been drawn to my attention. We're stepping on toes and it's dangerous. And you don't want to get hurt, do you? You understand what I'm saying, don't you? This is the end. You get out. End of.'

She opened her mouth to shout him down again when the waiter arrived with their orders and Tomaz dived in, loading one of her naans with curry and stuffing it into his mouth. Her hunger deserted her again.

He didn't understand. Hardly his fault. She was a stranger to him. This new Tess was almost a stranger to her. But the old one, the one that was revving back to life, that Tess never followed orders.

The next day she was back at work. Of course she was. Sod Tomaz. The stubborn streak, the iron determination was strong in her again. She even raided her own wardrobe for a transitional outfit. She wanted something that was not quite the full Tess, that would have been too much too soon, and she didn't want alarm bells sounding, but equally she wanted something that was hers.

'Wow,' Asha remarked the second she walked in. 'And there was me thinking you *were* a summer dress. Is this the new you?' Tess cursed herself. Why couldn't she do half measures? But once she had chosen the wide yellow trousers, a sartorial two fingers to the dreary autumn day, the bright blue top was too tempting, and then there was the signature chunky ethnic jewellery she made herself in a workshop in Rajasthan. And she had missed this. Missed it all. 'It's an interesting look,' Will said, 'not one I would have put together.'

'Shut up, Will, and get the coffees. No one's interested in your opinion,' Asha said.

And that was it. For the next few days at least. Tess went to work and came home and went to work again. And were it not for the fact she finally worked out Kyle's password, standing at a certain angle in his office, and logged in as him one evening when everyone else went home, she would have fooled herself this was a proper job and she had no ulterior motive.

Tomaz didn't call. This was a blessing, wasn't it? No questions to answer, no excuses to make. At first, all she wanted was a window of time, a few days at least, a week perhaps, to uncover more information and prove to him the value of ploughing on by feeding him the gold she was intent on mining. And she got her wish. The sun rose and fell, and the days shrank, summer burning itself out, autumn waiting in the wings, and it felt like a strange, safe kind of limbo, a half reality where Tess could carry on existing in her pretend world, waiting for Tomaz to accost her from an alleyway or on her way home, *What the fuck do you think you're doing?*, and announce its abrupt end. But after a week there was still no sign of Tomaz. He had gone quiet, and Tess took this as a good sign initially. And then later on, not so much.

It was a Friday that she experienced the first real slice of nerves. Kyle asked them to assemble in his office at two o'clock. He had something to tell them apparently. Her immediate concern was that she had been rumbled and the morning was spent in a high state of alert, her mind playing out the endless consequences of being exposed. When she could stand it no longer, she plucked up the courage and texted Kyle: *Very cryptic, any clues?* But his reply, *It wouldn't be a surprise if I told you*, did nothing to relieve her anxiety. She would have stormed his office and used some of her guile to extract it from him, but he wasn't even there and his office was locked. There was nothing else for it but to sit and stew, watching the clock, wondering whether she should just pick up her things and walk out while she still could.

*

Two o'clock. It felt like forty-eight hours had passed. Every minute had sauntered by, with Tess trying to second-guess if anyone knew anything about the impending annoucement. 'No one tells me anything,' Joe said, which wasn't strictly true, simply that he appeared to retain very little beyond what was required for the task in hand. She refused to give Will the satisfaction of asking, knowing she couldn't trust what came out of his mouth anyway. And Libby? Well, she wasn't going to ask Libby, given that they weren't speaking; Libby was barely speaking to anyone, in fact, not even Joe, poor guy. Instead, her face was set with a ferocious focus that discouraged any interruptions or interaction.

When she broached the subject with Asha, she guessed her friend was not holding anything back. 'If this meeting clashes with the free yoga, I'm buggered if I'm coming.'

Finally two o'clock came. Tess lingered by her desk. It wouldn't do to be the first person in Kyle's office. She let Joe go before her, and Libby – still not talking – before she gulped a breath of air, held it in her lungs and took herself in to meet them, just as Asha was crashing through the door, dressed in leggings and bare feet. 'This better be good, I was just smashing the killer praying mantis,' she whispered to Tess.

Kyle was still tapping on the keyboard as they assembled, as if the task was too urgent, too important to be terminated prematurely. They waited, faces taut, the air strung with nerves. Tess was partly relieved to see she was not the only one who'd been affected by the information vacuum. 'Are we in the shit?' Will asked, his voice uncharacteristically quiet.

'You're always in the shit,' Asha said.

Finally, Kyle stopped, looked up in surprise as if he'd only just noticed their presence.

'Was it something I said?' He laughed. 'Relax. I have good

news.' Tess expelled the air from her lungs, but the hammer beat of her heart would not be stilled. 'You've been together for what . . . seven weeks now, and I have to say, you're working well as a team.' *You can't fault the American enthusiasm,* Tess thought, even when it was wildly misplaced. There had been a friction in the office all week, like someone had scrubbed the air with sandpaper. And yes, Tess accepted some of the blame. Tess and her spat with Libby, but really that was Libby's fault. Then there was Will whose only goal in life was to rub everyone up the wrong way. Surely Kyle hadn't failed to notice the tensions?

'But there are always things we can improve upon. We can work better as a team. Sure, we all have our individual projects but we need to be a unit. Anyway, I think you're going to love this . . . We have a place in Sussex.' His diction stretched it into two words, Suss Sex. 'You'll love it, I promise you. There's nothing there . . . OK, there's a pub about four miles away, but apart from that it's just this amazing barn, a lake and miles and miles of the most beautiful countryside you've ever seen.' Tess felt a stab of irritation. She knew where Sussex was, knew the county. She used to go camping there with her dad, but the way Kyle was talking you'd think he'd discovered it all by himself. 'Five days, all expenses paid. I hope you're going to say yes, Christ, you'd be mad not to. It's going to be awesome. What d'you say?'

Tess waited for someone else to answer first. She had a lot to say but nothing for public consumption. The voice in her head was shouting that she needed to get out of here, rustle up a killer excuse as to why, on no account, could she go to deepest Sussex with her colleagues.

'I'm not overly fond of the countryside if I'm honest, Kyle,' Asha said, and Tess could hear the hiss of relief in the room. Asha would tell it how it is. 'I've never really seen the point of it. Where is it we're going to stay? Because I don't do camping. Or paintballing. I'd end up killing someone if I was made to do paintballing. Anyway, that kind of team-building stuff, it's all old school now, isn't it?'

'Thank God we have you, Asha, to say what everyone else is thinking.' Kyle studied them all one by one, tittering to himself. 'Where's your sense of adventure? Come on, this will be brilliant, I promise.'

'But the camping?' Asha said. 'Are we camping?'

'Let me reassure you, we are not camping. You might change your mind when you see the accommodation.' He pulled up the photographs on his iPad.

'Jesus, Kyle, all you had to do was show me this,' Asha said. Tess moved in for a look, Libby craning over her shoulder. It was impressive, spectacular even, if it had been a barn once, it didn't look like one now. It was a series of glass structures held together by slices of grey concrete.

'The pool is heated all year round, before you ask,' Kyle said. 'We like to treat our staff well at Freetech, didn't I tell you?'

'It is a bit over the top for a work retreat,' Libby said.

'I'm sure we can find you a tent if you want to camp in the woods, Libby,' Kyle said, and Libby's eyes turned glassy, like she might cry. 'But the rest of us will be very happy to stay in luxury.' He turned to Tess. 'You in?'

He was playing them off against each other. Tess could spot these tactics a mile off and she stood, daring to withstand the heat of his gaze. Part of her wanted to say yes just to compound Libby's irritation, but she couldn't. She was not in. She was most definitely not in. She needed an excuse, a good one. And fast. *My mum is sick.* That used to be an old favourite, one she trotted out before her mum was really sick, and then she felt like the worst daughter, like she had personally jinxed her health. *I have a dog to look after.* But there was no dog and knowing Kyle he'd probably want to know its name and pedigree and arrange kennels for the imaginary pet.

I'm not who you think I am and I want out.

'Come on, Tess, don't let me down.'

'Yes,' she said. The word defied her. She defied herself, wasn't thinking straight, distracted by the end result, the goal, the desire to finish what Tomaz had started no matter the cost. She wasn't thinking about the cost. She never did. 'Yes, I'll come.'

Fourteen
Day 1

Joe

Did I want to go to Kenton Thorpe and spend five days team-building with people I barely knew?

Do you really have to ask me that question? Even Libby was reluctant, having broken the silence between us to complain. 'Five days in that house in the middle of nowhere, it'll feel like an eternity.'

'We don't have to go,' I reminded her at home later. The imminent retreat had done us a favour, created some much-needed common ground between us. I'd cooked a curry as a peace offering and we were sitting in the living room, plates on our laps, binge watching *The Affair*. 'We got a job, we didn't join a cult.'

She stabbed a piece of chicken with her fork and held it suspended in mid-air.

'We have to go.'

'Why?'

'Because that's part of being an adult, you know, doing things you don't want to do.'

'He can't make us.'

'You sound like a child.'

I could feel it again, the shared ground shifting like a melting iceberg. A better person would have stepped back, taken the heat out of the situation.

'That's rich coming from you.'

'What's that supposed to mean?'

'You've had it in for Tess pretty much since the beginning. It hasn't exactly made for a happy working environment.'

She picked up her plate and walked into the kitchen where she scraped it into the bin before slamming the door into the bedroom. I could have gone after her. I could have extinguished the fire with a few carefully selected words to soothe and defuse. But my rage was greater than my love. I wasn't just angry with her, I was angry that we'd found fault lines in our perfection. We were becoming those people who fought and squabbled over petty, tawdry things when the whole point of us was that we were better than that. So instead of going to Libby and saying, *None of this matters, all that matters is us*, I spent the rest of the night alone on the sofa watching Dominic West and Ruth Wilson career into a crazy, unjustifiable mess of an affair in the name of love.

Two days later I was in a car travelling to Kenton Thorpe in Sussex. What can I say? I'm weak. I'm pathetic. She said sorry, I said sorry. We had reconciliation sex that was almost worth the argument. A team-building retreat. I was beginning to understand that love cost.

And yet looking back now, there was something off-key about Libby right from the beginning. On the journey down to Sussex that Sunday, her mood was upbeat, theatrically so, and in direct contrast to her earlier reservations. 'It will be amazing . . . and the fresh air . . . and the skies.' I let her babble on, not wanting to appear pedantic by pointing out there was only one sky, and it was the same one above Sussex as London. I suspected she was nervous, a little strung out, and if she wanted to kid herself it was going to be heaven on a stick, who was I to burst the pretence?

*

Kyle hadn't lied to us. Kenton Thorpe was an impressive place if you like concrete and glass. There were three blocks knitted together by glass structures that reflected the sky and the trees and the blue shimmer of the swimming pool, the illusion so powerful you might have dived into the glass to cool off.

'Hey, guys, down here.'

It was Kyle, waving up from the terrace. 'Come and join us.'

We tumbled downwards through the long grass, my foot squelching in something I would later identify as fox shit. The sky was wiped blue, not even a wisp of cloud to score it. 'Kyle probably arranged this too,' I told Libby. 'The perfection, you know, to lure us into a false sense of security.'

'Shut up, he'll hear you.'

'You've made it!' Kyle said. He walked towards us, beaming his welcome with a show of white teeth and a bare chest. A predictably smooth and ripped chest, I should add. He'd obviously been for a swim but it was not a hot day, certainly not the kind of temperature to merit a bare chest for any length of time. I couldn't shake the feeling he'd set this whole scene just so he could star in it.

'You said two o'clock, are we late?' Libby's voice carried a note of alarm and I wanted to say, *It's Sunday. Technically this is a day of rest. We're not even being paid.*

He raised his hands. 'Tranquilo, we're all chilled as you can see. You coming in? It's heated.'

He pointed to the pool. An infinity pool, as Libby would later tell me, although there was nothing infinite about it, it was simply another illusion, the water appearing to pour over the side and into the field. I had no intention of getting semi-naked with my colleagues, but clearly Asha didn't share my reservations. I spotted her starfishing on the skin of the water, her bobbed hair fanning out like a dark orb around her face.

'My swimsuit is in the car,' Libby said by way of an excuse, but Kyle wouldn't drop it, had mastered the art of making you feel lesser if you didn't join him in whatever he suggested. 'Hasn't stopped anyone else. Come on, don't tell me you're not tempted.'

And then she was stripping off, down to her knickers and T-shirt before she disappeared into the depths, leaving me to watch her glide through the water as I stood holding her clothes.

We'd started drinking early on, Libby uncharacteristically enthusiastic with the booze, and by the time Kyle dropped his first bombshell we were pleasantly inebriated. 'Listen, guys, I had a thought, and I know this is going to freak you out but bear with me.' Kyle loved a preamble, liked to make his audience wait for the big reveal. There was a safe in front of him and he opened it and put his phone inside. Alarm chimed in my head. 'How about it? Let's go without them for a few days. In our jobs especially it's important to detox, take time to clear our minds. Get creative. I wouldn't ask you to do anything I'm not doing myself. Who's in?'

I turned to Libby, *whattheactualfuck?* At the very least, I expected a beam of understanding. Her face was a blank.

Asha was the first one to fall. 'Mine's knackered anyway, I dropped it by the pool,' she said, placing her smashed iPhone down. Even if it hadn't been broken I sensed she would have given it up. Not because she was weak, but the opposite. She could live without a phone, refused to be ruled by tech. I had greater hopes for Libby. Libby was forever cruising Instagram, recording how many likes her posts garnered as if she needed the reassurance. Not a chance she would part with it so easily.

And yet.

She smiled at Kyle and I waited for her to pull out a line that would excuse her. But no, Libby ducked down into her bag and extracted the rose-gold phone. 'Here you go,' she said as if it didn't hurt one bit, was not akin to severing a limb.

There were three of us left. Tess and Will and me. My phone

was my friend, a constant companion; it came with me everywhere, to bed, to the loo. It was there when I had my haircut, playing me inane YouTube videos, keeping me up to date with the uni friends I'd all but stopped seeing since Libby through our WhatsApp group. It gave me my mum's voice every three days, the same routine, questioning me about the weather where I was, *Mum, I live in London, five miles from you*, I'd say. And she'd say, *Oh, I would never have guessed, it's been one/two/three weeks since I saw you, I thought you'd moved to the other side of the world.*

I could not relinquish my phone.

I watched Tess hesitate. What would happen if she said no? *Nothing*, I wanted to scream. *Nothing will happen. This is bullshit.* My eyes drilled into her. Just say no. Say no. But then, to my despair, she put it in the safe. My only hope was Will, a dire situation in which to find myself. I was encouraged by his twitching, like an addict being denied a fix. 'I don't think, I mean, I've got to check up on—'

'Will, it's only for a few days. You can do this, I know you can do it. Don't let us down, hell, you might even enjoy it.'

Will shook his head, an overgrown child who refused to give up his sweets.

'How else will he watch porn?' Asha said and everyone laughed except Will. And me, because I knew that comment sealed it.

'Here you go,' he said. 'One day only.'

'One day at a time,' Kyle said, winking at the rest of us.

And then it was my turn. All eyes pinning me down. Do what you're told. Follow the pack.

I felt the cool, hard outline in my pocket, considered legging it out of the kitchen and into the car, driving back where I had come from.

And then I looked around at the expectant faces and I laid my phone on the table.

*

The house. What about the house? Over to Kyle, conducting the grand tour, a tour designed to elicit oohs and aahhs and *oh my God, one day!* 'It's incredible, right?' Kyle said, running his finger along the polished concrete of the kitchen island. We were back where we started having been upstairs via a huge concrete spiral staircase that had been designed with little concern for safety. On one side it was enclosed by a frameless glass banister that looked like it wasn't there, the other side was completely open. It was like a test, forget which one was which and you'd be a goner.

'Our problem,' Kyle continued, 'will be getting you lot out of here at the end. You won't want to leave.' I begged to differ. No question, it was a step up from our one-bedder in Clapton, Albert Square to Buckingham Palace. But . . . there was definitely a but, I just needed to locate it. I surveyed the scene again: the huge vaulted ceilings slotted with industrial metallic pipes that sent a rainstorm of light showering down; the stainless steel cabinets reflecting the sun so harshly I had to close my eyes; and the mercury-smooth floor surface, the whorls and swirls moving like a river as they caught the light. It all made my head swim. I was too hot, an ant frying under a magnifying glass. Was it just me? Tess was staring into the middle distance, trapped in thought. Will was pawing the surfaces, marking his territory, and Libby was studying the series of framed photographs on the wall, pictures of the house that tracked its transformation from the original barn, to the demolition and finally, the new building.

'I hate it here,' Libby said when we were shown to our rooms. 'It's soulless and empty.' She shivered and I attempted to hold her but her body was tight and rigid. 'I'm scared to breathe.'

And this was it, exactly. Libby had nailed it. Everything we did in this house would leave a trace, a fingerprint, a footprint, an echo.

Fifteen

Tess

'Hey,' Kyle said. 'Ever foraged before?' It was evening and on Kyle's instructions they had gathered on the terrace again. He was addressing Joe but the mention of foraging made Tess freak. Surely he didn't mean they were to source their own food? The phone was one thing, but this?

And she was hungry, hangry, bloody starving. No change there, then. Her eyes scavenged the terrace for food, or signs of food preparation, plates, a wrapper, anything. Found none. There was a barbecue to tease her but no coals firing, no smell of meat cooking. Would it be rude to ask? She was considering a neat way around it, *What can I do to help with dinner?* when her pocket buzzed and her heart set off on a sprint. She feigned a coughing fit, precisely the wrong thing to do because a) her phone was on silent and b) she wanted to avoid attention, not attract it.

'Everything OK, Tess?' Kyle said.

'Uh-huh.'

'I can go foraging,' Joe said. 'Why not?'

'You?' Libby said. 'What have you foraged before, Joe? Searching the reduced bins at Tesco doesn't count.'

'I've been plenty of times, if you must know.'

'I can help,' Tess said, suddenly desperate for the gig, to get out of eyesight and earshot, to have a moment alone. 'I've done it before.' This was not strictly true, not unless you counted watching Hugh Fearnley-Whittingstall do it on TV.

'Great, let's go,' Joe said and Libby shot her a look, *Don't try to encroach on my territory*, that made her even more determined.

'For the record, I have never searched the reduced bins at Tesco,' Joe said when they were on their way, trampling through the field in the direction of the hedgerows.

'No shame if you had. By the way, do you think he's going to feed us? I mean, this isn't going to be the main source of sustenance, is it?'

'I hope not, I haven't a clue what I'm looking for.'

'But you—'

'Yeah, I lied. And now I'm relying on you.'

'I hate to break it to you, but—'

'Shit, then we're really stuffed.'

They were faced with a sea of green; yellowy greens and deep greens, faded greens, green turning orange in the early autumn, but nothing that obviously shouted *Eat me, I'm green*, like a head of broccoli or cabbage. 'I'd kill for a rotisserie chicken now, or a freshly baked baguette.'

'I reckon we could make a run for it while no one's looking.'

She was only half joking. *I shouldn't be here. I shouldn't be here.* The voice kept nagging her. In her defence, she had tried to wriggle out of the trip directly after she said yes. Twenty minutes after, in fact, once she had selected an assortment of excuses from her black book, *friend's birthday, can't let her down*, visit to her mum's (sorry, Mum), and then there was also a dentist's appointment, a particularly lame one she wheeled out because she was desperate. But Kyle was persistent, steam-rollering every excuse she mentioned, *It's only a few days, the dentist can wait, your mum will understand, you're part of the team, is there something you want to tell me, are you not enjoying it, do we need to talk?* She felt him prying deeper and deeper, sensed he would plough on, driving the questions under her skin until she squealed. And she couldn't squeal because that would be the end of everything, so she did the only thing that made him stop. She said OK all over again.

And now her weakness had left her exposed. She tried calling Tomaz, yesterday and again today before Kyle picked her up (he insisted on giving her a lift with Asha) but it went straight to answerphone. She left a message, *I need to talk, I've done something*, and now she wished she'd made it less cryptic. He needed to know she was here. The fallout, the bollocking, the consequences she could deal with. Being four miles from the nearest village brought her stupidity into sharp relief. Tess just needed to know someone was watching her back.

But Tomaz hadn't replied. She knew this because the phone she had given Kyle wasn't her personal one. As if she would have willingly parted with her only link to the outside world. She still had the other one in her pocket and the real reason for the foraging expedition was to try calling him again.

'I reckon the hedgerows would be a good place. I'll head over there, and by the way, I'd steer clear of mushrooms unless you know what you're doing,' she said.

Joe was crouching down analysing a fungus at the foot of an enormous tree. 'Where's your sense of adventure?'

She walked along the bushes, pretending to study whatever they had to offer, which happened to be very little. It was probably the wrong time of year anyway, Kyle had probably set them up, to reveal the gag to everyone later. Not that she cared. All she wanted right now was to hear Tomaz's voice, an irony not lost on her.

She spotted a gap in the hedges, cast a look over to Joe, still enthralled by the mushrooms. No one else was around. She took out her phone and redialled the previous number.

'Tess?'

'Why haven't you replied to my calls?' The sound of his voice triggered relief that quickly gave way to anger. He shouldn't have left her like this. He had promised, hadn't he? Right at the start, he would protect her.

'I called at your flat today,' he said. 'Where are you? And by the way, we shouldn't speak on the phone.'

'Why not?' How else were they going to speak?

'You did as you were told, didn't you? You got out. You left. Tell me you left.'

'We were getting somewhere . . .'

'Fuck getting somewhere. I warned you. This is over. Where are you right now?'

She didn't like his tone, the panic that was ripe within it. It told her in capital letters, through a loudspeaker, that she had been stupid, idiotic, reckless. But more than that, and this was the engine of her fear, it told her that the game was over. Except she was still playing it.

The regret came in a flash of pain, pure and toxic, an amalgamation of every mistake that had brought her here, alone, in a field. Vulnerable.

'Tess!' Tomaz was shouting but there was someone else saying her name too. Someone closer to her, his hand on her shoulder, his breath on her neck. He was spinning her body around to face him. She closed her eyes. 'That's not a phone you have, surely?' the voice said. *Kyle.* She knew from the tenor of the accusation, from the sense of dread that drummed through her body. It was him.

'Shit, I didn't mean to give you a fright.'

Not Kyle. Joe. His face packed with concern. 'You're shaking.' This was true. She had melted into a puddle of nerves, and try as she might to stretch her mouth into a smile, it would not oblige. She could feel the tears rising, surging. And then Joe laid his hand on her shoulder, awkwardly, it had to be said, because it was obvious he wasn't comfortable with the show of emotion spilling out in front of him, but he was a kind man. This was as clear as the sky. And his simple act of kindness was her undoing.

'Don't cry . . . I mean, fuck, cry if you want to. I'm not a fascist when it comes to tears or anything. I'm just saying it can't be that bad, can it?' He delved in his pocket and produced a tissue, one she suspected was second-hand, but even this she was willing to overlook in the face of his concern. 'I won't tell anyone about the phone, honest. I'm more likely to ask to borrow it, dial a Dominoes to save us all from starving to death. We'll be eating the furniture by tomorrow, if there was any, that is. By the way, you didn't even say goodbye.'

'What?'

'Whoever you were talking to on the phone. You didn't say goodbye. I'm a firm believer in hellos and goodbyes.'

She stared down at the phone in her hand. The call had ended. Had he ended it or had she? Not that it mattered. She hadn't told Tomaz the one crucial piece of information. She hadn't told him where she was.

'Anyone important?' he asked. She gulped the tears down. Tess was not a crier by nature, not even at sad films, with the exception of *Free Willy*, which got her every time. But she was beginning to understand limits and where hers were. How it felt to go past them.

'Just a guy.'

'Boyfriend? God, I'm nosy. Tell me to butt out. It's none of my business. But for the record we're not worth it. Just ask Libby, I think she hates me.'

'She definitely hates me.'

'Yeah, sorry about that. You've generated a strong reaction in her.'

'I thought you were going to tell me I'd got her wrong, that she loves me really.'

'Not at all. She genuinely dislikes you.' Tess's face creased. 'Was that the wrong thing to say? I'm not very good in these situations. But I like you.' There he was again, his kindness tripping her up. 'I mean, not in a pervy way, not in a way that should worry you. Don't cry, I'm really not that bad, I promise.'

In the absence of any foraging knowledge they played it safe, collecting a few berries, one Tess identified as rosehip, and blackberries, along with a sweep of nuts from beneath a beech tree, before they headed back.

The thick smoky aroma of the barbecue hit them as they approached the house. 'My stomach is weeping,' Tess said, practically breaking out into a run. 'If they haven't left us anything I won't be responsible for my actions.'

'Ah, the foragers return,' Kyle shouted, waving barbecue tongs in the air. 'You've been gone ages, we're all expecting wonders.'

Tess looked down at her bag, 'I wouldn't get too excited, we bring blackberries and little else. But they're fat and juicy and I'll happily give you the whole bag in exchange for a sausage and a beer.' She handed it to Kyle and grabbed a bottle from the ice bucket.

The beer made her bilious and curiously light-headed, but then booze on an empty stomach never agreed with her. She eyed the sausages. How long did it take to cook a sausage? Five minutes? Ten? They looked done to her, they looked delicious. Ready to be eaten. For fuck's sake. This was torture. She shoved the beer bottle in her mouth again to stop her begging for one.

Finally, they ate at the large table on the terrace with lights spraying up from the carefully manicured borders. It was chilly by now, the sharp coldness that descends on the countryside without buildings and office blocks and micro climates to insulate. A jumper would have been advisable but Tess couldn't move until she'd eaten, was worried she might be blown away without something heavy in her stomach to tether her down. Judging from Libby and Asha's praise, the food was delicious, but Tess didn't chew hers long enough to detect any flavour. Oh, and by now she was pissed.

At some stage the beer, the food, the music, sent her to sleep. This was not unusual, Tess was an Olympian sleeper, known to pass out at the table, on a chair, standing up. But it was a pity her body allowed it on that particular night. She was not with close friends or family accustomed to her traits or the strange noises they told her she made when asleep, *like you're chewing on the air.* And afterwards she considered whether her staying awake would have prevented what happened next but she really couldn't see how. She couldn't have stopped it because it wasn't her fault, despite everything Libby said to the contrary.

Sixteen

Libby

Tess was asleep, passed out at the table, emitting an odd choking noise. Libby hoped she did choke. OK, not really, that was a bit strong. She would never wish a fatal accident on anyone, but Tess had been doing her best to wind her up this evening and it hadn't gone unnoticed. *Oh, I'll come with you, Joe. I've foraged lots of times before.* Libby could quite believe it was the kind of thing that Tess might get up to in her spare time. She was a bit alternative, a bit off centre. *Look at me, I pick my own food, I sprout my own beans.* All this Libby could have forgiven, it was none of her business if Tess wanted to stew chickweed, or culture alfalfa sprouts, or wear organic cotton farmed in India. But what she did object to was her making a move on Joe because that's what this little foraging expedition was all about, even if she was the only person to see it. And the chumminess between them on their return was notable, like their friendship had ratcheted up a gear in the hour they had been gone. They had even been giggling when they approached the house. Giggling! Joe was not a giggler. Not lately, anyway, and the image of the two of them stung her and it throbbed throughout the evening, no matter how much she drank to numb it. 'Tess was great, she knows her onions, or knows her berries rather,' Joe had said. It was a very poor joke and Libby was not at all amused.

After dinner they left Tess at the table and moved further down the garden to sit under a wooden canopy decked with string lights like super-sized stars. In the middle was a fire pit, sunken and roaring, fighting the chill of the autumn evening. Kyle had excused himself to do some work.

Libby stood up to grab another bottle of wine and crashed into the table before righting herself and filling her glass to the brim. 'I'm just hazarding a guess here,' said Joe, 'but I'd say you're going to regret that in the morning.'

His tone was not unkind but she took issue with it all the same. He did not get to tell her what to do. Besides, she was not drunk. A bit merry maybe, but definitely not drunk, unlike some around here. She sharpened her eyes, stabbed them in Tess's direction once again. *That woman.* 'I have not had too much to drink,' she said, irritated that the slur of her words failed to back her up in this respect. 'I'm perfectly fine.' And to prove it she took a generous swig from her glass.

'So much for Bear Grylls,' Will said. He was holding aloft Tess's bag of blackberries. 'I was expecting some magic mushrooms.' Libby was disappointed too, hoping for a poisonous berry or weed that someone would identify and expose Tess's incompetence in the process. But blackberries she liked. Will chucked a few in his mouth and let the juice drip down his chin like blood. 'Anyone?' he offered.

'Watching you eat is more than enough for me,' Asha said, tightening the string of her hoodie against the cold so she was reduced to two dark eyes.

'Go on then,' Libby said, and she could feel the burn of Joe's stare, surprised Will's eating was not enough to put *her* off. But he wasn't inside her head, couldn't hear what she could hear. The voice that was telling her to push her hand into the bag, the one that said, *There, remember that,* when she did. The berries were glued together and they stuck to her fingers just the way she hoped they would and she smeared the juice on to her lips. And the voice said, *I told you they were delicious.* They were more than delicious, they were much more than a taste. They were sticky and sharp on her tongue and they puckered her face. They revived autumn afternoons and the trudge of welly boots through wet leaves. They were simple pleasures, a different Libby. They were before. They were her mother. And now she couldn't eat them fast enough, immune to Joe's caution that she could make herself sick, her hand scooping out more and more to feed the ferocious hunger that had exploded within her. They weren't a taste. They were a treasured memory, long buried and denied.

She didn't think of Tess again until later. She was happy. Warm on the inside, giddy almost, her raw edges planed and smoothed. And her mood brought a rare insight: she should learn to let stuff go, stop nurturing grudges. Maybe she *had* overreacted. Maybe Tess was not the devil and there was another explanation for the newspaper story. No one, not even Kyle, had blamed her. What harm had been done? Her uncle had warned Libby of jumping to conclusions too, had not accused her of being negligent. And she sensed, increasingly, that Joe was tiring of her ways, the ongoing suspicion. She needed to relax a little, get some perspective, ingratiate herself with the others, because despite what she told Joe to the contrary, there was an element of truth in what he had said. If it wasn't for her and her hostility towards Tess they might not be here in the first place.

Her mood held strong for an hour or so. Libby was flying. She could do this! Even when Will produced a guitar and said, 'I played in a band in sixth form, but they got rid of me for a blonde with enormous tits,' and he cupped his hands in front of his chest, she forgot to tell him what a misogynous git he was. And when he started to strum something that sounded like the bastard love child of Coldplay and Metallica, she did not plead for mercy. She left that to Asha. 'Fuck me, I've died and gone to hell.'

The racket must have woken Tess out of her stupor because

she came down and joined them, revived and springing to life, dancing to the unrecognisable beat. The top half of her body swayed, arms held out to either side, head moving between them, as if she was in some kind of a trance. Libby wished she could master that abandon. Wished she could hold a room (or a garden) in thrall like Tess. All eyes were locked on her, feeding on this energy of hers that had charged the air. Well maybe she could; this new relaxed version of Libby could do anything. Joe moved closer to her, stroked her back. 'Dance with me,' he said. And she wanted to, she was desperate to let herself go, but she reminded herself, *Libby doesn't dance.* Ever since the cool girls at school said her dancing reminded them of a chicken pecking at the air, any vestige of rhythm deserted her, never to return. But why should they hold her back? Libby could do what she wanted to do, and those girls could go fuck themselves. She started to dance, without any grace or rhythm it has to be said, and with very few moves to rely on. But she danced all the same. She danced and she loved it. The tension running out of her body, the heat of Joe's next to her and the sense that nothing else mattered, not the future, not her plans, the stifling sense of duty and debt. Nothing mattered but him and her and this moment.

And then, it happened.

Will was still playing and murdering 'Paradise' when the first round of vomiting hit mid-chorus. They all carried on dancing because honestly, there wasn't such a big distinction between him singing and retching. It was only when he threw his guitar to the ground and bent over that she saw the spray of regurgitated food at his feet. She should have offered to help, it was what Libby would normally have done. She was good in a crisis, but she found herself repelled, gripped by a sensation, like a fist closing tighter and tighter around her intestines, squeezing them until she squealed in pain. And she didn't have to look at Will again to know exactly what was coming her way.

The pain in her stomach was something else. Like a fire. She wanted to put herself out. Wanted to take Joe out, and *her* too. She had no room in her head to say her name. Anger expanded, pushed up against her temples. Later, she would have room, would make her pay.

But now.

Libby looked down to her feet to see the remnants of the barbecue churned up. Joe was buzzing around her like a fly. He wasn't good in an emergency. She hadn't known that before, but she did now. 'Do you want water? What can I get you? Do you need air?' As if she had decided to stop breathing just because she was sick. 'This is your doing . . .' What had they picked? Why had they been so stupid? She tried to shout but the effort, sucking in the breath, gathering the steam for her outburst, made her retch again.

Joe held her hair back, like he'd read the good boyfriend manual, like he cared. But those gestures were empty, cost nothing in the grand scheme of things. He always joked he had a stomach of iron. He could hold her hair back all night and through the night and still it wouldn't buy him credit. He needed to hurt.

On her forehead, sweat beaded and dripped, the toxins in whatever the hell she had eaten stoking the furnace. She might die. It was possible, wasn't it? Anything was possible. Anything except Joe being useful.

A doctor. That was what she needed. Not air for fuck's sake. Not water that she would simply gulp down and then hose out again. Why couldn't he see what she needed? She heaved once more. It wasn't even food coming out now, it was her stomach, the very fabric of it surely. She was only petite, and always measured her calorie intake, so it wasn't possible there was this much inside her. The fact that gluttony was not in her make-up made her decision to try Tess's offerings particularly hard to stomach, no pun intended.

Libby hated herself. Hated herself more than she hated Joe and Tess, and that was saying something. She had indulged in a moment of weakness, allowed herself to reminisce and gorge on the past, and she'd loosened and relaxed and the relief of it flooded her system, and drugged her. It was this place, being here, in the countryside again, the memories it stirred, the emotions it revived, too potent to resist. But she should have known, no good ever came from looking back.

Seventeen
Day 2

Joe

Libby wasn't in the right frame of mind to listen to my arguments that night, and I valued my life too much to attempt to tell her it wasn't Tess's fault she was ill. I watched Tess pick blackberries and rosehips and neither make you violently sick.

I had higher hopes for the next morning. The visits to the loo had eased in the early hours and she had managed to sleep. I prayed it was something we might laugh about, and I had a few gentle jokes at the ready to coax her into a good mood. Let's just say I didn't get to use them.

'She tried to poison me.'

The *she* being Tess, no need to clarify. We were sitting outside, Libby keen to escape the smell of fried eggs that coated the kitchen air. I had brought her a black coffee. She said thanks but it didn't sound like a thanks. It sounded like *I blame you*.

There were a number of issues with Libby's poisoning theory, the first being me as the witness. 'I watched her pick blackberries and rosehips,' I said. 'Nothing else.'

'And how would you know if she slipped something else in when you weren't looking, unless you didn't take your eyes off her?'

This was a trap, delicate and subtle but a trap nevertheless.

Libby had constructed an argument I couldn't win. I either admitted there was a possibility Tess could have tampered with the blackberries or I admitted I was obsessed with her. I decided to do neither and moved on to issue number two. 'How was she to know you were the one who was going to eat them? She was asleep. It was Will who brought the bag down to you and then you stuffed . . .' Her eyes warned me off going too far, ' . . . you ate a lot of them. And why would she want to poison Will as well? Isn't it possible you were just unlucky?'

Her silence told me that as far as she was concerned, this was not a possibility she was prepared to entertain. 'Tess isn't who you think she is. It's a shame you can't see that.'

'How many of us are, Libby?' Her eyes were rubbed raw with tiredness and I couldn't work out whether it was disappointment I saw in them, or fury, or a mixture of the two.

With Will there was no such confusion. His rage was as strong as the stench of last night's beer from his pores. 'You need to watch your back, mate,' he said. 'I am not amused and my guitar is wrecked.'

'Does that mean you can't play it any more?' It was unwise to goad him but the open goal was hard to resist. He grabbed my T-shirt and squashed his face up to mine. His breath alone almost ended me.

'Your problem is you think you're so fucking smart. You did this, didn't you? That's why you warned Libby not to eat so many.'

'Don't be ridiculous, why would I try to poison you?' I said, as plenty of reasons sprang to mind.

'Because you think I'm a threat.' I pushed away from him and took a few steps back out of range of his breath.

'You?'

'That's right. Threatened at work because I'm better than you. Threatened because Libby likes me, Tess likes me.' I noticed he didn't mention Asha. Even for Will, that was a delusion too far.

'Must be hard being you, Will, what with all these women throwing themselves at you. Who knows what it is that makes you so attractive? It's certainly not your singing or your looks, or your clothes, or your personality.'

He lunged forward, raised his arm as if he was going to use it, but a stomach cramp saved me. I walked away as he doubled over. If I was going to poison anyone, Will would be right up there on my list of targets.

Kyle referred to it as last night's *unfortunate incident* and gave us the morning off, advising us to conserve our energy for the afternoon. 'Dom is coming to put us through our paces,' he said without telling anyone who Dom was or what paces he had in mind.

I fancied a walk to decompress. It was a dull day, the sky doling out measly portions of sunshine only for the clouds to snatch them away again. But still, anything was better than the atmosphere in the house. And besides, I wanted to find Tess because so far that morning she had proved elusive. It wasn't that I believed Libby – the poisoning accusation was in the realms of the ridiculous – but what I wouldn't admit was this: the more I got to know Tess, the more I sensed something about her didn't add up. Her arrest for hacking Westminster Council's system and leaking her findings to the press was an open secret on campus, and it was troubling me. I had expected the person responsible to be a bigger, stronger, more fearless version of the Tess I was getting to know. I couldn't help but think she had been diluted, jumping in fear when I appeared behind her, shaking, sitting on the edges of conversation, too scared to dive in. Perhaps that was what time in police custody did to you. Chipped away at your self-belief, reminded you no one was invincible, that for all you were young, the consequences of your actions were adult in scale.

I did a loop of the lake, trudged through the woods, careful to avoid the scene of last night's incident and its debris. There was no sign of Tess but I crossed Kyle's path on his morning run, all sweat and testosterone and ruddy cheeks, grunting as he swept past, and me burping up last night's beer. I was struck again by the contradictory feeling of hating him while wanting to be like him.

The sighting of Kyle put a downer on my walk, leaving me as it did with a sense of inadequacy. Clearly, it wasn't enough to be outside enjoying the morning, not when I could have been achieving and progressing and getting somewhere fast. I headed back, cold and in need of the loo. There was one on the ground floor at the far end of the house next to Kyle's room. I removed my muddy boots and padded along the hallway, turning the corner towards the bathroom. Tess. *There* she was. I opened my mouth to call her but her name sat on my lips, silent. Why was she here? She was standing outside a room. Kyle's room, her fingers twisting something long and thin, metallic, into the lock.

I was almost upon her when she spun at the sound of footsteps, her face replicating the fear and fright and panic of the night before, the moment I had caught her with a phone. It was emblazoned with guilt. But the footsteps she heard weren't mine. Mine were socked and silent. There was someone else coming with heavy trainered feet down the hallway.

Kyle.

She reached out and gripped my arm, leant in to me.

'Help me.'

98

Eighteen

Tess

What to do? *Run.* The word flashed up in her mind like a warning. But if she ran that would be the end of it, no going back. She might as well hold her hands up and confess everything. And then what?

No, Joe was her only option. Joe and his kindness. She was exploiting him and she didn't like it, but she had no space for guilt. Guilt wasn't going to help her, but Joe might.

'Help me,' she said, stepping away from Kyle's door.

She reckoned her chances were fifty-fifty but his expression downgraded them to thirty-seventy. He was not amused. His face accused her. His kindness was outraged. *And to think I trusted you*, it said.

'Guys,' Kyle was out of breath, his T-shirt dark with sweat, sticking to his chest, hair glistening. She could almost see the steam rise from his body. 'You came to see me?'

Tess nodded. 'We have a problem.'

The words tumbled out. Libby blamed her for last night. Libby believed Tess had done it on purpose. 'I'm trying my best but I don't think she likes me and I just thought it might be worth flagging up given the whole purpose of this is team-building.' She spoke fast and without looking at Joe because she didn't dare. She was waiting, expecting him to correct her, to say, *This is a diversion, a smokescreen. I saw her trying to get in to your room.*

But he didn't.

The kindness. She was right to exploit it.

'Is that why you're here, Joe, to back her up?' Joe shifted away from her. This was going to break him. She was asking for too much. Asking him to turn Judas. 'Libby has a problem with Tess, is that it?' Kyle pressed.

The silence between them stretched until it was ice-thin. And then he said, 'I think that about sums it up.'

Tess walked back down the corridor in silence, fearful that a single word would smash the lies she had told and rain them down on her head. When they made it outside Joe spun round.

'Don't ever do that again,' he said.

'I can explain but . . .' She glanced around. 'Later, OK?' She needed time to get her story straight, work out how much of it to ration out to Joe. As little as possible but something, she had to give him something, because if she were to see this out, if she wanted him on her side, she had to give him a morsel of the truth.

'You need to because I won't cover for you again.' He went into the house, leaving her alone to consider his likely reaction if she came clean. It was perfectly possible she was a fool to trust someone she barely knew. And she was still calculating how fast she would have to move if Joe didn't take it well, if he threatened to expose her, when Kyle called them to the kitchen.

'I want you to meet someone,' he said.

In the kitchen, Tess found a man, arms in perfect Vs sitting on his hips, legs apart, occupying more space than was strictly necessary. 'This is Dom,' Kyle said, and patted Dom on the back. Dom smiled in a way that suggested he did not smile a lot and did not like being thumped on the back by over-zealous Americans. He had a scar that ran out of the right side of his mouth. 'Dom used to be in the army so don't expect any mercy. He'll be putting us through our paces this afternoon.'

'Hello,' Dom said. He also used his words sparingly as if they were in limited supply. 'Good to be here.' He was a chunky man, almost as wide as he was tall, and cast his eyes around greedily, like he was deciding which one of them to eat first. 'We're going out on the Downs this afternoon, see what you're made of.' At this, a grin flashed on his face before disappearing as quickly as it had appeared. 'We're going to split you into teams. Girls v boys. We're leaving straight after lunch so I suggest you take something warm with you. At this time of year the temperature can drop quickly.' He nodded to the window and the clouds beyond. 'You're not in London now.'

'OK, listen up.' They were standing at the top of Devil's Dyke, Tess attempting to appreciate the view while her mood sullied it. Had she been in a different frame of mind she would have taken a photo of the huge ravine that opened up in front of her and the sky brushed with greys and blues, and the horizon studded with churches and windmills, the fields in patchwork colours. She might have said, *Well, isn't this the tonic after London,* like her father used to when they visited her grandmother. But she was flat, her excitement battery exhausted. All she could think about were the teams, boys v girls. An afternoon of physical activity with Libby.

'I have a little surprise for you.' Kyle was still talking although she sensed she hadn't missed much by tuning out for a few minutes. She had come to realise he was a master of the art of talking a lot while saying very little. 'To make it more interesting, there will be one person on each team who belongs to the other side. Your job is to work out who it is and avoid them sabotaging you, while bringing your team home first.'

'And the purpose of this is what?' said Joe.

'There's always a purpose. We want to see how you work as a team but also how you function on your own. Let me tell you this, there's a misconception about teamwork. Most people think it means you have to carry the weakest player. That is not how it works. Teamwork is about everyone pitching in, pulling their weight, but if that's not happening you have to be strong enough, brave enough to get rid of them. That's when teamwork gets hard. If you want your team to succeed, and we all want that, right, then we can't be afraid of calling someone out and saying you're not good enough.'

Joe's brows were knitted together in a scowl, like he was struggling with the deconstructed version of teamwork Kyle had presented.

'It's not that hard, Joe. Let me put it like this: you're here to win. Everyone is out to win. We all want to do well in life, in our jobs, in our personal life, but not everyone can win so that means we have to beat the rest.' He flung his arms out. 'You have to beat these people here. We can't blindly trust each other. People are way too trusting; it's one of the reasons our clients lose millions of pounds because Jonny in the Chief Exec's office trusts some guy who calls up pretending to be the global head of HR. He lets them into the system, and then BANG! It's too late. To do this job we have to toughen up, we don't let emotion hamper us, we don't listen to sob stories, we don't pity. We stay focused, single-minded, determined. Disciplined. Now tell me that doesn't make sense.'

It was two o'clock when they started, the girls huddling in their group, away from Will, Joe and Kyle, to discuss tactics. Tess was strung out, hated competitive sport, anything where a timer was involved, any activity that demanded she move quickly. But what she lacked in speed and agility she would make up for in map reading, or so she thought, until it was revealed that an orienteering map didn't look like any map she had seen before.

'Well, this is a good start. Anyone got a clue what's going on? We're going to get spanked otherwise,' Asha said. She had tied her hair back in a bandana and was dressed in combat trousers, like she had joined a militia.

'I did orienteering in Guides,' Libby told Asha. Guides, Tess thought, that figured. She could picture Libby collecting her badges, sewing them on her sleeve, irrefutable proof that she was one of society's good eggs. Tess had half expected her to cry off today. She was still pale from blackberrygate, her hair scraped back from her face, skin red and mottled, her voice strained as if the vomiting had scoured her throat. But any natural pity Libby's condition generated was short-lived. She had blamed Tess for the poisoning. *Me!* Tess had been outraged to the point of combustion when Joe told her. 'Is she mad?' she had asked and he simply shrugged, as if to say, *It's quite possible she is.*

Now it was just the three of them, Libby directed her speech at Asha, refusing to acknowledge Tess's presence. 'Woodland is marked white,' she said, having laid the map on the ground like a picnic blanket, 'unless it's dense and then it's green. Fields are yellow. The narrow green stripes are undergrowth. This is north and this is west.' She tapped it with a pencil like an army general planning her advance. 'The first control point should be half a mile north from here. I say we go there first.'

They set off at a brisk jog, much to Tess's distress. Were they planning to keep this pace all afternoon? Asha was surprisingly strong and despite Libby's sickness, it was apparent she was fit too, at least far fitter than Tess, who had never been in a gym in her life. And Libby was out to prove a point, that much was evident. Prove herself a martyr. *You tried to hurt me and look at me now, I can still outrun you.* 'Why are we running? Surely we don't want to peak too soon?' Tess asked.

'Did you miss the part where Kyle said speed is key?' Asha said. 'The idea is to beat the other team. Not saunter in three hours later . . .' Tess could hear Libby's mind turning over. *Unless you are out to sabotage us.*

They had been running for ten minutes when the first control point appeared, just as Libby promised it would, just as Tess was about to expire. 'Thank fuck.' She sat down, pulled an energy bar from her bag, took one bite, and was considering whether to offer it around or eat it all herself when Libby barked at her.

'It's not picnic time. We have ten of these control points to hit. Preferably this week.'

Despite herself, and despite Libby, Tess began to enjoy the task. She found her stride, a more sedate one than Libby's who stuck to the front of their little group, and fell into a rhythm alongside Asha. They didn't talk much, saved their breath for the task, and Tess found the quiet beauty of the countryside calmed her anxiety. The churning sky. The whip of the wind. The inclines and peaks, her knees folding under her as they sank down hills, the squelch of mud underfoot, the deep satisfaction when the landmarks shot into focus on the horizon just as the map predicted they would, all this occupied her mind, stilled the jitters that had plagued her. She enjoyed the challenge, one she could undertake without any obvious danger. And she relished the certainty after months of unknowns. There was a logic to this process, a definitive answer at the end. And lately, Tess had been starved of answers.

After the fifth control point, at the edge of a wooded area, Libby permitted a break, 'a few minutes, no more,' she said, looking at her watch to time them. Tess's feet were throbbing now and she could feel the pinch of blisters sprouting on her heels. While Libby and Asha gulped water to drench their thirst, Tess headed into the woods. 'A free wee,' she said. 'I'm desperate.'

She was mid-flow when she turned to her left and spotted a rabbit staring at her. Did rabbits stare? This one was definitely staring. Staring and not moving like its survival instinct had deserted it. She zipped up her trousers and moved towards it slowly until she was so close she could see it twitching. There was a reason it hadn't scarpered away. It couldn't. Its foot was stuck in a trap.

She ran back to the others. 'I need your help,' she told Asha and Libby. 'There's a rabbit in there, caught in a trap, we need to get it out.' She was breathless, her heart hammering. Tess never could stand the sight of any creature in pain. Even as a seven-year-old, when they had a mouse problem she would go around unsetting the mouse traps every night until the problem became an infestation and her mother threatened to ground her for the summer holidays if she didn't desist. 'Come on,' she said. They exchanged a look, Libby to Asha, Asha back to Libby, and Tess wanted to scream because all she could think about was the rabbit twitching in the trap and its life ticking away with every passing second. 'What's the matter with you?'

That knowing look again from Libby, stirring the suspicion. *Nice try. We're not falling for that one.*

'Oh for fuck's sake, really? You really think I'm trying to win some stupid game by making this up? There's an animal in there and it's dying and I'm asking for your help to save it. That's all. No ulterior motive. I'm really not that inventive.' She turned to Asha. Asha was her best hope. Asha liked her, or at least hadn't shown any obvious signs of hating her in the way Libby had. 'Come and see for yourself.' Asha took a step towards her but Libby put her hand on her arm, shook her head. 'She's lying.'

'Well, there's only one way to find out, isn't there? It'll cost you all of a few minutes.'

Tess swore she saw Libby's face thaw, a softening that told her Libby wasn't that hard, not really, that deep down she wasn't the sort of person who could walk away from an injured animal just to win a game. And then Libby peered upwards from their position at the bottom of the valley and Tess followed her gaze. At the crest of the hill, a thick, stocky figure stood. As wide as he was tall. *Dom.* It had to be him. Following their progress or lack of, ready to report back. And Tess, hearing Kyle's words roll back to her, could imagine his disdain: *We don't pity. We stay focused, single-minded, determined.*

Libby's face changed again, like a mould hardening, and she rubbed her temples as if to dislodge a pain. 'That's nature for you. Survival of the fittest. We don't have time, the weather's changing.' They glanced up to the sky, the clouds forming in dark masses above them. 'If she wants to stay here alone, that's her choice.'

That was it. They walked away, heading upwards, leaving any vestige of kindness, of heart, behind. At least Asha had the decency to mouth *sorry* before she left, although when Tess thought about it, sorry made it worse, because it meant Asha knew it was wrong and still did it. She could stick her apology up her arse.

Tess tramped back into the woods, counting the trees to lead her to the rabbit. Eight trees in, four to the left. That was what she remembered, had imprinted in her mind. Eight and four. Or was it four and eight? What had been certain was now scrambled in her brain. The rabbit wasn't there anyway. She must be wrong. Tess spun around, walked back towards the opening again. Counted four trees in and eight to the left just in case. But that got her nowhere either. Tears pressed against her eyes. She was tired. Bone tired, had exhausted every atom of energy in her body. But the image of the rabbit wouldn't release her. She couldn't walk away and abandon her mission. If she did that how would she tell herself apart from Asha or Libby?

It was darker now, harder to see her way through, but she kept moving. This time she counted too many trees, way more than eight, and it seemed to her they were sprouting and springing up simply to mess with her head. The rain started, rattling and shaking the trees, their branches dipping down to touch her, to tease and whisper, *You're lost*. Was she lost? She most certainly was. She had done so many rotations, Tess wouldn't have been able to say which way was north or south, east or west. Which was the way out. Finally, she slumped down and cried. Cried hard because there was no one to hear her. No one to help her. She had never wanted this in the first place. And now she wanted out.

Tomaz. She would try him again. He would be pissed off with her but she would explain why she had done it, the pressure to say yes, the lack of opportunity to leave. He would understand. And if he didn't, so what? It was of no consequence. She just wanted him to come to get her out. As soon as possible.

Tess delved in her bag. Her phone was buried in a small zip pocket. She'd managed to charge it a little while she was awake last night. Couldn't risk leaving it in case someone came in and saw it while she slept. There were six missed calls. Number unknown. One voicemail. Two bars of signal. Nothing short of a miracle considering where she was.

Tomaz.

His words lashed her like a whip. A torrent of obscenities and threats. She edited them out, gleaning only what she needed to hear. The import of his words. It was all her fears and paranoia, all the shadows that populated her dreams, all the worst-case scenarios thrown together and multiplied to the power of one thousand. And the urgency, the rawness of his voice, drained the blood from her.

'They know. Get out. They know.'

She called his number. But there was nothing. No answer. No connection to him. She sent a text. He might see that, at least. She wanted him to know where she was.

I'm at a house called Kenton Thorpe in Sussex. Closest village Wivelton.

She waited for the speech bubble to appear, evidence of him preparing to reply.

Nothing.

Run!

It wasn't the first time this had occurred to her, but now it was imperative. She scanned around, had the sense she wasn't alone, that the woods were alive, their branches snapping at her, the trees sealing her in, the sky disappearing. She pushed her phone back into its case, into the pocket at the bottom of her bag, and she moved, faster than Tess had ever moved, than she thought possible. No sign of tiredness now, fear had given her fresh energy. Tess could have run for miles, run all night if it meant she could escape.

All night, if she hadn't stopped.

If something hadn't hit her.

If she hadn't hit something.

Which way was it? She could never say.

All she remembered was a smash of pain in her head. A brightness into which everything else dissolved. And the rabbit's dead eyes staring into hers telling her she had failed.

Nineteen

Libby

Libby felt the lack keenly in this house. It was empty and soulless. Yes, there was space in abundance, but it had no real reason to exist if there was nothing to fill it. And Libby had been here long enough to know there *was* nothing to fill it. No furniture, no atmosphere, no colours beyond white and grey. Its heart had been ripped out, stripped back to its bones and its bones crushed and reformed. And yes, Libby knew houses weren't supposed to have feelings but she didn't care. She knew, could tell right from the beginning, that this one was restless and disturbed. She lay in bed and tried to imagine what it was like originally, the 'before' photograph in the kitchen, before the destruction was wrought and the great sheets of glass were craned in and the concrete poured to turn the surfaces hard and shiny and unforgiving. But she couldn't. She couldn't summon up its past so she lay in bed and listened to the house speak in whispers and creaks and clunks like it was trying to tell her something, a story she needed to understand, one she could not yet decipher.

Sleep wouldn't come tonight. She had given up closing her eyes, willing it to arrive and sweep her off. It wasn't going to happen. No matter that her limbs were singing with exhaustion and tiredness was beating against her skull. Her head was too full of today, the things she couldn't scrape out of her brain. *Bad things happen here*, she thought and then berated herself. She had made bad things happen. Libby had not been a passive agent. She didn't get to absolve herself of blame. She deserved to suffer, to be reminded, *This is your fault. This is what you did*. Libby had left Tess alone and now Tess was missing. Added to that – there was plenty more to add to her shame – she had persuaded Asha to collude, insisting it was Tess working against them when she knew this to be a lie. Libby knew it was a lie because it was Libby who was on the other side. And she did all this because she had wanted to win. Libby liked winning because her achievements were hers alone. They would never desert her.

This was how it had come to pass. This was why, instead of recognising the task for the stupid game it was, she allowed it and her dislike of Tess to consume her. The rabbit was the final straw. She didn't doubt it was real, that it was in pain and trapped; the desperation that leaked from Tess's face told her the truth. All Tess wanted to do was save the damn rabbit. And it was this that Libby couldn't handle. The compassion. Libby didn't want Tess to be compassionate. It suited her perfectly well to cast her as the villain, the thief, the manipulator, the woman who was out to sabotage their work for her own gain. But the rabbit, the bloody rabbit, demanded she reframe her opinion of Tess. Recast her in a different light. And the funny thing was Tess had almost won her over. You'd have to have a cold heart not to be moved and Libby's heart wasn't cold, it was big and warm and open. She *was* going to help her. And then she saw Dom on the horizon and wondered what he would think, what Kyle would think if they abandoned the task to save an animal. They'd think less of her, and Libby always wanted people to think more.

So she walked.

It was that easy.

'We've left Tess down there trying to rescue a rabbit caught in a trap,' she told Dom, her tone thick with disdain. And he shook his head just as she had predicted and his expression (because Dom didn't do subtle) said: *Fucking softie, an animal, for fuck's sake!* Libby had scored a small victory but instead of giving her a buzz in the way her victories normally did, it made her feel toxic and dirty. It taught her something about herself too, and it was this: She liked to win, but she liked to win clean, otherwise it didn't count.

When Tess didn't return Joe had asked for her assessment of the situation.

'If she was in the woods surely they would have found her by now,' he said. *They* were Dom and Kyle who had stayed on the Downs to search for Tess. The others had gone back to Kenton Thorpe in a taxi.

'Are you blaming me?' she said. *I blame myself.*

'Of course not.' And he gave her a hug but it was cold and hard, just how she imagined her heart had become.

Asha was no longer speaking to her. 'It was part of the task,' Libby had tried to tell her. 'I was supposed to fool you. How could I do that without lying?' But even she didn't buy her excuses.

'You're a first-class bitch and I hope they find her, because we'll never live with ourselves if they don't.'

It was fair to say none of this was going to plan. Libby had come to Kenton Thorpe because she was asked. Before that, she had embarked on this whole adventure because she wanted to please. Please her uncle mainly. Repay him for all he had done for her when her mother left, the education, the money, his presence, always being there for her. Perhaps if her mother hadn't died it would have been very different. Libby might not have felt the need to overcompensate, jump through hoops to help others, to be accepted. She wanted to be good. It really wasn't that difficult to understand. That's why she was here. That's why she hadn't been entirely truthful with Joe or the others. But it was a little white lie, not even that, it was more a harmless omission, and nobody needed to know. So why couldn't she shake the nagging sense there was something more, out of her reach, on the periphery of her vision that was about to swamp her?

She was being stupid. Of course she was. Over-analysing again. Thinking the worst because Libby of all people knew the worst could happen. It was Tess's disappearance that had set her mind in freefall, that was all. She was worried and her anxiety opened the door to the flurry of negative emotions, the endless tragic permutations. Tess's return would set her world straight again. Libby dialled up the God she'd long ago ditched, bartering to keep Tess safe: *I'll give up the job if she's OK. I'll go and work in an orphanage. Become celibate. I'll become less . . . less driven, less critical, more forgiving.*

By two in the morning her relationship with him had soured once more. He wasn't a giver, this God; when had he ever helped her before? Had he helped her mother? Had he brought her back? Had he cared? No. No. No. She must have been desperate to turn to him. But then she heard the sound of a car on the drive, pulling to a stop, its engine falling silent. They were here! Libby dived to the window. Her bedroom light was out, she didn't want to be noticed, but she needed to know, to see if Tess was there. Kyle got out of the car first, the driveway lights spraying his face with a cold glow, and then Dom leant in to the passenger seat and helped someone out. A huddled figure, stooping and shuffling as Dom pulled her along. *Tess.* Libby's tears came in a torrent that almost choked her. Tess was alive. Libby couldn't take her eyes off her, saw her face, blown up in a bruise, her eye swollen to a slit and blood caking her head. She must have fallen, but how? Libby razored in, absorbing every tiny detail of the scene before her. And like one of those images that turns into something else if you stare at it long enough, she saw it all differently. It struck her with such force she couldn't breathe. Dom was not helping Tess, he was pulling her, dragging her along, and Kyle was allowing it to happen.

Libby rewound back to when she had deserted Tess. 'She's down in the woods rescuing a rabbit,' she'd told Dom. He was the only other person who knew where she was. But why, she wanted to know, why would he hurt her?

Twenty
Day 3

Joe

Tess had hit her head on a branch and passed out, Kyle told us at breakfast. 'Lucky Dom found her when he did, it was cold out there last night. Just reinforces the importance of teamwork and sticking together, don't you think?'

I opened my mouth to correct him. Which particular brand of teamwork was he referring to? The one where people supported each other or the one he had championed where we were all out for ourselves? 'Actually, Kyle, I think you'll find you said we were to ditch those who were holding us back. That is the polar opposite to what you're saying now.'

Kyle shook his head. 'Listen, Joe, you must have misunderstood me. I mean, I tried to explain but obviously you didn't get it. We stick together, right? Libby has already apologised. I don't think we need to indulge in the blame game, that's not going to help Tess now.'

I had hoped one of the others might back me up, but Will was only too happy for Kyle to give me a hard time and Asha had no intention of stepping into the breach, given her role in leaving Tess. Libby's eyes were fixed on the floor, willing it to crack open and suck her into a black hole. I dropped it for her, but I wasn't buying his doublespeak.

'I'd like to see Tess,' I said.

'She needs her rest right now, she had a bit of a scare.'

'Don't you think she needs a doctor?'

'Where do you think we were last night? She's been seen to, we've got this, Joe. No need to stress. Dom is on hand if she needs anything.' He moved on, closing down that line of investigation. 'After the excitement of yesterday, you'll be pleased to hear we're going to have a relaxed day. But we have something planned for tonight. More details to follow, but I think you're going to love it.'

'I want to see Tess,' Libby said when we were outside. 'I need to apologise.' She hadn't slept, the exhaustion drawn on her face in dark shadows, bloodshot eyes. The coffees she'd been necking all morning hadn't helped; they had set her nerves on edge.

'Do you think she'll want to see you?'

'I wouldn't blame her if she didn't. But . . . Dom, I don't think she'd want him either.' Libby wouldn't look at me straight, her gaze settled elsewhere. She was right, Dom was an unlikely choice for nursemaid, stationed outside Tess's door, but I knew there was more to it than that.

'You going to spit it out?'

'I just want to make sure she's OK, that's all.'

We agreed I would go. Tess had no reason to turn me away and besides, Libby's skills of persuasion were needed to distract Dom.

We waited until Kyle set off for a run, gave it five minutes or so until he was out of range. Dom was in his car, on a call when Libby ran up from the garden and shouted that Kyle needed him. 'He's down in the far field, I think he might have hurt his ankle.' Dom jumped out of the driver's seat and broke into a run, Libby alongside, pointing in the direction of the field. I knew she wasn't comfortable lying, but in the absence of any alternative ideas she didn't have much choice. Besides, I told her she could blame it all on me, I was past caring what Kyle thought of me. After this morning's debacle, I was of the view he deserved a taste of his own medicine.

From the garden, I watched them disappear and walked back towards the house, passing Dom's car en route. It was one of those flash four by four numbers. Pristine too, not even a coffee cup or an empty packet of crisps. But there was a red rucksack on the back seat, one I recognised as Tess's. I'd have expected a man like Dom to be security conscious, even in the middle of nowhere, but in his haste to help Kyle, he'd left the car unlocked. I grabbed the bag to return it to its rightful owner.

'Open up,' I hissed at Tess's door. 'It's me, Joe.'

I waited. Heard nothing. Knocked again. 'Tess, I don't have much time. If you're there, open the door – I have your rucksack, but if you don't want to see me, I can leave it outside.'

This time footsteps shuffled across the floor. 'Wait, please, don't leave it there.' There was a desperate note to her voice. 'I'm locked in.'

Anger spiked me. What was this? 'Do you want me to kick it in?' I said, having never kicked a door down in my life.

'Hang on, I have a hair clip.' She fiddled with the lock for what seemed like an eternity and I shifted nervously, casting my eyes down the hallway to check no one was coming.

Finally, the door opened and Tess's face stared into mine. 'Your bag,' I said. And she pulled it tight into her chest like it was the most precious item she possessed. And then she started to cry.

'I don't know what happened,' she said. She was sitting on the bed, having recovered her phone from the lining of the bag and hidden it in the wardrobe. There was a bruise on her forehead, ripe red and purple, but it was the fear leaking out of her that made me sweat.

'I was running and then I passed out. The next thing I knew I was in Dom's car.'

I studied the gash on her forehead. 'Why didn't you have stitches at the hospital? It's deep enough.'

'I didn't go to the hospital.'

'But Kyle said he took you to the doctor's.'

She shook her head, tears soaked her face. 'You need to help me get out of here.'

It started with the hack, she said, the Westminster Council hack and the leak to the newspaper. 'I was careful, honestly. I know what I'm doing.'

'So how did they find out?'

'I gave the story to an old friend on the *Herald*, Clara George. I trust her. I don't think she would have shafted me, but the police had her phone records and my number was in there. They must have been watching us because they even had photos of us together. She swore she told them nothing.

'And you believed her?'

'She's an old family friend. Honestly, she was more upset than I was. Anyway, they had all the evidence against me they needed. And it was terrifying. You know, to be there, being interviewed for hours on end and knowing that you might go to jail and that your criminal record will be with you forever. I realised I was such a fake. All my life I thought I was brave and fearless, some kind of warrior against social injustice, and the next thing I was thinking of a trial and prison and suddenly I was just a girl crapping my pants and crying for my parents. They could have suggested anything and I would have done it.'

'Done what? What did they make you do?'

'This, all of this,' she waved her arms around. My brain was swelling, overheating. I could handle numbers and equations and sneak my way around any computer system, but this was overload.

'Well, that's not entirely true. She said I wasn't supposed to be here. The operation is over, dead.'

'What operation?'

'The police. I've been working for the police. They approached me, Detective Sergeant Tomaz Ramsay was my contact. I'd already applied for this job when I was arrested. I was giving them some sob story about having a future and when they found out the company I'd applied to, they completely changed tack. That's how I got away without a criminal record, on the basis I helped them.'

'You're helping the police?'

'They think Freetech is a shell company, a front to hack and sell on confidential information. The deal was I accepted the job, handed them whatever information I could find and in return they wouldn't prosecute me. Only now I'm in here and somehow Kyle and Dom have found out who I am and what I've been doing.'

I shook my head. There was a wasp trapped inside somewhere, buzzing around my brain. Tess had had a knock to the head, she wasn't thinking straight, confusing reality with fantasy.

'Tess,' I tried to reason. 'We're pen testing clients . . . ethical hacking. Why would they shaft their clients?'

'You don't get it, do you?' She was scarily lucid. 'How do you know they even have clients? How do you know we've not just been hacking into systems? We've only got Kyle's word for it. Think about it, we were some of the best students in our year, we all had previous hacking experience. We're smart, just not smart enough to see what's really going on. They've blinded you with talk of money and opportunity and ambition.'

I wanted to resist this version and the humiliation that came with it. I was an intelligent guy, for fuck's sake, not some loser who was easily fooled. And yet my brain churned over, casting up the debris of the past weeks. 'The newspaper story, the one about Marc Zimmerman. Libby thought that was you.'

'It wasn't me. Yes, I was at her desk, yes, I was prying but not for the reasons she thought. I wanted to know what she had on Zimmerman; I needed to know what information she'd sent to Kyle so I could prove what they were doing. And when it turned up in the newspaper a few days later we knew we were on to something. Kyle leaked that story. That's the whole point of Freetech.'

'But . . .'

She grabbed my hand, dug her nails down into the flesh. 'They know who I am, Joe. They know what I've been doing. You think this was an accident?' She stabbed her finger towards her wound. 'I need to get out of here and you need to do the same.'

Before I could say anything, the thud of footsteps rolled along the hallway. 'It's him,' she said. 'What are you going to say?'

What was I going to say? The excuse I had lined up was simple. I had wanted to see Tess. End of. It was a free world and I could do as I pleased. If it incurred their wrath so be it, I was more than happy to live with Kyle's disapproval. But Tess's revelation destroyed my excuse. It relied on them being reasonable. And reasonable people did not smash up a woman's face and lock her in a room.

My brain buffered. They were almost here now, the noises outside cranking up, footsteps getting closer and closer. I couldn't pull any words out of the mess and even if I could, I wouldn't have trusted myself to speak them, so I let my actions do it for me. Just as the door flew open, I leant forward and kissed her.

Twenty-One

Tess

The kiss. Tess had not expected that. There was no romance involved, it was not *that* kind of kiss. It wasn't as if Joe was making a crude pass at her. He was simply trying to rescue the situation and managed to drop himself right in the shit in the process.

His tactic worked, to an extent. Dom's anger gave way to a perverse pleasure, the warped thrill of catching two people in the act, made all the sweeter because he wasn't alone. He was with Libby. Tess imagined Dom would have called it poetic justice if he knew what poetry was.

'You sneaky bastard,' he said. 'Couldn't stay away, could you?' And to Libby, whose eyes were knifing her: 'You're better off without him. They deserve each other if you ask me.'

At least Tess didn't have to manufacture her alarm. That was steaming off her skin, one hundred per cent pure; it was just that the kiss and being caught out were not the cause of it. Given her current predicament, one treacherous kiss was the least of her worries.

'I'll give you two a minute to compose yourselves and then Kyle wants us downstairs for lunch.'

Tess told Dom she was feeling better and please could she have some lunch? She sounded like Oliver Twist, meek and beseeching, thanked him for helping her the night before. 'I'm such a fool,' she said and he nodded his fat head in agreement. If she was to get out of here the pretence would be everything. And if Dom and Kyle could keep it up, so could she.

Lunch proved a tougher test. The air so brittle she thought it might shatter. 'Fucking hell, look at you,' Will said.

'I'm sure Tess doesn't need to be reminded of her accident,' Kyle said, baring his white teeth in her direction. She shuddered. Only a few days ago she had found it easy to be close to him, flirt even, in order to extract what information she could. Now he repelled her, and her reaction to his presence was a physical one, like insects marching across her skin. 'There's a place for you there,' he pointed to the chair next to Joe's. *He's enjoying this, the bastard.*

Asha and Libby were bunched together, trading their disgust. Neither acknowledged Tess's presence, their glares pitched in Joe's direction instead, like cameras trained to monitor a suspect's reaction. Libby had told Asha about the kiss, Tess concluded. *Whatever.* She no longer had the energy to care. Kyle was busying himself in the kitchen. It smelt disgusting whatever they were having.

She put her hand in her pocket to feel for her phone. To remind herself that all wasn't lost, that she still had a chance to get through to Tomaz, to anyone on the outside who could help.

'It's feta and sweet potato,' Kyle said, plonking a huge dish down on the table. He looked around expectantly, like he was waiting for a round of applause.

'Feta and sweet potato, my favourite, said no one ever,' Will whispered to her and for once she was inclined to agree with him.

Tess loaded her fork and filled her mouth with food. It was as tasteless as it looked, possibly worse, but again, the pretence mattered so she chewed as if her life depended on it. She chewed and chewed, like she was in the chewing Olympics, but it wouldn't go down. It coagulated into a foul ball of matter, clawing at her throat. *I'm going to choke. Death by sweet potato.*

'Excuse me.' She coughed, threw her hand over her mouth. 'I have to go to the toilet.' Her interruption caused a murmur of surprise, reminding everyone they had been eating in silence.

Tess ran down the hallway, her hand never leaving the cold, hard metal of the phone, her last line of defence. At the bathroom, she locked the door, allowed her body to slide down the back of it. She could hardly bear to look. Couldn't cope if she did and saw the battery had died.

Fifteen per cent.

Another missed call.

Another voicemail.

It was Tomaz again, although thanks to his slurred speech this was not immediately apparent.

I'm sorry, Tess, I'm sorry. It's my fault they know who you are. There was nothing I could do. I had to tell them. You don't understand what's going on. It's a fucking mess. A mess . . .

Was he pissed? He was definitely pissed. Pissed and morose. She hated a teary drunk, hated a teary drunk who had fucked her over even more.

They knew we had someone on the inside and I had to tell them. I'm sorry. I didn't want the money. I didn't do it for the money . . . you have to believe me. I did it because there was no other way out.

She forced herself to breathe, sharp intakes of air that pierced her lungs. Tomaz was paid to out her. Was that what she'd just heard?

I'm over, finished. I've quit. I'll hope you'll forgive me . . .

He wanted absolution. From her? She let out a weird animal wail that bounced off the tiled walls of the bathroom before she stuffed her fist into her mouth to silence it. Detective Sergeant Ramsay would soon be no more. He'd taken the bribe, the pay-off, was probably drunk on pina coladas in Portugal, calling her to assuage his momentary guilt. But tomorrow it would have passed, and he'd be basting himself in Ambre Solaire once more, raising a glass at the end of the day, *this is the life.*

She would simply be a loose end. A project that went tits up. And so what if she got hurt? Shit happens.

He was still talking. Tess couldn't listen to any more of it, her finger about to press END when his words pierced her anger.

Maybe you'd understand if I told you what's really going on. It's way bigger than you think, Tess. People involved in a way you would never guess. I had no idea and I'm going to tell you so you'll understand and you'll get out and get as far away from this as possible . . .

Her mind turned black. What Tomaz explained was too much. The names, the plot, the high-level corruption, she could not absorb. She leant forward, the cold stone tiles against her face as her body was beaten by a fresh terror. She wanted to believe none of it, not a word, but why would Tomaz lie? His pleading was not an act, it was the desperation of a man who had nowhere to turn. And although she did not forgive him, not entirely, she understood the colossal force of what he had come up against.

It was obvious to her why the police operation could go no further. How could they get around what he had just told her, the monumental pressure they would have faced? The police were trying to uncover something that was never meant to be exposed.

No one was allowed to know the scale of the deceit.

No one could know who had contracted Freetech to hack the accounts of political figures, campaigners, journalists, dissenters.

Because the people who were bankrolling the theft of information were the very people who were running the country.

They would kill her if they got half a chance, that much was clear. She wondered why they hadn't already. They could have done it in the woods because it was obvious she knew too much now. How easy would it be to dispose of her without too many questions? She knew the answer: it was easy enough to get away with any form of corruption and violence when you had the force of power behind you.

She wanted to scream. Scream for all of them lured into this trap, brought here to this house, miles away from anywhere, for reasons still murky and unclear, but sinister, no doubt. And she wanted to scratch the eyes out of those involved, who had taken their trust and used it against them, cruelly, callously for their own ends. Tears of rage bubbled up. *Do not cry. Don't you dare cry.* Crying would only reinforce how pathetic she had become. Highlight the scale of her folly, the trail of her mistakes, one after the other, starting with the moment she was arrested. The police had plied her with horror stories of prison, of broken people and ruined futures. But really she knew it wasn't their fault. It was hers. Fear had tripped her up. The terrifying novelty of it. Tess had always been emboldened by the injustice of whatever cause she was advancing. Fear didn't touch her. And that made her different, better, set her apart from the masses; a student superhero with a nose ring and a loudspeaker voice.

And then she found herself sitting in the interview room, the air stagnant and stale, the walls the colour of a tea bag, and the cold eyes of the detectives dismantled her outrageous self-belief piece by piece as if it were nothing. And all that was left of her was a girl, an ordinary girl, nothing special at all, and this terrified her more than anything else. To see herself laid bare.

So when, two days later, she was brought to a room with another officer, a Detective Sergeant Tomaz Ramsay, and he offered her a way out, made it seem easy, told her they'd be watching her back all the time, she said yes. She was up to the job. It wouldn't be hard to pretend, would it? Not now she realised she had been pretending all her life.

Now look at her, slumped in a bathroom in a house where at least two people wanted her dead. By rights Tess should have been down and out, hands raised in surrender, but she was stubborn, always had been, and instead of rolling over she asked herself this: if there was no substance to her then why had it been so hard to pretend? If she had no spirit, why had it been so painful when it was crushed?

Anger. That was what she needed. A fire to weld herself together again. Lucky then that she was possessed by an anger even she did not recognise. Tess would find a way out; she would not entertain the possibility of failure, not for a single second. And then she would expose every last person involved in this sordid scandal. This time, the knowledge of her weakness no longer scared her, it made her strong.

But first, one call, to her friend Clara George. Even the theft of the information she had passed her about Westminster Council made sense now. The state was spying. But that explanation would have to wait.

'Hello.'

'Listen,' Tess whispered. 'It's me, Tess. Just listen, no time for questions . . .' She told her friend where she was and what had happened, the police, Tomaz Ramsay, Freetech. 'This will be the biggest story of your life.' She spoke over Clara's *whatthe-fucks* and *you'rekiddingme* and *areyouok?* and ploughed on until she heard someone coming along the hallway towards the bathroom. 'I've got to go,' she said. 'I'm going to leave tonight. Meet me tomorrow, midday, Westminster Pier.'

'OK . . . but . . .'

Tess hung up. She hadn't told Clara everything. She hadn't got to the part about the powerful figures driving the corruption. But she would. Tomorrow.

'You OK in there, Tess?' It was Kyle. 'Come back to the kitchen when you're ready. We've got a bit of a problem and I want to talk to you.'

Twenty-Two

Joe

Kyle was the master of the drip feed, liked to make his audience salivate.

'I'm going to find Tess, I'm afraid there's something important we need to discuss,' he said, when everyone had eaten their fill of lunch. And he left us like that, fermenting our worries and insecurities and fears. It was a control thing. A power trip, and it made my hatred of Kyle balloon like an abscess.

This is it, I thought. *Must be the moment. He's going to expose Tess, parade her in front of us, reveal her treachery, only spinning it to place her firmly in the wrong.* I predicted him fanning and stoking the hurt and betrayal to turn the others against her until all sense and reason deserted them, until they became capable of anything. I was ready for a reimagining of *Lord of the Flies* in the depths of Sussex.

The sound of them pacing back along the hallway escalated my panic. Then they were here, Tess following Kyle into the room, and me trying not to stare but my eyes sticking to her, scanning her face for a reaction, a sign, the smallest hint that this was the end. Her expression held no clues. If she was bricking it, she was hiding it exceptionally well.

'We have a problem,' said Kyle. He was on his feet, cultivating a solemn expression, using his full arsenal of tactics, the pregnant pauses, the uncomfortable meaty silences, the beady stares pinballing from one to the other to inject maximum drama.

'You're all aware that the work we do here is confidential.' He waited for us to confirm via a nod or blink of the eye. Everyone obeyed his silent orders. 'That was made absolutely clear to you before you even started at Freetech. It might have been one of the very first things I said to you when we met back in the hotel. I thought you got it but I'm afraid and saddened – disappointed – to tell you we believe someone, someone in this room, has leaked highly sensitive information about one of our clients to a national newspaper.'

The room shrank in fear, stupefied by the revelation. This prize Kyle had held aloft, the job, the wealth, the instant success – all of which we thought was our right – was under threat. And looming on the horizon was the spectre of something else, something none of us was accustomed to; the alien concept of failure. A murmur passed between us, followed by the vigorous shaking of heads. *Not me. It wasn't me.* I played along. Tess too. But it was agonising, this complicity. If I had doubted Tess and her crazy story, this was the moment those doubts were obliterated. I saw Kyle for what he was, a charlatan, a charismatic demagogue who had spun a web of lies so elaborate most of our group could no longer see the truth. He was to blame for the Zimmerman leak and this witch hunt was nothing more than a ruse to cover his own tracks.

'Well, it wasn't me,' Will said.

Kyle ignored him and continued. 'As you know, we work alone. No one else in the company could have accessed any of our client's systems. And of course, it could be a coincidence that someone hacked them at the same time we were running tests on them. But that would be a very big coincidence, don't you think? And one which our client is unlikely to buy.'

'Whose client was it?' Asha asked. 'Surely the suspicion should only fall on that person and not the whole group.'

I tried to shoot Libby a look of solidarity but she was concentrating on her fingers, picking debris from her nails.

'Thanks for your observation, Asha . . .' Kyle stood arms knitted in front of him, back poker straight, 'but if you don't mind me saying, that's a rather simplistic view. It relies on many things, mainly that none of you have been discussing your work.'

'But whose client was it?' Will asked.

Kyle sighed. 'It was Libby's but that does not mean Libby is under any more suspicion than the rest of you.'

Libby was forced to meet their stares now, her eyes bulging with tears. 'I can categorically say I had nothing to do with it but I have a good idea who has.'

'That's enough, Libby. Unfounded allegations have no place here.' Kyle raised his hand in the air to silence her, claiming the moral high ground for his own.

'So what happens now?' Asha said.

'I was getting to that. Listen, I know this is a shock, but believe me, we're working hard to get to the bottom of it. That person, one of you, has let you all down, let themselves down, and they know who they are. But we are going to carry on as normal, for now at least. Tonight, it's Halloween and we're out in the woods, divided into teams, a kind of adult *Manhunt*.'

'And then what?' Will asked.

'If no one owns up,' Kyle said, 'and we can't find out who it is, we'll have to let you all go.'

After that bombshell, there was something of a stand-off, no one was willing to be the first to move as if a speedy exit would be a sure sign of guilt. I played my part in this collective paralysis for a few minutes before I shook myself out of it. This was what he was doing to us, exerting power in a million subtle ways until no one knew their own mind, no one trusted themselves to make a simple decision like leaving a room without wondering how it would be construed, what points they would win or lose, measuring every action against Kyle's imminent approval or otherwise.

'I'm going outside,' I said and as I left I could hear movement. The spell was broken. The rest followed suit.

Solitude. I craved it, needed a place where I could be alone and unravel my thoughts. I walked and walked until I found a rare untended spot where the weeds pushed up through the gravel in quiet protest against the perfection of the house. I gulped the air, let the wind beat my face. Hanging over me was the sweet temptation to drive my suspicions away, convince myself Tess was lying, that everything was going to be OK. But as soon as I considered this possibility, the facts beat it down. Tess had been attacked in the woods, locked in a room. Everything about her made sense in the light of her revelations – her caginess, the spying, the inexplicable fact the police hadn't charged her with hacking Westminster Council's system. And then there was Kyle's dark charm, his lies and doublespeak. We had to get out of here. Me. Tess. Libby. All of us.

'Now do you believe me?' The sharpness of the accusation sliced through my thoughts.

'Shit!' I jumped at the sight of Libby standing over me.

'Surprised to see me? I suppose you were waiting for someone else.'

Suddenly, I was weary, fatigued deep into my bones. We didn't have time for this pettiness.

'No, Libby. I wasn't waiting for Tess. I've already told you, it wasn't how it looked.' I tried to coat my voice in calm.

'And I know what I saw,' Libby said with a tone so cold and devoid of emotion it felled me.

I could have launched into another explanation, told her she was simultaneously right and wrong, that the kiss was real but it didn't mean anything, or it did mean something, just not what she thought. I could have told her everything I knew about Tess but she wouldn't have believed a word of it. That had to come later, once we were out of here.

'Libby,' I refused to rise to her bait. 'We need to leave.'

She looked confused, disappointed even, as if she was expecting more of a fight and wasn't prepared to let the argument fizzle out.

'What's wrong? Don't tell me you've embarrassed yourself.'

'It's got nothing to do with the kiss.'

'You can do what you want, but you're on your own. I'm not going anywhere.'

She left me alone again, wondering how it had happened, how it was that weeks ago we fitted together like a bespoke creation, specially made for each other, how we had marvelled at the unique perfection of us, extending our sympathies to the poor sods in the Argentinian Steakhouse, or Ranzi's Tandoori on a Friday night, with not a single word of conversation to offer each other. *Would you look at them? Can you imagine?*

I guess what hurt the most was not Libby's anger, but that reality had destroyed our magic. We were one step away from the couple in the steakhouse. And this, I reckoned, was the real cruelty of love. It made you feel special only to show you how ordinary you really were.

I was walking back towards the house when Tess approached me. There was no sign of her earlier composure. Her face was crawling with nerves. 'I need to talk to you, away from everyone. Meet me by the lake in ten minutes.'

We found each other having arrived by different routes, and pressed ourselves into the bushes out of sight of the house.

'I'm leaving this afternoon. I need to know if you've said anything to Libby?' She hurried the question, kept it low and hushed.

'I saw her before—'

'Did you tell her anything?'

'I said we should leave.'

'And that was it?'

'She wasn't really in the mood to listen.' She cast her eyes around, grabbed my hand.

'I'm sorry, OK. I'm sorry for what I'm going to tell you.'

She was worrying me now. Terrifying me. This whole situation had run away from reality, torn up the neat, structured life in which I starred, and cast me in a role I never wanted, never asked for, was not equipped for. 'What's the matter?' It was a stupid question. Lame as hell. Everything was the matter: Dom, Kyle, the fact they wanted to hurt her, the police who had abandoned her, but I knew there was something else coming, the something that had taken her fear up a notch, made her eyes fizz with panic.

'He left me a message, just before, Detective Sergeant Ramsay, and now I know what's going on. What's really going on. It's bigger than I thought. You need to listen, Joe . . . what the fuck!' Tess jumped up, her feet clearing the ground in fright. I sprang around to find Will standing behind my back.

'Oh please . . .' He had plastered a fat smile on his fat face. 'Don't stop talking on my account, unless it's something you don't want to share, that is. Why've you gone red, Joe? You look like a man with something to hide. Don't tell me you were the sneaky little shit selling information and turning us over. If I lose my job because of you, you'll be very sorry.'

'Leave us alone, Will,' Tess said.

'Us?' He broke out into a laugh. 'Jesus, Tess, if you were that desperate you should have told me.' He swaggered towards her, arms out at his side, like the prize catch he wasn't. 'I'd have been willing to help.' He was close to her face now, almost touching it with his. 'But I retract my offer now you've been near him. I have some standards. Even his own girlfriend won't shag him, and who could blame her?'

I am not a violent man, but there was no reasoning with Will. Every time Tess stepped back to clear some personal space, he invaded it again. My anger was on quick boil, the guy was a

131

twat, harassing her. I'm not claiming to be a model of chivalry but someone needed to rein him in.

I pulled him away from her. Or at least that was the intention. I had underestimated both his bulk and my own weakness. The only thing I achieved was a rip in his T-shirt.

'That cost two hundred quid, you bastard.'

He was quick, credit where credit's due, Will wasted no time in lunging towards me. My body tensed, braced for an impact that didn't arrive. Little relief, because what he had in mind was worse. The lake. That's where we were headed, not that I had any choice. Sure, I tried to fight him off, kicking and lashing out pathetically as he hauled me towards the water, Tess too, but neither of us made any impact.

And then I was in. The water iced my limbs, made them scream in pain. Will grabbed my hair and pushed me under, held me there, a shark drowning its prey before devouring it.

The cold pounded my head. Pressure surged behind my eyeballs. My lungs burnt. *Stay still. Stay still, conserve your breath, he won't drown you.*

I was right. He loosened his grip, allowed my head to break the skin of the water while I snatched at the air. And then he thrust me under again.

You're going to kill him.

Tess's voice was worlds away. And so too was Will's muffled reply. Pithy, to the point.

Good.

I was going to die. It was a possibility, growing stronger by the second. *Do something.* But I couldn't think what. My body was limp, my muscles starved of oxygen. And then my hands brushed the side of his leg.

An idea.

My only one.

I thrust my hand out and upwards and clenched. The effort emptied me. It would kill me if it didn't work.

Will let out a wail, relaxed his hold on my hair sufficiently for me to kick away, out of his reach.

'You fucking pervert, you touched my fucking knob.'

Later, I would tell him it wasn't a pleasure, as far from a pleasure as I have experienced, but at that moment I had no breath to speak.

Tess dragged me out of the water as Will screamed into the air, 'You fucking deviant!' And then Kyle appeared, running down the bank with Asha.

'You need to grow up, the pair of you,' he shouted. 'Joe, you come with me, Asha and Tess, you stay with Will.'

Twenty-Three

Libby

The kiss. Libby was not going to let that drop. She buffed and polished her rage all afternoon, rehearsing her imminent confrontation with Tess, refining the salient points until they were pin-sharp. To think she had wanted to relent, to mellow. To think Tess nearly had her fooled with the bloody rabbit and the show of compassion. God, she'd even been concerned for her wellbeing, began to imagine all kinds of sinister occurrences when she saw Dom pull Tess out of the car. And the terror, the raw, unadulterated terror of that image had stalked her through the night, dragged her out of a pitiful sleep the next morning, and forced her, against Kyle's express wishes, to seek out Tess. Because Libby had begun to believe that something untoward was unfolding, and once that seed sprouted it grew like a weed, colonising her head, killing all the happy, mellow thoughts she had planted. She had wanted to see Tess with her own two eyes. She needed to know she was OK. But then Joe had persuaded her it was best that he go, and she distract Dom. And she'd done it, willingly, because she thought he was trying to help, didn't think for a single second it was because he wanted a good old snog.

The kiss told her she was a fool. Granted, Tess looked like shit, but beyond that she was fine. Better than fine. She was snogging Libby's boyfriend. Libby's mind had been playing her for a fool, that's all, teasing and wrong-footing her like it had done so many times before. Like it did with Joe, chanting, *he loves you, he loves you, he loves you*, on repeat until finally she believed that maybe, just maybe, he did. Maybe she wasn't so hard to love after all. And no sooner had she allowed it in, this blissful acceptance, this glorious, addictive calm, than her mind began to undercut it, exposing it to reality, to this place, Kenton Thorpe, where they had gone into freefall, culminating with that image, in agonising technicolour. Joe kissing Tess. Tess kissing Joe.

The humiliation coated her tongue with acid. It made her retch.

Now it looked like she was right about Tess leaking information too. She had expected to find a degree of vindication in Kyle's announcement. She had warned him, after all. She had warned Joe, and no one had taken her seriously. And surely now it was only a matter of time before Tess would be revealed as the perpetrator. But mainly, Libby was furious. Furious that people hadn't taken her seriously in the first place. Furious that Kyle hadn't even so much as acknowledged she was right. Furious with herself for carrying on as normal, maintaining the façade, the smile, the *gosh isn't it a glorious day* Pollyanna vibe she had perfected. Good Libby didn't like to rock the boat, stick her head above the parapet. Good Libby didn't like confrontation.

Good Libby could go fuck herself. Good Libby had brought her nothing but angst, the devastating sense of never quite being enough. The other Libby was in charge now and at some point today, she would hunt Tess down and do what, she hadn't decided. But she was not going to let this pass.

An opportunity, she only needed one. To catch her alone and deliver her judgement. But Tess was ephemeral. Darting about. An illusion, almost. Several times she had her in her sights only for her to vanish. Libby could have caught a fish with her hands more easily. It was as if Tess was frightened of being in one place for too long in case the air trapped her and kept her prisoner.

By four o'clock the light was sinking, rinsing the fields and the wood with a dull bluey grey. Kyle and Dom were skirting through the trees with Will and Joe, talking through the game. Libby had no stomach for more games, least of all ones that involved chasing after people in the dark. 'Trust me, there's a reason for everything we do here,' Kyle had said but Libby couldn't see it. Truth be told, the whole experience was wearing thin. Despite what she'd told Joe earlier, she wanted out too. She'd been avoiding him since, avoiding their room when she'd heard him in there. And Kyle had kept him busy all afternoon, insisting he build the bonfire pyre with Will. She took some comfort in this, a fitting punishment.

It was Tess's coat she saw first, a sheath of green fabric, the colour of the trees. She actually thought it *was* a tree until it moved down the garden towards the gate. Tess. Where was she going? Libby didn't care. She just needed to catch her.

'I want a word,' she said, out of breath from the sprint. Wished it sounded less *EastEnders*. Tess jumped. She was past the gate now, tucked around the corner. The bruise around her eye had turned yellow, giving her a partial jaundice.

'What is it?' She wasn't looking straight at Libby but beyond her, scanning the garden. Didn't want anyone else to witness the exchange, Libby figured. Couldn't say she blamed her.

'You really have to ask?'

Tess made the calculation, Libby saw it in her eyes. *Give her what she wants to shut her up.*

'I'm sorry. I don't know what else to say. There really is nothing going on. I mean, I like Joe, I really do, but not like that.' If Libby had thought about it, there wasn't much more Tess could say. But she wasn't in the mood for reason. And Tess's tone didn't measure up to a fulsome apology. Reeled off too fast and without feeling. One eye on her escape. Libby wanted more.

'And that's it? You think that's good enough? I'm just supposed to say, no worries, Tess, you made a move on my boyfriend and that's OK?'

'I said I was sorry, what more do you want?' Tess tried to move around her but Libby didn't budge.

'Where are you going anyway? The game starts soon.' She glanced down to Tess's feet, saw a red rucksack tucked behind them.

'Nowhere.' But Libby sensed her unease and smelt blood.

'Why don't you show me what's in there?' She reached down and snatched Tess's bag from behind her in a single deft movement. 'I'll have a look, shall I?' She dangled it in front of her like a threat. A glassy panic filled Tess's eyes. This was pleasing. A genuine reaction at last. Libby had found a pressure point. She was making Tess squirm.

'See, I thought we were friends, Tess, but friends don't behave like that.'

Tess laughed, a spiteful, mocking laugh. 'I would never be friends with someone like you.'

Like me?

Libby felt a throb of anger building in waves, threatening to overpower her.

'You think you're too good for me?' She had the zip between her fingers, started to pull it open. 'Is that it?'

'I know why you're here and what you're doing. What I don't know is how you live with yourself.'

Hang on a minute. She did not get the upper hand. That belonged to Libby. How dare Tess make a play for it? 'What are you talking about? I'm not the one who has been spying on my colleagues and stealing their information to leak it.'

Tess snorted now, a sound ripe with sarcasm. 'You keep on telling yourself that, one day you might actually believe it.'

Libby still had the bag, her arm knitted around it. Not that she cared what was inside, but Tess had taken everything else from her, and she wanted something in return.

Tess lunged towards her, attempting to snatch the bag out of her hand. The force pushed Libby to the ground, but she wouldn't let go, scrambling along the ground away from her, until she felt the tread of Tess's trainers on her fingers.

'Bitch.' Tess pressed down hard and the pain travelled in electric currents through Libby's hands, down her body.

Finally, Tess relented, crouched down so her head was aligned with Libby's. Her voice was quieter, beseeching. 'Why don't you care? How could you sit back and let this happen?' She might as well have been speaking in tongues for all Libby understood. The woman was insane. Her moral rectitude unfathomable. How could any of this be Libby's fault? But then she saw Tess's expression change, her rage giving way to something much worse.

Pity.

'Christ, you really don't know, do you? You don't understand.'

What? she wanted to scream. *What don't I understand?* But she was forced to silence her questions because Tess started pulling her upright, brushing her down. 'You OK?' she asked, hitching her lips up, trying to conjure a smile. It was poor disguise for the fear thrashing beneath her skin.

Dom. He was here. A few metres away, his presence freezing the air.

'Ladies.' His voice stopped them like a Taser. 'What's going on?' They were standing so close together, they were almost touching, the rucksack hidden behind them. Instinct made Libby kick it into the bushes as Dom trained his mechanical stare on Tess. One, two, three beats. Then he turned to Libby, 'Is there a problem?'

She hesitated. There *was* a problem, Libby just didn't know what it looked like. She could feel it but couldn't detect its shape or colour. And all the while she considered Dom's question,

Tess's heartbeat drummed the air between them, harder and harder.

'No,' she said. 'No problem at all. We were just discussing tactics for tonight. Boys v girls again?'

'No, we're shaking it up, making the teams more even. It's got to be a fair fight, after all.'

They followed Dom back to the house, Libby walking behind Tess, aware of the droop of her shoulders, the reluctance of her steps. But it was the temperature of her panic that chilled her to the bone.

Something was wrong, something beyond Libby's understanding, and she needed to find Tess again tonight, to root the answer out of her.

Twenty-Four

Tess

'Why are you still here?' Joe was barely audible, a ventrilo-quist hissing out the sounds without moving his lips. They had assembled by the huge pyre at the bottom of the garden, piled high with old furniture from the shed, chair legs sticking out like dismembered limbs. Kyle doused it in petrol and a rich, chemical tang filled the air before it fizzed to life, its flames climbing higher and higher to score the dark.

'An unexpected intervention,' she said in a similarly hushed voice. 'Libby saw me.'

For fuck's sake, this time he formed the words with his mouth. Kyle saw him. As far as Tess could tell, Kyle saw everything.

'What's the matter, Joe? You're not scared, are you?' he said, opening his eyes wide and staggering forwards, his hands raised in front of him, prodding at the dark. Tess couldn't decide whether the effect was terrifying or ridiculous, or both, a sinister sweet spot where the two conflated. Kyle was made up as a zombie. White face, blood, open wounds, the full works. It was a Halloween theme. It would add to the fun, apparently.

'Far from it,' Joe said. 'A game of zombie apocalypse was just what I had in mind when I agreed to come here.'

'Good,' Kyle said, bypassing the sarcasm, 'because Asha is waiting for you.'

Asha was in charge of make-up, a task she embraced with surprising zeal. When it was Tess's turn she appeared to have forgotten her dislike and chatted breezily. 'Halloween is by far my favourite day of the year. I mean, fuck Christmas and the elves and Cliff Richard, I've never been a fan. But, this, this is the business.' She sponged Tess's face with grey paint. 'How about you?' Asha paused for a moment, stood back to examine her work before attacking Tess with a darker paint, 'For the eyes. It's all in the eyes with zombies.'

Tess told her that yes, she did love Halloween, and accepted the tube of fake blood Asha foisted upon her, *in case you want to go for a more gruesome look later on*. Tess knew she wouldn't. This was more than enough, her absolute zombie limit, but she accepted it anyway, loath to stop the flow of chatter that had brought her a welcome sense of respite and calm. Asha worked away, her incessant babbling, *There really wasn't much work to do on Will, the guy's scary enough as it is*, dampening her myriad fears. Fear of tonight, fear of Dom and Kyle, of the dark. Of everything here. Even the fight between Joe and Will had achieved the impossible, raising tensions further when Tess would have sworn they were already dialled to their highest. The threats were coming from all angles. And Libby. What of Libby, who had blocked her escape but then covered for her in front of Dom? Libby needed some serious unravelling. But that would have to come later. Tess did not have the mental resources for it now.

The teams were Dom, Libby and Joe, and then Tess, Asha, Will and Kyle, a discrepancy in the numbers because Dom counted for two people. He smiled when Kyle said this and his scar smiled with him, like he had two mouths. Each one eager to consume her.

They were gathered around the fire again having been issued with a bottle of beer, 'to get you in the mood,' Kyle said. *Because a bottle of Kronenbourg always puts me in the mood for killing zombies*, Tess thought. But she drank some of it all the same, clenching the bottle, making sure no one saw her shake.

'The rules are simple.' He was forced to shout above the roar of the fire. 'One team has to capture the other. You have to work out your tactics, who your leader is, if you have one. And we play until we have a victor. Each of you will have your own weapons,' he held a luminescent gun aloft. 'Paintball, yeah, I know, sorry Asha, it's old school, but you've got to admit, it's fun.'

He went on, *Remember, no eyes, no face, no one comes to harm, don't get carried away*. And then they were off.

Will was nominated leader, a suicidal choice but the only one available given that no one else wanted it. He headed deep into the woods, prowling the terrain for enemies and hostile fire, furnishing them with an excruciating running commentary: *On the lookout for bogeys, check to the left, and right, all clear.*

They were hypervigilant, listening out for every noise, every snap of a branch or rustle in the trees that might signal an attack. But there was nothing. Will took them deeper and deeper into the dark, stumbling over roots, sinking into the thick mud underfoot. A fog had descended and the cold sneaked under Tess's clothes and wrapped itself around her. The night. The night filled her with unease; its scuttling creatures and the shadows alive with threat and the trees blunting the view ahead all ate into the last vestiges of bravado. And Tess felt herself drift out on to the periphery, here but not quite here. How would anyone find them, when they could barely find themselves?

CRACK.

A bullet smashed on to the tree next to her, spilled luminous paint down the bark. Like Predator's blood, she thought, and the sight of it jump-started her senses.

'There's someone over there,' she heard herself say. *There. Somewhere.* She tried to point in the direction it came from but her hand felt light, unable to withstand the gust of the wind, and it fell back to her side.

'Where?' Will shouted.

She shrugged, not that anyone would have seen her. *I don't know*, she wanted to say but the words were trapped inside her.

Another bullet, another crack, this time finding a human target, Asha, a few paces in front of her. They weren't supposed to hurt, these bullets, wasn't that what everyone said? And yet Asha shouted, *fucking hell*, and called someone a bastard. Tess should help her. Teamwork and all that. And she thought of Asha chuntering on about Halloween and taking the zombie make-up a little too seriously and she felt a shot of guilt. Asha was nice. Plain and simple. And in any other situation Tess would go to her and wipe the luminious blood from her body and heave her upright and say, *Are you OK?* and *sod this game, let's go inside and have a beer.* But her predicament, the precarious balance of her situation, scrambled her priorities. Tess could only think of herself. And her escape. She seized the moment and slipped into the darkness.

Which way to go? She had no idea. Yes, she had tried to keep track of the direction they were taking, she wasn't completely stupid, but it would have been easier to count grains of sand on a beach. She closed her eyes to reset. Recalibrate. Nope, that was no use either. Swirls of red and blue, hot oranges and greens danced on her lids, a kaleidoscope of colours, pretty in the right circumstances. But not tonight. Not here. Christ! Was she drunk? She'd only had one bottle of beer, barely finished it. It tasted bitter. She wasn't in the mood. *Bitter.* Kyle had given her the beer. *Surely not.* Alarm tore through her. Surely he wouldn't have spiked her drink. Focus. Tess was trying, with every fibre in her body she was trying; it just wasn't enough. There was silt clogging her veins, weighing her down, tying her to the earth. The ground was grabbing her, the harsh grass scouring her ankles, the mud sucking her in.

No no no no no. She would not allow surrender. Mind over matter. She planted one foot on the earth and then another. *How hard can it be?* Pretty damn hard as a matter of fact. She was a candle melted to its wick. Spent, wasted. Useless.

Tess took a minute. Five. Ten. She couldn't hold on to time any more. Her mind fastened to the sounds of the night; the rustling and crunching, the whine of the wind, shrieks and squawks from the undergrowth. She told herself it was the air, the restless countryside air tearing through the branches. But still, her heart hammered. The night was turning on her, circling.

Where the hell was she?

Somehow, she went on, pushing through the dark until her attention snagged on the sound of water. It wasn't the lake. She would have recognised its specific rhythm, the gentle push and suck. This was water rushing over rocks, in a hurry, not unlike herself. She tried to clear a space in her head, draw a mental map of the house and its surrounds. There *was* a stream. She'd stumbled upon it once with Asha when they'd gone for a walk. Diagonally left from the house. The relief made her weak. She was heading, if not exactly in the right direction, then not far off. By her calculations she wouldn't be too far away from the road that led to the village. And then—

'Tess?'

The sound of her name jolted her body.

'Tess?'

Was it Joe? Joe was worried about her. She knew that from the looks he shot her around the bonfire. He wanted to help her. Kind, generous Joe. Had he found her? She prayed he had. She craved the security of a friendly presence. Turned and saw a beam of light spraying on to the ground behind her.

'Who is it?'

The air echoed the question back to her. But no answer came. She needed to get to the road, imagined feeling hard ground below her feet, the physical proof of escaping the clutches of the house and its inhabitants. She couldn't be far. Surely.

'Tess, it's me.'

The tone was gentle, persuasive. She knew that voice.

Did she?

Joe.

She hesitated. Until she saw his face she should keep going. But her body was drowned with relief. It wouldn't move. It wanted Joe. It wanted help.

'Where are you?' She barely recognised her own voice, thin and weak. She asked but again, no answer came back, just a rustling, a heavy movement in the trees. And then a figure came into view, face burnt out by the glow of the gun.

'Don't go.'

Two words. Ice in her bloodstream. Enough to tell her the tone wasn't right. And the time to escape had passed. She had let that one slip through her fingers like everything else. Stupid. Stupid. Stupid. But she tried anyway, started to run, no more than three paces before she fell on to a rock, its sharp edges gouging her head, blood oozing from her hairline, thick and sticky.

And then he pulled her upright.

No kindness there.

A hand on her shoulder and then around her neck. A shoot of pain through her body so hot it melted her bones. Tess put her arms out, pointlessly clawing at the figure in front of her. They found flesh but no victory. She grabbed at the air for breath.

'Joe!' She tried to scream. Distantly, she could hear Libby calling her name, but it was too late now. Her mind flooded with a blackness and she tried to resist. Tess tried because she was a fighter and she was stubborn and her Tessness would not allow anything else. She tried until she could no longer find a way around it and the urge swept her away.

There was a weird animal noise coming from the bushes, she registered that, and then her legs buckled under her, and the last thing she felt was a strange sensation, a paintball stinging her like a bee. She saw a flood of bright light spread over her body before she fell to the ground, like a star that had dropped from the sky.

Twenty-Five
Day 4

Joe

I awoke cold and shivering to find myself caked in blood. A considerable amount of blood, the source of which I traced to a gash on my head, just above my right ear. The wound was open and oozing and for a brief moment I thought my ear was hanging off, so sharp was the pain. But my ear was still intact; it was my head that was buggered. My head and my face. On further inspection I discovered a wound running down my left cheek. I didn't need a mirror to confirm I was in a state.

I was also in the woods.

All in all, it wasn't a great start to the morning.

Tess. Her name cut through my thoughts. Where was she? I hauled myself upright and scanned around, grabbing on to a tree to steady myself. The simple act of moving blinded me with pain. 'Tess!' I shouted. Her name hurt my throat. What had happened? I slumped down again and tried to revive the memories of the night before.

This is what I remembered.

Getting lost, about two minutes into the game. Libby following Dom as if they were Velcroed together, moving fast through the dark. I tripped early on and righted myself only to find them gone. No loss to me. It was Tess I wanted to find. I remember thinking, *I'm no expert on* Zombie Apocalypse, *or whatever the hell it is we're supposed to be playing, but I recognise a problem when I see one.* We didn't have enough players. It would have been possible to track through the woods all night and not encounter another soul.

I couldn't say how long I spent walking around, the ridiculous paintball gun branding the night with strips of luminescent light. A few times, out of desperation I called her name, 'Tess! Tess, it's me.' And once, when I swore I heard a reply roll back through the wind, I ran forward to meet the source of the sound. But that was the last thing I remembered, running, then a dull thud and my body rinsed with pain. I must have run straight into a branch.

I considered running again, right now, out of the woods towards the road, flagging a passing farmer down, hitching a ride. But it wouldn't be easy to flag anyone down in my current state, what with the zombie make-up layered with blood and dirt; I was more likely to get arrested. But mainly, I wanted to know Tess was safe. If she hadn't made it out there, I couldn't leave her there alone.

'Joe?' Asha said my name like a question, *Is that really you?* At the mention of my name Will and Kyle swung around. I had slipped in unnoticed half an hour before, checking Tess's room first. The bed was made. She might not have come back last night, or she might have made it this morning. It told me precisely nothing, so I showered, sluicing the grime and filth away, cleaning the blood from my fingernails, the soapy water sinking into my cuts, making me wince. And then I had headed to the kitchen.

They stood, the three of them, Kyle, Asha and Will, gawping like imbeciles. 'You should have seen me before,' I said but no one laughed. I didn't even raise a smile.

Will stepped forward from his station at the hob, brandishing a fish slice, the bacon spitting in the pan behind him. The air was thick and fatty.

'Where's Tess?' I said.

'Why don't you tell *us*?'

'Hey, Will,' Kyle placed himself between us. 'I'll deal with this, OK?'

In the kangaroo court of Kenton Thorpe they skipped the arrest and the trial, overlooked the fabricated evidence and went straight for the verdict.

I was the guilty party. The Cheat. The Liar.

'Was it the money?' Kyle asked, shaking his head in disgust. My head burnt. I needed water to lubricate my brain. 'You realise you've fucked everyone over, don't you?'

'You might want to tell me what I'm accused of first, that's generally the way we do things here.'

'You know exactly what you've done, but if you want me to spell it out just to be clear, you sold information on Libby's client to the newspapers. You are responsible for the leak. With the help of your friend—'

'Where is Tess?'

'Drop the act, Joe. How much did they pay you? Or did you do it for kicks? You've screwed everyone over, but then you know that, don't you? Sure, we can try some damage limitation, tell our clients it was just some schmuck who slipped through the net. But trust is a big thing in our game. Once that's gone, we're finished. So well done, great job of work.' He started a slow hand clap.

'It wasn't me.' I sounded pathetic. Weak, which was about right because I wasn't feeling too great. Less than great. I had the shakes, needed water. Not that a drink was going to solve my problems wholesale but at least my mouth wouldn't have felt like it had been coated with glue. I stepped forward to get to the sink. Kyle intercepted me.

'The least you can do is be man enough to own up, that would be a start.' He had turned on his good cop routine, cleaned the venom from his voice. *I'm all heart, really.* The sad thing was I wanted nothing more than to believe his act. I was tired, really fucking tired, and all the mind games, the tedious fighting with Libby, the endless revelations, had messed with my head. I had fallen in love with a girl, got a job. That was my crime. It wasn't supposed to be this difficult. I never set out to change the world, I just fancied upgrading my car. Until a few months ago, that was the summit of my medium-term ambition. Now I was in over my head except I didn't really know what the hell it was, this engine of everyone's craziness.

Kyle was still talking. The man never shut up. He'd probably scripted this whole show last night when the rest of us were running around the woods pretending to be zombies. He was the puppet master, pulling our strings, and the worst thing was the rest of them couldn't see it, Asha, Will, Libby. A smoke-screen, that's what Tess had called it, a distraction technique. Push the blame on to someone else while they got away scot-free. And yet I couldn't see the endgame, what exactly it was they wanted from this, and my chances of working it out today were slim to non-existent. I needed a rest.

'You owe them an apology. You need to look them in the eye and say sorry,' Kyle said. If I had more energy I would have punched him.

'I'm not sorry.'

'I'm gonna fucking kill you.' Will made it past Kyle this time, grabbed hold of my T-shirt and pulled me in towards him.

'He's angry, Joe.' Kyle was not normally one for understatement. 'He's put in all this hard work, Asha too, and now it looks like it's going to amount to nothing because of you. And you know what, Joe? I'm angry too. The least we deserve is an explanation, don't you think? Tell us why you did it.'

'I'm not telling you anything because it wasn't me.'

'Yeah, nice. That's the way to go, but my friend here doesn't seem at all satisfied with that explanation.' Kyle watched on as Will lifted me up by my T-shirt. 'Don't make this harder than it needs to be.'

'You haven't actually said how you know I did it. Or have you completely dispensed with the need for evidence?'

'Oh, don't worry about that, we have plenty of evidence. Asha and Will and Libby are already party to that information. They know you're a liar, Joe. Libby is particularly upset, let me tell you. Why don't you say it, spare us all the grief? I. AM. A. LIAR.' He turned to his audience, Asha and Will, who had now returned my feet to the ground. Both of them were wide-eyed, hypnotised by the unfolding spectacle and by Kyle's potent, persuasive oratory. They wanted to believe him too. Why wouldn't they? He was a man with all the answers in a world with none. You can hardly blame them for falling hard.

'Where's Tess?' I said.

'Fuck Tess. I don't want to talk about Tess. She was in on it with you,' Will said. 'I want to hear you say sorry.'

'You're going to have a long wait.'

The door. Back where I came from. I needed to make it to the door, leave this place, away from the eyes that were stuck to me and the smell of frying food and the wild, manic energy Kyle had infected everyone with.

'Oh no you don't.' Will pulled me back.

'Take your hands off me. I'm leaving.' I tried to shrug off his grip, to no avail. He was pumped up with rage and I was the source. I began to feel like a daddy-long-legs in the hands of a belligerent child. Will would happily strip me of my limbs and watch me suffer.

'For God's sake, I didn't do it. Have you lost the power of rational thought? Has he . . .' I stabbed my finger in Kyle's direction, '. . . indoctrinated you so much that you believe anything he says?' I don't know what I was expecting, some evidence of my words registering, touching a nerve, a glimmer of life in the cold, glassy eyes that assessed me. Either way I found nothing at all.

'You're a piece of shit,' Will said.

I should have seen it coming, but as old-fashioned as it sounds, I still believed there would be a modicum of restraint, of keeping up appearances. That no matter how pissed off you claimed to be, lamping a colleague in front of your boss was not the thing to do.

Turned out it was.

My head sprang back at the force of Will's punch, the tendons in my neck straining to stop it snapping off entirely. I tried to right myself when another came my way, and another, until I lost count. I'm sure there were protests, shouts from Asha, but I can't say they registered. All I could hear was the pounding in my head, the sound of my own demise. I cowered, huddled into myself using my arms to form a shield over my head.

Another blow landed, black spots clouded my vision and now the sounds that had been drowned out rose to a frightening pitch. A cacophony of shouts and screeches tearing at the air around me. I had descended into hell, an inferno of misery. I hit out, kicking and clawing at whatever and whoever came close.

'You fucking asshole,' Kyle said. I would have recognised that twang anywhere. 'I was trying to help you.'

Dark enclosed spaces. My worst fear. Remember that? He'd forced it out of me the very first day at the hotel. It could have been a coincidence. Well yes, I'd be inclined to agree, were it not for the fact Kyle didn't do coincidences. He schemed, and he planned, and he plotted. He connived. Nothing happened by chance.

The miracle was that he managed to take so many people

along with him. No, not a miracle. He wasn't Jesus fucking Christ. He simply exploited a fundamental weakness in the human condition. He'd shown us the gold and then set about persuading us that we wanted it, that we were the chosen ones, the brilliant ones, that everything we wanted could be ours.

And when you want something badly enough, you'll do anything to get it.

Anything at all.

I don't suppose they were thinking of how far they'd fallen when they locked me in the cellar. The mind is an able accomplice, willing to block out inconvenient truths. Will and Asha didn't protest as I was shoved downstairs, as I bit and scratched and struggled. Libby did. Her voice, right at the end, hit me like one of Will's blows. *Make sure he has some water.* She was all heart, this woman I loved.

'He can come out when he calms down,' Kyle said as he locked the door.

And if I didn't?

What then?

Twenty-Six

Libby

Libby kept learning things about herself she'd rather not know. Today's lesson: she could stomach more than she thought possible.

She was a pacifist, the kind of lily-livered creature who would rescue a fly thrashing against glass and set it free. Once, much to her housemates' fury, she released a rat they had caught on to the street. 'Why would you do that? They piss five hundred times a day,' Hani had asked her.

'I don't like cruelty,' she replied. It was simple really.

And now look how far she had come. She had stood by, watched on as Kyle threw Joe in the cellar and locked the door behind him. Libby barely recognised herself.

In her defence, there was a plan. Or at least there would be when Libby had concocted one. *Dark enclosed spaces*. Joe's biggest fear. Funny that he was now trapped in the cellar where there was a high probability of him encountering both. It was almost as if Kyle remembered. Come to think of it, it wasn't funny at all, not in the slightest. She had lost all sense of humour where Kyle and Kenton Thorpe were concerned. She had no intention of leaving Joe in there for a moment longer than necessary.

Trust. That was the nub of the issue. She'd cut Kyle slack, much more than he deserved, but the slack had run out and all that was left was disgust at her own actions. Dom, she had never liked from the beginning. There was something polluted about his air that made her want to steer clear and his eyes gave her the willies, the way they never betrayed any emotion. Not a single trace, like they'd seen too much and there was nothing left to surprise or appal.

She'd kept her own eyes on him last night in the woods. Sellotaped to his back. It was no easy task and one that meant she had to ditch Joe when he stumbled. If she had waited, Dom would have shaken her off. And despite the rules that stipulated they stick together as a team, it was obvious shaking her off was exactly what Dom had in mind. Dodging one way and then the other, doubling back on himself to wrong-foot her. Ramping up a gear to wear her out. His behaviour quickly disabused her of any notion they were on the same side. The only side Dom played for was his own. And having fought in Iraq or Afghanistan, faced down snipers and militia, he would have been excused for thinking that he could outwit a former head girl in a wood in Sussex, no bother at all.

Except he hadn't reckoned with Libby.

As it happened, Libby hadn't reckoned with herself.

She wouldn't take her eyes off Dom, that was what she had told herself after he had sprung up on her and Tess earlier that afternoon. She hadn't liked the vibe, the weird, toxic energy that flowed between them. Sure, she was not Tess's biggest fan, but she liked Dom less and less as the evening wore on, some feat considering the bar had not been high to begin with. Every time she approached Tess either around the fire, or after Asha had done her make-up, Dom would appear, thwarting another opportunity for Libby to ask Tess: *What is it I don't know?* And she'd see the smile rising on his lips, never bothering his eyes, and down another notch in her estimation he'd drop. He must have mistaken her public school diction, her good girl love of the rules, for some kind of idiocy. She knew he was up to something, and she damn well intended to find out what it was.

At one stage in the woods, when an enemy paintball narrowly missed them, Dom stopped. 'We should split up, better that way.'

'I disagree.'

Even in the dark, close up she could see the lines in his face tense, the muscle twitch in his jaw. He wasn't accustomed to dissent. 'We stay together. Those are the rules,' she said with an iron will that pleased her.

'Jesus.'

'Unless there's a specific reason you want to be on your own. I mean, it's only a game after all. It seems you're taking it very seriously.' Her tone was clipped and extra prim to rile him.

He opened his mouth to say something but decided against it and started moving again. A few minutes later he slowed his pace before stopping completely.

'I think there's someone up there,' Libby said. She'd heard a noise, footsteps, she was certain of it.

He shook his head. 'It's just an animal.'

'How do you know?'

'I need a piss. I'll go up there and check, shall I?' he said, ignoring her question completely. 'You can stay here, unless you want to watch me.'

She waited, eyes trained on the bright stripe of his gun until it faded into nothing. The air was misty, like walking through cigarette smoke, and the cold, barely noticeable at first, was the type to seep in slowly, take up residence in your bones. She thought she felt a raindrop pattering against a branch and waited for a deluge to follow but none came. After a few minutes she knew Dom wasn't coming back. The likelihood was he didn't need a piss at all, it was simply an excuse to get rid of her. She swung her head around, illuminating the path to her right and then left. And that's when she saw her.

Tess.

The sight of her long blond hair flashed into vision.

'Tess,' she called.

She was supposed to shoot at her, wasn't that the point of the game? Libby was done with the game. She wanted to speak to Tess and that was what she was going to do. She started running towards her but the night was thick and unforgiving, revealing a glimpse of something only to hide it away again. Where had she gone? Libby turned one way and then the other before she stopped, defeated. A mewling, somewhere beyond her. Where was it coming from? Where? A fury whipped up inside her. She wanted to take an axe and hack the trees down and pull the sun up again with her own two hands. She wanted to see what was going on.

She pushed on, the rage driving her forward, but her only reward was to see an outline of Dom crouched down in the bushes. Oh God, was he having a crap? She raised her gun and aimed at him in the vague hope it would hit him clean on the arse. And then she ran away.

This morning Kyle had woken her with the news that it was Joe and Tess who were involved in the Zimmerman leak. 'Tess appears to have left sometime last night. We think Joe might have done the same.' She turned in the bed. Joe's side was cold and untouched. 'I owe you an apology. You were right, we should have listened to you in the first place.'

He watched Libby's expression, willing her to smile. She could have made him grovel, *I won't say I told you so, but . . .* and he would have indulged her. But Libby had no intention of smiling. She had wanted to be right and now she didn't. She hated the taste and the touch and the smell of it. It was all wrong. Joe wasn't that person. He wouldn't have betrayed her. A kiss was one thing. This deeper form of treachery she would never believe.

'I understand it's hard. I know you and him are a thing.' He rested his hand on her hair and she felt invaded. *A thing*? Was that what they were now? Their relationship reduced to a shapeless, amorphous thing. She let him drawl on about evidence and email trails and when he said, 'Is there anything you want to ask me?', she said, 'Can I have my phone back,' and then, 'don't ever touch me again.'

She called her uncle. Who else was she going to call? The man who could fix everything. 'I don't like it here,' she said. 'I don't like Kyle and I don't like Dom.' She could hear the regression in her voice, the slippage into petulant teenager. 'And they're blaming Joe for the leak. What's going on?'

He sighed. The sigh was loaded with so many unsaid words it hurt. It said, *Darling I don't have time for this, and do you always have to call me for everything, and when will you grow up and get on with the job in hand?* It did not say, *Don't worry, I will sort this out.* It did not make everything OK. And this, though she didn't realise it at the time, was the biggest favour Richard ever did her.

The rest of the morning passed without incident. After Joe was locked in the cellar, that is, because as incidents go that one was hard to beat. She didn't see Dom, didn't want to mention his name and dirty her mouth, she'd just brushed her teeth. Asha and Will and Kyle discussed the plans for the day, a five-mile hike up towards Ditchling, puncturing the morning with cups of coffee and rounds of toast. And Libby waited for the epiphany to strike, for them to stand up, and shout, 'Shit, what have we done? What possessed us to lock Joe in the cellar?' She kept snatching looks at Asha, expecting to see her broken by guilt, because Asha, she knew, was a kind person. At her heart, she was caring and considerate. But something had happened, something that made this behaviour acceptable. Kyle and his zeal had possessed her. At the point she heard them discuss the relative merits of the custard cream and the bourbon biscuit Libby knew they had slipped into a parallel universe.

When she could stand it no longer, she faked an excuse about losing her watch last night and going out to look for it in the woods. As she passed through the kitchen, she stood by the window, made some glib comment, *Doesn't the sky look wonderful*, and dipped her hand in the plant pot where she knew the spare key to the cellar lay before moving towards the cellar itself.

She was a few feet away, considering her next move, when she felt his breath on her neck. 'Everything OK?' She jumped. Kyle moved without making a sound. She was increasingly convinced he was not fully human.

'Perfect,' she said, and supposed somewhere in a parallel universe it was.

Outside she ran into the day, let the wind push up against her, spin her around, shock her into life. She needed this, a connection with reality, with nature. To know that the trees were green and the sky was blue and wrong wasn't right. When she reached the gate at the bottom of the drive, the site of her altercation with Tess the day before, she glanced around before shoving her hand into the foliage where she had kicked Tess's bag the moment Dom had appeared.

It was still there.

Inside she found a phone, a notepad, her wallet. A clean change of clothes, toothbrush. The bare necessities. Guilt bloated her mind. Tess had been leaving and Libby had stopped her. It was obvious now she thought of it, and it would have been obvious yesterday if her logic hadn't given way to anger. And now where was Tess? Without her phone, without money, a clean pair of knickers, God forbid. Libby stuffed the phone and the wallet and the notepad into her pockets and headed down to the woods where she'd last seen her.

★

Daylight had turned the woods friendly, smaller, welcoming. Bars of sunlight fell through the trees and scattered the ground and for a few minutes it had the effect of clearing Libby's mind, planting her in the moment. She tuned into the gentle chirrup of the birds and felt the tension run out of her. She studied the trees, their branches shaped by centuries of rain and storms and gales, but still standing, still here.

It was going to be OK.

'It's going to be OK,' she said out loud.

And she knew this with certainty because this was Libby's life and the worst had already happened.

On she walked in the direction of where she had spotted Tess. Not that Libby could have told you why she was heading there, or what she expected to find. She simply needed to go, and that was that.

It was no use. *You have to have a goal, otherwise you'll never get anywhere*, wasn't that what Richard always said? And he should know, the man with everything. Libby's mistake was to wander randomly through the woods without a plan. Really, a vague notion of finding *something* wasn't going to help. She should go back to the house. To Joe. Oh God, Joe! She was hit by a wave of horror. Unless Kyle had suffered an attack of compassion, Joe would still be in the cellar. What was she doing out here? The lunacy of it felled her. Why hadn't she just marched to the cellar door and opened it and told Kyle to fuck off, that she wasn't going to stand for any of his games, his cruelty? *Because you're scared, that's why*, her inner voice shouted back at her. And yet there was no need to be scared, the whole thing was quite clearly a nonsense. Tess was probably feeding her lines to frighten her and throw her off the trail of her own misdemeanours. Well, if that was her plan, she'd done a good job because Libby didn't know whether she was coming or going.

★

Through a break in the trees she caught sight of the road and this triggered a memory. She'd heard a passing car as she was waiting for Dom – who incidentally returned in a fury, accusing someone of firing while he was answering nature's call. She must have seen Tess close to the road. Libby checked her watch. Two more minutes, that's all she'd give it, just in case, and then she'd turn back.

Two minutes in which her folly nagged her. She told it to shut up, that she'd do as she pleased thank you very much. And still it needled and poked fun at her. Who did she think she was, one of the Famous Five, trudging through the woods to seek out a mystery of no importance at all? But what few people realised, and Libby often forgot herself, was that for all she was straight and proper, her stubborn streak was something to behold. Even when the snap of a twig, the crunch of leaves, a bird squawking overhead set her heart thudding and she had the creeping sense that someone else was here, Libby carried on. She might have been stupid, but the stupidity was hers alone.

Two minutes were up. *Admit defeat. Retreat.* She slouched against a tree, her hands resting on the bark, her folly deafening now and she raised a hand to her head to massage the noise away.

Her hands were red. The colour of blood.

Blood on the bark of the tree.

Blood on her shoes.

And close by, the remnants of a paintball bullet splattered around.

Twenty-Seven

Libby

Libby screamed, a formless roar, a noise unlike anything she had ever produced. She was going to vomit, wanted to; this need to purge her body of everything it contained possessed her. She bent over to empty herself out, but nothing came. *Blood.* The solid, irrefutable presence of it pulverised her. She stared at her hands, brown and sticky with its residue. *Tess appears to have left sometime last night,* Kyle had told her. But her trust in Kyle had dried up, there wasn't a single particle of it left, and in its place a question thrashed against her skull: what if Tess hadn't made it out of the woods? What if they hurt her in retaliation for the leak? A few hours before Libby would have said no. *No no no no no.* It was an outlandish theory. There was no point in her life that intersected with criminal acts. She would never be involved in anything untoward, not even as an unwitting bystander. Hers was a life of privilege and private education and expensive holidays; the man who brought her up was a well-respected businessman. It was inconceivable. Full stop.

Except, today's developments had erased the full stop, added another clause to the sentence. Libby had already witnessed violence this morning, and its casual acceptance diluted everything. Joe was still in the cellar, beaten and bruised. And here she was in the woods where she had seen Tess last night, surrounded by blood.

And she *wasn't* alone.

The sound of a foot crunching on leaves alerted her to

another presence. Her heart rate soared. All those gym classes, the ones racked up on early mornings and late nights when she really couldn't be stuffed, this was her payback. She ran fast and hard. Someone had followed her, she knew that with certainty now. Those noises she passed off as birds and wind pushing through the trees, the soundtrack to the country, they belonged to someone. They were a threat hunting her down.

It's going to be OK. That statement belonged to another life, not even Libby would fall for it now. Not with the blood and what she was holding in her hand. Tess's hairclip, the bright yellow flower.

Not so bright now.

If it hadn't been for Joe she would not have gone back to the house. It went against all her instincts. But she wasn't going to leave him at the mercy of Kyle and Dom. She wasn't going to leave him full stop.

She snuck in, the house eerily quiet, and headed upstairs to their room where she grabbed a change of clothes, money, a phone charger even though Kyle still had their phones, stuffing everything into one bag, along with Tess's belongings, her phone, her notepad, her wallet. And then she went to the bathroom to clean up, scrub the blood away. She checked in the mirror to make sure it had gone, no mark left on her face. She *was* clean, tick. Her skin red and raw but something was missing, something that made her insides collapse. Her mother's antique diamond stud gone from one ear.

'I'm not feeling well.' She found Kyle downstairs examining a map. She rubbed her stomach. 'Cramps. I'm going to lie down for a bit.'

'But . . .' he began. Libby shot him a look packed with defiance. *Try me.* She was good at putting up a front when necessary, her childhood had taught her this much.

'Looks like we're one down,' Kyle announced to Will and Asha before turning back to her. 'If you need anything Dom will be right here.'

She retreated to her room, listened to the door slam, peered out of the window to make sure they hadn't dragged Joe out of the cellar just to inflict more damage. And when she watched them shrink and disappear down the garden, she lay back in bed and waited, staring at the blank white walls. Time was glue, each minute stretching to twice, three, four times its length. She hated this house, its harsh, unforgiving lines, the precision of everything, planned and plotted to look the best. She hated being here, the memories the countryside dredged up, its unique smells, the endless skies, the vast open views that changed personality with the light. Everything about it signposted her loss and reopened a wound she thought long healed.

A noise distracted her from her internal rant. Dom crashing about downstairs, except now he was moving, the footfall coming closer. If there were any drawers she would have pushed them in front of the door but everything was hidden here, built-in cupboards, storage tucked away. So she waited. Waited as the footsteps stopped outside her door, aware of the rasp of her own breath, the air constricting around her, the stream of panic dragging her down.

And then she heard the lock turn.

Relief was an odd concept. Technically relief should not be a man locking you in a room against your will. But next to the alternative, a direct, potentially violent confrontation with Dom, this relief was so solid she could touch it.

Better still was what came a few minutes later: the sight of Dom's car clearing the driveway.

Libby grabbed the rucksack and went to the window, then pulled it open without thinking. It was like her body, her muscle memory was one step ahead of her mind. *You used to do this*, it reminded her. *You used to do this before.* And so she did. She had the skills, there, deep down, imprinted in her childhood. Her mum had an old house in a state of graceful decay where things only worked sporadically. The doors stuck, the locks refused to turn, the roof leaked. Libby was fast and nimble and could scale the wall like a home-grown Spiderman. *My secret weapon*, her mother used to call her.

She could do it then, and she could do it now. And to the voice that reminded her she was fifteen years older, considerably larger and no longer a daredevil, she said, *Shut up*.

The drop from the flat roof was five or six metres, but what of it? She wasn't going to let anything stand in her way. She reached for the guttering, prayed it would resist her weight and swung her legs over the side. Halfway down she lost her footing. Nothing for it but to jump. She tried to relax in readiness for the moment of impact – broken bones would not advance her cause – and it worked to an extent. When her feet hit the ground, the pain juddered through her. She waited a second, checked she could still move. Her arm was grazed, bleeding from where she'd dragged it down the wall, but beyond that, nothing serious.

At the cellar door, she fumbled for the key. It had to fit. Surely. Except she knew there was no surely about it. No definites or givens any more. The world wasn't out to do her favours, she'd learnt that to her cost. She pushed the key in. Twisted it in the lock. It didn't give. She tried again, pulling the handle towards her. This time she was in.

She lodged the door open with her bag, waited for a chink of light to fight its way in. Joe wasn't there. It was as if the walls had absorbed him.

'Joe.' A whisper, not a shout. 'Joe, we have no time.'

And then, she saw him, pressed into the wall. He gave no response as she inched closer, the smell attacking her senses. Dampness overpowered by urine. 'Joe!' she hissed, and leant out to touch his arm. 'It's me.'

'Me?' he said.

The full horror of what they had done assaulted her. She had to get him out, get out of there herself, or there would be consequences. *Consequences.* The word caught fire and tore through her head. There was nothing Kyle wouldn't do. She hated him, but until that moment, until she stared into Joe's eyes, took in the pitiful sight in front of her, the depth of his cruelty had been an abstract concept. She had credited Kyle with a basic level of human decency he didn't possess.

'Drink,' she said, holding the bottle of water she had brought to his lips. 'We need to hurry.'

He glugged the water, before cupping some in his hands and pouring it on his face. The shock seemed to bring him round. 'Libby?' His voice was thin and weak.

'We need to go. I have your things.'

He stood up, surprisingly quickly given his state, like he'd flicked a switch and turned himself back on.

They moved together, crouching low on the ground in case anyone caught sight of their outlines, only standing upright to run down the hill. Neither of them had the breath to talk. The exertion and panic had squeezed it out of them.

In the woods, Joe fell back. He was wheezing, rounding it off with a hacking cough that seemed to have no end.

'We can't stop,' she said. 'Not here.' Even fully fit, he wasn't the fastest.

They started moving again, him dragging his feet along the ground, kicking up earth, stumbling like a drunk. 'I can't. I need to stop.'

'Not here, just a few more minutes, we'll find a place to stop,' and true to her word she came across a ditch, alongside the hedgerow, hidden from view. She felt the mud soak through her clothes as she hunkered down.

'Why?' It was a short word but it came out long with his breath. 'Why did you do it?' His hand felt for her face, clasping at her jaw. She'd expected tenderness, relief, not this. 'Why did you let them do it?' he said.

'It wasn't me. It was Kyle and Will and Asha. They put you in there.'

'You saw me go in and you left me there. Hours and hours and hours . . .'

He wasn't lucid; semi-delirious, dehydrated, hurt and hurting. He squeezed tighter. 'You're frightening me,' she said.

'I'm frightening you? You've frightened me every day since we got here. I look at you and can't work out where you've gone, or whether I just imagined you in the first place. Was that it, you were pretending to be someone that didn't exist? I fell in love with someone who was an illusion.' He slipped his hand down from her jaw to her neck and pulsed it, his eyes drilling into hers, offering no mercy, no warmth.

'It's terrifying, isn't it, believing you know someone only to find out you haven't a clue who they are. Nothing makes sense after that. You don't even know yourself.'

He released his grip and pushed her back. She hit her cheek on a rock and it burst open. Blood on her hands. He didn't offer to help. He didn't know what he was doing. Joe wouldn't hurt her, not in the real world.

'We have to go,' she said.

'We? There is no *we*. You're not coming anywhere with me.'

'But I can't go back, they'll . . .'

He snatched the bag from her. 'If you follow me, I won't be responsible for my actions.'

She believed him, the venom in his voice cut to her bones.

'That,' he prodded the air, pointing towards the house, 'is part of your making. You allowed that to happen, you wanted it. So you go back and live with the monster you have created.'

She started to shiver uncontrollably. She wouldn't go back to the house. Didn't want to. Couldn't. 'Please,' she begged. 'I'm sorry. I'm so sorry, I didn't mean for this to happen. I love you.' It was the truth, and the force of it winded her. All this time she had doubted, dampened her emotions with practicalities and promises she had made, and now in her despair, she saw it with absolute clarity. *I love you.* Joe was good and kind and maddening, yes, but decent. He was a good man. And he'd loved her. Past tense. Perhaps the only person who did.

She reached out for him, but he shook her off. 'Have you ever really loved anyone? I don't think you know how to, I don't think anyone has ever shown you.' The words pummelled her. They weren't true. She had been loved, truly, but in the intervening years she had forgotten what it looked like, the touch and sound and feel of unconditional love.

Joe wasn't just a good man, he was perceptive too. And she had no response, nothing to throw back at him, because he was right.

That was it. He was gone, his departing figure, broken by the house, by the people inside it, by her. She mopped up the blood on her cheek with her sleeve. Her jumper would be ruined. And she cried. Instead of running away, she cried over a ruined jumper and a ruined opportunity, and she couldn't say how much time passed before she heard the shouts and the commotion, but she knew they were coming to find her.

There was still time to escape but stacked against her was the fading light, the shadows that jumped with life, her own weakness. And if they caught her running away . . . when they caught her, what then? What story could she spin to convince them she was still on the right side? On their side? She just needed to convince them long enough to get help from her uncle. He would not let anything bad happen to her. She still had leverage there.

The wind bit her face and fear whispered its doubts in her ear, and she sat in the ditch considering her options long enough to rule them out entirely.

There was no time left.

They had found her.

PART TWO

Twenty-Eight

Richard

Since everyone else is giving their side of the story, it's only fair I give mine. I'm Libby's uncle, her knight in shining armour. The one who makes everything better.

What you need to know, before we go any further, is that I have a huge affection for the girl. Love. Yes, of course I love her. I've brought her up as my own daughter. How many men would do that? I was in my early thirties, my prime, when she first came to live with me. Imagine that, a single man of considerable and growing means with more invitations than I knew what to do with, women aplenty, and I was forced to take charge of my nine-year-old niece. A month, that was what I said at first. A month until The Priory (at my expense) got my sister back on her feet. But sadly, it wasn't to be. There was an awful incident and we lost Ruth, Libby's mother, and with no one else – a motor bike accident had seen off her wastrel of a father – she came to live with me.

She was a sweet child, always rushing to the door to greet me when I came home like an excitable puppy. I have to say the unconditional affection was addictive at first. Every other woman in my life wanted something from me, expensive dinners, plush hotels, sex, a ring, marriage, blood, but Libby just wanted to see me. She wanted to hear my jokes, play board games (or bored games as I came to think of them), she wanted me to chase her through the garden and rewarded my efforts with that infectious cackle of hers. For the first time in my life I could see the point of children.

Was she sad? I suppose losing your mother at such an impressionable age must have had an effect but I can't say I noticed. I always got the smiles and the hugs. Sometimes the nannies would report bad behaviour or tears but I left them to deal with that. It's what they were paid for, after all.

What changed? Life changes. 'It's not a straight line, that's part of the fun,' I told Libby, but I don't think she shared my enthusiasm. Dana was coming to stay. Dana was to be my wife. She even asked Libby to be bridesmaid on my suggestion, but the girl didn't take to her at all. I'd go so far as to say she was jealous. We muddled through for a few years, an awkward accommodation really, every night Dana relating a fresh tale of woe: *She refused to do her homework/eat dinner/she called me a bitch.* I told her Libby was always perfect around me but Dana would not let it lie.

It came to a head when we had Max, our firstborn. Naturally Dana was protective, overly so in my book. She would not let the boy out of her sight, it was like she had grown an appendage. There he was wriggling in bed with us at night, suckling on her breasts long after I thought it strictly necessary. She had imbibed some godawful book about attachment parenting, skin-to-skin contact, the kind of guff that gives mothers a bad name. I couldn't get near even if I wanted to, although I can't say I did given the deterioration in her appearance. My God, now I understood the con of marriage. You marry a siren and end up with a frump for a wife. I tried my best, bought her sexy underwear as a hint, and she cried, not tears of joy either. I booked her favourite restaurant but she insisted the boy come too, and of course I relented, only for him to fill his nappy just as the foie gras starters were served. Dana spent a good twenty minutes in the bathroom cleaning him up and returned with a suspicious patch of yellow smeared on her dress. She blushed when I pointed it out and claimed it was part of the pattern of her dress. But floral patterns don't smell of shit. That much I know.

Anyway, I digress. I admit that I paid Libby five pounds one day during the summer holidays to take Max on a long walk to get him away from Dana. It was for her own good. She needed a break, to go cold turkey on the boy for a few hours. It was also for the good of our marriage. I really didn't want to look elsewhere, but we were fast approaching that critical point where circumstances might have forced me. So Libby agreed to take him off when Dana was showering. She was a good girl in that respect, always happy to help. She only went down to the village and around the park and it wasn't like he was starving. He had a rusk, for Christ's sake, and a bottle of expressed milk from one of those labelled bags that crammed our freezer. But Dana didn't take it in the spirit in which it was intended. All hell broke loose. The stupid woman called the police.

By the time I arrived home, Max had been found, which was hardly a feat since he wasn't lost in the first place. Libby was in the sitting room crying and Dana was in the kitchen, firstly because she was talking to the police officer but mainly because she couldn't bear to look at *that girl*.

'She says you told her to take Max out.' She'd been crying furiously and her face had puffed up. I noticed there was a stain around her breasts where milk had leaked and then dried. 'But I told the officer you would never do that. She's eleven years old, for goodness' sake, what father would entrust a six-month-old baby with an eleven-year-old for a whole morning? You should have seen his nappy when he came back.'

Max's nappy was the last thing I wanted to see. The officer appraised me as I formulated my response, as if trying to deduce if I were the type to do such a thing, and I found myself in something of a predicament. I could hardly admit I was the sort of man to indulge in child neglect, even if I didn't see it as neglect at all. Libby was almost twelve. The world had gone mad.

Still, if I've learnt anything it's that you have to read each situation carefully and adapt your responses accordingly. 'It's tricky,' I said to the officer. I glanced at Dana and fought the urge to tell the man in front of me about the marriage con and the baby taking my wife prisoner and the ill-fitting clothes and endless breastfeeding, and myself, relegated to the sidelines, on the cusp of having an affair through no fault of my own, and the simple act of giving Libby a fiver to take him off for a few hours. 'My niece gets very jealous,' I said. 'She lost her mother a few years ago and the arrival of a new baby has been hard for her.'

At the end of the summer holidays Libby went to boarding school. Berrybourne House, an amazing place, swimming pools, theatre, sport pitches galore, even stables for the girls to house their own horses, not that Libby had one. And it was only five miles from home. 'So why do I need to board?' she asked. What a shame Libby was becoming as demanding as all the other women in my life.

'It's for the best. I know it seems hard now,' I said. She would acclimatise, grow used to the set-up. Look at the Royals, it worked out OK for them. Besides, there was no alternative now. Dana and I had brokered a deal and Libby was the key. In return for me sending her to Berrybourne, Dana had agreed to a nanny, an end to the breastfeeding. She would start taking care of herself again. Not that I put it quite so harshly. There was no need. She discovered my affair around the same period. I suppose she knew it was time to up her game.

But don't think for one moment I forgot about Libby. Far from it. I gave that girl everything. The best education, the best holidays, the best opportunities.

It's hardly my fault she squandered them.

Twenty-Nine

Richard

I'm not going to lie. I'm a successful man. The company I run was started with a modest inheritance from my father in my late twenties. I have the trappings of wealth, the big house in Surrey, acres of garden I never see, a swimming pool and a tennis court, although don't ask me when anyone last used it. I'm not expecting sympathy, far from it, but this is not a lifestyle one achieves without complications and pressures. Once you have it, you're damned if you're going to give it up, and occasionally the very thing you've worked so hard to create scares the living daylights out of you. There are days when it sucks me dry; the school fees, the house in the South of France, the socialising, the cars, the staff. It's endless. The interior updates, the rugs, curtains, all in constant flux. Dana's wardrobe budget alone could feed a small nation, and if I ever complain she spits back: 'This was what you wanted, wasn't it, darling?'

We had a rapprochement after Libby left, no question, a second honeymoon of sorts. Hats off, she did a great job of putting herself back together, so much so I agreed on another child, reluctantly in theory but in practice, well, it wasn't so hard to convince myself.

I didn't intend to have another fling, certainly not while she was pregnant with Matilda, and morally speaking, I accept it was a low point. But it was nothing more than a moment of weakness eked out over a month or two. And it didn't mean anything. Dana was understanding, or so I thought, quietly contemplative when she found out, none of the dramatics and the tantrums of the previous time. That should have made me suspicious, but what can I say? Women are my blind spot.

It was different with Matilda. Dana didn't suffer from the hormonal madness she had with Max. Attachment parenting was never mentioned, and to my surprise she declined to breastfeed. She took care of herself, went straight back to the gym where she spent endless hours with her friends. She bought clothes that were a little risqué even for my taste, and upped the nanny's hours. But she was distant in a way that is hard to describe. Brittle almost, like she had erected a veneer and would not permit me access. Ironically sex was good, better if anything, but I had the unnerving sense that it was not my wife I was making love to, but someone else who had taken her place.

It was over dinner one evening that it finally became clear what I was dealing with. The day had been packed with stress; a deal in which we'd invested heavily was in danger of turning sour. I made some flippant remark about selling up and moving to Cornwall for a simple life. I'd always been fond of Cornwall; it was just too far from London for my liking.

'You can do what you want, the children and I are staying here.' I studied her face, searching for the trace of a joke, thinking it wasn't her style. My wife was known for many things but humour wasn't one of them.

'I'm serious,' she said.

'I think you're misunderstanding my point. I'm talking about taking our lives down a gear or two.' I was fed up, riled at having to explain a throwaway comment. I had no intention of moving to Cornwall or anywhere else, but I was damned if I was going to be told I couldn't.

'You know, we could grow veg, keep chickens.' I was winding her up now, just for the fun. 'I can see you knee-deep in the mud, collecting eggs of a morning. If I went you'd have to come too. You can hardly support this lifestyle on your own.'

She set her knife and fork down. 'You really should give me more credit. Remember, I own one of the businesses.'

'You are a director in name only, darling.' This was true. I was already a director of three companies. It made sense to put Dana's name on one for tax purposes.

'Well,' she said, leaning forward, 'why don't I tell you how it is?'

For the next half an hour Dana laid out everything she knew about the business in her name, and the others too. She had compiled a dossier of all the assets and taken legal advice; one of her gym friends was a divorce lawyer on a sabbatical, just my bloody luck. Dana knew exactly what she could take me for, and worse, she knew where the bodies were buried. Figuratively speaking, of course. The shady deals, the kind every successful businessperson dabbles in to stay ahead.

I couldn't take my eyes off her. She was beautiful, no question. But there was something disturbing about her perfection, the white teeth set off by the light gloss of a summer tan, the toned arms, the flawless skin. She had given me exactly what I wanted. And sold herself to achieve it.

'Our marriage is a deal, you made that very clear some years ago. And I agreed to it. But I did not agree to a turgid little half-life somewhere in the sticks. It's time we were honest, so you know exactly where you stand. All this,' she waved her hand around her, the three-carat diamond ring catching the light and laughing at me, 'is what I get in return for keeping my side of the bargain.'

You may be surprised to know that our marriage functioned like a well-oiled car until this recent drama. Since I had no intention of divorcing and living in middle-class poverty in a two-bedder in Staines, seeing my children every other weekend, it was simply a question of adapting to circumstances, changing to suit your habitat. Survival of the fittest, I suppose you could call it.

It started to go awry when the business was hit by a bad overseas deal. We'd bought into an Asian tech company, over-paid at the same time their economy hit the rafters. We'd been too hard, too aggressive, too confident, and now we were paying the price. Everything I built started falling down around me, but I'd been around long enough to know something would come up. A rescue plan, an investor, a huge contract. Something. Business is for optimists.

I didn't tell Dana. Dana was the last person I would tell. And it wasn't like we were great talkers anyway, we didn't do pillow talk. We exchanged notes, timings, logistics: *Max has cricket at ten on Saturday, Matilda has gym, barbecue at Christy's on Sunday.*

Who the hell was Christy?

'You know Christy and Matthew Collingwood, friends with Soline and Pierre. You met them at Janey's for dinner.' This was Dana's style, confuse me to the point of surrender.

'Whatever,' I said.

I turned up dutifully, armed with a few excuses. Half an hour and then I'd be out of there.

I didn't use my excuses. If anything, I probably overstayed my welcome. Matthew Collingwood was a fascinating character and astoundingly well connected, exactly the kind of person I needed to ingratiate myself with. By the time the food was ready, I was racing ahead, working out which contacts of Matt's (*all my friends call me Matt*) I needed to meet, what I could get out of them.

'I've just signed a big deal myself,' he said. 'I think our areas of expertise could complement each other, what do you say we meet next week?'

★

And that was how it started. Matt Collingwood wanted to buy in a niche set of skills. The best brains, young and agile. And the money he was willing to pay made my heart sprint.

And since his company was contracted by the government, I really didn't think we could go wrong.

Thirty

Libby

Libby lay on the sofa, withstanding a steady flow of tea and food and questions. The aim was to suffocate her, she was certain, with attention and concern. She had not been left alone for a second.

'Did he hurt you?' Asha asked, studying the ripe red mark on her cheek. Libby shook her head and gave her tears free rein. The others could read into them whatever they wished.

She had told the story as briefly as possible, without embellishment. Embellishment would trip her up. Kyle was too smart and she was too shaken to compete.

It went like this.

She had opened the door to him because he needed water.

Joe had pushed past her.

She ran after him, to persuade him to come back.

But he wouldn't listen.

It was as straightforward as that.

She also had a request. 'I want to go home,' she told Kyle, whose unnerving smile had held through the telling of her account as if it were set in glue.

It was a simple request. 'I want to speak to my uncle,' she said. 'He'll come and collect me. I'm sure he wouldn't want me to stay here if he knew I was hurt.' She produced her phone, still in her possession from earlier and went to make the call.

Kyle nodded as if in agreement, as if her request had registered and he was going to see to it, quick smart. And her heart soared, only to crash as his hand removed the phone from hers.

'You're in shock, let me call him. And I don't think you should be travelling anywhere in this state. Besides, we're all leaving the day after tomorrow.' He made it sound as if she was considering an expedition to Australia, not Surrey. 'You need to rest. And Libby,' he whispered this, as if it were a little secret between them, 'we all make mistakes, it's how we learn from them that counts.'

She worked the mental anguish excuse until it ran out at around eight in the evening when they were serving dinner. She refused food – the smell alone made her stomach clench – and retreated from the leather chair, a sorry, uncomfortable excuse for an armchair, back into her room. There she stood at the window, running her fingers along the black aluminium sill. She had compressed her rage all evening. Packed it into every muscle and sinew of her body, and now the pressure of it shook her. How dare they? How fucking dare they? Did they know who she was? What a massive, career-ending mistake they were making by treating her so abysmally? She had it all racked up, every incident, every cruelty, the stories she would relay to Richard. This was not how it was supposed to be. He would not stand for this. He was a powerful man. He would destroy them.

But first, she needed to get the hell out of here. That had to be her focus. The rage could wait, detonate like a bomb afterwards, but not now. The air inside the house was choking her; she was existing on short, shallow breaths, the strain of which was dizzying. Another two nights here? She couldn't face another minute. The window was her only option. She'd done it once today. She could do it twice.

Except, she would have to cross the drive and that was directly in front of the kitchen. But what was there to lose? And the fact she didn't have her phone, or that Joe had nicked off with the rucksack and her wallet, was a handicap, but not a reason to stay.

Except, the window was locked.

She pulled it with all the force she could muster but it wouldn't budge.

She screamed. It ran out of her unchecked. Brutal, visceral. The noise of rage.

'Something wrong?'

Libby swung round.

Richard.

She ran towards him, light with the relief of his presence.

'Hey, it's OK,' he said, and he held her and she smelt his scent, the woody, musky scent so familiar to her, the one that had rescued and protected her and sometimes forced tough choices on her, but all for the best. Always for the best. 'Everything is OK,' he said. 'I'm here.' His reassurances dissolved the dread inside her. Libby let him hold her, felt the steady rhythm of his heart slow hers, and the clouds that had been crowding her mind began to part. And then he said, 'Kyle called me. He was worried about you. He said you weren't coping very well.' Libby wasn't really listening, not properly, just to hear his voice was enough. But her mind snagged on the end of the sentence. The words weren't right. She replayed them but it was still there, the blame. The accusation like a knot tightening around her. *You weren't coping very well.*

'He locked Joe in the cellar.' This was the truth, she was not going to be persuaded otherwise. She clung to it as the room pitched.

'Yes, he did mention that.' *Mention.* As in casually throw it into conversation. *Mention.* The word diluted and downgraded the cruelty of the incident to the point of irrelevance. She stared at the man in front of her, willed him to redeem himself. To be the man she expected.

'I think it's fair to say he overreacted. He should not have done that.' Libby exhaled. Of course Richard wouldn't stand for that kind of behaviour. She should have more faith, and she softened once more.

'But I understand Joe was out of control.'

No no no. He didn't get to unpick the criticism until it wasn't a criticism at all. This time she found her words, her indignation freshly minted. '*Kyle* is out of control. He let Will beat the shit out of Joe and then locked him in the cellar.'

'Darling,' he laid his hand on her head to calm her. Libby had no intention of being calmed or patronised or being told the sky was green when one glance out of the window told her it was blue.

'I know what I saw.' She spat the words out before he said anything to soothe her.

'It's upsetting, I can see that. Painful too. I know you had fallen for him, but he was in the wrong. Kyle has the proof Joe was responsible for the leak. The truth is he is not the person you thought he was. I know . . . I know, it's hard to believe someone you loved would betray you, but darling, I'm afraid that's life. It's a hard and painful lesson to learn. All Kyle was doing was trying to calm him down and keep everyone else safe at the same time. With good reason by the looks of things.' He leant in and lifted her chin gently with his hand to study the cut on her cheek, 'Did he do this?'

God, he was good. So deft and precise, nailing the target, the exact spot of her weakness with one single shot. 'No,' she said, her hand immediately covering her cheek to guard her injury from further inspection. 'I fell. He wouldn't hurt me. And I don't believe he would have sold the information on Zimmerman either.' But she felt the cut pulse and throb, the doubt was awakened.

His eyes leaked sympathy, as if he was privy to an insight that still eluded her. *Poor delusional Libby.* And she wanted him to be wrong but, and it was a big but, she wanted him to be right.

There lay the central conflict, the circle she could not square. He loved her. He was there for her when no one else was. This was the foundation on which everything else sat, the roots from which she had grown. She needed to trust him because if she didn't, if that trust was shaken, or destroyed, there would be nothing left of her.

Reluctantly, she rewound, specifically to the few minutes she spent with Joe in the ditch. And there she found it, the ragged, uncomfortable truth that her desperation to get out of this house had pushed into the background. Joe had frightened her. Beyond frightened. What she had experienced was darker, deeper, an instinctive response. He had put his hand around her neck and for a second, a single terrifying second, she had believed it was over. She'd believed he was going to kill her.

She felt herself cave. Richard's subtle logic was intoxicating, but . . . the image filled her head and her body tightened. The blood. What about the blood?

'There's blood in the woods right in the spot where I saw Tess last night. And Kyle says she left but what if they've done something to her?' Richard hated tears but she was crying now regardless, pathetic snivelling tears that did not advance her cause one bit.

He planted his hands on her shoulders firmly, so she could feel the strength of his grip. 'I think we both know your fears are the product of an overtired, overactive imagination. I'll say this once because that kind of talk doesn't merit further discussion, but think back, Libby, use your brain. It was Halloween, you were all made up as zombies as I understand it, with fake blood. Fake blood, Libby.'

Fake blood. It was true, Asha had given everyone a tube of fake blood. Libby felt her whole skeleton collapse, as if there was nothing left to hold her up. Her humiliation was complete, her resistance to Richard's logic obliterated.

'I'm sorry this has all been too much for you, darling, being here, shouldering the responsibility. I should have known.'

'Can we go?' She wanted him to stop talking because every word he spoke pointed to her failure. It wasn't just the house she wanted to escape any more, but this level of scrutiny that turned her inside out. She needed distance and peace and calm to think. To reassess and reassure herself she wasn't useless. She wasn't a bad person either. It was simply that circumstances beyond her control had ruined everything.

'Later. My car is coming back later. But for now we'll have dinner and relax and I promise it won't seem so bad. Don't let Joe cock it up for you. You have to deal with setbacks, learn to overcome them.' Joe was relegated to a setback now, no longer the man she love/d, the one she'd fallen for hard and fast. Was this what Richard did? Parcel up his emotions, seal them up and move on. It would explain how he bounced through life, sliced through troubles like butter. But she wasn't sure . . .

'Please, Libby, I'm asking you to do this.' His request cut through her thoughts. And there it was, the trigger to prompt a Pavlovian response.

She couldn't say no. Ever helpful, ever agreeable, that was Libby's role, the one she had carved out. It wasn't for her to be demanding, not when Dana was never satisfied and Max and Matilda were never content, no matter what he did or how much he gave them. Early on, Libby had spotted a niche, and settled into the empty space where gratitude and usefulness sat.

Come to think of it, it was the only reason she'd got involved in this mess in the first place.

'Can you repeat that?' she asked when he was finished detailing what was required of her. They'd drunk two bottles of wine in Mama Rosa's and she was struggling to get her head around his request for help.

He was setting up a new cyber security arm of the business. 'Ethical hacking. It's where the growth is, Libby, big profits to be made.' His excitement was contagious. This was the Richard she knew, solving problems, spotting opportunities.

'The recruitment is tricky, though, which is where you come in. Think of it as a talent scout,' he said. 'I need the best young graduates, you know the kind, the people who don't want your usual corporate role, the ones who can hit the ground running. The sort who've dabbled in small-time hacking. I bet there are a few of them on campus. You're doing a computing degree, the place must be rife with them.'

The next day, when the hangover subsided, Libby called Richard again, just to make sure she hadn't dreamt it.

'Think you're up to it?' he said. And she said, yes. She could rise to the challenge and prove her worth.

'Good, because you're going to be a silent director of this company and it could make you very, very rich.'

Libby didn't waste any time, drew up a shortlist of potential candidates. It wasn't as straightforward as targeting the students with the best grades. There was a combination of skills required. Subversion in one form or another. A disregard for rules, and most importantly, previous experience of hacking.

Asha was the first one who came to her attention. Libby soaked up the tales of Asha's cyber revenge that raced around the faculty. Of course her ex-boyfriend could have gone to the police when he discovered that she had hacked his accounts and changed his passwords, but Asha had guessed, correctly as it transpired, that he wouldn't. Not if it meant him having to explain why he plastered intimate photos of her all over the internet.

Will had been more of a conundrum and she had dithered over putting him on her shortlist. He was not an immediately likeable character. He seemed arrogant and without empathy, eager to cream as much money as possible from his dubious online activities. But the reality was those traits made him the perfect fit.

Tess was known on campus for her campaigning and there was also a rumour that she'd put her tech skills to use, hacking corporates who had incurred her wrath, including Westminster Council. When she was arrested Libby thought it was doubtful she'd make the cut, but somehow Tess managed to walk free.

And then there was Joe. The go-to person for any tech-related issues, no matter how difficult. An ordinary guy with an extraordinary brain. It was just a shame she had already fallen for him. A shame she got him involved and that she had thought, wrongly, that the lie she told him was tiny and inconsequential.

Not that Libby had wanted to deceive anyone. Given the choice she would have been upfront about her role, told them exactly what she was doing, but Richard had counselled against it. He suggested the crack-the-code competition to make it look like a regular recruitment process. 'It's hugely sensitive work we'll be doing. I've got an expert to run the company. Kyle Nowak. He's a great guy and he'll be in charge on a day-to-day basis so you'll just be one of the team, albeit one who is my eyes and ears.'

And she wanted to be one of them. The sneaking about wasn't her thing, or so she thought. And then Tess's behaviour raised her suspicions and Libby found she had a talent for the sneaking and reporting back after all.

Tess was always the problem, right from the start. And even now she had gone, she was still causing Libby angst.

How could you sit back and let this happen?

The weight of the accusation was too heavy for Libby's crime, if you could call it a crime at all. Sure, Libby had been a little underhand in the recruitment, but she had also presented them with a golden opportunity straight out of university.

Christ, you really don't know, do you?

You don't understand.

As she headed down to dinner with Richard, Tess's questions deafened her.

Thirty-One

Joe

L ibby. I thought of nothing else after I left Kenton Thorpe.
Well, apart from sleep and a bath and food, but you get my
drift. I thought of what I had done to her, that thing with my
hands around her neck. And I thought, *Who the hell am I? What
was I thinking?*

I wasn't thinking. Therein lay the problem. When Libby let
me out of the cellar, I was broken. I barely knew who I was.
And when I came to, I didn't recognise myself. I was possessed
by a wild fury that burnt through reason and logic and love.

It was all her fault.

Dark enclosed spaces. *Leave me there to rot why don't you.*

Except she hadn't. It was thanks to her I got out. I could still
be there rotting had she not intervened. But this was the voice
of my reason, too quiet, too scared to stand up to my rage.

I headed straight to the village. It wasn't a long way but at some
stage I must have stopped, surrendered to a short, fitful sleep.
My eyes were heavy, weighted by worry, and the pain of my
injuries was beating my body. There was nothing that didn't
throb, but no good dwelling on it if I wanted to get away from
Kenton Thorpe. I had to keep going.

I stuck to footpaths and bridleways. The road was too dangerous a proposition. I imagined Kyle, alerted to my disappearance,
out and prowling the countryside to find me.

It was early evening by the time I reached Wivelton, one of

those quaint places where Tudor buildings push up against each other, drooping under the strain of the years. The sky was still a weak grey, the air fresh and snapping at my skin. I stared down at my clothes, caked with mud and blood, my jeans stiff and cold. I guessed my face hadn't fared any better. I was a mess, but I was a mess in a hurry. Train first then a wash. Thankfully it was almost empty. No one to scream in alarm at my appearance.

It was the bag that burst my rage, those small things that have a knack of getting to you: the deodorant, the toothbrush, clean clothes for both of us, and her favourite T-shirt, an old green one she'd bought at her first festival, the one she wore on lazy Sundays. All those little items spoke to me and they said: *You're a fucking fool, Joe.*

The guilt stung more than the cuts. Would I have hurt her? Here's the honest answer: Yes. In that moment, sitting in the ditch, covered in filth and shame, listening to her weak apologies, her entreaties, my hatred for her was so complete, so utterly consuming, I could have happily smashed in her skull.

I was pondering this truth and what it said about me as I rummaged through the bag. I found a phone I recognised as Tess's. Why did Libby have Tess's phone? The frustration of the unanswered question gnawed at me, as did my own stupidity. If Libby had been here she could have explained but my temper had seen to that. There was also a green notepad, the paper light brown and recycled, on its fifth life no doubt. It was neither mine nor Libby's and contained scribbled appointments, timings and venues mainly. There was one final entry.

Clara Wednesday 12 p.m. Westminster Pier.

Clara. The name sounded a bell in a corner of my mind. *Clara.* The reporter friend whose story about Westminster Council got Tess arrested. Had Tess planned to meet her as soon as she left Kenton Thorpe? She needed someone to help her if she couldn't turn to the police. Her police contact was the problem, not the solution. So why not Clara who could try to blow it all out in the open? Harder to act in secret when the blaze of public attention is raining down on you.

I felt the first stirring of relief, and my mind, fed a diet of lies and fear and conspiracies over the past few days, began to feast, if not on positive outcomes, then marginally more upbeat ones. Perhaps Tess had met up with Clara and they were working behind the scenes to end this dirty little saga. Quickly, I got carried away, picturing her in a newsroom somewhere in Canary Wharf plotting the exclusive with Clara, spilling every last detail of her narrow escape, the scandal of selling confidential information. Perhaps a photographer was there too, working at the edges of their conversation, capturing Tess's injuries before they faded. Tess would be wearing her pissed off face, the only suitable attire when a rogue police officer put your life on the line.

And Libby? This was how it was going to end: there would be tears, hers and mine, and we'd say sorry and argue over who was the sorriest, until we agreed we were both idiots and therefore deserved to be together.

I took myself to the train loo, washed as best I could and changed my clothes. That helped. So too did the positive thoughts. When I sat back down, my shoulders unbuckled and my head calmed a fraction. I stared out of the window, soaked up the high-speed view as night fell. The glow from the trackside houses, glimpses into kitchens, snapshots of evening meals. Family life. Normal life. Before long the city lights began to appear, crowding the sky line, plugging me back into a power source.

Tess's phone was ringing.

I stared at the screen, startled. No caller ID. My hands shook as I swiped, the simple task of answering a call had me at my limit.

'Hello?'

'Who's this?' A woman's voice.

'Who am *I* speaking to?'

'I just asked *you* that question.' This was growing tiresome.

'I'm Tess's friend.'

'And do you have a name?' She said.

'Yes.'

'That's normally the point where you tell me what it is.'

'Joe,' I said. 'My name is Joe. Your turn.'

'Clara. Clara George.'

Clara George ruined the evening with one question. 'Do you know where Tess is?'

'I was hoping she was with you.' A cold slick of dread crept through me, rinsing away all the positive outcomes. There was no newsroom, no photographer, no exposé in the pipeline.

'Can you tell me why you have her phone?' She said.

'I could but there's only ten per cent battery left. I'd need at least forty per cent for the full story. Can we meet instead?'

She hesitated. 'First tell me how you know Tess.'

'We work . . . we worked together at Freetech. We've been away in Sussex since Sunday but Tess left last night. I was hoping she'd met you.'

She sighed, as if considering the veracity of my story. 'You could be a nutter.'

'Fair point. We could meet somewhere public, and busy, where people would hear you scream.'

'That's not funny.'

'It wasn't my intention.'

We decided on Grosvenor Gardens close to Victoria Station. I went to the toilets first, to see if I could make myself less terrifying, but my face was a wreck, one eye cut and swollen, closed over to a slit thanks to the combination of Will and the cellar stairs. The buzz of Victoria dizzied me. It had only been a few days since I was in London but my pace had slackened, I was moving at the wrong speed, a swathe of commuters, faces drained by the day, scuttling around me, running for trains, swearing as cancellations were announced, haranguing guards simply because their anger, their exhaustation needed an outlet. All this life and movement, it winded me. I spied a bench, considered rooting myself to it for the next few hours, days, for no other reason than I could not be arsed to move a muscle. My body was empty. And then I spied the yellow and black sign of the Cornish Pasty Company and remembered how I'd sworn, throughout my late teens and university years, that there was no situation, no crisis or disaster that a steak and ale pasty could not make better. This would be the ultimate test. I found my legs and pulled myself across the concourse to order one for me, one for Clara, although I suspected from the tone of her voice that she might be a vegan.

'Hey you!' I'd found a bench in Grosvenor Gardens and was tucking into my pasty when a man stumbled towards me carrying a can of Special Brew like a tonne weight. 'This is ma patch, OK? You can't just move in and think you can take over.'

I knew I wasn't looking my best, but this was an all-time low.

'I'm just sitting down. I'm not after your spot.'

He squinted, 'Aye, right.' He eyed me suspiciously. 'You always look like this, then?'

'Only on good days.'

His laugh turned into a bronchial cough. 'Here, get some of this down you, by all accounts you need it more than I do.' He slung the Special Brew in my direction. 'A'm starving. Are you eating both of them?' He pointed to the second pasty. 'A'm Jimmy by the way.'

'Joe,' I held out my hand and we shook. 'You can have it.'

For the next ten minutes Jimmy listened as I told him everything that had happened, how we'd been tricked, Freetech's illegal activity, the zombie game in the woods and the grand finale of my imprisonment in the cellar. He was a good listener.

'Fuck me, that's some shit you've been taking,' he said when I finished.

'I'm not on drugs.'

'Right you are. And a'm fucking Kublai Khan. Anyway, I'd say your lady friend is here now.' I looked up to find a pocket-sized woman hovering over us.

'Joe?' she asked.

I raised my hand. 'That's me.'

Jimmy stood up. 'A'll let you have ma bench for a while because I like you, Joe, you're a good man, even if you are a fucking headcase.'

Clara was an unusual creature, not much older than me and tiny, miniature in every way apart from her hair which was an extravagant affair piled on top of her head and swaddled in a bright patterned fabric. It wobbled as she moved, giving the impression it might topple at any time.

'You weren't joking then,' she said, sitting down next to me, her face initially puckering in distaste at the sight of my injuries, and then relaxing as if she was reassured I was on the right side. 'They did this?'

'Them and the cellar stairs. They're quite vicious.'

'And you say Tess left before that?'

'The night before. We were playing a game in the woods, dressed as zombies . . . yeah, I know.' She'd hitched one eyebrow so far it was touching her hairline. 'Not my idea of fun. Anyway, I thought I spotted Tess in the dark and I started running towards her, and next thing I knew I was waking up the following morning in the woods. I must have run into a branch, or . . .'

'Someone knocked you out.'

We let the thought percolate for a moment. 'I was hoping Tess was safe with you. I have her notepad.' I showed her the book, the memo to meet at midday. *Westminster Pier.*

'Yeah, I was there but Tess never showed up. Two hours I waited, I must have taken about ten photographs for Japanese tourists in that time. I was ready to kill her, honestly. She's always late. But the thing is she always turns up in the end, totally oblivious to her appalling timekeeping. She's annoying but she's not rude.'

My mangled brain tried to keep up with Clara as she raced through what she already knew about Freetech and Tess working for the police thanks to a two-minute phone call from Kenton Thorpe. 'Anyone else and I wouldn't have believed it, but Tess, she has a knack of getting herself into these situations. This time, though . . . she's totally outdone herself.'

She made it sound like an acrobatic feat that Tess had achieved.

'I'm worried about her, and Libby,' I said. 'My girlfriend is still there.'

'Hmm,' she rubbed her chin as if weighing up the situation.

'They're not the kind of people to mess with.' I fingered the cut on my cheek to remind her what they were capable of, hoping to elicit a bit more concern.

'The thing you need to know about Tess is she's crafty. Good crafty, not bad crafty if you know what I'm saying. She's been getting into shit all her life and she always manages to escape unscathed.'

'I wouldn't call these particular circumstances escaping unscathed.'

She studied me, her expression flickering between irritation and pity.

'Listen, I'm not saying this is an ideal situation, but what are you going to do? Sit around examining your injuries or actually do something to help?'

'I'm sensing there is only one answer.'

Let's just say I was beginning to understand that you didn't say no to Clara George.

'I made some calls to the police after I spoke to Tess.' She was bringing me up to date with everything she knew, cutting my exhaustion no slack whatsoever. 'I mean, they tell you jack shit at the best of times so I wasn't exactly holding my hopes out for a full-on confession, but they denied there had ever been any such operation. I explained to them it was a secret investigation, so perhaps it did exist, they just hadn't been told, and they said they knew about all the secret operations, and I said well, if that was the case they wouldn't be secret. As you can see, I wasn't getting very far. I even called my contact on the cyber crime team but he's been conspicuously silent. It's like he's ignoring my calls.'

I exhaled, prayed for Clara to slow down. She had bright, erratic eyes that flitted about as she talked. Whoever this contact in the cyber crime team was, he had my sympathy. If I were him, I'd probably ignore her calls too. 'The thing is when they ignore you, that's when you know you're on to something.'

'Maybe he's just on holiday, annual leave, working on a murder case.'

'Were you not listening? I said he works for cyber crime, not murder.' I raised my hands in surrender. 'Anyway, it's not all lost yet. I have his address.'

'You're going to visit him at home?'

'Not my contact. The officer who roped Tess into all this. She gave me his name and by the power of the internet, I've found out where he lives. Fancy a trip to Barnet?'

As it happened, I did not fancy a trip to Barnet. I have never knowingly fancied a trip to Barnet, but I got the distinct impression it would require less energy to agree to Clara's plans than resist. 'Yes. But not like this. I stink. I really need a shower.'

'I didn't want to say anything, but you're pretty offensive.'

'Thanks.'

She shrugged. 'My flat is en route. You can use my shower as long as you promise not to leave any pubes.'

Clara's flat was styled in what I believe is called an eclectic fashion: brightly coloured throws and mismatched cushions in loud patterns, junk yard finds, an old table, a pineapple-shaped table lamp, a battered leather armchair. It was compact, like her, but equipped with more than everything you needed. I showered, collecting any stray hairs as instructed, while Clara agreed to wash my filthy clothes. 'I put them on boil,' she said. 'Although really I think they should be burnt. Anyhow, I need your help.'

Her laptop was fired up on the table, along with tea and toast. 'Don't worry, I'm not usually this hospitable, it's just because I want something from you. I've got plenty of skills, but me and computers, we don't see eye to eye.'

I took a swig of tea, braced myself for Clara's next request. 'Tess mentioned Freetech was a shell company. She said its parent company is Foresight Solutions, run by this man, Richard Gilligan Thomas. You know the sort, moves in powerful circles, shits out gold. At least he did. The company was valued at thirty-five million pounds a few years ago but they've had a crappy time of it – I know this because I asked our business editor – some big deal went tits up and it seemed like Richard had bitten off more than he could chew. Anyway, it would make sense, some guy setting up a dodgy subsidiary company to bail his failing one out. But the thing is I can't see the connection. Richard isn't the director of Freetech. And nor is his wife Dana.

It's under the ownership of someone else entirely and I need you to find out who this woman is.'

Clara shifted the laptop in my direction so I could see the name on the screen. I stared at it. And looked away, my insides collapsing. Then I stared at it again and willed the letters to rearrange themselves into a different name entirely.

ELIZABETH GRACE SUMNER.

Libby.

Thirty-Two

Joe

Libby.

It couldn't be her. The scale of the deceit was too big. It destroyed everything, everything we had together, the whole concept of us. There *was* no us if this was true. Not a pair or a couple, just one person lying to another for their own gains.

'Elizabeth is my girlfriend.'

Clara whistled. 'Fucking hell. Are you sure? Absolutely certain? Elizabeth is a common name.' It *was* a common name. Thousands of Elizabeths out there. Millions. OK, so the middle name and the surname narrowed the chances of pure coincidence substantially, but still, Clara was right, there must be a chance, a shard of hope.

We carried on searching. Helpfully, there were plenty of stories on Richard Gilligan Thomas, the business pin-up, the charity donor, the guy with a perma-tan and white teeth whose smile said, *Wouldn't you just love to be me?* He was happy to pose in the grounds of his pad in Litchfield (tick) with his children, Max and Matilda (tick), with his wife, Libby's nemesis, Dana (tick). One by one the chances of coincidence narrowed until there was no coincidence at all. Just cold hard fact.

It was Libby.

'There's always the possibility she doesn't know,' Clara said, only to scrunch up her face in a way that suggested the opposite.

There wasn't a chance, was there?

I considered the regular phone calls, the trips Libby made to her uncle's house, my invitation always conspicuously absent. But more than anything it was the way she talked about him, this life and soul, this goldenballs that made everyone feel better just by his presence.

'She knew.'

Detective Sergeant Tomaz Ramsay lived in a seventies terraced house not far from Barnet High Street. Clara insisted on driving there in her yellow 2008 G-Wiz. 'No point taking the Tube. What if he's not in? This way we can wait for him without being noticed.'

It was late when we arrived, around ten, and DS Ramsay was in, or at least someone was in his house. Clara spotted a figure at the upstairs window when we pulled up. But if it was him, he wasn't in a hurry to answer the door. 'I don't think he wants to talk,' I said.

'Of course he doesn't want to talk. Our job is to give him no option.'

She carried on ringing the bell for a good twenty minutes until a shadow appeared behind the frosted glass of the door telling us to piss off.

'I'm sorry, I can't piss off.' Clara's voice was unnaturally loud. 'I want to talk to you about the money you took.'

This time the letter box opened, the warning clearer: 'I'll call the police if you don't get off my property.'

'Well, that would be interesting, wouldn't it? Me telling your colleagues about the money you took to identify an informant.' No sooner had she spoken than a door flew open and a hand dragged Clara inside.

Tomaz Ramsay was off work with stress. To be fair he looked the part. Hollow sleepless eyes, his skin tight over his cheeks, a smattering of spots lining his forehead. He brought us through to his kitchen, though I wished he hadn't. It was strewn with beer cans and empty bottles, the smell of half-rancid bins overpowering.

'I don't know who you are or what you want—'

'Listen and I'll tell you who we are. We're friends of Tess. Remember her?' His cheeks beat out heat. 'Good, because I can't stand lies. Tess has disappeared. My friend Joe here saw her at Kenton Thorpe last night and she hasn't been seen since, and obviously we'd call the police, but since the police dropped her in the shit in the first place it didn't seem like a very good place to start.'

'Tess will be OK, trust me.'

'Yeah, and you're right at the top of my list of trustworthy people.'

'Do you know where she is?' I said, and caught a flash of Clara's disapproval. *Is that the best you can do?*

'You were supposed to be covering her back,' Clara said. 'You got her into this in the first place. What did you get? Ten grand? More? Twenty? Thirty? Shit, you really hit the jackpot. Shame that the guilt will eat away at you and ruin your career.'

'You don't understand.' He closed his eyes, pressed his fingers down on to the lids.

'Then why don't you explain?' Clara said. 'Why did you do it? You can either tell me or I'll find out. I'm already halfway there.'

He stood up straight as if he was hit by a charge of electricity. 'You're the reporter, aren't you?'

'I'm afraid so.'

He walked towards her, rage steaming off him. And it occurred to me it wasn't the smartest move to find yourself in the home of a bent copper then threaten to expose him. 'You're the one who's been asking all the questions. Have you any idea what you're doing? You need to stop. You're making it worse, for fuck's sake.' He was shaking her now, his face puce, eyes bulbous, and Clara's cool slipped.

'Take your fucking hands off me.'

Whether he would have followed her orders, I couldn't say, but whatever his intention, the fist pounding on the front door stopped him in his tracks. 'Get the fuck out of here, do you understand? Take the back door, and don't come back.'

I can't remember running, just the boom of my heart and the quick, rasping breaths that didn't feed enough oxygen to my body. I thought the fear was going to knock me out, leave me to my fate, lying in Tomaz's takeaway squalor in perpetuity. 'Move it,' hissed Clara. At least someone was thinking for both of us.

It was dark in the garden, no lights to aid our escape. I pasted my eyes on Clara's headgear, followed it, running out to the alleyway and turning back on to Tomaz's street once more. There was a car parked outside. A black saloon, nothing too flash. Clara pulled out her phone and took a picture of the registration, the flash creating a burst of light. 'Wouldn't it be better if we just left?' I said, gasping between words.

'We're not leaving,' Clara said. 'We're going to wait here.'

Here was the yellow G-Wiz, London's most conspicuous car. It wasn't even possible to sink down into the seats, to stay out of sight. It was not designed with leg-room in mind.

We waited, despite my pleas. A tight band of pain had wrapped itself around my chest. 'It's probably a panic attack,' Clara said when I told her I thought I was going to die. 'Just breathe.'

But the air was too thin to breathe, not enough of it in the G-Wiz for the two of us.

'How much longer?'

'As long as it takes.'

It took seventeen minutes of pure torture before two men emerged from Tomaz's door. Their faces were barely visible in the dark but I could see they were wearing jeans and jackets, smart casual. Nothing out of the ordinary. Nothing strange to report. It didn't stop Clara snapping them with her camera, flash off this time at my insistence. At least she was small, only her hands visible at the window. If they had looked it would have been my face they saw.

I closed my eyes and prayed to God they didn't.

Clara gave it two minutes after the car had cleared the cul-de-sac before she opened the door. 'Where are you going?' I asked.

'To see Tomaz,' she said, as if she was a guest invited to his party.

The small matter of no answer at the door was not going to put Clara off. She went straight back where we came from, round to the alleyway, through the garden where she marched up to the door, turned the handle and let herself in, beckoning for me to follow.

The crunch of glass underfoot was the first sign that Tomaz's visitors had not come to enjoy a cup of tea and a slice of cake. Every cupboard door was open, the contents of each thrown over the floor. The dirty plates and glasses that had lined the worktop were now smashed, the remnants of takeaway containers littering the ground.

Tomaz was not in the kitchen.

He was not in the living room.

'Listen to that.' Clara stopped in the centre of the room.

They were coming back.

'There's water running upstairs.'

Tomaz was in the bath. Fully clothed, hands tied. A luxuriant soak this was not. His blood had turned the water a ripe red.

'He's dead.' I backed out of the room. I didn't want to look but it was too late, the image of Tomaz semi-naked, and the blood, ruled my vision. This could not be happening. Not today. Not any day, for fuck's sake, but definitely not today. Today was all my nightmares, all the agony and pain and fear, every horror story you know will never happen in real life, dished out in one massive, inedible feast.

'He's not dead.' Clara was leaning over him trying to pull him upright. 'But he will be soon if you don't turn the water off.'

Clara wouldn't accept weakness. Not hers, obviously, but mine. 'Don't just stand there like an idiot,' she said, 'help me.' So I did. I went into autopilot, used reserves of energy I didn't know I possessed and together we hauled him out of the bath, laid him on the floor. He wasn't a great-looking guy to begin with, his face had too much going on, like his features were in competition with each other, but now it was carnage, impossible to tell where his nose stopped and his mouth started.

Clara found the last few clean towels, insisted on drying him. 'I'll be fine,' he managed to say, but she wouldn't listen.

'I'm a qualified first-aider and it's ages since I got to practise. Don't think you're getting away that easily.'

And I don't know whether it was the relief of being alive, the pain of his injuries, or Clara's back-to-front brand of kindness, but Tomaz Ramsay started to cry.

'Now, I don't want to blow my own trumpet but I'd say we might just have saved your life,' she told him.

'Thank you,' Tomaz said.

We were sitting in his living room, the place unrecognisable from a few hours before thanks to Clara's insistence that we clean and tidy it.

I had protested, mainly because I hated cleaning but also because he wasn't deserving of our help.

'You're right, he isn't,' Clara had agreed, 'but he's going to get our help anyway and then he'll feel so pathetically grateful he'll tell us exactly what's going on.'

'Thanks is easy to say, Tomaz,' Clara said now, although in

his case it wasn't true. The *th* was pronounced with a whistle due to the loss of two teeth. 'Much better to show your appreciation.'

He stared at Clara's empty mug. 'Cup of tea?'

'I've had my caffeine quota for today, thanks. I was thinking more of what you can tell us.'

He flinched, drew back into his chair, not easy considering his ribs were most likely broken.

'Why did they come back if they've already paid you to be quiet? Don't they trust you?'

'The quethions,' he said with his toothless lisp, 'the quethions you've been asking. Ith making it difficult. They're worried ith going to be exposed and they can't have that. Ith too big. They need to clothe it down.'

Clara's eyes flitted about, as if they were the engines of her thought. 'Bigger than one company selling confidential information obtained illegally?'

His silence said everything. His arms were folded as if to contain himself but Clara wouldn't let him go, not now she had him where she wanted him. 'I'm dead if I tell you.'

'I reckon you'll be dead if you don't. They're not going to let you go, you know too much. The only way to stop them is to expose them.'

He reached out, took a gulp of cold tea, his hand barely able to hold the mug, and he took the deepest of breaths to sustain him while he told us everything.

And then we understood.

The scale of it. Why they would keep it quiet at any cost.

Thirty-Three

Richard

Let me say this: Libby was only too happy to get involved. There was no arm-twisting or pressurising. No haranguing on my part. I didn't even have to bribe her with money. I'm sure she would have obliged even if I hadn't offered to make her a director of Freetech. She was that kind of girl. Amenable. But still, she stood to make a small fortune if it all came off. Imagine being set up for life in your early twenties. I thought that would be enough to focus her mind on the task.

Obviously, I was wrong.

If only she'd been more selective in the people she recruited, I could be in a very different situation right now. Kyle had expressed his doubts but I assured him Libby was to be trusted, she knew these people from university, she had done her due diligence. But my trust was misplaced. She left me looking like a fool. And worse, much worse, instead of solving my problems, Freetech spiralled them out of control.

Let me explain. Matt Collingwood said he was working for the government but this wasn't strictly true. He was working for the political party in power, and even then he was only subcontracted by a small division of that party with a clear remit: to help them remain in power.

My job, via Freetech, was to give him and them the edge, while remaining very much below the radar. It was an information game because in twenty-first-century politics information is king. And the confidential information you have on your rivals trumps everything else.

In order to bring our project to life, we needed the young guns, the people who had the skills but wouldn't necessarily ask too many questions. They would deny it, I'm sure, but it helped that they believed in their own brilliance, that they had a strong sense of entitlement. *Of course we deserve to earn fifty grand a year straight out of college. We're IT wizards, we can walk through walls, our ingenuity knows no bounds.*

We're special.

Don't make me laugh.

They were going to do exactly the opposite of what they believed they were doing.

They were going to be played.

We were hacking into the systems of key public figures, political figures, journalists even, all of whom supported the opposition, in order to obtain the kind of information that would bring them down, or tarnish them at the very least should it find its way out into the public arena. Sometimes it would simply be a case of spying, keeping tabs on what they were up to. Sometimes the information would be used to destroy them.

The way I saw it, this kind of business had been going on for years. The smears, the stings, the manufactured downfalls, they were part and parcel of the dark arts of politics. All we were doing was giving it a modern twist.

One last word on the recruits: no one forced them into anything. Sometimes people are blind because they don't want to see the truth. It really is that simple.

Was Libby blind? Well, I admit this was partly my fault. I told her a half-truth, a white lie, whatever you want to call it. I spun her the line about ethical hacking because I had very little choice. For the scheme to work I needed her help, and as I said before the girl was eager to please, but a rule breaker she was not. Her finely tuned sense of doing the right thing would not have embraced my proposition. But I had banked on the money and success eventually loosening that strict moral code of hers. Everyone has a price and my thinking was that when Libby saw the millions in the bank, she was hardly going to walk away.

Was that the only reason I didn't tell her the whole story? If I scratch my soul for the answer perhaps there is something else. Perhaps there is another truth I have kept hidden even from myself until now. Through her eyes I saw the best possible version of myself, the man I would never be. No one else held me in such high regard. It was a form of delusion, I suppose, but how lovely to have this raw, unfiltered adoration from one person in my life. Perhaps, underneath everything else, that is the real reason I lied to her.

The first indication that our scheme was unravelling came from Matt Collingwood.

'You have a problem,' he said. We were in the Packhorse pub on the outskirts of Cobham, a dingy little place but one where we were certain we would not be noticed. I'm not sure what I expected next, Matt to laugh and tell me my shirt was the wrong colour or my car was too flash. He was that kind of guy, liked a joke, a bit of banter.

Except there was no trace of a smile on his face.

'With one of your people.' By now he had my attention. The emphasis on the possessive pronoun, *your*, made me tetchy. As far as I was concerned, everything was going to plan at my end. Better than that, we'd just delivered a dossier on Marc Zimmerman that was going to run in the *Herald*, destroying the man's reputation and any political influence he had. Surely gratitude and praise were the order of the day, not criticism.

'You have a mole.'

'What are you talking about?' *Spit it out, man*, I wanted to shout. This rationing out of information was infuriating.

'There is someone in Freetech who is passing information to the police.' It wasn't a joke, nothing funny about Matt's ice-cold tone. I stared down at the scampi I'd ordered. It hadn't been appetising to begin with but there was no way I was going to eat it now.

'How do you know?'

'It doesn't matter how I know, the fact is my source is very well placed, he has high level contacts in the police. They're running an undercover operation for fuck's sake, or at least they were. It'll be closed down, that's already in hand, but . . . and here's our problem, the detective in charge won't hand over the name of his informant, the person he has inside your outfit. You need to find out who it is. And fast. Do you understand what I'm saying? My government contacts will make sure the police operation doesn't go any further. They can't afford a scandal of those proportions. Your job is to make sure there are no leaks from your end. Otherwise . . .' He let the ellipsis sit between us.

Otherwise.

Was that a threat?

The trip to Kenton Thorpe was Kyle's idea and initially I can't say I was happy. That house was a model of perfection built to my exacting standards. It stood for everything I had achieved and I was loath to throw the doors open for a team-building retreat or whatever the hell it was Kyle had sold them.

Libby also registered her protests. 'Why do we have to go there of all places?' She had a thing about the house, the memories of her mother and grandmother – the girl was hopelessly nostalgic. But Kyle wasn't budging.

'Where else are we going to find an isolated house within driving distance of London by Sunday? If you want me to find out who it is, this is the only way, take them out of their comfort zone, break down the loyalties. No phones, no way out. We'll get there, I promise you.'

I believed him and left matters in his capable hands. He could get his dirty, that's what I paid him for.

Mine were going to stay clean.

I wouldn't say I relaxed when I heard they were safely ensconced within the walls of Kenton Thorpe (and had removed their shoes as per my instructions – the polished concrete floor was ludicrously expensive), but I had the sense the situation was, if not under control, then certainly in the process of being tamed. And yet no sooner had I settled down to a whisky in my study, than the phone rang. It was Matt Collingwood.

'Have you got a name yet?' It was only Sunday evening. How fast did the man think we worked?

'We're getting there.'

'I don't think you have understood the urgency, Richard.' He rolled the R in my name to labour his point.

'I'll get you a name,' he said, his tone sour. 'Everyone has a price.'

Fifty thousand pounds was the price of the detective's morals. In return he handed over the identity of the informant he had vowed he would protect.

Tess Langton.

The very person Libby had told us she had suspected of the newspaper leak. In a funny way she had been right and completely wrong at the same time.

'Whatever happens from now, if any of this ever gets out, you need to know this won't come back to the government. You need to deal with it or they'll hang you out to dry,' Matt said in a phone call.

'Hang on a minute, you approached me in the first place.'

'Richard, you have no proof of that, no contract, no emails. And you'll find the payments you've received aren't traceable to me. I'm afraid this is a mess of your own making.'

And that was it. I was cast adrift as the storm gathered on the horizon. I placed my phone down on my desk and poured myself another whisky, my hand shaking with the unfamiliar fury of being outplayed.

Thirty-Four

Richard

Dana found me in my study. She says I was crying but this is just another example of her bogus recollections. I was upset, of course I was, but I was trying to think of a way out, a solution to the crisis. My first mistake that evening was to confide in my wife, and my second was to listen to her.

'We've got a table booked at Pierre Gabriel in half an hour.' She was standing in the doorway attempting to prod me into action.

'I can't go.' I had no appetite, and the prospect of spending an evening making small talk with one of Dana's friends turned me cold. It was one such evening that had been my undoing.

'I don't ask much, Richard, but to cancel at the last minute really is the height of bad manners.' On she went, barely taking a breath, listing everything she did for the family, for me, keeping the housing running, the children healthy and well educated. None of it thanks to me, obviously; the school fees and the mortgage and the bills all magically paid themselves. God, the woman could moan, whipping up a storm of regrets and marital injustices just so I would bloody well agree to going to Pierre Gabriel. I don't even like French food.

'I'm in a spot of bother.' I only said it to shut her up. A schoolboy error.

Her sharp eyes appraised me, as if to deduce the severity of the bother to which I referred. When she had decided it was serious enough, she sat down next to me. 'Do you want to tell me about it?'

Her concern unpicked my defences. I needed to unburden, to offload, and while my wife would not have been my first choice, she was the only choice I had.

Once I started the words spun out of me thick and fast. At the time I thought it was the delight of catharsis that drove me to tell her everything, from the deal going wrong and our precarious financial situation, to Matt Collingwood's proposal, to Libby's involvement, but now I suspect it was simply the whisky talking. When I was finished I surprised myself by saying, 'Are you going to leave me?' I did not want her to leave me. I can't say I loved her, but I needed her. I did not have the bandwidth to endure anything else crashing down around me.

She took my hand, softly, in a way that made me want to cry, not that I did, and she said, 'I'm not going to leave you.' There was no doubt in her voice, no hesitation, and her certitude was the balm I craved. 'There is no way we are going to lose everything. But if you want my help, you have to do as I say.'

Dana stood up, took a sheaf of paper from my desk and a pen and started to write, asking me for names and connections, informing herself of the finer details of the predicament into which I'd landed. Her eyes were bright, cut with a steely determination, and I realised there and then I had underestimated my wife. Quite woefully. All this time she'd busied herself with gym classes and soft furnishings and fashion when it was apparent she had been primed and prepped for a much greater challenge. I watched her in awe, the gratitude slicking out of my pores. At that moment, I was even thankful for the time she had spent rooting around in my business. She knew the staff I used when I needed a problem to be resolved in a less than conventional manner; there was no need to explain to her what was possible. 'Call Dom,' she said. 'Send him to Kenton Thorpe. If anyone can scare this Tess character into silence it's him.'

I hesitated briefly. 'Dom doesn't do subtle,' I said.

'For heaven's sake, Richard, I think we are past the point of subtlety now, don't you?'

And so Dom was dispatched. The following evening he reported back that Tess had suffered a minor concussion while they were out on the Downs and he was keeping her under surveillance.

Again, I experienced a brief respite, sent Collingwood a terse message to update him and insist the matter was under control. I had twenty-four hours of relative calm, and treated myself to a game of cricket with Max and Tilly in the garden, enjoying their shrieks and cries as they celebrated a run. We were heading in, Tilly having sustained a thumb injury, when another call came. It was as if the man had a sixth sense and was out to destroy my hard-won equilibrium.

'Your mole has contacted the press,' Matt said. 'A reporter by the name of Clara George. She works for the *Herald* in case you are interested.' He was speaking in code again. 'You *should* be interested, I don't have to tell you that much. So much for containing this. If you don't close this down it'll be your name in the paper this week, your door the police will be banging down.'

Collingwood hung up, the pleasantries overlooked now our business relationship had officially disintegrated.

I stood in the kitchen, the children's chatter spinning me out. 'Can we have a hot chocolate?' Tilly asked.

'And watch a movie together?' Max said.

And I stared at those expectant little faces, still ruddy from the garden, eyes looking to me to deliver. 'Whatever you want,' I said, and felt a cord tighten around my neck.

★

I settled them in front of a movie, and called Dom, the instructions I gave him both clear and open to interpretation. 'It appears Tess is playing you for a fool. Your persuasion techniques were clearly too subtle,' I told him. Always best to make it personal with Dom, to wind him up like a toy. 'We really can't take any more risks, I'm afraid. I have to know, one hundred per cent, she won't be speaking to anyone any more.'

Of course, Dom went too far. Much too far. He called the next morning with news of his ambush in the woods. That is the exact word he used, I swear to God, like he was fucking Rambo, taking out a bloke, Joe, and then slaying a woman in the dark, expecting praise or a generous bonus or a goddam award for services to brutality.

'Tell me you're kidding,' I said. But I knew he wasn't. He had no sense of humour for starters. What was he thinking? My whole body tensed with dread. All I had done was instruct him to clear up a mess and he had created an entirely different one of catastrophic proportions.

'I hope you've cleared up after you.' I moved swiftly into damage limitation mode.

'Don't worry, Massey has seen to that.'

This was not the reassurance I wanted. Far from it. 'I thought I told you not to use him again?' Massey had let us down badly once before, nearly dropped us in the shit.

'Funnily enough, it's not that easy to find people who are willing to do his line of work.'

I didn't appreciate his tone. 'You better hope to God he's done a thorough job this time,' I said.

After that the speed of the unravelling gained momentum, as if Dom and his murderous ways had doused me in bad karma. Joe escaped from Kenton Thorpe thanks to my niece's misplaced compassion. Libby herself was increasingly suspicious and Clara

George was still making the phone calls, asking the questions, like a bloodhound chasing a scent. And the calls from Collingwood were reduced to threats of no more than a few words.

Do something.

It was half term. The children were in the garden. I opened the window to hear their voices, to soak up the sound of normality. I only wanted to escape from my head for a moment, one solitary moment of respite. Was that too much to ask? Tilly and Max were in the tree house, only their legs visible. My eyes snapped the scene before me, taking a mental Polaroid, and I turned away for no more than a second. I swear that's all it was.

And then I saw her.

And him.

Tilly screaming in delight as a man dangled her over the edge of the tree house by her feet, a good eight-foot drop, and my only focus was the veins in her temples pulsing red and then purple, and what would happen if the man let go? Her head, her beautiful, perfect head would smash on impact.

I ran out and saved her, that's what I want to tell you. That's what any decent father would do. But I didn't. I didn't move, my feet were stuck in cement, as the man's eyes locked with mine and he raised a smile.

And in return, I nodded. My surrender.

Because I knew. Not who he was, but what he was.

And whatever he was asking, whatever he wanted, I would do it.

He was polite, well spoken. Precise but firm in his oratory.

If the story got out it would bring down the government, cause a threat to national security.

The project was to be closed down entirely, as if it never existed at all.

And the people involved? I asked.

They were all to be at the house tomorrow night. Every single one of them.

Call it a party. The final supper. Whatever.

And what if I couldn't get them there?

To this he said, accidents could be arranged.

Your home.

Your wife.

Your children.

You.

Thirty-Five

Libby

'No one is more upset than me the way all this has turned out,' he said. 'That's why we're laying on a special party here, tomorrow night. What do you say?'

Libby was sitting at the kitchen island with Richard, her abandoned dinner plate in front of her. What she wanted to say was, *Are you insane? Have you listened to anything I've told you in the last hour? Have you understood a single thing? Why on earth would anyone want a party?*

'Oh, don't look like that. You always had to be persuaded to have fun, too serious for your own good. Come on. Don't be a quitter. There's always a way out of any situation. It's just about . . .'

Adapting.

She knew what was coming before he uttered the word. How many times had he given this nugget of advice? *You only have to look at nature, those who adapt survive. Same in business, Libby. Same in life.*

But Libby wasn't well disposed to adapting right now. Unlike her uncle, who was happily slicing through a chicken breast, topping his glass with yet more wine, she wasn't ready to gloss over what had happened to Joe. And what about Tess? Fake blood. Fake blood, she told herself. And yet once the initial acceptance had passed, the doubts pushed up like weeds. She thought of its texture, the way it had sunk into the lines of her palm and remained there no matter how many times she scrubbed her hands. It had a certain viscosity, a stickiness that insisted it was real blood. Tess's blood.

'I don't think it was fake,' she said, 'the blood in the woods.'

He laid down his fork and shrank her under the power of his glare. Not indulgence, not love, not affection – what was it she saw? Impatience, irritation, resentment. Her statement was an affront to his maxim: keep up, move on, don't linger on the small things.

But Tess was neither small nor a thing, and this fact bolstered Libby to press on in the face of his disapproval.

'Don't you think it's a bit suspicious, the blood in the exact spot where Tess was?'

'You don't even know she was there, for Christ's sake. It was dark.'

But she did. 'I found her clip at the same place.'

He shook his head. It was clearly an inconvenience, this constant questioning when there was a party to plan. A party. FFS. Even Richard's megawatt enthusiasm could never persuade her that dinner with six people, many of whom she disliked, would amount to a party.

'Listen to me, if Tess was hurt, if she was frightened, tell me why she's coming back tomorrow for the party?' He ran his hand through his hair, flustered as if he had just let slip a secret.

'Tess is coming?' Libby couldn't compute. Tess's return did not fit with her theory, with the worst-case scenario doom-mongering that had taken her hostage.

'That's what I said. She's been in touch with Kyle to apologise, but . . .' He sucked in a breath, steeling himself as if what was coming next was going to hurt. 'I'm afraid it was Joe who she wanted to get away from. Joe and his unwanted attentions.'

A white heat filled her head, and whooshed down her spine, and the need to escape was so ripe, so full, she thought she might expire, combust right there in front of him. It was lies. All lies.

Why was he spinning them when he knew how much they hurt?

Richard reached out to pat her down, like a disobedient dog, and she saw his nails, perfect as ever, and felt his soft hands, and she marvelled at that charismatic glaze, his bristling masculinity. But she also noted the quiver in those hands, the strain breaking out through the mask, a muscle twitching in his cheek, his impatience fermenting. And she felt her own stubbornness solidify.

'I'd like my phone back to call Tess.'

He thought it was over, the game all sewn up. He did not appreciate Libby's last minute demands. 'Oh for pity's sake,' his real mood finally escaped and was now on the rampage. 'What do you think this is? Of course you can have your bloody phone. Be my guest, phone Tess. Then you'll know who to call a liar, and it isn't me, I can tell you that much.'

Richard drained his wine and stalked off to find Kyle and locate her phone *so they could put this nonsense to bed once and for all.*

Libby was left to pace the kitchen, trying to raise her memories of the old house, her grandmother's house, what it used to be like before Richard tore it down. The exact layout escaped her, she was nine years old when she last saw it in its original guise, but she closed her eyes and slowly the smell and the feel of the place bubbled up in her mind. It had been warm and homely, the walls pinned with postcards and cards, notes of love and good wishes from distant and not-so-distant places. And owls, her grandmother had a thing for owls and everyone *knew* Rose had a thing for owls, so wherever they went, they'd bring one back as a present. 'You can never have too many owls,' she used to say, squeezing another one on the shelf. Libby's mother didn't share the love, 'they give me the creeps,' but Libby liked those big friendly eyes watching her eat, watching her bake cakes, watching over her.

She wondered where they had gone, when the old barn was demolished to make way for this new monstrosity. And then she caught the shard of a memory, a skip full of ceramic eyes and feathers, cast out because they didn't fit with Richard's vision of the future.

He returned with her phone. And when she turned it on she saw there was a message waiting for her.

From Tess.

> Sorry, I seem to have been the cause of worry!! My bad to do a runner but it was all a bit too much. Will explain tomorrow at the grand finale.
> See you then.
> Tess. Xxx

The confusion must have been painted on her face. 'Who's it from?' Richard asked.

'Tess.' She said her name quietly, reluctant to broadcast her defeat.

Richard leant over her to read the message. 'Well, thank God for that. You almost had me with all that sinister talk.'

A thought rattled through her mind. Tess's phone had been in the backpack Joe had taken.

'But she doesn't have her phone.'

'She had two, apparently. Cheated on the detox. You youngsters, can't live without them.'

She tried to find the space in her head to untangle the confusion, work out the logistics of how that could have happened, but Richard snatched her attention away.

'Listen, I'm sorry, OK. I can see you're upset about Joe, and it's all very easy for me to say you should move on, but I've been there too, believe it or not, and it's no fun having your heart broken. Why don't you contact him, see if he'll come

back tomorrow and we can make amends? Maybe all is not lost.'
This was his skill, bringing her off the boil with a few carefully
chosen words. He cared. At the heart of everything, that was the
truth. Yes, sometimes people emerged bruised and battered from
their exchanges with Richard, beaten by the relentless pace of
his mind. But eventually, he'd stop and go back to find the
people he'd left behind.

'But Kyle . . .' She couldn't shake the image of Kyle locking
Joe in the cellar.

'Kyle can apologise. He shouldn't have behaved like that. I
hope you didn't think I was trying to make excuses for him.'

'Joe will never agree to it. Not here.'

'Well, why don't you arrange to meet him somewhere
tomorrow? I can get my driver to take you. I want to make this
up to you, Libby. Send him a message. If you really love him,
it's got to be worth a shot.'

And she did, didn't she? Libby loved Joe, it really wasn't any
more complicated than that. And if you loved someone you
didn't just give up. OK, she hadn't really felt the love during
their last encounter, not in the ditch with him threatening her,
but this place had knocked everything out of shape. And she was
prepared to write it off as an anomaly because Joe wasn't violent
or evil, he was just Joe.

'I'll think about it,' she said, reluctant to concede too easily.
Instead, she accepted a refill of wine and then another as Richard
told her about Max making the cricket team and Tilly's dancing
performance that took everyone's breath away.

'How's Dana?' she asked, out of duty, not interest.

'You know, the usual whirlwind. Even busier of late, believe
it or not.'

And Libby imagined gym classes and nail bars and trips to the
hairdresser for highlights, and the float spa that she swore was
the reason for the good mood Libby never witnessed.

'I'm sure she is.'

'Speaking of which, I'm afraid I have to get back. You're OK to stay until tomorrow, aren't you? Let me know what Joe says and I'll send someone to collect you.' He scooped up his jacket and kissed her on the forehead before she could protest. 'Sleep tight,' he said.

Libby finished the wine, and then cracked open another bottle. She wasn't what you would call a serious drinker, mainly because she liked to keep a clear head, but the giddiness that filled her tonight was pleasing and she didn't want to let it go. She thought of tomorrow, the slim but real prospect of meeting Joe and resetting themselves away from Kenton Thorpe. In fact the prospect of leaving this house and these grounds alone made her spirits soar. Yes, the potential for failure was great. He might not want to see her. He might hate her. But the wine turned this kind of unhelpful chatter down to a low murmur.

Eventually she staggered up the spiral staircase trying to remember which side the banister was on. Right or left? Lean to one side and she would fall, lean to the other and she'd be safe. Trouble was she couldn't get a handle on what was before her. The huge pendants were no use, throwing spots of light here and there without illuminating the whole area. It really shouldn't be that difficult. She was almost at the top when she felt herself sway and teeter over the drop, and her body braced itself for the pain of impact.

But somehow she recovered, righted herself at the last possible second, and it made her think of the ghosts of her grandma's owls, their big glassy eyes still watching over her, keeping her safe.

She crawled into bed, her body light with exhaustion. Before she succumbed to sleep, she took her phone and composed a text.

I'm sorry. That doesn't even begin to cover it.

Can we meet tomorrow for lunch?

Rocco's Café near St Paul's. Remember the one?
Libby xxx

She waited, stared at her screen until her eyes surrendered to sleep, and when she woke the next morning the first thing she saw was this:

I remember the place.
One o'clock.

His brevity stung but she told herself it was a start. Better than nothing. She would win him over. Make him love her again.

Thirty-Six
Day 5

Libby

Today was going to be a better day, Libby would not have it any other way. The sky agreed with her, showing its best face, the kind of vivid blue that energised and revived and made you thankful for everything from a good sleep to a hot shower, to a cup of tea. Libby was even grateful for her colleagues and the bacon sandwich one of them placed in front of her.

The bacon tasted exceptionally good, cooked to the perfect degree of crispiness. Asha and Will were in a better mood. Everything was good, things would be sorted out. One extra night here to restore harmony. She could do that. No problem.

'Tess is coming back,' Will said. 'And we're having karaoke.' And Libby glanced at Asha who smiled and rolled her eyes.

'What are you going to sing?' Libby said, instead of, 'God help us.'

Nothing was going to ruin her mood.

She was meeting Joe and she was going to London, diving back into the busyness and the hustle and the noise, away from Kenton Thorpe. But mainly she was meeting Joe, and afterwards, they'd have a party.

She went up to shower. If she'd had the full complement of her wardrobe she'd have chosen the T-shirt Joe liked and the skinnies and the white Stan Smiths and worn no make-up at all.

He liked her natural and real, but the spots on her chin were a bit too real for her liking so she applied a tinted moisturiser and a concealer and a dusting of blusher. What he didn't know wouldn't hurt him.

The simple act of putting herself together further enhanced her mood. She was herself again, her mind clear as the sky. Her stay at Kenton Thorpe was nearly over. Tomorrow she'd be going home. But the next time someone mentioned team-building at work, she'd tell them where to stick their paintballs.

'Hey, Libby, can I have a word?' Kyle said. The new day seemed to have worked miracles on Kyle, rendering him normal, borderline likeable, his tone sincere. 'I'm about to go,' she said. And so she was, coat on, shoes on, her bag on the island in front of her.

'It won't take a minute.' He invited her into his room which doubled as a makeshift office where he maintained a level of military tidiness that was completely beyond her.

'I wanted to say I'm sorry, I acted like a dick.'

'I'd like to disagree but—'

'You don't want to lie. Don't worry, I get it. I got a bit carried away. Actually I got a lot carried away. Genuinely, I was worried about what he might do, but that's no excuse. Thanks for getting him out of there. You did right.'

The bluntness of his apology muted her. All she could do was replay it in her head for signs of insincerity. She found none.

'I'd like to say this to Joe in person but I totally understand if he doesn't want to come back, I wouldn't if I were him. Maybe you can pass on my apologies. I want him to know he's welcome tonight. And the cellar is out of bounds.'

'Thanks,' she said finally. She wasn't ready to make a joke of it yet but she gave him something. 'We all make mistakes.'

'And when we do, we have to pay for them.' He held her stare for a little too long and it made her question what was in store. Was Richard going to sack him? She didn't know and she had no intention of asking either. She was just grateful Richard had worked his magic again, made everyone see sense and was bringing them all back to a more peaceful reality. Not for the first time, she was glad to have him on her side.

'You came,' she said. They were sitting opposite each other in Rocco's Café, in the back streets near St Paul's, the same one they had stumbled into one day three months before as the heavens opened. Then they'd eaten chocolate cake and drunk coffee while the windows steamed up and it tipped down. 'Simple pleasures,' Joe had said with chocolate icing dusting his top lip.

'You didn't think I would?' He'd been there when she arrived; the sight of him had her on the point of collapse, so great was the relief. She smiled, waited for him to beam a greeting back in her direction, a hint of warmth, a trace of what had been, something that would give her hope they could erase all that had happened between then and now.

'Hi,' was all he had said as she sat down, the word stiff and starched like a new shirt on its first wear. And all her hopes crashed because she knew that the familiarity accrued from their time together had been squandered. There was nothing between them now but a bruise, the pain of something that had already happened.

'I hoped you'd come . . .' her mouth was dry, sucking up the words she wanted to spill out, 'but I wouldn't have blamed you if—'

'Why did you want to see me?' He cut through her meanderings, swift and businesslike.

'To say sorry.'

'Well, now you have, maybe you can tell me where Tess is.'

Tess. The name pierced the last bubble of hope. Was that the only reason he came?

'The last time I saw her was in the woods.'

'That's the last time anyone saw her.'

She didn't like his tone, the heavy load it carried. She turned away from him, couldn't bear to see the disgust in his eyes because she did not deserve it. Not his bile or his hatred. She had made a mistake persuading him to come to Kenton Thorpe, made a mistake going there herself. And she should have acted sooner to help him. But beyond that? Libby's eyes scanned the café for a diversion. There was a tiny young woman a few tables away with extravagant headgear dunking a herbal tea bag into a cup of water, and a man ploughing into a cooked breakfast while peering at his newspaper. Beyond that they were alone.

'I called out to her but she didn't respond, and then . . . well, it was dark. I didn't see her again. But she's coming back tonight.'

'Who told you that?'

'She's been in touch with Kyle.' He was shaking his head, rejecting everything she was telling him, his face full of sneer. 'She said it was you she wanted to get away from.' Libby sat back, waiting for that bomb to explode.

'Drop the act, just tell me what you've done with her.'

'I'm telling you the truth.'

This set him off, laughing at her, not with her. 'Shit. I honestly don't know how you fooled me.' He reached over, grabbed her wrist, pulled her towards him and hissed at her: 'Where is she?'

Joe had lost it. He was beyond insane. Delusional. Accusing her, Libby, of hurting Tess.

'I don't know. What the hell do you think I've done?'

'The problem with lying is that no one believes you when you tell the truth. I know about your lies, Libby. I know the job was a sham.'

He knew. Somehow he had found out about her involvement in Freetech. The lies had seemed so harmless to begin with, so small and trivial and completely without consequence. It was their love that made them toxic. You can't build a relationship on a lie, no matter how small. She should have known.

Libby steadied herself, dug her remorse out of the well of her anger.

'I should have told you. I'm sorry. It was stupid of me. I should have been honest and given you the choice.'

'The choice?'

'To take the job or not, go in with your eyes open.'

His eyes bulged, as if she had sprouted three heads. 'You really think I would have agreed to that kind of work? Christ, I don't even know you. You're a stranger to me.'

Once again she had the sense that his rage didn't fit her crime. It was out of proportion. It was cruel. And his blind refusal to listen to reason, to see her for who she was, the woman he had loved, broke her in two. She'd come equipped with all the apologies, for Kenton Thorpe, for Kyle, for the damn cellar. Everything. She was prepared to be humble, to persuade him to give them one more chance. And she wasn't beyond begging, but this, this was too much. It ignited her fire once more.

'Since you mention strangers, why don't we talk about your behaviour? I thought you were going to kill me. I tried to help you and in return you hurt me.' Instinctively her hand went to her neck.

'That was out of character.'

'And that makes it OK?'

'I'd been left in a filthy dark cellar all day, I'd been beaten up. I didn't even know who I was. And I thought you were in on it.' His laugh came out hard as rock and glazed with sarcasm. 'I thought you were in on it. And now I know.'

'I had nothing to do with putting you in the cellar. Yes, I didn't tell you about my connection to Freetech. Yes, my uncle owns the company. I am sorry. I wish I had been honest, I wish I could turn back the clock and tell you the truth, but let's stop acting like it's a huge deal. You got a job, and you liked the job until everything went wrong. You're making it sound like we were running some kind of murderous campaign.'

His mouth was a fat O of indignation and Libby braced herself for a tirade.

But before he could speak a Star Wars ringtone cut through the air between them.

'Yes?' he said.

Libby heard a muffled voice on fast forward. It lasted no more than a few seconds after which Joe rose to his feet, his eyes glassy and dark.

'You disgust me.'

And then he was gone.

Cups and plates clattered and the coffee machine shhhed its steam and a woman stumbled in, laughing into a phone, turning to the girl behind the counter (she looked like a girl, barely beyond teenage years) as if she was surprised to find herself in a café. 'Oh . . . I'll have a soup to go and a macchiato.' She carried a handbag in a rare aubergine colour that caught Libby's eye. The tiny woman had left. The man two tables down had finished his breakfast, a clear plate save for three button mushrooms cast to one side. His skin bore the imprint of acne and he had dark eyes that scuttled away like beetles when they met hers. He got up to leave. Libby took all this in, the tiny granular details of the scene before her. These were the components that kept everything before her real and solid, and she grasped at them in a vain attempt to keep herself afloat.

The words they had shared were all wrong. They were hard, cold and destructive and they had cut her to the bone. It was the vehemence with which he spoke to her that had blocked any decent conversation, any progress. Perhaps if she'd had more time, another ten minutes say, she could have defused the situation, brokered some kind of amnesty that would have allowed her to explain in full. But his departure was so abrupt, it left no time and now all the unspoken explanations sat in her throat, pickling in regret.

She stood up slowly, testing her legs, surprised to find they could carry her, and walked to the door.

'Are you going to pay?' the girl called after her. She turned back, reached in her pocket, felt for a note and laid it on the counter.

Thirty-Seven

Joe

My meeting with Libby did not achieve a single one of my goals. I wanted her to tell me where Tess was, and I wanted to appeal to the woman I love/d to intervene, turn herself in, turn her uncle in. But really I wanted her to look me in the eye and tell me there had been some awful mistake, that she was not involved in such a corrupt scheme. No way had she lied and tricked us to be part of it. I wanted her to scream, *How dare you suggest such a thing!* I wanted to witness a wild indignation in her eyes that would tell me, beyond all reasonable doubt, that she was not to blame. That she wasn't a liar. Instead she said, *I'm sorry.* An admission of guilt so straight and pure it killed my hope. Killed me. And if that wasn't pain enough, she tormented me with the casual accusation that I was overreacting. Nothing could be rescued from that. There was no going back. I didn't want to waste time trying to understand her warped moral code. From there our conversation descended into recriminations and acrimony. We'd reached a new low.

Or so I thought.

Until my phone rang. Clara had insisted I bought a pay as you go before I met Libby so I was contactable at all times. She spoke even faster than usual, telling me there was a man in the café watching us and a car outside waiting. 'I have a horrible feeling this is a set-up,' she said.

Libby wouldn't do that, would she? *Would she?* The crushing truth was that it lay within the realms of possibility.

Libby. I could barely form her name. It was poison in my mouth. The layers of our relationship, the memories, the fun, all the moments we spent together, unpeeled like skin until there was nothing left but a raw, weeping sore. Pride made me want to believe she had loved me, that at some point what we shared had been underpinned by truth. But who was I kidding? Her lies reduced everything to rubble.

'You disgust me,' I told her.

Outside the sun sneaked through the clouds, its brightness stinging my eyes. I pushed through the crowds to get as far away from the café as possible.

I was halfway up the street when I heard someone call, 'Hey, you left your wallet.'

I swung round without stopping, narrowly avoided crashing into a family posing for a photograph. It was the Full English man from the café.

'Your wallet,' he said. He was standing a few metres away. I was supposed to stop, thank him for his trouble. It was a kind gesture after all, or it would have been except my wallet was in my pocket.

I broke out into a run, fuelled by panic. Everything was possible. I had been beaten and locked in a cellar. I had seen the police officer who shafted Tess left for dead. My girlfriend – ex – was a liar, a manipulator. Nothing was real except my fear. I ran and ran, ploughing through office workers out for lunch, turning back only a few times to check where he was. Losing ground. Thank fuck. My lungs were on the point of exploding by the time I weaved my way into the quieter back streets. On and on, until finally I had no choice but to stop. My body wouldn't give any more.

And then the horror of what had happened settled over me.

The final blow.

Libby had set me up.

Tomaz had warned us, hadn't he? This was more than one rogue company selling information. It was a state-sponsored attempt to steal and control information.

And we had found ourselves in the thick of it.

'You should be worried,' Tomaz had said. 'You know too much. And where Clara is concerned, they know you know too much. You need to stop with the questions, lay low, forget any of this happened.'

Clara had bristled, her indignation greater than any thought of self-preservation. 'So what, I just sit on the truth and let them get away with it, is that what you're saying?'

'Put it this way, you're not much use to anyone if you're dead.'

Tomaz had packed his things in front of us that night and left his house. He was in a pitiful state. 'No point being a sitting target.' He wouldn't tell us where he was going, he didn't know himself, but he gave us his number, 'For when you need it.'

When. Not if.

I should have listened to him. Meeting Libby did not constitute keeping a low profile. It was prancing around naked in the street, screaming at the top of my voice, alerting everyone to my whereabouts.

I blamed it on the invincibility of youth, the innocent misplaced sense that I would come to no harm. The same sense that told me the state and the police were always there to protect us.

Funny, now I think about it.

I called Clara, didn't wait for her to say hello, just raced through what had just happened.

'That's nice,' a man's voice said. Not Clara. 'Your friend is here with me, keeping me company, although I have to say she has a foul mouth on her, this one. We're on Bread Street by the way, just round the corner from where you're standing, if you want to join us, that is.'

My head thumped, dread echoed through me. *Clara*. They had her. And they knew where I was, their eyes trained on me at this very second. I spun around, looking up at the windows of the office blocks that crowded me, left and right, up and down the street. Where were they? Who was watching? It was hopeless. Too many places for them to hide, and yet I couldn't find a single one for myself. I felt for my phone. The police, 999, still my first instinct, and then my mind swung to Clara, sitting in a car with whoever had picked her up. Waiting.

I turned the corner into Bread Street, my body tensed as if waiting to be struck. A few seconds later a car pulled up alongside me, the window wound down, a man's face peering out. Black hair, pocked skin. The Full English man.

'Glad you could make it.'

He opened the door and Clara shook her head.

'Don't,' she said.

'You're not going to leave her all alone, are you? Don't tell me chivalry is dead.'

I got in. What else could I do?

'Where are you taking us?' I asked.

'I'm told there's a party back at Kenton Thorpe,' the man said. 'We wouldn't want you to miss it.

'Well done,' Clara hissed in my ear. 'Now we're both fucked.'

Thirty-Eight

Richard

Where were we? Ah yes, Libby's meeting with Joe. Of course I didn't believe any of that guff about second chances and love triumphing. Do I look like a fool? But Libby was soft. I knew she only needed a little light encouragement and then she would be off, baring her soul, begging him to come back to her. And I was right.

Of course there was always the danger he wouldn't reply and the meeting wouldn't take place. And I'm told there was a Plan B for that eventuality, but there was no need when Plan A worked so beautifully.

No love like young love.

Bringing Joe and Clara George to Kenton Thorpe was not arranged by me, but I can't say I wasted any sleep over the arrangements. In many ways they brought it upon themselves. As I understand it, the girl had been warned to desist several times but she failed to heed the warning. And this was a matter of national security. I don't buy all that nonsense about the truth at all costs. Sometimes our political process needs a little push, a helping hand. What was it Winston Churchill said? The best argument against democracy is a five-minute conversation with the average voter. People don't know what's good for them, that's the problem if you ask me.

My task was to organise the party, an area in which I was known to excel. *Richard gives a bloody good party*, that's what they all said. Dana and I have thrown some belters in our time, fancy dress, music, enough food to feed a small nation, the bigger the better as far as I'm concerned.

This one was rather pitiful in comparison but I did my best: champagne bottles in trugs of ice, cocktails, dirty burgers, whatever they are. A karaoke machine, a smoke machine. On it went. Whatever you might think, I genuinely wanted it to look the part.

Did I give much consideration to the after party arrangements? In all honesty I thought the idea was to get them all together, give them a damn good fright and that would be the end of it. Don't forget, my niece was there too so I was hardly going to condone anything violent. To be honest, I thought it was about time Libby was taught a tough lesson, dragged into the real world. She'd had it too easy. Mea culpa. I honestly had no idea there were other plans.

Thirty-Nine

Libby

On the journey back to Kenton Thorpe Libby plugged herself in to her iPhone and played 'Royal Blood' on repeat. Not because she liked it, but because it fuelled her mood. All that screeching and screaming and the guitars stretched her nerves nice and taut, just how she wanted them.

Tess and Joe, what a pair! They wouldn't know the truth if it bit them on the arse. She'd had enough of trying to fathom their lies, the red herrings, their manufactured outrage. They had been up to something from the start, plotting against her in those exclusive little chats they shared.

Tess left because she wanted to get away from Joe? That allegation had winded her at the time but it was obviously a lie. She had witnessed the kiss. Did she see Tess try to fight him off? No, she did not. Did Tess ever mention Joe's unwanted attention at any of the various opportunities Libby presented her with? No, she did not.

Libby didn't know what they were up to. And she no longer cared.

And that was the lie she told herself.

The light was sinking by the time she arrived back, the sky grey and moody, the morning blue wiped as if it had been an illusion. She studied the house on their approach, its insolence striking her afresh. No nod to its surroundings, no attempt to blend in, just hard, harsh lines and a blank exterior sticking two fingers up to the countryside. She got out of the car and shivered. Winter was closing in, turning the season in the space of a week. She didn't want to be here, and she was most certainly not in a party frame of mind.

Once inside, she found the light was too bright, like a stage before the show. Will and Asha, who were busying themselves with food preparations, glanced up to say hi. They'd already started on the beer. She wanted to get Asha alone, talk to her about Joe and tell her that everything was turning to shit. She wanted Asha to feed her one of her pithy answers that would make her laugh, puncture the stress, *For fuck's sake, Joe has moobs, you're not allowed to grieve for a man who has moobs*. She studied the pair, Will and Asha, Asha and Will. An unlikely alliance had sprung up between them and it sidelined Libby. She was an outsider. Always had been. And what with her uncle coming later, they were bound to find out Libby's connection and think less of her for it. Best to keep her distance.

She peered into the hallway and found Kyle up a ladder hanging festoon lights and a few coloured lanterns. The effect was cheap make-up on a haggard face, his efforts doing nothing for the house.

Bottles of champagne and vodka were stacked up in the kitchen, way too many for their number. And a huge cardboard box of fireworks sat in the corner. Richard's doing, no doubt. *It's not a party without fireworks*. It was all too much, everything about the day had been out of proportion. First Joe's anger, now this. Libby was walking through a hall of mirrors, her grip on reality warped.

'Is Tess here yet?' she asked Kyle. She'd resisted the question for all of four minutes and even that delay tested her.

'She rang to say she's going to be late,' he answered quickly, almost before she'd finished speaking, like he'd anticipated the question before she'd asked.

She spied the bottles of vodka, decided there was only one way to get through tonight and that was to drink, starting right now. Something had to take the edge off her mood. She poured herself one and then a second. Closed her eyes as she felt the warm flush chase through her system ordering her body to relax.

The vodka encouraged her to make an effort, a shower at the very least and a douse of perfume. She reapplied her make-up, heavier this time, the full works with smoky eyes to boot. Libby was not trying to impress Joe any more, there was no pressure to be her natural self. She was never that fond of that version anyway. She'd reached the lipstick stage, the grand finale of make-up application, when there was a knock on the door and Richard's voice spoke to her from behind it.

'It's me.'

She braced herself. 'Come in.'

'Wow, look at you, stunning!' Rather than lift her mood, his enthusiasm punctured it. Her uncle was the only one who would be complimenting her tonight. Joe's absence throbbed like a sore. If only she could remove him erase him from her memory, cell by cell. Love was too painful to carry around when the object of it had gone. Libby had learnt that lesson years ago.

Richard handed her a glass of champagne. Did vodka and champagne mix? If it got her pissed quicker, it did. She took a swig, the bubbles gathering in the back of her throat.

'How did it go today?' Richard said. There really was no escape. Joe was still dominating the conversation in his absence.

'Badly. I shouldn't have gone.' *Shouldn't have let you persuade me*, she wanted to say, but that would have been her anger talking, searching for a target to blame. 'He wanted to know where Tess was.'

'Oh . . . I'm sorry.'

How she hated that throwaway line, packed full of pity, him jumping to the right conclusion immediately. *He's only interested in Tess. Why can't you see it?* The answer was that she had wanted to believe. She'd discounted the kiss and everything else and still clung on to the belief that Joe loved her. The mind, she thought, what fools it makes of us.

'He accused me of hurting her. And he knows, he knows that I lied to him about you and Freetech.' She tried to keep the accusatory note out of her voice. 'He said I disgust him.' The words came back to torture her. Disgust, such a violent word to be thrown at someone you once loved.

No, she didn't want to cry. The tears were physical evidence she still cared and she didn't want to care. If she had one wish it would be not to give a flying fuck about Joe Hemsley.

Richard sat next to her on the bed and pulled her into him. Her smoky eyes were running into his suit but she was past caring, and when Libby thought about it he deserved a bit of eyeliner on his lapel, because her lies were his. He had told her what to say, what not to say. And that was how she found the question deep inside her, the one that had been there from the start, the one that love and adoration and eagerness to please had buried alive.

'Is there something you haven't told me?'

His arms tightened around her like a vice and she felt her bones being crushed before he pushed her away, held her out in front of him for inspection, and she could see the sadness in his eyes. It looked like grief. She had broken something precious between them that could never be repaired.

Forty

Joe

'Make yourselves at home, you're going to be in here for a while.'

The door shut. The men who'd escorted us in here left us in the dark. From what I could make out, it appeared to be a boiler room, as hot as hell.

'Well, this is cosy,' Clara said when we bumped into each other feeling our way through the dark. 'Do you think we're the surprise guests?'

I didn't want to think. Thinking led me to all the various combinations of violence that were stacking up in my head.

From beyond the door, I could hear Will's voice speaking through the microphone, *testing, testing*, Libby telling him to put a sock in it. It was surreal, a bad dream I couldn't shake off.

'Is he for real?' Clara said.

'Unfortunately.'

We'd barely spoken on the journey – the atmosphere wasn't conducive to conversation – but it was clear from Clara's body language and her initial outburst that my choice to get in the car did not meet with her approval.

'Why would you do that?' She let rip now. 'Why not just take the reg or follow me?'

'I was on foot.'

'You could have hailed a cab.'

'That would have cost a fortune.'

'Fuck off.'

'At least we're not tied up.'

'You're easily pleased. What do you think they're going to do with us?'

'They seem to have organised some kind of a party.' We'd spied boxes of champagne bottles and beers in the hall as we were taken from the car to the store. It would have been easy to shout, to grab attention, if it weren't for the hands around our mouths.

'This isn't a party,' Clara said.

'Well, not for us, it isn't.'

'Not for anyone.'

'Listen . . .' Will was at it again. 'They've even got a karaoke,' I said to prove my point.

'It's weird how you can be so intelligent and yet so thick at the same time. Haven't you worked it out yet? With these people what you see is the opposite of what's going on.'

'But . . .' I admit, my brain was struggling with the concept.

'They might want it to look like a party, but they're not doing this because they're generous, fun-loving guys, are they?'

A bulb illuminated in my head and I saw what I didn't want to see. A party, a gathering of friends in one place. 'They want everyone here who knows about Freetech, and then . . .'

'Let's not think about the then, shall we?' she said. 'Let's put our energies into getting out of here.'

They'd chosen the room well. Far enough away from the main house for no one to hear us scream. No windows to smash. No obvious method of escape. It was just an airless box filled with more boxes and a boiler. The fierce, dry heat sucked the moisture out of my system. I was already down to my T-shirt but the sweat was still dripping into my eyelids. We needed water but strangely enough they hadn't provided refreshments.

'There must be something in here we can use to get out.'

We felt our way around as best we could, not knowing

exactly what it was we were searching for: a key, a sharp object, anything that could assist our escape.

Time. The ticking seconds stirred up panic but I couldn't surrender. Panic would get us nowhere. I tried to swallow but my mouth was parched, my tongue like a foreign body. *Think*. Problem-solving was my thing. I could always think my way around a problem.

I sat down on a box, wasting a few more precious seconds. *The boxes*. 'What's inside these boxes?'

Clara was on it immediately, ripping one open, muttering expletives as she fought her way in. 'It would help if I could see,' she said. 'I don't know what these are.'

She handed me a heavy, thick object, and then another, and another. Different shapes and sizes. I held one to my nose. Charcoal and sulphur.

I knew what they were.

'I think I might have just worked out their plan.'

'Fireworks,' I said. 'We're sitting on boxes of fireworks.'

'You don't seriously think . . .'

'They're going to blow us up like Guy Fawkes.' I laughed. It wasn't the time for laughter but I didn't want to cry and it was one or the other.

'Jesus Christ, I'm already writing the story in my head. Graduates die in—'

'Spare me the details.'

'They'll turn it into a tragic accident. Fire rips through party, I can see the headlines. And it'll look like you and me slunk off for a snog or a fag or something and set the whole room alight. Bang. We're history.'

'I said I didn't want to know.'

'Well, maybe now you do know, you can think of a way to get us out of here.'

'Why me?'

'You should never have got into the car, that's why.'

Two steps in one direction, two in the other. I paced backwards and forwards as if I was expecting the motion to trigger a reaction in my brain. For her part, Clara thumped on the door with her fist and screamed until her body was empty of fight and her voice had grown thin. Thanks to Will's singing, no one heard a thing.

'Joe,' Clara said.

'Yes?'

'I don't want to scare you, but I think it's over.'

That killed the conversation cold. I had nothing to add, beyond *I think you might be right*, so I chose to remain silent. I may not have been capable of speech at any rate; by now my T-shirt and trousers were soaked, my head dizzy from dehydration, my eyes pressed shut, tired of fighting the dark.

I just wanted it to be over.

And it was.

The bang told me as much.

A firework going off under my backside, that was my first thought. And then I was flying out of the room, shunted by a force greater than myself, my eyes still locked shut, too scared to witness my own demise.

Forty-One

Joe

Not a firework.

Someone solid and muscular, dragging me out of the room, into the garden, pulling me down a path and into the overgrowth. A hand clamped over my mouth. No noise. No screams. No scene to attract attention.

Better that way.

The shock whiplashed me, recalibrated a new outcome, one where I was taken into the woods, left for dead, for months, years, while the rain and mud slicked over me. A modern-day Tollund Man.

Being trapped in the house had been bad. The idea of exploding on a pyre of fireworks wasn't great either, but now it seemed almost civilised by comparison. At least it would be quick. Instant, even. Better than having this malign presence, this solid mass next to me, hissing orders and threats. My bones melted in fear, my legs buckled under me. The only part of me willing to put up a fight was my teeth. *Well done, teeth.* One hundred metres or so from the house they sank into the flesh of my assailant's hand.

'What the fuck are you doing?' He jerked me back but didn't let go. The voice. I recognised a frailer, weaker version of it. And then I opened my eyes for the first time since the bang and I saw him.

Tomaz.

'You . . . what are you doing here?'

'Out for a picnic, what does it look like? Just do as I say.' His tone was hostile as he pulled me close to the bushes for cover.

Whose side was he on?

My brain couldn't formulate an answer. Too many unknowns. The known unknowns and the unknown unknowns. How did he know we were here? Where was he taking us? Had they asked him to do this, to end us? They'd paid him once, why not again?

'Why would you hurt us?'

He stopped suddenly and with a single push sent me flying back into the foliage.

'You might be better leaving him here,' he said to Clara. She was here, had been all along, moving silently, without encouragement or physical force. Clara was the chink of light. Clara and her willingness to follow Tomaz. That must mean something but what I couldn't have told you.

'He'll be fine.' Clara stood over me, the whites of her eyes locking with mine. 'A bit slow on the uptake, maybe, but he gets there in the end.'

'Get up, Joe, for fuck's sake,' Tomaz snapped. 'In case you haven't realised, we don't have time to lie in bushes.'

I pulled myself upright, my feet sliding in the mud as I tried to steady myself.

Hope. I felt the shoots of it bloom. I didn't want hope. Hope was the killer. Been there, done that. This time I wanted something more substantial, something concrete by way of confirmation. I needed answers.

'But can you tell me—'

'You either believe me or you stay here. Understand? The questions can wait.'

The questions were never asked. They resolved themselves with the sound of a car that knifed the night's eerie silence.

We'd reached the edge of the drive when we heard it. 'Get down,' Tomaz breathed.

This time my body obeyed. No arguments. The car stopped only a few metres from us, the heat of its engine chilling me. Through the branches I saw a man emerge, talking into his phone, eyes fixed on the house.

I'm here. All set. Time to get Richard and Kyle out.

My heart was a hammer, banging so violently I could have sworn it was echoing into the night. The man ended his call, stepped close to the area where we were hiding, eyes searching the bushes, his head cocked as if listening out for the slightest vibration, a breath, a murmur, a heartbeat.

And then he walked away, treating us to the sound of an ignition being switched, and drove on.

We sat there, the cold night sinking into our limbs. The sky was stuffed with stars, oblivious to the tiny, inconsequential drama playing out a million light years away. It came to me then in an acute flash of insight. We didn't matter. We weren't special or different, whatever grades we achieved, the intelligence nature's lottery had granted us, the money we accumulated, the empires we built. These were simply the lies we told ourselves to plaster over the terror of being nothing. And the bigger lie, the greater folly was to kid ourselves they could insulate us from life's chaos. *This can't be happening to me. I'm too good to die. Do you know who I am?*

It isn't who we are but what we do that sets us apart.

'We'll have to wait for the car to come back down again. If we move now we risk them seeing us on their way out.' Tomaz was right. I told myself this again and again. And I made myself wait with them, too scared to talk, too scared to give voice to my thoughts. Finally, our patience was rewarded by the sight of Richard, lit by the wash of bright light from the porch, scurrying out of the house and into the car, followed by Kyle.

The car that took them down the drive, away from the house and sank into the night.

'Let's go,' Tomaz whispered. 'My car is about a quarter of a mile away, the only place I could find that wasn't obvious.' Tomaz was talking but his words were rinsed out as if I were hearing them underwater, at a remove.

'Hurry up,' he said.

I breathed. I had to speak now, I couldn't hide any longer. 'I'm not coming,' I said.

Richard and Kyle in the car. Richard. Kyle. The driver. No one else. The image pressed deep into my brain until it hurt. And the hurt found the doubt that had already taken root in my mind and together they began to unpick everything. Libby. What was the level of her involvement? She was not in the car with Richard and Kyle. Libby was still in the house. Whatever they had planned for us tonight, and I didn't doubt that something *was* planned, Libby was part of the deal. No get out of jail card for her. Her status was not going to protect her.

The hurt was on to something now, travelling like a tornado through my head, ripping up everything I'd pinned down in the last few days. Libby had betrayed me, betrayed everyone. She was a liar, said as much herself, callously trying to downplay the gravity of what she had done.

And yet.

And yet.

The hurt said this:

Libby is still in the house.

Awaiting a fate unknown.

Why believe the worst when the evidence veers the other way? She let you out of the cellar. She wanted to come with you. To escape.

She love/d you.

What if she is a victim too?

249

What if Richard used her, like he used us, withheld the full truth of what he was doing? Obtaining passwords, hacking emails of political campaigners, activists, the opposition. That's not Libby's style.

Your anger has left no space for reason.

Think about it.

Think hard.

Think of her Lady Macduff in Macbeth. The worst actress you have ever seen.

She couldn't fake her love.

Couldn't fake her indignation when you accused her.

She lied. But she thought her lie was small. No harm done. What if Richard lied to her?

'I'm going back,' I repeated.

'You're fucking kidding me? I've just risked my life for you. I owed you this, you saved me. But we're quits now, do you hear me? You get yourself into trouble, you find a way out. Alone.'

'I can't just leave her in there, Libby . . . any of them. We can't just leave them and run away. They could all be dead soon.'

'Listen, this isn't fucking *Die Hard*, OK? We can't get everyone out of there, it's too dangerous. We've got more hope getting to my car and getting help.'

I thought about this. A fire engine, if a fire was what they had planned, how long would that take to arrive, out here, miles from anywhere? They'd all be gone before anyone could reach them. That was the beauty of the plan. The warped genius of it.

'He's right,' Clara said but her normal certainty had deserted her. 'At least we can do something if we're not locked inside the house.'

She was right. He was right. I no longer cared. I couldn't leave them. Couldn't leave Libby. And that's how it happened, before I even knew it myself, before they could stop me, my legs were carrying me back towards the house.

Forty-Two

Libby

If Libby hadn't been so drunk she would have been angry. Beyond angry, livid in fact. Some party, she thought as she poured another glass of champagne. Tess was late, and now Richard had gone to collect her from the station in Wivelton, taking Kyle with him as if it were a two-man job. 'We've got an urgent business call to make on the way,' was his reason when she pressed him. Business was always prefixed with urgent where Richard was concerned, a sure way to close down any questions.

And that was that, she was left with Will and Asha. And Dom.

Why was he here? She had specifically requested that Dom not be invited because he was a creep with violent tendencies and he stared in a way that unsettled her. Richard had appeared troubled when she first told him, though not quite troubled enough for her liking, but still, he had nodded in agreement and said *of course I understand*, when clearly he hadn't understood a damn thing because Dom was here.

'You promised,' Libby reminded Richard when she saw Dom's bulky frame walk through the door earlier that evening.

'Not everything revolves around your needs, Libby, hard as that is to understand.' And just like that she was cut down to half her size. She'd heard Richard speak in that manner before, to Dana, to his secretary, even to Max and Matilda. But never to her. His words were always honey-coated and soft and in return she covered him in adoration, like icing a cake, making him more appetising than the raw ingredients deserved.

At least Richard's frostiness and subsequent departure solved one problem. Asha and Will had not guessed their connection. She presumed that her colleagues would have detected an intimacy between them and Libby would be forced to come clean, *Did I not mention my uncle was the boss? I got the job fair and square, though*. Whatever explanation she tried out, nothing rang true. She sounded like the fraud she was. And then Richard came to her rescue, treating her with such cool disdain there was no suspicion to answer and Libby couldn't decide whether she was outraged or relieved.

Define the word party, she challenged herself. It certainly wouldn't be this. There was nothing in the dictionary that mentioned eating two packets of Kettle Chips, half a dirty burger (which tasted like every other burger she'd ever eaten) and drinking . . . she'd lost count of how much she'd drunk. The only bonus was Asha keeping her company, matching her drink for drink, and the pair of them enjoying a decent chat about men and the perpetual disappointment that came with them, and how the next time someone in Freetech mentioned team-building they'd be sacked on the spot because this had been such an unqualified disaster.

And then Will turned on the karaoke and started singing Chesney Hawkes and that was the end of that.

Her head demanded she go to bed. Sod Tess, keeping them waiting all this time. Libby couldn't even find her anger any more, it had sunk into a pool of vodka and champagne. Best wait till the morning to confront her. By that time she would have the mother of all hangovers and there would be no need to search for her rage; it would be there waiting for her when she woke.

'I need to go to bed,' she said to no one in particular, but Asha caught her words and pointed to her watch.

It was only nine thirty.

And Dom heard her too because that was his job; to watch and listen all the time.

'You can't go now, we've got the fireworks.'

Libby did not like being told what to do. Least of all by Dom. If she wanted to go to bed that was exactly what she was going to do. The prospect of fireworks was not going to change her mind. Why had she never told Richard she hated fireworks? Right from the time when her mum was still around and their labrador Mavis would cower behind the sofa and poo herself in fright at the rockets and the Catherine wheels whizzing by their window. So fireworks didn't make Libby think *PARTY!* They made her think of a dog whimpering, her mother down on her hands and knees cleaning up a mess, and the lingering stench of shit.

She ignored Dom, moved towards the door and watched him step towards her, a small jerk as if he were man marking her in a football match.

'I'm going to the loo, for God's sake. Do you want to come too?'

This was not a complete fabrication; at this stage of inebriation there was never a time when Libby did not need a wee. She walked to the downstairs bathroom, pulled her trousers down and experienced the sweet relief of her bladder emptying. It was when she was washing her hands, considering her face in the mirror, the heavily applied mask of make-up beginning to slip, that she became aware of voices outside, a car's engine dying.

They must be back.

Quickly, she washed her hands, re-emerged into the hallway. It was empty. But she detected a fractional change, evidence of recent movement in the air. Her eyes travelled up the spiral staircase in time to see the back of a head melt into the darkness of the landing.

She moved fast, negotiating the stairs as quickly as possible, but by the time she reached the first floor whoever was there had gone. All she heard was the gentle closing of a door. She went straight to Tess's room, knocked quietly at first and then louder. No answer. Libby turned the handle, poked her head inside, flicked the light switch. Tess wasn't there. She moved along the landing, listening at each door for the sound of life. She knew Will was still downstairs because she could hear him murdering U2. She opened the door to Asha's room. The mess of it raised a smile, the polar opposite of Kyle's extreme tidiness. And then she closed the door again, moved down the corridor to her own room, pressing her ear to the door as if listening out for an intruder.

There was an intruder.

Her senses, dulled with booze, were awakened now. Who the hell was in her room? She imagined Dom rooting around for what, she had no idea, but he seemed the type to be where he wasn't welcome. She'd warned Richard about him, hadn't she, only he'd paid no heed. Well, this was the final straw. She would not stand for this.

Her hand shook as she opened the door, the expletives lined up ready to fire.

But the man who was in her room wanted her to be quiet – why else would he have his finger over his mouth? And she didn't scream or call him a prying bastard. For a moment she said nothing at all, because the man in her room wasn't Dom.

It was Joe.

'What are you doing here?' She forced the words out finally. She wished she could draw the alcohol out of her system to think straight, talk without slurring.

'We need to go.'

We. That was news to her. There *was* no we. He had spelt that out with words that cut and ripped and destroyed whatever they had left.

You disgust me.

254

World Population/Time Abroad

Country	Population in Millions	Capital	Hours Fast or slow on EST
Argentina	28.4	Buenos Aires	+ 2
Australia	14.9	Canberra	+15
Belgium	9.9	Brussels	+ 6
Brazil	121.6	Brasilia	+ 2
Canada	24.6	Ottawa	EST
Chile	11.5	Santiago	+ 2
Colombia	27.1	Bogotá	EST
Egypt	44.7	Cairo	+ 7
France	54.0	Paris	+ 6
Germany (FR)	61.6	Bonn	+ 6
Greece	9.7	Athens	+ 7
Hong Kong	5.2	Victoria	+13
India	676.2	Delhi	+10½
Indonesia	150.5	Jakarta	+12
Israel	4.0	Jerusalem	+ 7
Italy	57.2	Rome	+ 6
Japan	117.7	Tokyo	+14
Luxembourg	0.4	Luxembourg	+ 6
Malaysia	14.4	Kuala Lumpur	+13
Mexico	71.2	Mexico City	– 1
Netherlands	14.3	Amsterdam	+ 6
Nigeria	79.7	Lagos	+ 6
Peru	18.8	Lima	EST
Philippines	50.7	Quezon City	+13
Saudi Arabia	9.3	Riyadh	+ 8
Singapore	2.5	Singapore	+13
South Africa	30.1	Pretoria	+ 7
South Korea	39.3	Seoul	+14
Spain	37.9	Madrid	+ 6
Sweden	8.3	Stockholm	+ 6
Switzerland	6.5	Berne	+ 6
Thailand	48.5	Bangkok	+12
United Kingdom	55.8	London	+ 5
USA	229.8	Washington	EST
USSR	267.7	Moscow	+ 8
Venezuela	14.3	Caracas	+ 1

Countries included in this table are selected according to volume of trade with the USA.

HOLIDAYS IN THE UNITED KINGDOM 1989

Year	England and Wales	Northern Ireland	Scotland
New Year	Jan. 1✝, (Jan. 2)	Jan. 1✝, (Jan. 2)	Jan. 2, Jan. 3
St Patrick	—	Mar. 17	—
Good Friday	Mar. 24≠	Mar. 24 ≠	Mar. 24
Easter Monday	Mar. 27	Mar. 27	—
May Day	May 1	May 1	May 1
Spring	May 29	May 29	May 29
Battle of the Boyne	—	July 12	—
Summer	Aug. 28	Aug. 28	Aug. 7
Christmas	Dec. 25 ≠, Dec. 26	Dec. 25 ≠, Dec. 26	Dec. 25, Dec. 26

≠ Common Law Holiday   * Holiday falls on a Saturday   ✝ Holiday falls on a Sunday

She wasn't going to forget that in a hurry.

'Go where?' Her tone didn't convey adequate levels of indignation, but it was the best she could do in the circumstances.

'You have to get out of here.'

'Why?'

'We don't have time for questions, just believe me, you need to get out. I'll explain later.'

No, you won't.

Libby was done with being patronised by men, men who thought they could order her around: her uncle, who made her stay here when she wanted to leave, who told her what she thought and who she was, *sweet, helpful Libby.* And Dom, who was some kind of self-appointed minder. Now Joe too.

She wasn't having any of it.

'You expect me to jump when you click your fingers. Just like that. No explanation, no apology.'

'I'm sorry,' he said. That was a start, at least. 'But it's for your own good.'

Whoa! Did he really just say that? *For your own good. I know best.*

'How fucking dare you!'

'Libby,' he tried to inject his voice with a tenderness that she knew was not one hundred per cent genuine. There was something else simmering beneath it, an impatience, a frustration. She studied him. He wasn't quite right either. Wasn't a lot right. His T-shirt was caked in mud, his hands filthy, nails black, his eyes glazed with a kind of mania that frightened her.

Should she scream for help?

'Please don't make a sound.' He could read her mind, she used to love that about him once. But that was before.

He moved one step closer to her. And another.

She moved one further away. She was threatened, exposed.

'Libby, you have to come with me now.'

'Or else?'

'Or else you're going to get hurt.'

The threat. Clear as day. Dark as night. He was going to hurt her if she didn't do what he said.

Now she screamed, tried to at least, but she'd barely let out a sound when Joe was upon her, his hand over her mouth. 'Shut up,' he said. 'I'll explain, OK?' But he didn't move his hand.

'You don't know what's going on, do you?' There it was again, the patronising *poor Libby doesn't understand*. But he wasn't done; on he went as the anger possessed her. 'I thought you knew, that's why I said all those things earlier. Your uncle is being paid millions to hack the accounts of influential political figures and activists. That's what we've been doing, Libby. We're not working for our clients, we've been attacking them. He conned all of us.'

'No,' she said. It came out as a grunt.

'No what? No, you knew, or no, you don't believe me?'

'No,' she said again. It was impossible to explain the no. She would need days, years. A lifetime. It meant everything. Who she was, what she believed in. The love and trust, every single memory from the age of nine. It had to be no.

'They're planning something tonight. They were watching us in the café, do you know that? Someone followed me out and brought me and Clara back here and locked us in the boiler room. Clara is a reporter . . . Oh, for fuck's sake, we don't have time for all of this, there's too much to explain. We need to get out.' He removed his hand from her face and she snatched at the air for breath.

'What about Tess?'

He shook his head. 'Tess knew. She was passing on informa-tion to the police. And no one has seen her for days.'

A tide of nausea washed over Libby. The police, a conspiracy, illegal activity, Tess. Joe was dangling her over a dark and bottomless well, and if she listened, allowed the allegations space to roam in her head, she knew that would be the end of her.

'No,' she said again. All the other words had been wiped from her vocabulary. She was reduced to a single denial.

'Think about it, Libby. Think about it. Tess was in the woods. I saw her and went to find her, that was when I was knocked out. The next thing I knew I was waking up in the morning and by that time she was gone.'

Libby opened her mouth again to repeat the denial only to find it had been stolen. Stolen by the blood in the woods, the blood that found its way on to her hands and clothes. The blood in the spot where she last saw Tess.

Fake blood. That was what Richard had said, and she had wanted it to be plausible, and for a while it had seemed so, his explanation dressed with such confidence it was hard to argue. But she'd known, at her core, that distant place she rarely looked, Libby had known it wasn't true. And now she *was* looking, right down inside herself in microscopic detail, and it wasn't a pretty sight. It was like she'd lifted a stone and found her doubts seething like insects underneath. The party that wasn't a party, but a stage for something else. Richard's departure. Tess's no show.

'I don't care if you hate me,' Joe said. 'I don't care if you never want to see me again after this, just come with me now. Get out of here while we still can.'

'Why?' she said.

'Why what?'

'Why would you bother with me? If you're that worried, just go without me.'

He looked at her, that doleful, wide-eyed stare he used to give her, and she thought of everything they had wasted, could never recover.

'Because I love you.'

It was obvious then. Nothing had ever been clearer.

He loved her. She loved him.

And because she loved him she couldn't go with him. She had to stay.

'I knew,' she said. It was the only way.

He shook his head violently to empty it of the words she had just spoken. 'No, you didn't,' his voice carried a cold authority, his pupils dark like bullets. He was not going to be easily fooled. She'd have to try harder.

'I knew all along,' she pushed the words out, each one cutting her deeper than the last. 'He's my uncle, for Christ's sake. I'm a director of the company, I knew everything right from the start.'

'You're a terrible actor, Libby, you wouldn't be able to fake it.'

'Don't make this harder than it is.'

'You're coming with me.' He grabbed her arm, his grip pinching her skin as he pulled her across the room.

'Joe,' she pushed him off, wrestled free and stared straight into his eyes. She had to say it, no matter the hurt. 'I don't love you. I never did.'

Confusion clouded his face; he couldn't make sense of what she was telling him. His eyes were dark and still. It was his body that shook, as if an internal explosion was taking place, obliterating everything he felt, everything he knew, all he believed.

She couldn't bear to look. This was what she had done.

'Get out of here,' she screamed and she pulled at his filthy T-shirt, ripping it, clawing at his skin to make him move. But he wouldn't give in.

'Not without you.'

She almost caved. It would be easier to give in, wouldn't it? Her body softened, teetered on the cusp of surrender. She was so tired of this useless defiance, utterly enticed by the alternative. *Go with him. Get out. Leave Richard behind.* God knows she was terrified of staying, of what lay in store. And yet she knew she had to.

But still, he wouldn't leave her. This time he dragged her across the room more forcibly. And in turn she did everything within her power to fight him off, shake herself free, clawing, kicking, scratching. And that's how it happened, she supposed. Neither to blame. Both to blame. They were locked in a tug of war and all he did was relax his grip, suddenly, so suddenly that it sent her flying backwards towards the floor and the moment of impact. She remembered the noise, a strange, unexpected sound of something breaking within her and a constellation of stars exploding in her head.

Forty-Three

Joe

Libby was knocked unconscious, either by the porcelain floor or by my own hand, it really depends on which way you want to look at it. I'll admit to erring on the side of the floor because it put me in a better light. I was not a violent person. But the truth is we all surprise ourselves at some point in our lives. Depravity is not a stranger, it's part of us; all we have to do is create the right conditions for it to flourish.

Libby had turned me into a man I didn't recognise, a man I despised, and I wanted to hate her. But loving her wasn't a choice, it was a reality I couldn't escape. It was part of me.

In hindsight I think that's why I was slow to react. To touch her, to shout for help, to do something would have made it real, and I didn't think I could withstand the pain. So I waited, suspended in that agonising moment, unable to act, yet knowing that time was running out. The noises outside finally broke my paralysis. Footsteps on gravel, a car door opening. At the window I saw Dom and one of the men who had brought us here getting into a car. And then a few seconds later they were gone. The night had devoured them.

By my calculations that left me and Libby plus Asha and Will. I ran out of the room and that's when it hit me, the smoke rising upwards, rolling towards us.

I told myself it was the smoke machine for no other reason than I wanted it to be true. It's one thing to anticipate an imminent threat, another to face it head on at the point where it's no longer a threat, but real. The realest thing you've ever dealt with in your entire life.

It wasn't the smoke machine. Smoke machines don't dispense clouds of blackness that spread within minutes and seize your lungs with such force you can't breathe. I tried to shout but nothing came out, no air in those lungs, and the heat, the heat was racing across my back and filling my head.

I retreated. Back to the room. Slammed the door. Libby on the floor. She hadn't moved. Of course she hadn't. I grabbed her arms and hauled her towards the window. If I could get her out on to the roof she'd have a chance, a small one at least. But all the power had run out of me, my legs weak, my arms limp and my body collapsing. *Open the window. Open the window.* But the window was locked and there was no key, only screams now, carrying upstairs on the wings of the smoke and Amy Winehouse's distant voice on the karaoke lulling me into the blackness.

Forty-Four

Libby

Libby stirred, tried to open her eyes, but all she could see was a dark shroud descending. And she couldn't remember how she'd ended up on the floor of a room in a house that stood for everything she had lost: her mother, her grandmother, the warmth, the familiarity, the comforting clutter, the ceramic owls and their big watchful eyes, but here she was. And even in the treacle blackness, with the heat, the fierce, alien heat spreading over her body, she could see everything for what it was, brighter than she ever had.

The only thing that confused her was why it had taken so long.

And now what? Had Joe got out? She couldn't see him but then she couldn't see anything at all. She hoped he had. Hoped with such a fervour it hurt. *I don't love you. I never did.* That was for his own good. In this case she knew better than him, not the other way around. He needed to go and Libby needed to stick it out.

Joe wouldn't have understood and she didn't have time to explain, but she had to make up her own mind, see with her own two eyes what was going on. That was the crux of it. She needed to know because Richard had been her foundation, shaping her with his version of the truth: her mother taking her own life, leaving her only daughter behind, him having her best interests in mind, sending her off to boarding school for her own good. And now this, the doubts over his business activities, him telling her one thing, the evidence pointing the other way.

Every scrap and morsel she had been fed for the past thirteen years had come from Richard's table and that was no way to live as an adult. It was time to fend for herself.

But first she needed to know. There was power in knowledge and even if everything else was ripped from under her, at least that would remain. Besides, if this *was* a mess, it was one she had helped manufacture and Libby did not get to walk out on it early.

Now here she was. On the floor, unable to move. And she knew. The truth was all around her, in the blackness and the heat and the smoke choking her lungs. She knew everything. She knew who Richard was. What he had done. Only the truth wasn't empowering in the way she'd envisaged. She'd cocked that one up royally, arriving at the truth too late when the fire had already stolen the power. Libby lay there and thought, *Well, this is it.* There wasn't much more she could do. And when she felt herself being lifted and carried she didn't fight; all the fight in her had gone because the fire had the power and there was nothing she could do to wrestle it back.

Forty-Five

Richard

I know what you're thinking, how convenient that I left the house directly before the fire. Well, let me say this: there is proof of a business call to Australia from my phone on that night, about five minutes after we left. You can't seriously believe I knew the house was going to go up in flames. It was *my* house, remember. Three years fighting planners and goddam nimbies for permission and another one year for the build. That's not even taking into account the money, treble what it should have cost once Dana got involved with her Italian stone this and concrete that. I would have been mad to destroy it.

And of course, my niece was in there too.

The call came close to midnight that evening. Dana and I were in bed, having sex for the first time for months. It was a furious, urgent encounter, the kind in which to hide yourself. We'd only just finished when she said, 'It's going to be OK, I'm sure of it.'

And then the phone rang.

I should have known never to trust a thing that woman said.

It was the police delivering news of the fire. I held the phone away from me, barely able to listen for fear of what they might reveal. Dana was clawing at my arm, *What is it? Who is it?* and I shooed her away, concentrating on the details the officer was imparting: Libby was in hospital, rescued from the fire by a man called Tomaz Ramsay.

'I'm afraid to say she has not yet regained consciousness.'

Tomaz Ramsay. I knew that name. He was the police officer to whom Tess had been passing information. What the hell was he doing on my property? I was told he had been dealt with.

'You have a lot to thank him for,' the voice said. 'He's in a bad way.'

'How bad?' I asked hopefully.

Questions, the police fired so many at me in those first twenty-four hours it was a miracle I managed to contain my anger. How many people were in the house? Why were they there? Had I any idea how the fire could have started?

'Often it's a faulty appliance to blame,' said one of the fire officers.

'I can assure you all my appliances are of the highest quality.'

They counted four out. Joe, Asha, Will and Libby.

'Just the four?'

'That's right. Is there someone unaccounted for?' I was thinking of that reporter who'd been causing all the problems. And Joe. They were there too. 'My mistake,' I said, 'I forgot the fifth guest left a few days earlier.' And I closed my eyes and tried not to think about charred remains.

Then there was *Tess* to contend with. Gone, but very much the topic of conversation. Her parents had reported her missing a day earlier after trying and failing to reach her. Word must have reached the police that she was last seen in the woods, because before I could raise an objection an army of officers was combing the area, picking through every last twig and branch.

They wanted to question me about her too. I told them I had never set eyes on the girl but they assured me it was all routine.

'What are we going to say?' Dana asked. She'd dropped the reassurance act and reverted to type, expecting me to provide all the answers.

'We're going to say nothing, nothing at all beyond offering our condolences.'

'Wouldn't that suggest we knew what had happened to her?'

'For goodness' sake, Dana, you know exactly what I mean. We offer them tea and assistance and nothing more.'

The detectives were perfectly pleasant in a provincial way, a woman and a man. Dullards, I suppose, the kind you'd rotate the room to avoid at a party.

As in most situations, the woman did the lion's share of the talking. She had a yappy voice and two protruding front teeth, and I listened to her with a degree of bemusement as if she were a terrier barking out the questions.

Dana stuck to the script for all of two minutes before veering dramatically off piste. What is it about women that they feel the need to overshare?

The detective, I can't remember her name, asked if we knew anything about Tess to which Dana replied, 'Only what our niece told Richard.'

The detectives' eyes drifted to me. 'And what did she tell you about Tess, Mr Gilligan Thomas?'

'She wasn't fond of her,' Dana answered on my behalf. 'She thought at one point she might be selling information, you know, for her own gain. It would have been very valuable in the wrong hands. And Libby is such a stickler for the rules she would not have stood for any of that nonsense.'

'Nothing was ever proven,' I added, training the heat of my stare on Dana.

'Oh, and she thought Tess was trying to steal her boyfriend. I suppose you could say there was a bit of jealousy. They're all insecure at that age, aren't they? Always seeking out a drama.'

'Do you know when your niece last saw Tess?'

'Yes, she told Richard. She saw her in the woods the night of the zombie apocalypse game . . . I know . . . my idea of hell.

She wanted to talk to her because they'd had an argument that day.'

'I see,' said the officer as if a picture had just become clearer.

'What the hell is the matter with you?' I demanded after the police officers left. I was spoiling for a fight but Dana made me wait, her head deep in the fridge selecting a bottle of wine.

When she emerged she looked at me with something akin to pity. 'You have to give them something, Richard, otherwise they'll keep prying. You'll thank me for it soon.'

I revisited this exchange many times, both in the days that followed and later. Dana wasn't just feeding the police some throwaway lines to keep them happy; my wife knew exactly what she was doing. She had her target within range. So if you ask me if I feel bad about what happened subsequently, I'd say yes, of course, but the truth is she brought it all on herself.

PART THREE

PART THREE

Forty-Six

Joe

Lewes Police Station
October 2017

Libby wasn't the only one Tomaz rescued from the fire. Whatever he said to the contrary, he definitely had notions of *Die Hard* that evening. Me, Libby, Asha and Will have him to thank for our lives. Only he's still in hospital, hooked up to a ventilator, unconscious. The thank-yous will have to wait. But I'm certain he'll pull through. I can't entertain any other outcome.

I was in hospital for a short spell with smoke inhalation. The food wasn't great and it's impossible to get a good night's sleep but I could have stuck it out another few days if the police hadn't had other ideas.

Libby has a head injury. She has not regained consciousness. And I was the only person in the room with her. They think I wanted to hurt her and judging by their expressions, nothing I've told them in the last eight hours has changed their minds.

My solicitor is slumped in his chair. He is a friend of a friend of an acquaintance of my parents brought out of retirement for one last appearance. DS Blaine rubs his eyes, his partner, DS Mirchini, stifles a yawn that reminds me I haven't slept. For how long? One day? Two? It's impossible to say. Time has lost its structure. I need a shower. My own body odour is offensive, and my teeth are coated in fur. Basically, I'm emitting fumes from all orifices. These things shouldn't matter given the gravity of the situation, but strangely they do. As if me being clean and fresh can revive Libby and Tomaz, locate Tess.

There is a knock on the door and a head appears from behind it.

'Can I have a word?' It's a detective I've never seen before.

DS Blaine stops the tape, gets up and leaves the room.

The vague hum of their conversation is audible but its contents are not. I suspect DS Mirchini is as curious as I am. He sits up straight, leans his body towards the wall as if he can ingest its substance from there. A few minutes pass before Blaine enters the room again and calls Mirchini out. The energy is shifting, banishing the sluggish air that has been sedating us, not that my solicitor seems to notice. His eyes are shut, arms crossed. He must be missing his afternoon nap. I stand up, stretch my legs, encourage the blood flow to my head. My radar tells me I need to be alert, something is heading my way.

'Can you think back to last Tuesday night?' DS Blaine is present once more. The interview restarted.

'I can,' I say. Although I'd rather not.

'A game of zombie apocalypse, is that right? You were all out in the woods playing.'

'Yes.'

'Did you see Tess Langton in the woods that evening?'

'Yes.'

'And did you speak to her?'

'No.'

'Did you approach her?'

'I tried to.'

'You tried to?'

'I saw her and ran towards her because I knew she wanted to get away.'

'Why did she want to get away?'

I sigh. We've been over this countless times. 'I've already told you, she was a police informant and Kyle knew what she was doing. She was in danger.'

They exchange a look and I know what's coming next. 'And we've already told you there is no record of any such operation, or government links, or a conspiracy to silence political campaigners.' A smile rises on his face. They think I'm delusional.

'She wanted out and I wanted to help her.' I tone down the story for their consumption.

'And did you?'

'No, because I was knocked out. I was running towards her and the next thing I knew I was waking up in the woods hours later with a cut on my head.'

'We've found evidence of Tess Langton's blood in the woods.'

Tess's blood.

I want to run as far from this room as I can, to escape from what they are telling me. But instead, they have me trapped, searching my face for a reaction, and I don't know what it reveals or how my features interpret my emotions, but I know this: my insides are shattering.

I summon her image, the dancing on the first night, the jokes that cut through Kyle's crap, the face tanned by the sun, a riot of freckles. Did I love her? I think I did. But not in the way Libby suspected. I loved her because beneath the fear I could see she was funny and offbeat. She had spirit and fight and courage.

DS Blaine, whose large white face has acquired a sheen of sweat, asks, 'Is there anything you want to say?'

Do you think she's dead? This is what I want to ask, but I say nothing. The set of Blaine's face tells me he has a question of his own.

Did you kill her?

Forty-Seven

Libby

L ibby is awake, her body heavy and sore and her vision slicked with a film of Vaseline, but she is awake nevertheless. She enjoys a few minutes of peace before her revival is noted and causes a stir among the nurses.

'Hello,' one of them says, peering into her eyes. 'You've had us all worried.'

The next few hours or days (time is hard to pin down) float around her, punctuated by nurses administering medication, taking her blood pressure, her stats.

The fire.

This she remembers mainly because she can still taste it in her mouth, like she's feasted on burning plastic. The nurse whose name is Trudie has also explained she has a head injury, and Libby can see an image of herself in the room at Kenton Thorpe lying prone on the floor, as if she is watching herself from above.

They do not explain how she came to be lying on the floor, though she wishes they could. In the passage between unconscious and conscious her memories have burrowed themselves deep into the recesses of her brain, and for now, at least, it hurts too much to excavate them.

'You're stronger than you look,' says one middle-aged doctor with a bald red head and unfortunate teeth. She can't work out whether he's being patronising or complimentary before deciding she doesn't care either way. Libby is woozy and light, like she's drifting on clouds. Somewhere, she can hear the distant echo of her anger, but what it is saying, what it is telling her she can't discern. Her mood flows on a straight trajectory, no bumps or blips.

It could be the blow to the head. Libby knows there are legions of stories about people who have turned volatile and aggressive as a result of a head injury – damage to the frontal and temporal lobes the culprit. But the other way around? It could be the drugs, pulsing through her system, turning her into a better version of herself. Placid, calm. Chilled out.

The arrival of the police has the potential to ruin her zen, but since only a few questions are permitted at first, they don't trouble her.

'Joe was in the room with you when this happened,' one of the detectives tells her. And Libby knows this to be true as soon as she hears it, the statement triggers a memory. She nods in the direction of the female officer whose name has floated straight out of her grasp.

'Were you arguing?' she asks.

They were. She can see a snapshot of his expression, the concentrated rage in his face.

'Did Joe try to hurt you?' Libby thinks about this, casting back to what seems like a century ago.

'No,' she says. That doesn't ring true, her instincts point in the opposite direction.

'Are you sure?'

'Yes,' Libby says. And slowly, fragments of that night present themselves all jumbled up, like someone has scrambled the pieces of a jigsaw puzzle.

'How did you hurt your head?'

'I fell.'

'Did he push you?'

Libby hesitates. *Did he?* She can't say one way or another with any certainty.

'I don't think so.'

'You don't think so.'

She wants to expand but every word scratches her throat. She has to use them carefully.

'You don't have to protect him, you know.'

'I know.'

They want to press further but something beeps on a machine and Nurse Trudie marches over, her blond ponytail swishing and swinging like a propeller.

'You'll have to come back later,' she says.

'When can I go home?' she asks the doctor but he only shrugs as if it isn't his decision.

'It's above my pay grade,' Trudie says when she directs the same question at her. At some stage Richard appears under a cloud of concern armed with grapes and flowers. Libby doesn't like grapes and the flowers are rejected according to hospital policy, but it's the thought that counts.

She should be pleased to see him, overjoyed at a friendly face smothering her in sympathy and well wishes, but her reactions are limp. She blames it on the drugs and the trauma. Maybe she'll never get exercised about anything again.

Richard grips her hands in his, a little too forcefully, to be truthful, but she will excuse him; he must have been beside himself with worry these past few days. He has bags under his papery white skin.

'Thank God you're OK,' he says. 'Dana sends her love.'

The police return, each visit incrementally longer, the questions probing deeper, furrowing in wounds and disputes, raking up throwaway comments as if they meant something. They want to know what went on at Kenton Thorpe. *Was it harmonious, or were there rivalries? Did they fight?*

What can she tell them about her relationship with Tess?

★

Tess. The name unleashes a vortex of emotions and she tries to sift through them only to find at the very centre there is one more pressing, more urgent than all the others: an absence, a loss, her disappearance.

'Have you found her?' she asks.

'You knew she was missing?'

'She left, but . . .' There is a but and she pauses to allow it to come into focus. 'But Kyle said she was coming to the party.'

'She didn't turn up, though, did she?'

'No.'

'Did you like her?' The directness of the question slaps her. Did she like her? No. The honest answer is Libby did not. *Shall I tell you all the things I disliked about her, starting with her floaty dresses and her flowery hair accessories, the dancing, her enviable magnetic energy that hogged all the light, the kiss she shared with Joe? The fact all anyone cares about is Tess, Tess, Tess.*

'She was perfectly nice.'

'Nice, that's a damning word,' the male detective says. And she feels it, the smallest prick on her skin, the air sharpening, a knife turning. 'Did you argue with her?'

'We had a few misunderstandings.'

'Such as?'

'I walked in on her kissing my boyfriend.' Too much information, Libby knows this as soon as the words are out there, but it's like she's swallowed a truth potion. She cannot lie. Not any more.

'I'd say that is more than a misunderstanding. I'd say that's enough to make you pretty angry. Did you confront her?'

'We had words afterwards.'

'And when was this?'

'On the afternoon before the zombie game in the woods.'

'Did you physically fight?'

'She pushed me.'

'Why did she push you?'

'I had her bag. She was trying to get away and I just wanted to talk to her.'

'You stole her bag and when you refused to give it back she pushed you?'

'I didn't steal it, I was going to return it.'

'And all this happened a few hours before she disappeared,' the woman says and leaves the statement there, sitting like an unexploded bomb between them.

Later, as Libby is considering the soup, a watery offering masquerading as potato and leek, the detective and her partner return. She expects Trudie to tell them to go, let her eat in peace, but she simply swishes out of the room and leaves them alone.

'DS Foley and I have a few more questions,' says the partner, another one with a name she can't remember. What else is there to ask? Surely she's been over everything. No wonder the police budget is stretched.

'I honestly don't—'

'We've found Tess Langton's blood in the woods.'

The detective's mouth is moving but Libby can't hear a thing. Her senses have shut down, short-circuited with the power of the news. A drink, that's what she needs. The thirst is burning her throat. There is a bottle of Coke by the side of her bed but she can't turn her head to locate it, or summon the energy to speak. She feels herself slipping away, drawing a commotion of doctors and nurses into the room as she goes.

When she comes round, she finds the questions have been patiently waiting for her, stacked up neatly, one on top of the other.

'Can you think of anyone who would want to hurt Tess?'

Her mind backflips to a conversation with Joe, one that has flown in and out of her mental radar; each time she dismissed it as a fantasy, as something her drug-addled brain had conjured up, but now, in the absence of anything else, she offers it to the police.

'Joe told me Tess was working for the police . . .' Libby stops. The sudden, rushing sound in her ears is deafening. And worse, much worse, are the locked-away memories hurtling from their hiding places to bombard her. She can see it now, in blistering technicolour, exactly where the sentence is taking her, the final destination in which Richard cheated and lied and is party to criminal activity. Her heart rate gathers pace, sweat pools underneath her hospital issue gown, under her arms, in the middle of her back. The room sways. She doesn't want to go there but there is no other way, it is the only route available.

'We've found no record of any such police operation,' DS Foley says. And Libby exhales. She can't trust her memories. Can't trust herself.

'If you don't mind, I'm tired now,' she tells them.

Forty-Eight

Richard

I tried calling Matt Collingwood to ask him about the Tomaz guy and what the hell he was doing at my house, but his number was unobtainable. Bastard. I rued the day Dana persuaded me to go to that barbecue, because if I had refused, I would never have met Collingwood and succumbed to his hospitality and agreed to enter into his dodgy scheme. I wouldn't be where I am now. Dana has a lot to answer for.

Not that you would have guessed from the way she stalked around the house like everything was under control, not a hair out of place, fully made up, smelling of flowers, her boobs, the ones I gifted her, sticking out like pistols daring me to cross her. I don't know what it was I wanted; it definitely wasn't her tears – the woman is a hell of an ugly crier – maybe just a small acknowledgement that we were one step away from calamity.

I went to visit Libby in hospital. 'You're awake, thank God,' I said. I brought grapes and flowers but I can't even remember her thanking me. I didn't stay long, she wasn't up to much conversation. On my way out I charmed a nurse into giving me an update on Tomaz Ramsay. 'Well, I'm not supposed to, but . . .'

He was still unconscious. Not much of a hero now, I thought.

On my return from hospital Dana was waiting for me with a barrage of questions. She disguised her intentions with a gin and tonic and a bowl of olives, and another of pretzels – my favourites – and then she started.

'How is Libby?'

'She's awake.'

'Yes, we knew that already, Richard. Have the police been in to see her?'

'I didn't ask.'

'You didn't ask.' She had a habit of repeating me in order to underline my stupidity.

'That's what I said.'

'Remind me what it was Libby asked you about Tess's disappearance, that thing she said about the blood.'

It was all very tiresome but when Dana was in one of those moods there was no escaping. 'Libby told me she went into the woods and found blood in the area she'd last seen Tess.'

'Anything else?'

'She stood in it, it was on her hands and her T-shirt. Why are you asking me all these questions?'

'Never mind,' she said and poured me another drink.

Later, I went out for a run and returned to find Dom sitting at my kitchen table talking to Dana. 'What the hell is he doing here?' I asked. I didn't want Dom anywhere near me. If he had been a bit more subtle with his persuasion, the police wouldn't be crawling around the woods at Kenton Thorpe asking questions about Tess's disappearance.

'Dana wanted to see me.' On top of my rage, I experienced a flicker of jealousy at being excluded from this little tête-à-tête. Surely they weren't having an affair. And then I looked at Dom again, the gracelessness of his bulk, and shook my head. No way would my wife consider him when she had me.

I was right. Dana had something much more important on her agenda, and if I'd even had an inkling of what she was up to, I swear I would have stopped her.

Forty-Nine

Libby

'Do you think Joe could have harmed Tess?'

Libby has begun to think the questions will never end. That the rest of her life will be one long Q&A until she caves and admits to doing something terrible, just to make them shut up.

'No,' she said.

'Why not?' They were asking her to explain a certainty that ran through her like blood. She could give them any number of reasons, tell them he was very fond of Tess, although that sounded all wrong.

'Because he's not a violent person.'

'But he did this to you.'

'I've already said that was an accident.' She handles her answers like a loaded gun. One wrong word and she'll take someone out.

'Your relationship with Joe fell apart, didn't it? Why was that?'

'He blamed me for things I had nothing to do with.'

'Such as?'

'He blamed me for Tess leaving.' She blurts it out without thinking and immediately feels the pain, the shot to her foot. *Stupid. Stupid. Stupid.*

When Richard appears like a vision she doesn't attempt to contain her tears; they surge forward, a burst dam of emotion.

He sits beside her, silently, patting her head, offering a tissue. She can smell the cold air, his aftershave, him. The small, familiar memory keys that when pressed lift her out of her nightmare and plant her back in reality. How could she have doubted him? This is the man she knows and loves.

'They're questioning me like I had something to do with Tess's disappearance.' Richard is the man who can make everything better and he needs to work his magic on this particular shit show. Quick fast.

He listens to her vent, interjecting now and then to pin down the detail. 'Have they found anything else other than her blood?'

'I don't know.'

'Anything else at the scene?'

'I said I don't know.' She should appreciate Richard's attention to detail but instead she feels under fire all over again.

'Have they mentioned forensics?'

'No.' His interrogation pounds her head like friendly fire. In the brief gaps between his questions, when she's not scratching her brain for responses, she regards her uncle. There's an intensity to his mood that unsettles her.

'They're still questioning Joe,' he says. At last, he speaks without demanding an answer. 'They've got an extension.'

'He didn't hurt me on purpose.'

'You don't know that.'

'Yes, I do, I was there.' He's doing it again, telling her what to think, what to believe.

'I don't understand why you're sticking up for him; he doesn't care about you.'

'Thanks.'

'Oh for goodness' sake, Libby, the truth hurts sometimes but it's what makes us stronger.'

He's right, she thinks. The truth will make her stronger if she can find it. But to find it, she has to look.

'I remember us arguing before I hit my head,' she starts

slowly, her voice barely more than a whisper. 'We were arguing about you.'

'Me?'

'Joe said we were at Kenton Thorpe under false pretences.' She studies his reaction, doesn't care that it makes him uncomfortable. His cheeks redden, his ire ignited.

She could stop right here, on the precipice, retreat and pretend this has not happened.

But she doesn't because she needs to know.

'He said the plan was for you to make large sums of money by mining commercially sensitive or confidential information and then selling it on. Ethical hacking without the ethics.'

He thumps the bed, hitting her leg, too lost in his fury to notice. 'Are you telling me so I know what this crackpot is claiming, or are you asking me if he's correct?'

The day has been long and hard, and the prospect that some terrible fate has befallen Tess has put everything into perspective. Libby's fears are small by comparison. Her loss would be too. The truth wouldn't kill her. So, she won't turn away and she won't retreat, no matter the look Richard is firing in her direction, *Go on if you dare*, and she sees right there, that his love is not unconditional, it is bought at a price. *Make him proud, do what's expected, don't challenge or speak out.*

'I'm asking you if it's true.'

'After everything I have done for you, you have the gall to ask me that question? Who do you think put you in hospital? Joe did this, no matter what fantasies you want to cook up. He did this because that's the kind of man he is and you can't see past it. Now I'm going to say this and you need to listen. If you want to get out of this you'd better stop sticking up for him, because as far as I can see the police think it's either you or him are responsible for Tess's disappearance. Yes, that's the truth, Libby. You need to wake up. And it's even more dangerous for you because you've admitted to fighting with Tess on the night she was killed, and then you went into the woods and got what turns out to be her blood on your clothes and your shoes.' He stops, breathless and gulping at the air. 'Now, I'm going to get a cup of tea and I want you to give this some serious thought and work out who's on your side. Do you understand?'

He disappears through the door and she waits for his footsteps to fade out until she sinks back into the bed. It's the sound she hears that shreds her nerves, a beep too faint to be the monitor or a dripping tap. It is the ticking of a bomb. She searches for its source just as it detonates.

On the night she was killed.

Richard's words.

But no one knows Tess is dead. Not yet. And even if she is dead, without a body, how could anyone know when she died?

She tries to hide from the answer but it hunts her down. Richard has orchestrated the whole thing. The meal at Mama Rosa's, the casual mention of his troubles over dinner. Would she help? Of course she would. She wanted to, needed to prove her worth. His return on investment.

And what an astute investment she has turned out to be. She said yes to everything, asked no questions, obeyed orders with blind trust. Best of all, she's standing in the firing line exactly where Richard and his henchmen should be.

All his questions make sense now. The light has snapped on in her head and she can't look the other way. The questions are for his benefit, not hers. He's trying to gauge how much the police know and if he and his cohorts are in the frame.

Would he do that to her?

She knows he could. He did it once before with her mother when she started to cause him problems, their argument over the inheritance, who got her grandmother's house in Kenton Thorpe. Her mother wouldn't give up, she'd already lost her mother and before that the love of her life, and still Richard

285

drove her to madness, threatened her with everything. That's why she started to drink and drink until she couldn't take it any more. Ruthless, that's what her mother used to call him. *Richard is loving until he's ruthless.*

And Libby couldn't believe her. Not after she had gone, because Richard was all she had.

Footsteps crash into her thoughts, grow louder as they edge closer. She watches the handle turn and his face appear from behind the door. He's wearing a smile, part conciliatory, part reprimanding.

Have you learnt your lesson? it says.

Libby assesses him, the bare bones of who he is, rather than the person she wants him to be. Her chest thuds as he approaches her bed. Just him and her. No one else around. Would he hurt her?

All bets are off.

She feeds him a smile of her own. Chastened. Remorseful.

Just play his game.

'Now then, where were we?' he says.

'I'm sorry,' she says. And he smiles.

One thing she knows, her capacity for anger is stronger than ever.

Fifty

Libby

*M*urder. The officers launch the word into the air like a rocket.

'We are working on the theory Tess could have been murdered last Tuesday night.'

All the worst-case scenarios have become real, the bad thoughts Libby had stuffed to the back of her mind, telling herself she was being ridiculous, always looking on the bleak side of life.

'You don't look surprised,' DS Foley says.

Did she not? She'd have to work harder, work out the correct way to arrange her expression in order to convince them neither she nor Joe had anything to do with Tess's death.

'I've been worried, that's all. You told me she hasn't been seen since Tuesday.'

'Is that the only reason?'

'Yes.' She stares down at her palms, swears she can still see blood in the tiny rivulets and lines of her hands.

'Are you sure about that?'

'Yes, I'm sure.' They're leading her down a dark alleyway, ready to spring something on her.

'We found Tess's blood on a sweater. Do you recognise this piece of clothing?' They show her a photograph of a baby pink jumper.

'I do.'

'And can you explain why your jumper has Tess's blood on it?'

'I went into the woods to look for her the next day.' She launches head first into the explanation, in full knowledge it will sound implausible, a likely excuse. 'Kyle said she had left, but I guess . . . well, I guess I was worried. I stopped by a tree to rest and when I looked down there was blood at my feet and blood on my hands.'

'And you didn't think to mention this earlier?'

'I didn't think it was relevant.'

Her comment lights a touch paper. 'We're conducting a missing person's investigation and you didn't think it was relevant?'

'I thought it was fake, my uncle—'

'Fake blood?'

'We were all made up to look like zombies, we had fake blood in tubes. I thought someone might have spilt theirs.' She speaks with no conviction. None whatsoever. The statement is weak and pathetic and it exposes her unforgivable stupidity. It is not what *she* believed, it was what Richard told her to believe. Libby knew all along the blood was real but she sacrificed reason for blind trust. And now it's too late. She can't recall the lie she has just spoken, it has been recorded on the tape, it has been wedged in the officers' minds and it is helping them form their conclusion, that she, Libby Sumner, is a liar and an unconvincing one at that. Her body starts to shake, her mouth is dry like every drop of moisture has been syphoned off, leaving her a crumbling, shrivelling husk. She considers pressing the nuclear button, launching into an explanation about her uncle and his insistence that it was fake, and how she always believed everything he said because that was how it had to be, the only way she could survive, but how she has the growing suspicion he has wronged her, not just in the past week, but from the age of nine. Except, they'd ask, *Where is your evidence?* And she'd shrink and be forced to admit she has none, just a hunch, an overpowering visceral hunch. And even Libby knows hunches don't survive in court, they don't wash in interview rooms, or hospital rooms doubling as interview rooms. This is not the place for feelings and regrets and grief over losing something she never had in the first place. It is a hostile environment where only cold hard facts and evidence survive.

'We have a witness who says he saw you on the ground searching it. What were you looking for?'

'I wasn't searching the ground. I was looking for Tess.'

'Was this what you were searching for?'

They present her with a bag containing a tiny diamond stud earring.

'It's your earring, Libby. You were right to be worried you'd lost it in the woods where Tess was hurt. Where you hurt her.'

The net has her trapped. And she tells herself, amid the rising panic that makes her heart boom and her head spin, that none of it matters because she did not hurt Tess. She is innocent. They must know that she could not commit murder.

'I didn't hurt Tess,' she says.

'But you've already admitted you did, on the day she disappeared.'

'That's not what I said. I said we had an argument and she pushed me.'

Libby is allowed out of hospital, her head injury deemed to be minor. A cause for celebration in different circumstances, but not these ones. She is moved to Lewes Police Station for further questioning and her nightmare darkens. The upbeat, positive side of her personality hopes that someone will spring up behind her sometime soon, announce that it is a joke, admittedly one in terrible taste, but a joke nevertheless.

But the joker hasn't materialised. And the upbeat, positive side of her personality has disappeared. She's been here four hours, trapped inside the walls of the interview room, brown like the butterscotch Angel Delight she used to make with her mum. Richard has sent a solicitor, a woman who can't be much older than her and is called Clemmie Cabidis. She sounds like a sexually transmitted disease which pretty much sums up Libby's day.

Did Richard send this young, impressionable solicitor to do her worst? She reminds Libby of a scared rabbit, fidgeting, flighty, unfamiliar with her habitat. And she has an infuriating habit of running her tongue over her teeth every time Libby is asked a question. Libby presumes she is being paid double, triple the going rate for her troubles to spy and report back to Richard, and this suspicion adds another layer of complexity to the situation. She needs someone to help her negotiate her way around this minefield but she can't trust the advice Clemmie gives. The predicament is playing with her head, stretching the fabric of her mind until it tears.

All she wants is to go home.

But she doesn't even know where that is any more.

Bar the earring, the evidence against her can only be circumstantial. She knows this with utter certainty because she did not kill Tess. She doesn't look or talk like a murderer, however it is one looks and talks. She has a first-class degree, a future, if not mapped out, then roughly sketched. One that involves success and wealth, changing the world for the better, and maybe a few children with healthy complexions and good teeth.

'You wanted revenge, didn't you? Tess had stolen your boyfriend and so you sought her out and killed her.'

'No.'

No. No. No. No. No.

But they don't buy it. Her answers are like water running off balloons. And she gets it now. This is what they do. Wear you down until you will say anything, anything, to buy a moment's silence. The pair of them acting like a tag team, one picking up the baton while the other takes a breath, preparing for the next attack. And underneath all this, her distrust of Richard hardens into a white fury so hot she has to remind herself to breathe.

He *would* do this to her.

He *is* doing this to her.

'I think Tess knew what my uncle was doing . . . what Freetech is doing.'

'Did she?' the detective asks. 'And what is it Freetech is doing?'

'We were all told our job was to pen test clients, you know, ethical hacking, test their systems for weaknesses as a security measure, but I think we were doing the opposite. I think we were unwittingly stealing information so they could sell it on.'

'And you knew nothing about this?'

'No . . .' she raises her voice, her indignation is raw and sore. 'I would never have got involved if I'd known.'

'But you are involved, aren't you? You are a director of the company. Are you seriously suggesting you had no idea what was going on?'

They don't understand, why would they? Her name on the company records doesn't mean a thing; she assumed it was for tax purposes. 'Richard did that because it suited him. I didn't ask for it. I helped him recruit the others but beyond that I was just a regular employee.'

'Interesting.' The detective strokes the mush of stubble on his chin. 'You see, that's not what your aunt has told us.'

Dana.

Her name unleashes a fresh wave of despair. The weight of all the lies and half-truths are burying her alive. Dana never liked Libby. Right from the start she viewed her ten-year-old soon-to-be niece as a threat. And maybe she was right to, maybe Dana has always known that a man like Richard has a limited supply of attention and affection, that to share it would be to settle for a measly ration and resign herself to a love-starved marriage.

And now Dana has the perfect opportunity to erase Libby from the family picture.

'Dana is lying.'

'Is she lying about this too?'

They pass a printout across the table and Libby turns her head to the wall. She hasn't a clue what it is but she knows it will be yet more evidence to damn her.

'I suppose you don't need to look, not when you already know what's there.'

Finally she takes the paper and forces herself to study it. It is her bank statement, her name, her details, her address. And yet it can't be. Her eyes swim over the zeros, and she stares and stares, burning a hole in the paper, but they refuse to disappear.

'Looks like you were doing very well from this business,' DS Foley says. 'Are you still insisting you had nothing to do with this?'

She would insist but everything has gone, her fight, her will, her mind. There's nothing left of her.

Fifty-One

Richard

I didn't like it, not one bit. My niece in the firing line. That wasn't what Dana had sold me when she said she was taking care of everything.

'I can't have Libby charged with . . .' I stopped, couldn't bear to say the word.

'Murder. There, I'll say it for you.' Dana's capacity for cruelty was bottomless. 'You need to face up to what's going on here. If it's not her, it's you. And can you just admit once and for all you don't love her. You enjoy her adoration, Richard. Every time you look at her you can see a reminder of your power, what you won from your sister, the house, the inheritance. Libby reminds you of your greatness but don't confuse that with love.'

'What did you tell the police?' As soon as I ask I realise I don't want to know. The less I know about any of this, the clearer my conscience remains. But Dana isn't giving me an easy out. She doesn't want to share the load, she wants to make sure I'm carrying the lion's share.

'Very little. In fact, it was more careful suggestion than anything else. I told them Libby was a bit obsessive . . . Oh, for goodness' sake, don't look at me like that, you know she is, always skulking around, seeking love and reassurance. She must be exhausting as a girlfriend, I almost feel sorry for that Joe character. And of course they asked me if she had ever been violent.'

'Violent? For Christ's sake, Dana, Libby is many things but she is not violent.'

'What about that time she destroyed the peonies? I remember coming out and seeing their heads chopped off, every single last one of them. Such a wicked act.'

'She was ten, the girl had just lost her mother. And violence towards flowers doesn't count.'

'Or the time she stole Max? I was beside myself.'

I wished she hadn't dragged up that incident. It was not one of my finer moments. 'I paid . . .' I was on the brink of confessing over a decade late. *Dana, I paid her five pounds to take Max away from you for a few hours . . .* But then my wisdom stopped me. Now was not the time to inflame relations further.

'And I told them about the business.'

Dana was wielding a knife with these revelations, moving closer and closer to piercing my skin. I didn't trust her, not in the slightest. I don't claim to have been the perfect husband, and if she wanted to take revenge, she was looking at open goal. 'What exactly did you tell them about the business?'

'Only that Libby had been badgering you to set up on her own and you indulged her. You had nothing to do with Freetech apart from providing the initial set-up costs.'

'They'll never believe that, the money is—'

'In her account.'

'What?'

'I put the money into Libby's account when all this started.' Dana smiled like she'd just produced a winning hand.

'All of it?'

'All of it.'

'What in God's name—'

'Think about it, Richard. You don't want to be connected with this in any way. And the company is in her name, thanks to you.'

'But that was only for tax reasons.'

'No, darling, it was not. It was because you're exceptionally generous and when your niece came to you with a business idea you agreed to back it.'

I closed my eyes in an attempt to still my brain. I needed to arrange Dana's alternative facts into a coherent picture. But she wouldn't give me a moment to recover.

'I moved the money as an insurance policy because unlike you, I didn't think we could trust Libby not to betray you. If the company is in her name and the money is in her account, it gives her a motive to hurt Tess.'

I forced myself to look at her. Who was this woman I married, the mother of my children? Truthfully, I couldn't say I had loved her for years, if ever, but I had always thought her kind – all that charity work and baking and the aerobathons at the gym. She was gentle with the children too, our own at any rate, smothering them in kisses and cuddles and undeserved praise, *Oh darling, what a magnificent drawing! What a delicious cake!* Not that Libby ever received any of this. Libby wound her up, went out of her way to make Dana's life difficult.

Except. She didn't, did she? That was simply Dana's version, reforming the truth to suit her own ends, waging a campaign to get rid of Libby. And it had worked. I went for it, sent the poor girl away to boarding school to please my wife.

And now this.

She had gone too far. I would not stand by and see my niece destroyed.

'I won't allow you to do this.'

She regarded me with mild amusement. 'Oh Richard, you do make me laugh. You really don't know yourself very well, do you? You'll go along with this otherwise you'll lose everything. Take a look around . . . all this, the cars, the house.' She walked over to the door, opened it and called out, 'Max and Tilly, come and say goodnight to your father.' And in they trotted a few minutes later, bath-fresh and warm, eyes starred with tiredness. 'Your father's got a big decision to make, I think a hug might help.' And Tilly launched herself into my arms and I clung to her for dear life until she said, 'Dad, I can't breathe.' And then the same again with Max, his long, lean limbs wrapping around me.

'I'll be up in a second to kiss you goodnight,' Dana said shooing them out.

When they'd gone she picked up my phone and brought it to me, 'Are you going to call the police and tell them the truth?'

Fifty-Two

Joe

The guy in the cell next to mine is singing 'Auld Lang Syne'. He's pissed by the sounds of things, probably hasn't been sober since New Year's Eve 2016, but he can hold a tune and seems happy enough, laughing and talking to himself in between verses. I envy him. I wish I had enough drink in my system to blot out reality. But I'm not sure there's enough drink in London to achieve that.

Instead, I wait. There's no sleep to be achieved in this place, just different levels of consciousness, from screaming at the walls to quietly jibbering to myself, to the silent catatonic state I find myself in when the keys turn in the lock and the door swings open.

'You can go.'

I don't move. The despair and hopelessness sit like rocks in my stomach. They won't let me go that easily.

'Hey, you, did you hear what I said? You can go.'

I do that thing where I point to myself, *me?*

'Unless there's someone else in this cell called Joseph Hemsley.'

I scan the cell. There is only me and I answer to the name Joe Hemsley. They are letting me go.

Libby has told them I didn't push her intentionally and without any other evidence, they have no choice but to release me. The relief is chemical and overwhelms me with pure, liquid happiness. It's almost worth the trauma to experience it. Almost.

I want to ask about Tess and is she alive and if they don't think I hurt her, then who? But I'm too scared to remind them. One misplaced word could send me back to the cells.

I get one phone call. I should call my parents because I know they'll be worried sick, but they'd also insist on driving to the police station and battering me with questions on the way home; they'd want a detailed explanation of everything right from the start. And I can't do it. I've used up every grain of energy.

'About fucking time,' Clara says when I phone her. 'I was worried you were making a mess of things in the interview.'

'I'm fine, thanks for asking. Can I stay with you tonight?'

'That's not a come-on, is it? Because you're a nice guy and everything, Joe, but you're not my type.' She was trying hard but there was an undercurrent beneath the jokes.

'I promise.'

'I have to warn you,' she said. 'My flat's in a bit of a state.'

'You weren't lying then,' I say when Clara lets me in.

'I'm trying to look on the bright side, they found a stash of Dairy Milk I had forgotten about.'

Her flat is trashed, every drawer pulled out, cupboards ransacked, clothes strewn on the bed, mugs and plates smashed on the tiles, the contents of the fridge decorating the walls and sofa; a half-eaten cucumber, a Weetabix crushed on the carpet, a solitary rasher of bacon liberated from its pack now lying on the arm of the sofa.

'You've had visitors.'

'Uninvited guests.'

'Have you called the police?'

'What do you think?'

'I'll give you a hand.'

'I was hoping you'd say that, it's the only reason I agreed to let you stay.'

We work to the soundtrack of Clara's playlist, swinging erratically from The Bangles to London Grammar to Jamie T back through the decades to the Smiths. 'Sod the Smiths.' She turns it off when Morrissey starts up, 'I've got enough going on without him in my ear.'

The silence is unwelcome but we don't know where to start. There is too much to talk about, an overload of trauma. Clara orders a takeaway instead, opens a bottle of wine.

'Tomaz cursed you all the way back to his car,' she says once she has drained her first glass, 'and then as soon as we got in he drove straight back to Kenton Thorpe.'

I want to say I'm glad he came back. I wouldn't be here if he hadn't, and not just me, Asha, Will and Libby too, but then if he'd driven in the opposite direction, he wouldn't be lying unconscious in hospital. It's the kind of moral conundrum that pushes my brain to its limit. Clara senses my unease because it's hers too. She switches on the television for a diversion. We don't mean to watch the news, we need escapism, but Huw Edwards' face is there, set in a deep frown, telling us what we don't want to hear.

A woman has been charged with the murder of Tess Langton.

Her name is Elizabeth Sumner.

I start to cry, the kind of tears that fall so hard and fast I know they won't ever stop, will end up drowning me. And Clara stares at her takeaway, the lamb biryani that seemed so appetising a few minutes ago, and she lays down her fork and gives me a hug, and that hug, that simple display of tenderness from Clara, tells me this more than any words: this is seriously deep shit.

★

'You don't think she . . .' Clara asks. I shake my head.

'No, I don't.' And over the course of the next few hours, into the early morning, I spill out everything I know about Libby, everything we had done and shared, the small throwaway comments that meant nothing at the time but have assumed a meatier significance now, and we pore over it, searching for the signposts and clues that might lead us to her killing Tess.

There are plenty scattered around, right up to one of the last things she said to me. Her confession.

I knew.

And yet I can't believe it, it's like a fish bone stuck in my throat. It won't go down. I try to coax myself out of the delusion that I know her and I beat myself over the head with the words she screamed at me, *I don't love you, I never did*, but nothing works. I don't believe she killed Tess. I won't believe it.

I expect Clara to mock me, throw me a look that says, *You poor sod, when are you going to wake up?* But to my surprise, even after listening to all the evidence, she says, 'Remember what I told you, with these people what you see is the opposite of what's going on.'

We go to court the next morning for Libby's appearance. I don't want to go. I don't think I can watch her being charged with murder. But Clara insists. 'If you believe her you should be there. And I want to see Richard Gilligan Thomas's face, I want to make that bastard sweat.' I don't tell her that at five foot and one inch she's unlikely to frighten anyone because one thing I've learnt, you underestimate Clara at your cost.

Lewes Magistrates Court is rammed, satellite trucks parked up on the narrow pavements outside. As soon as I arrive, I know it is a mistake coming here. The photographers recognise me as one of the fire survivors and push their cameras into my face. I want to slam through them and scream for them to leave me in peace, but I just raise a hand to shield my eyes, put one foot in front of the next and keep going. By the time I make it to the public gallery everyone seems to know who I am, their eyes stabbing me like pins. It's too hot in here, tropically hot considering it's winter in Sussex, a close, sticky heat that makes me rush with nausea. The only thing I can do is look over to Clara in the press benches for reassurance, as if her presence is a weight to keep me tethered.

We wait and wait until I think I can't wait any longer and then a hush descends on the courtroom and the magistrates take their seats and the sound of footsteps coming from the bowels of the courtroom announce Libby's arrival. I should be watching her, studying her face for tics and nervous twitches, anything that will give me a yes or a no to the question, did she do it? But my attention is lured elsewhere, to the door of the courtroom and the figure of a woman talking frantically to the usher. I'm seeing things, obviously. It's been a tough few days. I draw my eyes away and then let them roam back again. But the picture is the same. And I start to move towards her as the usher casts around for someone to make sense of the information she has just imparted.

Fifty-Three

The power of television meant that at the very same moment Clara and Joe learnt of Libby's murder charge, millions of other people did too. One of those people was sitting in a tiny beach chalet in a small town called Seasalter in Kent. Not many people have heard of Seasalter outside Kent, and in winter not many people walked past the blue clapboard hut perched so close to the sea that it seemed the high tide might sweep it out into the English Channel.

Its solitude meant no one had seen Tess Langton sitting by the glass doors pocked with salt and spray, studying the churn of the sea, the sun rising and sinking across a flat sullen sky.

Had anyone walked past and noticed her and been so bold as to ask who she was, she would have told them she was called Louise. It was a nice straightforward name and there were enough Louises around to allow for confusion. But no one had troubled her. She had slept every night since she arrived and woken in the morning, dressed her wound, and made herself coffee and a few slices of toast out of the provisions Tomaz had left her. At lunchtime she had a cup of tea and a sandwich. It was a simple existence and one that might have suited her for a week or so. But the circumstances that brought her here meant it wasn't an existence at all.

Tess was a ghost; dead to her parents, her friends, the whole wide world, just to convince the people who wanted to kill her that their job was done.

The only person who knew she was alive was Tomaz and now he might be dead too.

It was *that* fucked up.

True, she'd had a love/hate relationship with Tomaz, mainly hate if she's honest. And who could blame her? Tomaz had revealed her identity and put her life in danger for fifty thousand pounds. At least that was what she thought initially. After he saved her life, she had allowed him to explain. It wasn't the money he wanted, it was his balls, the ones they'd threatened to cut off if he didn't tell them. His life or her name.

'I'm a coward,' he said.

Tess doesn't think Tomaz is a coward.

She remembers the moment last Tuesday evening in the woods when the night turned the deepest shade of black, dark like she'd never seen, and she remembers the rearing sensation when she looked into Joe's eyes and realised it wasn't Joe after all but Dom. And Dom's smile and the chill it sent through her is imprinted in her brain along with his bulk blocking her path, and his hands, the thick, strong hands stuck on his muscular arms, locking around her neck. Pressing. Compressing. Squeezing every drop of life out of her.

And then from somewhere in the woods Libby had called out, *Tess, Tess, Tess.* It was her last strand of hope and she would have liked to answer. Every fibre of her wanted to answer, but Dom had seen to that, no breath, no air, no words. She remembers him cursing, though, *for fuck's sake*, at Libby's intervention.

Libby hadn't found her, but thinking about it later, she saved Tess's life in a roundabout way with a single shot of the paintball. Tess would never have had her down as such a good aim, but that shot skirted Tess's arm and landed on the tree next to her and the luminous glow and Dom's expletive allowed Tomaz to locate them when Tess was down to her last remaining seconds.

This is where her memory tears, something to do with

passing out, lack of oxygen, but Tomaz filled her in the next day.

Thanks to the one text she had sent, Tomaz knew where Tess was, knew the name of the house and its rough location, although even then he'd had a bugger of a job finding it. He arrived late morning, spent the day casing the joint with the help of his police issue binoculars, the whole battery of his surveillance techniques coming into play. He'd witnessed Tess attempt to leave in the afternoon and witnessed the exchange with Libby turn into a fight. And when Dom approached and summoned them back to the house, Tomaz saw an opportunity to rescue Tess squandered. But he wasn't giving up. He watched Dom and Kyle in the woods – thank fuck for night vision binoculars – the pair planning and plotting as evening rolled in and the mist descended, knowing his chances of success were getting slimmer by the hour. By night-time, when he saw figures roaming through the trees, he took to scouring the woods himself. He wouldn't stop until he found her. He couldn't. And yet the task was impossible. He was losing her, he could feel it in the air, Tess slipping away, and it was all his fault. Her blood on his hands. The truth crushed him and he fell to his knees, praying to God for one more chance to save her. He didn't believe in God any more than he believed in Santa Claus but someone was listening because at that precise moment he saw the light. Not Jesus, but a divine intervention in the form of the luminous glow of a paintball. He trained his binoculars in the direction of the light. And there they were, two shapes filling his viewfinder, one drooping and falling to the ground. And he prayed again, for time to stop, to give him an extra second, two, three, to reach her before her attacker dealt the final blow. Tomaz rushed towards them, like a creature that had taken flight, and out of his mouth came a strange hybrid noise, half human, half animal. Later, he said it was because he wanted to scare her attacker off, but it was more basic than that, more innate. It was the sound of a last chance running out of him.

And it worked.

That great hulking lump of a man was spooked by the noises in the shadows, and thinking his job was done, he ran back into the darkness.

That was how Tomaz saved Tess. He took her to his car and drove her to Kent, to a chalet his family had owned for generations by the sea in Seasalter.

He checked her injuries, the deep cut on her hairline that needed stitches but was patched up with Steri-Strips, the bruising around her neck painful and black and blue but nothing life-threatening. And he filled the cupboards and the fridge and he left her money and a phone. No one could know she was here. Not her friends, not her family.

'Stay here until it's over,' he said.

More than anything Tess wanted to visit him in hospital and thank him and tell him their scorecard was even and will him back to life and say, *Don't you dare, don't you fucking dare leave now. It isn't over.*

But she couldn't go because she was dead and her premature resurrection would mean jeopardising everything he did for her, making it all for nothing. And it couldn't be for nothing. Not when he had risked so much. Tomaz told her to stay here until he sent word. She had money, he'd made sure of that. The fifty thousand pounds he received in return for revealing her identity was hers if she wanted it, which she didn't. She just needed enough to exist on until this ended.

But when she heard about the fire at Kenton Thorpe on the radio, and found out Tomaz was in hospital, unconscious, a question nagged her: how would she know when to leave if he couldn't tell her?

And then she watched Huw Edwards on the *Ten O'Clock*

News and he said that Elizabeth Sumner had been charged with her murder, and Tess knew her question was answered.

Now was the time.

The court usher doesn't believe her at first, shakes his head as if to say, I wasn't born yesterday. But she keeps on at him, *I am Tess Langton, you have to believe me.* And yet without a passport or a driving licence or any form of ID, the man isn't buying her nonsense. He is on the cusp of having her ejected when Joe shouts her name across the courtroom, *Tess! Tess!* and pushes his way towards her. A silence descends for a split second before it is broken by a commotion the likes of which Court One has never seen. The journalists rise to their feet, the solicitors stand mouths agape, and the magistrates attempt but fail to restore calm. The tremor travels to the very spot where Libby is sitting and leads her eyes to the epicentre of the disruption. The defendant sees Joe hugging Tess, the pair of them clinging to each other, an image that would have broken her heart days ago, but now, right now it is the most beautiful thing she has ever seen. It is the image that rips Libby from her nightmare.

Fifty-Four

Richard

'My wife and I never doubted Libby's innocence and we are grateful that it has now been proved beyond all reasonable doubt. But clearly in the coming days I will be asking questions about the police investigation and the wrongful arrest of my niece which has devastated our family.'

Dana and I stood outside the court, jostled on the thin strips of pavement by a hungry pack of press. They were vultures, ready to rip the meat from my bones. I gave them as little as I could get away with and pushed my way through their cameras and microphones to the waiting car. Libby had gone to hospital to be checked out having fainted in court. It bought Dana and me a few hours at least, time on our own to work through this latest development, although given the choice, the last person I would have spent time with at that juncture was my wife.

This was her fault.

Everything that had gone wrong could be traced back to her, right from that first meeting with Matt Collingwood through to Dom's involvement and her framing Libby. She had me sewn up good and proper; I had no choice but to go along with it.

'Dom said he—' I jabbed her in the ribs. I trusted my drivers but not enough to be party to this kind of talk.

'Shut up.' For once she did as I said and the remainder of the journey passed in silence, allowing me time to formulate my own plans for Dana and me.

*

Dom was standing in our driveway waiting for us when we arrived, his face a sweaty orb of panic. His presence was an affront. How dare he come here after everything he had done.

'You said she was dead.'

'I thought she was.'

'You thought?'

'It was dark, OK? She fell to the ground. And then Massey came to collect the body and he said—'

'Let me guess, he said he'd cleaned up and you paid him his eight thousand pounds of my money. He didn't tell you there was no fucking body. You fool, you fucking fool. I told you not to use him. He can't be trusted.' I started to walk away from him, heading into the house, but he tugged my jacket and I stopped, staring down at his grubby hands. 'Remember who you are dealing with,' I warned him.

'They'll know it was me, Tess is going to identify me. I'm fucked.' He was following me like a stray cat.

'That's not my problem.' I opened the back door and blocked his entrance. There was no way Dom was entering my house. The kids were away on a sleepover thankfully, they didn't need people like Dom in their lives. And nor did I.

'But you ordered this. You asked me to do it.'

The gardener walked by trying not to look, but he was no actor.

'Dom, I really don't think we can have anything more to do with each other,' I said loudly. 'Your work has been, let's say, well below par.'

'You think I'm going to take all the flak and not drag you into it?'

I spun round to face him, the gardener out of earshot now. 'Remind me of the exact conversation when I told you to hurt Tess.'

'It was . . .' His tiny brain creaked as it turned over. 'It was . . . Dana said you wanted me to—'

'Dana told you, did she? Did you and I ever have that conversation?'

He stared at me, his features painted with disgust.

'She's your wife, for fuck's sake.'

'I'm aware of that.'

'You really are the lowest of the fucking low,' he said.

I drove to Matt Collingwood's house that evening. I was probably over the limit but in the grand scale of my issues, a drink driving conviction was skirting at the very bottom. After the encounter with Dom I needed a few shots of whisky to cool my anger. It didn't work. I was still alight with fury, but on consideration, that was no bad thing. I needed Matt to understand I meant business, that I would not accept him freezing me out as if our partnership never existed. It was imperative he knew I would make life impossible for him if he didn't step in to help.

'I have nothing to say to you.' I caught him at the corner of his street, briefcase in hand, like he was returning from an honest day's work.

'That's fine, because I have plenty to say to you and I'm happy to have this conversation outside your front door if it's more convenient.'

That stopped him in his tracks. 'You have two minutes,' he said, casting around down the lane in case anyone was hiding in the bushes, ready to record our conversation. 'But I can't see a way out of this for you.'

I wasn't asking him to find a way out for me, I'd already done the heavy lifting as far as that was concerned. What I wanted was a guarantee of some official back-up, otherwise he needed to know I would create the biggest stink, use every penny I had to prove the link between him and the government. 'I have connections,' I reminded him. 'I know where you live, where your children go to school. I know people who will get their hands dirty for the right price. It really is in your best interests to have my back.'

'What exactly is it you are planning?'

We were over time but he granted me another two minutes to explain, his jaw slackening as he listened. When I finished I offered my hand for him to shake but he simply stared at it before scurrying away, as if he feared I was contagious.

I went to the pub on the way home, sank another few whiskys. It was a miserable little place, a live band tuning up. *One two one two*, the singer repeated into the microphone. He was wearing leathers as if he was some kind of rock god who had been washed up in Surrey. I was all for taking his microphone and ramming it down his scraggy neck, but I headed for my car instead. I had my reputation to consider. Petty violence never looked good. The countryside flew by as I raced round bends and corners, road signs flashing and zooming towards me. The drink had made me hyper alert, alive. Energised. All the journey needed was some musical accompaniment so I switched on the radio just as the news was playing.

Development number one: Tomaz had woken up.

Development number two: a thirty-seven-year-old man from South London had been arrested in connection with the fire at Kenton Thorpe and Tess Langton's attempted murder.

Dom was in his late thirties and lived in Croydon.

I changed the station, turned up the volume to its highest, but it couldn't drown out the undeniable truth.

Dana and I were finished.

Fifty-Five
Six months later
April 2018

Judge Rupert Harwood's sentencing,
Central Criminal Court, London

*I*t is clear from the outset you have lied and deceived and shown precious little remorse for what you have done. Rather than accept your crime, you have tried to shift the blame on to others in the most callous way imaginable. It is typical of the contempt you have shown for your victims and for the court.

Be in no doubt you will pay a high price for your actions.

Indeed there are a number of aggravating features in this case: you wilfully misled the police in the investigation into the disappearance of Tess Langton. You watched on as your own niece was arrested and charged with murder in full knowledge that you yourself had given instructions and paid for this young woman to be killed.

And when you were arrested and interviewed, you claimed your own spouse was behind this conspiracy, that you were just an innocent bystander with no knowledge of what was going on.

You had a lifestyle beyond the dreams of many, the cars, the holidays, a beautiful family. The irony is that in seeking to protect all this, you have destroyed everything you held dear.

It is for these reasons, Dana Gilligan Thomas, that in relation to the charge of perverting the course of justice I sentence you to thirty-six months in prison and on the charge of conspiring to murder you are sentenced to nine years. These sentences are to run concurrently.

Fifty-Six

Dana

The eyes in the courtroom are studding Dana's skin, measuring her reactions, the level of her suffering. Everything from her hair and clothes to her shoes has been pored over in this trial. She is still immaculately turned out, if you must know, but she won't be for much longer, and it is this, her imminent demise, that so delights her audience. It's why they're here, packing the public gallery, angling for the best view. The almighty fall from grace has long been the nation's favourite spectator sport, and court number three at the Old Bailey has put on a vintage show. Tonight, thinks Dana, all those people watching will trot home feeling better about their own pathetic lives.

From the dock, she searches for Richard. The sight of him – expensively suited, clean-shaven, wearing the platinum cufflinks she bought for their tenth anniversary – curdles her stomach. She might be sick, vomit all over the guard. That would give her audience something else to pick over. He catches her eye and stares right through her as if she never existed, as if they have nothing, no memories, no children, no love to bind them together.

Her stupidity dizzies her. Richard would do anything to save himself, isn't that what she used to say? Only she never thought he'd use her as collateral. Turn on his wife when all she had done was stick by him, try to hold their family together, retain the life she was promised. What no one understands is she made a deal with him years ago after she had Max, a quiet, unspoken deal but one they both understood. She had a choice: to leave, or stay and expect nothing from her husband beyond their wealth, the holidays, their lifestyle. And she chose to stay and do the best by their children, and she filled that loveless hole with gym classes and clothes and endless interior revamps. Losing it all was inconceivable. A truly terrifying prospect, because she knew that once it had gone there would be nothing left of her. She had sold everything else to the devil.

Tess's resurrection was the beginning and the end. After Libby was released, Dom was arrested and from there everything fell like a pack of cards.

Dom admitted Tess's attempted murder and the next thing Dana was brought in for questioning, Richard too. But something happened, in the quiet corners of the police station, beyond the reach and understanding of the detectives, something happened that erased Richard from the picture as another narrative took shape. Dana had been the driving force, the plotter, the arch manipulator. Richard hadn't known a thing. It was Dana who had ordered and paid Dom to kill Tess. It was Dana who had pointed the police in the wrong direction, leading them to suspect and arrest Libby. And part of it was true, and part of it was an outrageous lie, but the truth didn't seem to matter.

If only she'd gone in harder on Richard in those first hours of interview, instead of repeating like a mantra, 'My husband is a good man, he would never be part of anything like this.'

Loyalty, she had carried that like a burden, while unbeknown to her, Richard was feeding her to the lions.

When she understood the full depth of his treachery, she changed her story, told them everything about the shady deal to steal information, the off-grid government contract worth millions. She even named Matthew Collingwood. But it was too late, by now she was cast as the evil wife baring her claws when the battle was already lost. And every time she repeated her accusations, they closed her down. 'We've looked into this,' they said. 'And we believe you were the one responsible, not your husband.'

This was what tipped Dana over into the abyss, the cover-up, the closing of ranks, the invisible web of conspiracy winding around her. She knew it was there, somewhere, working against her, but not a single soul believed her. The invisible figures of the establishment had colluded in a campaign to damn her and cover up their own corruption and she couldn't prove a thing.

Richard didn't just stab her, he twisted the knife until she sang with pain. Dana had been acting alone, he'd said. *My God, I would never have condoned such violence.* He told the police that she had always despised their niece, forced him to send her to boarding school against Libby's wishes. He said Dana had demanded more say in the running of the business and that he had given in to her demands, reluctantly because he had sensed she was on the edge and needed something to occupy her time. Of course now he saw the colossal error of his ways. But what he would never forgive, was what Dana did to Libby. She used Freetech, a company in Libby's name, as a front to illegally mine information and sell it on. And when Tess uncovered her deceit, she sent Dom to kill her, framing their own niece for her murder.

Harwood dismisses the court and Dana sits until she is pulled to her feet by the guard. As horrific as this has been, she doesn't want it to end. The next chapter is prison. The loss of her children. She heads down into the bowels of the courtroom and tries to scream but when she opens her mouth she finds her voice has gone.

Fifty-Seven

Libby

The press want Libby to talk, they want her story.

I know it must be difficult, but speaking out might help.

They all say a version of the same thing in their emails and their phone calls and their doorstep entreaties, and in response she trots out the same reply: not yet, it's too raw, I need time to process everything that has happened.

When you're ready, they say, and hand her a card, remind her that they will pay a substantial fee for whatever she wants to tell them. As if Libby needs the money.

She has a good job, better than good, a job some people would kill for; she is back working for Freetech. Yes, she returned, as hard as that is for some people to understand. She never really left. But she is doing it on her terms, her way. Richard's company has survived. He employed a PR company to spin the crisis into a triumph. 'You have to adapt,' he told her. And for the first time in her life, Libby believes him. Despite everything, she is learning to adapt to her new circumstances. She is making the most of her situation.

Her ordeal focused her mind. She is a different person, no longer the nice, pliant Libby who is out to please. She has worked out once and for all what is important in her life. And if it means hurting others to get what she wants, so be it. Perhaps the blow to her head affected her personality after all.

She's back living with Richard too, a move he encouraged. Her presence helps rehabilitate his own image. She makes him more wholesome. After all, with her by his side, he can prove to the public they're still a solid family unit, pulling together as best they can after Dana's imprisonment.

Not that she has agreed to all his demands. She is selective, keeps one eye on the future. When he arranged a newspaper interview to speak of his torment, *my wife was a monster*, how he was trying to rebuild his life with his new girlfriend, she refused to pose for a photograph and sneaked Tilly and Max out for a pizza so they didn't have to endure it either. But by and large she doesn't rock the boat. She has won his trust, worked her way into his inner circle. And slowly but surely she is reaping the rewards.

She met Joe once, a few weeks after her release, in a Starbucks just off Bond Street, nice and anonymous. 'I'm sorry,' he said.

'I'm sorry too.'

'What you said about never loving me, was that . . .?'

She shook her head. 'I wanted you to get out of there. I wanted you to be angry enough to leave me.'

'Did you know about Freetech?'

'No.'

'Dana's taken all the blame.' He wanted her to admit that she knew Richard was involved too but Libby wouldn't do it.

'She has.'

'What will you do now?' he asked.

She shrugged. Libby knew exactly what she was going to do. She was going back to work for Richard. But she didn't want to explain it to Joe, not here in the middle of Starbucks. She was stronger, harder, more selfish, but Joe was her weakness. She couldn't face his outrage, to have him shout, *I will never understand you*, and leave her sitting alone because he couldn't stand to breathe the same air as her a second longer. That was a conversation for another day. A day sometime in the future, when she hoped Joe might give her another chance to tell him everything, to explain how she'd started to think about her mother and her death, and what Richard had done for her. But for now she kept her plans secret. Libby could be sly when she wanted.

He bought a chocolate cake, offered her half but she didn't accept. It didn't feel right, and ten minutes later they said goodbye.

She received a letter, two weeks later. It was from Joe, handwritten, something of a novelty these days, and all it said was, *How could you?*

Fifty-Eight

Joe

'How are you doing?' I get asked that question at least twice a day by my parents, my friends, random strangers who recognise my face from the news. My parents have taken to calling me first thing in the morning and such is the relief in their voice that I'm still here, still alive, haven't ended it all, I don't have the heart to tell them to bugger off and leave me alone.

I'm not going to end it, honestly, although I will admit there was a moment a couple of months back when it seemed like the answer. It was a few weeks after I'd met Libby. She'd appeared smaller than I remembered, thinner. Nervous too, her index finger chasing the rim of the cup. Clockwise. Anticlockwise.

I told her I was sorry.

She told me she was sorry.

I feared we'd get stuck in a never-ending circle of apologies so I bowled straight in and asked her if she meant it when she said she never loved me.

She shook her head. 'I wanted you to get out of there. I wanted you to be angry enough to leave me.'

'Did you know about Freetech?'

'No.'

I mentioned Dana taking all the flak and invited her to admit she knew what we all knew, including Asha and Will, who had been given the full story by Tess, that Richard had weaselled his way out of trouble but that he was to blame. It was all Richard's doing. She wouldn't, not in so many words, but her eyes said it all, escaping my gaze, fleeing the question. She knew. She knew. And that was enough for me, for the moment anyway.

I suppose I was hankering after a reunion. I would have jumped at the chance to have her back, to hold her and kiss her and smell her. To be us again.

But it was clear she wasn't ready.

She might never be ready for all I knew.

It's not John fucking Lewis.

I decided to give her time, sit on my impatience. She had been through hell, we all had, and I assumed she needed space to process everything. I just hated the thought of her doing it alone when I could have helped. Or maybe that was the problem. Maybe I was the problem. I tormented myself like this in the weeks after our meeting, running over all my mistakes, the things I could have done, the ways I could have supported her. But really it all boiled down to one simple thing: trust. I hadn't trusted her. Why would Libby ever want me back?

And then I was sitting with Rex in the Piper's Arms one Sunday. Rex was being remarkably, worryingly generous, offering to set me up with one of his girlfriend Amy's friends. 'She's a bit weird, you'd be the perfect match.'

'I'm not ready, mate,' I said.

'You were never ready but that didn't stop you before.'

I ignored the jibe, looked over his shoulder to the kitchen, willing our roasts to appear, when I saw someone holding a newspaper and I saw the headline.

ENTREPRENEUR RICHARD GILLIGAN THOMAS ON REBUILDING HIS LIFE AFTER HEARTACHE

I legged it over and relieved the man of his paper and that's how I learnt that Libby had gone back to live with him and she was now running Freetech.

Rex removed me from the pub, apologising to the man whose paper I'd nicked. 'She's just a girl,' he repeated all the way to my flat – our flat – because Rex wasn't big on emotions but give him his due he tried, even when I punched him in the face and told him to fuck off, he still insisted on taking me home, pouring me a vodka and demanding I drink it neat.

Rex tried to help, everyone tried to help, but the pain was too great, the cut too deep. I couldn't work out how to repair myself all over again. I was done with sifting truths from untruths. If you can't work out what's real and what's fantasy in life, you have to ask what is the point.

I directed that question to the vodka bottle and all it did was shrug and say pour yourself another.

I have Clara to thank for rescuing me. She tells me I will be forever in her debt, having saved me from choking on my own sick. But then she called my parents and they insisted I move back in with them for two weeks and they're still calling me every day to check I'm alive, so I reckon Clara and I are even.

I still hear from Will and Asha sporadically although we're never going to be bosom buddies, and last week Tess flew off to India with a backpack and a one-way ticket. Tomaz has moved to the Lake District and has joined the mountain rescue team. His CV looked good, four lives saved in one evening, they could hardly turn him down.

But the thing is, we're all watching our backs. With nothing resolved, we can't be sure the people who wanted us dead in that fire, don't still have us in their sights. And it's the invisible threat that messes with your world, turns innocuous situations like someone pushing you on a Tube platform into a near death experience.

Clara has left the *Herald* and is now working for UN-COVERED, a website, a bit like *Private Eye* for millennials. She's tried to get to the bottom of Richard Gilligan Thomas and his murky dealings, and for a while she was almost there but his lawyer took out an injunction and the website couldn't afford the legal fees to fight the case, not that she'll ever admit defeat.

'I swear to God, I'm going to get that fucker if it kills me.'

My only correspondence with Libby since our meeting was a letter I sent to Richard's home address. Three words.

How could you?

She never replied.

Maybe she doesn't know either.

Fifty-Nine

Libby

October 2018

Libby swallows hard. It's five in the morning and already her pulse is sprinting. Today is a big day. It has been planned, discussed, mapped out. She's left nothing to chance, dedicated months preparing the ground for this presentation. But my God, the fear is stalking her. The press are invited, en route already for the breakfast announcement, no doubt. A new product launch from Freetech, the emerging leader in cyber security. She has personally tweaked the press release. It had to be as enticing as possible. Maximum coverage, that's what she's after. And she knows they will come. Her face is still well known for the wrong reasons, *POOR LITTLE RICH GIRL ACCUSED OF MURDER*, just one of the headlines she remembers reading.

When she arrives at the venue, a hipster warehouse in Shoreditch, she turns off her car radio and takes a moment alone. Has she ever been this frightened? Being charged with murder in a police station is hard to beat in terms of raw fear. This is more complex but terrifying in its own unique way. She considers fleeing for no more than a nanosecond. Libby is no longer the girl who runs. She faces her fears and doubts head on. And whoever comes today, whatever coverage her announcement garners, no one will ever understand how much this means to her, the mental obstacles she has overcome to get here. Or perhaps there is one person who might. Her mind runs to Joe, wherever he is, and the huge gaping hole his absence has created. She hopes he will forgive her but maybe she's asking too much. Maybe she always did.

The place is already buzzing when she enters. Way more interest than expected. Who cares if it's because the press are still fascinated by her and the scandal surrounding her family? If it amplifies her message and achieves her aim, Libby is more than happy to capitalise on the infamy.

Richard is waiting for her out of sight of the photographers. When he spots his niece he beams, pulls her into a bear hug, 'I never doubted you, but this is something else. It's going to be phenomenal.'

When he releases her, she regards him with something close to awe. He is the man no one can hold down, a man who carries the sheen of success so effortlessly. A man who wants to pass it on to her. Libby's pulse races again. Her head is light and hot. Sweat beads her top lip. Is she really up to this?

She walks to the microphone, clears her throat. Richard is standing behind her, the proud uncle. In front of her, a sea of faces waiting for the performance. Among them, one is reassuringly familiar. Clara George, the UNCOVERED reporter. She smiles her encouragement. Nods.

All set.

Sixty

Libby

'I came back to work for Freetech eight months ago with a burning desire to lead the way in the prevention and detection of cyber crime. It's often an invisible crime, easy to hide, but one which has the power to destroy lives, paralyse the systems on which our hospitals, our institutions, our society function. Perhaps more sinister is its ability to influence the way we think, the way we vote. It can bring down governments, prop up others. That is why I have been working closely these last few months with Clara George from the website UN-COVERED to bring these corrupt practices to light, practices my uncle Richard Gilligan Thomas has been involved in, and stood to make millions from. We have amassed considerable evidence of criminal activity and government links through emails and payments, all of which I have on record. The UNCOVERED story has just gone live. We passed our dossier to the police an hour ago.

'I will be stepping down from my responsibilities at Freetech with immediate effect.

'I'm happy to take any questions.'

The hush in the room shatters, whispers erupt into shouts and Libby is blinded by the flash of cameras. But at the back, she sees two men and a woman file in and make their way down to the stage. They head straight for Richard.

You do not have to say anything but it may harm your defence . . .

Her uncle reaches for her, but Libby steps out of the way to make sure the cameras get their shot.

Sixty-One

Richard

March 2019

'Ritchie, shut the fuck up, man, I've heard this story fifty
times over.'

Cody is a decent listener, but there always comes a point
when he's had enough and loses his cool.

'It's all a mistake,' I say.

'Ritchie, there's no mistake.'

Ritchie.

I tried to tell him my name was Richard every day for the
first week until he held me up against the wall and said, 'If I
want to call you fuckface, I'll call you fuckface, OK?' In that
context, Ritchie didn't seem too bad.

'But the government . . .'

'Hey,' he shouts, 'James Bond here is talking about his secret
government work again.' A wave of laughter and jeers and
banging erupt down the corridor.

'You sure the doctors checked out before you came here,
Ritchie? I hear there's a bed in Broadmoor with your name on it.'

'I'm not mad,' I tell him.

'And I'm Prince fucking Charles.'

Cody is thirty-five but looks about fifty. The missing teeth don't
help his cause, and the ones that he hasn't lost are black and
rotten. I'd never met anyone without a single GCSE until I met

Cody but he's certainly not in the minority here. His speech is slow and slurred as if the drugs he was once addicted to have never quite left his system. Either that or he's sustained one too many blows to the head. I suspect it is a combination of both. He tells me he's clean now even though the evidence contradicts this statement. He doesn't look clean or smell clean. He needs a damn good scrub if you ask me.

Cody is my cellmate at HM Pentonville Prison. On arrival, I tried to explain to the guards that Cody and I were not a suitable pairing, given his low intelligence levels and his general demeanour. I was angling for a move to the other wing where they house the white-collar workers, the execs and embezzling politicians. My sort of people.

But they laughed in my face, like it was the funniest thing they'd heard in the whole of their wretched lives.

Oddly enough, we've reached a form of accommodation, Cody and I. He listens while I repeat my story over and over again like a curse. I'm teaching him how to read and in return he keeps me safe. It helps that I've promised him a job and a decent salary when we get out. Fortunately he lacks the mathematical skills to calculate the length of my sentence.

I could live twice over and I still wouldn't have enough time to serve it. Which brings me on to Libby.

Dana was right about one thing: Libby did not deserve the life I gave her. When I consider the wealth and opportunities I lavished on that girl, and what she has done to me in return, I'm possessed by such a violent rage I no longer know myself. She was such an obliging, obedient child, such a pliant teenager, it makes her barefaced treachery all the more breathtaking. I should have known the apple doesn't fall far from the tree. She is her mother's daughter.

The story exploded after the press conference. Libby made sure of that, everything perfectly choreographed and orchestrated.

And even though I had stood next to her as she dropped the bombshell, even though she watched on as the police led me away, I still could not believe she would do this to me. Such was my delusion, I wasted my only phone call from the police station to speak to her.

'Tell them it's a mistake,' I said.

And in return, in the face of my pleading and begging and grovelling, the offer of company shares and wealth, the reminder of my years of love and care, she said three words: *You appal me.*

As Matt Collingwood had predicted, the establishment closed ranks. The fallout for the government was confined to one rogue politician who was sacked and is now serving a term in jail. Collingwood got away scot-free, in some Houdini-like act of contortion. I insisted he was to blame, furnished the police with all his details, but guess what? He was gone. Poof! Moved house, no sign of his wife and kids. When they finally found him in the US, he claimed never to have met me, but said he'd heard on the grapevine (what grapevine?) that I was a fantasist, the Walter Mitty of Surrey. You couldn't make it up.

And then they threw in the murder charge.

Murder.

You heard that correctly.

Not Tess's murder. The last thing I knew she was swanning around India. No, this one is linked to my sister's death. Libby uncovered information relating to our inheritance dispute over our mother's house, Kenton Thorpe. My sister Ruth wanted to keep it, I wanted to sell. I needed the money for a fresh round of investment but she wouldn't budge, no matter how many lawyers' letters I sent her, no matter the threat of extortionate court action. She was doing it out of spite, that was blindingly clear. She had always been jealous of my success. In the end, I didn't even need the funds. An investor had stepped forward and stumped up the cash, but I was damned if Ruth was going to win.

I didn't go to Kenton Thorpe with the intention of killing her, we'd simply arranged to meet there to discuss a way forward. But the stupid woman came at me, shrieking and clawing the air like a harpy. She'd been drinking as usual, the smell of her alone was enough to inebriate oneself. All I did was try to silence her because the noise was unbearable. I threw her down on the grubby old sofa, grabbed a cushion and put it over her face. Admittedly, I left it there too long, but it wasn't intentional, I was simply enjoying an extended moment of calm. It was only when I felt her body go limp that I realised something terminal had occurred. Of course, I was shocked. I'm not completely heartless, but the truth was she looked at peace for the first time in years. You could say I did her a favour. The drink was going to kill her anyway, I just speeded up the process.

Anyway, I was forced to stay with her in that godawful house that stank of boiled vegetables for hours, waiting for night to fall, researching the various stages after death. The first one, algor mortis or the death chill, was nothing more than the body going cold. This was of no consequence to me. It was rigor mortis I was worried about. Ruth had let herself go, forever baking cakes and shovelling them into her mouth. As a result she was on the rotund side. I feared her stiff body would be impossible to carry down to the lake. Thankfully it was still limp by the time darkness came and we made it to the water where I filled her pockets with stones and submerged her.

It was a fitting end, I felt. She always loved swimming in that lake.

Poor Ruth.

Her death was officially recorded as suicide and everyone was happy until Libby started poking her nose around. She persuaded the police to reopen the investigation. Before I knew it they were exhuming Ruth's body. And that's how they found she died of suffocation, not drowning. The old investigating officer, whose suspicions I had silenced with a considerable sum of money, came forward to clear his nagging conscience. He was dying anyway and wanted to absolve himself of his sin, now that he was too ill to play golf and drink G&Ts on my account. I really have been too generous in my life.

After the trial, which Libby did not attend, not even for a single day, she gave her first and only interview to the press. There was a photograph of her on the front page, smiling and snuggling up with that loafer of a boyfriend. My downfall was the engine of their reconciliation, apparently. At the same time as I was sitting in the interview room, my world collapsing around me, she was calling Joe, begging for his forgiveness.

'There was nothing to forgive,' he said, nauseatingly. 'When I think of everything she has been through, I'm blown away by her strength.'

Then they spoke of their plans for the future. Travelling, they said. Thailand, Vietnam, the Mekong Delta.

It was a message, the final insult. Two fingers to me.

My reaction, the fury that swept through me like fire, earnt me two days in solitary confinement.

And even now, despite myself, I think of them every morning I wake, the clear blue seas in which they swim, the unspoilt beaches, the vast open skies of their freedom.

While I rot in prison.

Richard Gilligan Thomas. Father, husband, multimillionaire. Murderer.

Acknowledgements

My thanks to the following;

Kate Stephenson for the untangling.

To Alex Clarke, Jenni Leech and Ella Gordon at Headline.

To my agent Cathryn Summerhayes.

To the group of fellow crime authors, the most supportive band of people I could wish for. Thanks for the distractions, the research info and always being on hand with a filthy joke to brighten the day.

To readers and book bloggers who take the time to tweet, email and leave reviews, I am eternally grateful.

To Gianluca Stringhini at UCL for answering all my tech and hacking questions. Any mistakes are my own.

To my friends for always asking about the book, even when it doesn't seem like there is one.

To my family, Liz and Danny McBeth, Jacqueline McBeth, John and Margaret Curran for their enthusiasm and support.

To Finlay, Milo and Sylvie; for distracting me in the best possible way.

To Paul, for the tech support but mainly the love. Thanks as always.

AN ACT OF SILENCE

***SHORTLISTED FOR THE
CWA IAN FLEMING STEEL DAGGER AWARD 2018***

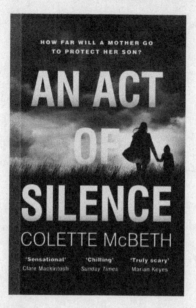

MOTHER. WIFE. POLITICIAN. LIAR.

THEN: How far did she go to conceal the truth?

Politician Linda Moscow sacrificed everything to protect
her son: her beliefs, her career, her marriage. All she wanted
was to keep him safe.

NOW: What will she risk to expose the lies?

When the voices she silenced come back to haunt her,
Linda is faced with another impossible choice. Only this time,
it's her life on the line . . .

An Act of Silence **is a story about the abuse of power,
the devastating effects of keeping the truth buried,
and the lengths a mother will go to save her child.**

THE LIFE I LEFT BEHIND

I know who attacked her. The same man who killed me . . .

Six years ago Melody was left for dead. When the body of
another woman, Eve, is discovered, Melody knows her attacker
is still out there. The only way she can survive is to follow
the clues of the life that Eve left behind.

**A twisty psychological thriller that will keep you
gripped to the pages**

'The plot is taut and compelling, and the writing is excellent'
Marian Keyes, author of *The Break*

'A well-paced, meticulously-researched thriller which is
not just gripping but compassionate, too' Paula Hawkins,
author of *The Girl on the Train*

PRECIOUS THING

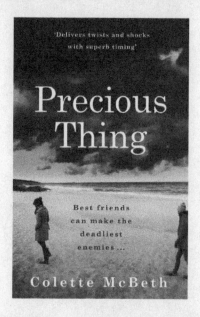

Remember the person you sat next to on your first day at school? Still your best friend? Or disappeared from your life for good?

Some friendships fizzle out. Rachel and Clara promised theirs would last for ever.

They met when Rachel was the new girl in class and Clara was the friend everyone wanted. Now in their late twenties Rachel has everything while Clara's life is spiralling further out of control. Then Clara vanishes.

Imagine discovering something about your oldest friend that forces you to question everything you've shared together.

The truth is always there. But only if you choose to see it.

THRILLINGLY GOOD BOOKS
FROM CRIMINALLY
GOOD WRITERS

CRIME FILES BRINGS YOU THE LATEST RELEASES FROM
TOP CRIME AND THRILLER AUTHORS.

SIGN UP ONLINE FOR OUR MONTHLY NEWSLETTER AND BE THE FIRST
TO KNOW ABOUT OUR COMPETITIONS, NEW BOOKS AND MORE.